GOLD LUST CONSPIRACY

LYNDA REES

lyndareesauthor@gmail.com

Website: lyndareesauthor.com

Publisher: Sweetwater Publishing Company

6612 Ky. Hwy. 17 North,

DeMossville, KY 41033

sweetwaterpublishingcompany.wordpress.com

Original Edition

Copyright © 2017 by Sweetwater Publishing Company

ISBN: 978-0-9990943-1-0

lyndareesauthor@gmail.com

Website: lyndareesauthor.com

Facebook: @lynda.rees.author

This book is dedicated to my loving husband Mike--the man of my dreams, my soul mate, muse and inspiration for this book. My incredible husband Mike's wacky, out-of-the-box, creative mind suggested this could've happened., and I believe it did. You are my hero. I would not be able to accomplish what I do without you by my side or pushing me forward. Because of you I'm achieving my dreams. I love you more than mere words can express.....forever, Yours.

Also, it is dedicated to my amazing brother Ernie Feltner, the most talented and one of the smartest men I ever met. Ernie, you left us too soon; but everyone you touched with your brilliance or humor was blessed in some way. You inspired me to write this story with talk of mining Alaskan gold fields. I will forever miss you. You remain always on my mind and in my heart.

This is a special thanks to my friend and editor, Linda Rankin. Thank you, Linda, for your help and even more, for your encouragement. You bolstered my courage when I needed it. Thank you to my critique team and everyone at Sweetwater Publishing Company who made this book possible.

CHAPTER 1

May, 1880

Spectacular wilderness sped quickly by--a thrilling sight. Lost in thought, Jessie Blackstone wrinkled her nose at the intoxicating scent of burning wood and intense pine blended in the sweltering summer air whiffing through the window. She flicked her fan to cool herself. Jessie would never forget the smell of the Wild West, so different from what she was used to.

"Mistress Blackstone," a soft voice uttered. It didn't register. Jessie tilted her head. After a pause the young woman spoke again. "Mistress Blackstone."

Jessie stared as people chatted quietly around her. Fascinated by the scenery and in awe of the modern steam engine, she hadn't paid much attention to anything else.

Before now, many had traveled west by more crude means—wagon trains, stagecoaches, horseback, and worse. A few years ago, who would've believed a contraption could speed from one coast to another? Thanks to her wealthy husband, Everett, and the Pullman Palace Car Company's new inventions, Jessie traveled in luxurious comfort.

"Mistress Blackstone? Are you all right, madam? I've tried to get your attention."

Heat rose to Jessie's cheeks as though she'd bent across a steeping teapot. *What a dunderhead I am.* She resisted hiding behind her lacy fan, and smiled sweetly at Lilly, a maneuver she'd practiced. The woman must think her a dodo bird.

Her chignon bounced from the movement of the train. She touched her hat to ensure the hatpin held securely. "I'm sorry, Lilly. I'm unaccustomed to my married name. At the academy, I was simply Jessie. Being Mistress Blackstone is new to me. What is it, dear?"

"It's all right, Mistress Blackstone. I was worried about you."

Jessie patted Lilly's hand reassuringly. "I'm splendid, Lilly."

"I'm glad we're back on the trail. Those angry picketers raisin' Cain at the Salt Lake City depot were frightening."

"Yes, strikes and riots protesting the railway have resulted in violence. The west is frightening enough without such silliness. Pinkerton guards hired by the railroad will put a stop to that nonsense, ensuring our safety," Jessie reassured Lilly. Unafraid of such things, she had seen worse.

"That's a relief."

"We're well away from it now, Lilly. Only minutes from the city, and already we're again in the wilderness. Why on earth are they launching an oil-burning engine when there's an endless supply of wood? Look at the forest, thick as can be." Jessie indicated the view out their window.

The most unusual things piqued one's curiosity. She must be careful around Everett, though. He'd never approve.

A lady steered clear of business discussions. *We mustn't worry our silly heads with such affairs. Needlepoint is more proper for a lady's discussion. Bah!*

"I suppose so. I never gave it much thought."

Lilly finds me strange to say the least. I can't help it. I'm curious about everything. "I'm sorry, Lilly, I'm rambling. You wanted something?"

"I'd like to pack your trunks for our departure. We don't need the whole boodle, with only one more night on the train. Is that all right with you?"

Lilly's fair skin glowed in the sunshine. A straight blonde braid hung down Lilly's back. Her grey dress, with its white collar and matching hat, were plain but still lovely. Lilly's bright blue eyes shone with pleasure, eager to please. Jessie had grown fond of the girl.

"That's fine. I'll refresh myself while you do that." Jessie hesitated, placing her hand on Lilly's slender arm, needing to discuss something with her even though it was embarrassing then whispered, "I'm grateful you're here. You were a blessing this morning, helping me get that dammed corset on. I appreciate everything you do. I'm not used to being waited on. You're good company. Thank you for coming. It would've been unseemly traveling alone."

Lilly blushed. "You're welcome, Mistress Blackstone. I'm pleased for the job as your companion. I need the work and hope to remain in San Francisco."

"Stay as my personal maid, then. I'll convince Mister Blackstone to keep you on. We're close in age, so this formality is strange between us. When we're alone, I prefer you call me Jessie."

"Yes, ma'am." Lilly blushed, glancing away before meeting Jessie's eyes. With a stammer Lilly whispered, "I'm nineteen, a year older than you. If you like, when we're alone I'll call you Jessie. I dare not in front of your husband. The headmistress who hired me said he's rather formal."

A rare giggle forced its way out. "You're correct. Everett wouldn't approve. Regardless, I'd like us to become friends. It'll be between us." Jessie winked. *Why upset Everett?*

They raised together, Lilly heading to the sleeper car. Jessie entered the secluded alcove near adjoining railcar doors toward the necessary. After dealing with her needs she exited to return to her seat.

Swish! Hot outside air assailed Jessie as the connecting doors between cars opened and closed. Before she could turn, rough hands gripped her shoulders. The intruder spun her around and she slammed against the wall. A stunned gasp escaped as her heart skipped and her shook to clear her vision.

"What in tarnation?"

A burly man in soiled deerskin leaned into her. A wicked grin exposed a few rotting teeth left in his mouth. An array of revolting odors assaulted Jessie's nose and she flinched then shivered, repulsed as the stench reeked of perspiration and something else—dried blood, urine? His smothering, steamy breath stank of cheap whiskey and decay.

The man sniffed Jessie's neck, pushing against her body. His guttural voice slurred, "Give old Wheezer a kiss. Will ya? One smackeroo will do. I ain't seen no white woman in more'n a year."

He licked Jessie from her neck toward her ear, sending tremors of fear along her spine. Heart racing, adrenaline pumping through her veins, fumbling for the fan hanging from her wrist, exposed a slim, razor-sharp dagger hidden within its ivory tines. Attempting to aim the blade at the disgusting man's side, Jessie groped for the hidden compartment in her skirt to withdraw another weapon, but couldn't reach it.

Suddenly, the connecting doors slid open and slammed shut. Hot air swooshed in. Jessie's attacker glanced behind him as she struggled harder.

Just in time to see a large hand catch Wheezer's neck in a chokehold. His tongue lolled out as he gagged and sputtered.

A statuesque man had pulled Wheezer off Jessie. The towering intruder's powerful appendage grabbed the back of Wheezer's neck and dragged the now-helpless tormentor toward the open connecting door, pushing him through it. With a zip-slamming rumble from the door, they were gone.

Free from her attacker, Jessie stood, shaking but erect. She smoothed her skirt, righted herself, and surveyed what she could of her appearance, bringing a hand to her hat to ensure it remained properly attached.

A lady must look regal in every circumstance. That lesson had been ingrained in Jessie during the last year.

Jessie stepped through the door, curious about the gallant stranger who'd come to her assistance, following him out to a walkway connecting the railcars. Throat still clutched in her rescuer's hand, Wheezer's feet swayed above the floor. Squealing, protesting, mostly gasping, he attempted to fill his lungs with sufficient air.

The man flipped Wheezer across the barrier, dangling him above the train coupling and the open rail like a weightless rag doll, while the train raced above a steep ravine to a shallow rocky riverbed at least a mile downward.

Jessie gaped at the spectacle. Would her savior drop the rude mountain man?

"Listen, old codger," The stranger spat, "if you accost this lady or any other on this train again, you won't receive a warning. Your miserable ass will be sent to hell. Understand?"

Wheezer's panicked eyes grew as big as saucers as he visibly trembled and frantically nodded. Between his parched lips, slobber drooled from his gaping mouth.

The scent of testosterone oozed from the impressive stranger, the essence of maleness. Powerful shoulders and arms threatened to burst his jacket seams. Her height barely reached the towering stranger's shoulder.

"You owe this lady an apology." He brutally shook the quivering Wheezer as Wheezer's head wobbled back and forth helplessly. All the fight had deserted Wheezer. He became limp as embroidery thread.

"What're you waiting for?"

Wheezer blinked at Jessie, seemingly forgetting her presence. Quaking, Wheezer rasped, "I apologize, ma'am." Wheezer appeared sorrowfully on the brink of tears.

Satisfied, her rescuer brought Wheezer back across the railing, settled Wheezer's feet gently onto the floor, and released him. The wretched bully scurried through the connecting door and disappeared into the next car.

Jessie's champion turned, chuckling low, his face actually turned pink. The spectacular male appeared embarrassed.

Intriguing.

A broad hand brushed back shaggy blonde hair which had come untamed during the tussle. His stunning face held a gracious smile. Flashing that adorable, dimpled expression at his mama, he could likely get away with anything.

Jessie tingled with a sudden desire to touch the appealing dent in his strong jaw. Hot blood surged through her veins.

Had someone fired the potbelly stove in the already s weltering railcar?

Heart pounding against the corseted restraints Jessie waved the fan over her face and pressed a gloved hand hard on her chest, as if keeping it from busting loose.

"Please forgive my rudeness. I apologize for my language. I don't normally speak that way in front of a lady. I had no choice." The stranger's head bowed nobly. Raising his face to Jessie, his smile exposed perfect white teeth.

Jessie gazed transfixed at those lips, unable to hold back an involuntary sigh.

"The old coot got himself liquored up and bent on mischief, so I followed him. He's a recluse, a mountain hermit. They rarely come out into public and don't care much for people. When they do their lack of social skills leads to chaos. Wheezer's sort only understands strong language and a firm hand." The stranger's voice held an apologetic note.

The handsome gent grinned. Had he read her silly thoughts? His eyes seemed to glint with an appreciative light as he inspected her from head to toe.

She should take offense. *Oh, hell!* She had ogled him, too. *Straighten up, Jessie. Act like a lady.*

He seemed unusually familiar, almost as though they were somehow intimate. She hadn't met him. She'd have definitely remembered . . .

Some unseen force surged between them Jessie couldn't put a finger on. Jessie didn't normally think much of men. She must learn more about the interesting fellow to understand this peculiar connection. It was a curious thing, oddly intriguing.

"No need to apologize, sir. I understand and appreciate your interference. Your chivalry is commendable, extremely gallant."

Jessie smiled congenially, trying not to appear taken aback by the bizarre experience. Compounding the situation was an odd compulsion to flirt. Jessie didn't flirt, had never wanted to. *How did one flirt anyway?* His effect on her constitution and being oddly drawn to the stranger was perplexing.

"Old Wheezer won't bother you again, ma'am." His gorgeous emerald eyes blinked almost shyly. He certainly knew how to use them. They pierced right through what little reserve remained. Did that sultry gaze read her innermost mysteries? It appeared so.

His dazzling smile spoke volumes about his appealing personality and warmed her insides.

He executed lovely manners, evidence of proper upbringing. Clearly he knew how to respect and treat a lady. His congenial, polished manner spoke with command, as though accustomed to leading. He appeared educated and cultured. No dandy, the man possessed genuine gentlemanly manners.

He certainly was brave and seemed used to taking care of himself and those around him. However, Jessie would wager he found violence distasteful. He had used it sparingly, treating Wheezer gently when he released him.

His muscular body emanated sensuality, virility and strength. Jessie wanted to sidle to him like a wanton. She stiffened. What was wrong with her? She didn't give a hoot about men. They were a necessary evil, a means to an end, a resource for survival in a man's world.

This man is different.

He sparked something none ever had. Every nerve sprang to life, on edge. Fireflies rustling within and a hand went to her belly to still the rumbling, taking a long breath.

Stop this nonsense. Gain control of yourself. Jessie held her head high.

The stranger's powerful, muscular arms evidenced manual labor. Yet he wore a gentleman's finery. His manner didn't seem to be of the worker class, either. Rather, an enigma.

I want to learn more.

"Thank you, kind sir." Jessie extended a gloved hand. His fingers grazed hers, and heat eased straight up her arm all the way to her cheeks.

He grinned at the fan poorly concealing her blush and nodded toward the slim dagger. Jessie's weapon remained exposed, the blade glistening.

"I see you can take care of yourself. I don't believe you need that knife, ma'am. You can put it away now. A lovely woman like you, I'm sure, finds it comforting. There's much danger to be wary of. You shouldn't be here alone. I shall escort you to your seat. Your companions must be worried." He reached for Jessie's arm.

She jerked from his grasp. "No need, sir, I'm fine on my own."

His eyes popped wide. "It is highly improper for a young woman to travel alone."

"Nonsense. It's none of your business, sir; but I'm traveling with my maid, on my way to meet my husband in San Francisco."

"Who you conveniently ditched." The man had the gall to argue.

"I beg your pardon?" Handsomeness and gallantry notwithstanding, he had no right to interfere. Jessie's blood simmered as she squared her stance, hands on hips.

The gent must've been impressed because he suddenly became contrite. "I apologize, ma'am. I've overstepped, worried for your welfare. I didn't mean to offend. My guess is, every male on this train's taken notice. Women are a rarity in many parts of the west. If you were my wife, I wouldn't risk your safety. Please accept my apologies."

"No harm done. Besides, this isn't my first journey."

The glint in his eye as he snickered showed he might doubt her capabilities.

Jessie pushed the button retracting the apple peeler blade into its hiding place inside the fan and felt the bounce of her curls as she tossed her head.

I'm acting downright dotty, but the man is perplexing. I'm not sure I like it. Resisting the urge to stomp her foot like a child, Jessie fought to remain a proper lady.

Observing with obvious curiosity, his tongue slipped out briefly and licked those perfect lips. Then he tilted his head, brows arched above sparkling jade eyes. "An experienced traveler, then. Are you enjoying our west?" He grinned wickedly.

Was he playing with her? Trying to extend their meeting?

It was a rather fun game, if indeed that was his intent.

"It's captivating. I'm bewitched by the scenery." Jessie's muscles relaxed; she'd been tensing them the whole time.

Mostly at ease with the handsome stranger, outlandish emotions surged through her so she lingered a spell to figure it out. Having kept to herself the whole journey, except for Lilly, a few minutes chatting with this welcome diversion wouldn't do any harm.

"Our western territories are admirably intoxicating," he offered.

"I've only lived in cities and never realized how marvelous the wilderness is. It changes almost constantly. For days after leaving Boston we passed a steady procession of one dreary town after another. Leaving St. Louis, lush forests and broad prairies appeared. Suddenly we were in the wilds. It's simply incredible. Each territory we sped through looked different from the last. Each had its own unique character, all breathtaking."

"I adore the wilderness myself, having been raised here."

"How fortunate for you. How can there be so much unsettled land? Immense woodlands far as the eye can see. Majestic mountain ranges rise above the tracks ruling the world." She clapped gleefully then a hand swept upward, exhibiting the heights she'd witnessed.

Emitting a low chuckle, clearly amused, he leaned against the wall, crossing long legs and arms.

Exhilaration blazed, evident in Jessie's descriptions. "The snow-topped, ragged, harsh peaks leave me breathless. Others are blanketed with lush pine stands, forests thick as hair on your head. No city or people, only wilderness and sometimes incredible creatures were visible."

"I'm in the timber business. These mountains and forests have been home to my family my whole life." He nodded and grinned.

She didn't need much encouragement. "Fascinating, but that sounds like a dangerous profession. You must be brave. These mighty mountains are nothing new to you, then. It's exciting from my perspective. I've never witnessed anything so spectacular."

Hearing her own words, heat rose and flooded her face. *Where's my fan? Can't be the weather doing this to me.*

Perhaps this man, with his scalding allure, affected her simply by innocently standing so near. Beneath her skirts, between her thighs, Jessie felt an unfamiliar glow. Her belly tingled oddly.

What the . . .?

"Our lovely mountains can be deceiving. Danger lurks as well as beauty."

"I've noticed. The mountains teem with wildlife." Jessie fought to keep her voice steady, flapping her fan to cool her body. Surely such an overheated state couldn't be a result of swooning about nature in front of a stranger.

"You met Wheezer. Not all peril comes from nature's creatures. The human element provides sufficient threat." He gave her a lazy smile.

Jessie ignored the warning, for she could have easily handled Wheezer. Instead she felt herself distracted by the strangest urge to run a finger across this man's chiseled chin. Smooth, or rough with stubble? Lips the color of honey appeared soft and inviting. Too bad she would never experience their texture and taste.

Stop dreaming. Stay in the real world.

He was certainly distracting.

Her mind deserting her, Jessie stammered, regaining control. *Stay on subject.*

"I've enjoyed sighting abundant wildlife. A bear fished in a stream. A rangy, awkward moose crossed the tracks. We sped by a herd of big horned sheep climbing a steep ravine, unafraid of the mighty steam engine." Warming to her narrative, Jessie spoke with animated liveliness.

"You've kept your eyes peeled." He nodded a pleasant sideways grin.

"Indeed, yesterday I spotted a wolf peeking from the forest. This morning a herd of buffalo grazed in open prairie. I can barely tear my eyes from the window."

Laughing heartily, he slapped his leg. "This western frontier is a hotbed of primal, untamed life."

As are you, Mister.

Hastily regrouping Jessie extended a gloved hand, ever the lady. "I beg your pardon, sir. I'm running on and on when we haven't been properly introduced. I'm Mistress Jessie Blackstone, wife of Everett Blackstone of San Francisco. I'm pleased to meet you. You are?"

He had visibly stiffened. An eyebrow flew up for the briefest of seconds, masking what looked like dismay. He straightened into a formal stance, scowling. Something about the way he stared made her temper simmer. His handsome face filled with what appeared to be trepidation, stared as though seeing her for the first time. His disposition became cold and proper.

Seconds felt like hours. What had changed making him behave strangely?

Finally he found his words and offered a slight bow. "I'm pleased to meet you, Mistress Blackstone. I'm Logan Pace from Oregon territory."

The spark which had attracted Jessie was absent from Mister Pace's voice. A cold wall had come between them, their connection lost; Mister Pace's attitude now stilted formality.

He graciously shook the extended hand, the contact muted by her glove.

How could a gentleman refuse?

Regardless, the gesture sent delicious sparks with it. Logan Pace had a potent effect.

Extremely curious.

Mister Pace dropped Jessie's hand quickly, as though her touch burned, and he appeared anxious to escape. Logan stepped backward toward the door, putting distance between them.

"I wish you a safe, comfortable journey, Mistress Blackstone. I must go now."

Turning, Logan swiftly entered the other car, leaving Jessie there with her mouth open.

"Good day, Mister Pace." Speaking to Logan's backside already through the door and in the other car before her goodbye was completed.

Peculiar how his congenial, friendly manner ceased, then exhibited disfavor at Everett's name . . . almost like he knows my husband . . . or knows of him.

Was it somehow distasteful to Mister Logan Pace? He'd lit out six ways to Sunday. Jessie sighed, her hands on her hips as she returned to her seat.

It didn't matter. Logan Pace had fled the scene.

What a shame. He'd evoked delicious sensations never experienced before. She'd liked it. Maybe Everett would provide similar pleasure once they were together. After all, Jessie was eighteen now. She'd matured into womanhood during the last year, as a married woman should.

About time she felt something for the opposite sex besides aversion.

CHAPTER 2

His encounter with the lovely lady peaked Logan's curiosity. He enjoyed the charming young bride—at first, anyway. Now, a sickening swirl in his gut ate at Logan.

Logan had concocted a plan to befriend the enchanting creature and stay by her side as long as possible. A seat nearby would've allowed a firsthand view, as she experienced the west.

But the bride wasn't alone. That was disappointing, though it eased Logan's mind.

Jessie Blackstone was a married woman. Logan couldn't push himself into her graces to satisfy a pining for Jessie's company. Still, Logan hadn't wanted their time together to end.

Yet it did, and in the worst way. Once Logan knew, he'd excused himself and left--fast.

Why had Jessie tied herself to such a clod? A waste.

Bile rose in Logan's throat at the mention of Everett Blackstone; and he wanted to puke. Logan couldn't get the vision of Jessie with that bastard out of his mind.

Jessie was a looker and a spitfire. *Old Blackstone's in for it. Hope he's up to it.* That woman would sure be a handful. Oh, to be a fly on the wall as their married life unfolded.

Jessie spoke with animated expressions and lively speech, exhibiting unadulterated pleasure. Her vibrant smile lit the deep green depths of her eyes, making them sparkle, and reminding Logan of tall pines.

Her contagious, daring spirit thrilled at every second of the adventure. Logan longed to view the world through her eyes.

The refined lady had waved her arms erratically. Her gloved hands swept about with child-like exuberance, observing the world through youthful eyes. She reminded Logan of his young niece experiencing some wonder for the first time.

Though young, Jessie was all women engaging Logan's senses and setting his nerves afire with anticipation and delight.

With her face aglow, her ample breasts rising and falling excitedly, her exotic beauty was captivating. The thick lashes, framing her almond-shaped eyes, fluttered when she spoke.

Her golden skin must be natural, for refined ladies avoided sun exposure.

He'd noted now her cheeks colored to soft pink when embarrassed. Logan longed to kiss her velvety lips, the color of peaches. Her long, slim neck invited his hand to surround it and pull her to him for a taste.

How I love peaches.

The satin ribbon on her gown, tied in back, accentuated her trim waist, its flamboyant bow resting enviously atop her buttocks.

Oh, to pull the ribbon loose, undo her dress stays and . . . What pleasure hides beneath those skirts?

Forget that. Logan could only dream about the sultry Jessie Blackstone, for he respected the institution of marriage. Logan would never pursue a married woman.

Logan's will to love had lain dormant since Amy's death. The raw ache in his heart surged anew each time Logan thought of

Amy. The young Blackstone bride had awakened senses Logan thought long dead, buried with Amy back home.

Apparently Logan was still capable of lustful instincts toward the fairer sex.

Logan sighed heavily. *Mustn't waste time dwelling on it.* He had bigger fish to fry.

* * *

The train jostled rudely back and forth on rough track and around sharp curves that seemed to bend in two. Jessie struggled to remain unscathed while it bumped and jarred, battling to sit erect. She must maintain an unbothered appearance . . . like a lady.

Her clothing aided her attempt. Damned whalebone stays in the miserable corset were killing her. If she slumped in the least they snagged her tender skin.

A lady never appeared unsettled. Jessie had learned that during the last year at the Boston School for Proper Young Ladies. She'd studied and practiced relentlessly, so Everett would be proud and happy he'd married her.

Sweat glided between her breasts, slithering like a snake against her skin.

Damn, it itches.

But a proper lady didn't sweat and never acknowledged discomfort. She endured, glistened or glowed.

Sweat? Heavens no.

The slight breeze didn't stand a chance of reaching Jessie's skin—not through the impenetrable high-necked, lace collar and bodice of her traveling dress. Heaven forbid someone see her arm or cleavage.

Who in tarnation decided a lady should wear such ridiculous garb? It must've been a man.

Who else would require a lady be clad at all times in a long-sleeved, high-necked, floor-length dress weighing at least forty pounds? Built for durability to withstand rigors of travel, the sheer bulk of substantial fabric in her ensemble flummoxed the mind.

Two crinolines held the skirt out fashionably. A chemise beneath the tight corset; pantaloons; stockings and above-the-ankle, kid-glove shoes sporting tedious laces, completed the outfit. It took forever just to get the silly shoes on. The world might end if some man got a look at her ankles.

Lounging comfortably around Mama's '*house,*' attire had been less formal.

Opening the fan hanging from her wrist, Jessie daintily waved the lace toward her glowing cheeks. A tiny hat perched atop her coiffed head, pinned slightly to one side above a chignon of finger curls that failed to stir in the slight breeze she created.

Would Everett regret choosing Jessie? He'd taken great pains ensuring she met his criteria. Their union began as a business deal—not yet a real marriage, but one of convenience for Everett. Not so for her, for this was to be a lifeline.

"Are you anxious to get home?"

"I am." Jessie made room for Lilly. *Definitely.* Her restless nature thrilled to be going somewhere, anywhere away from her past . . .

Also terrified.

"It must be awful for you, being separated from your husband since your wedding night. It must've been a dire emergency, keeping you from your groom."

"Indeed." Jessie tried appearing forlorn. Lilly wouldn't understand.

"This'll be an adjustment, I suppose."

"For sure, I keep wondering how it'll be, living with Everett. We only had our wedding night together."

"All brides must be nervous."

"I suppose, though I wonder about the silliest things. Is Everett quick to smile and joke? Will he be playful? I hope so. I want an easy life, full of love." They'd shared intimacies on their wedding night. They'd slept together that night, or at least Everett had slept.

"It'll work out. You jumped the broom with Everett, so you must love him. You'll build the life you want together."

"I suppose, Lilly. We both want a home filled with children. Everett especially wants a boy, heir to his fortune. I can hardly wait to become a mother. I'll be the best mama ever."

Not like mine. I'll be everything mine lacked.

"What's Mr. Blackstone like?" Lilly sounded nervous.

Good question. "Everett's a successful, powerful businessman in California." *He made it clear during negotiations.*

"Impressive. You must be proud of your husband."

She wished to know more about him personally, but that would come with time.

The life Everett promised hadn't been in Jessie's scope of reality, though Mama had been saving her for such an opportunity. This journey was an escape from hell.

"This trip's an adventure." Change the subject.

"Yes it is. I'm enjoying it." Lilly went back to her book.

They shared a love of western sagas, rags filled with tales of heathen Indians and bandits. Jessie read voraciously, treasuring any book bringing wonder into her existence.

Encountering Mister Logan Pace had been the most exciting part of the journey so far. Logan screamed vitality and virility, the kind of man others were eagerly drawn to.

Oh, to learn and unravel him like a suspense novel . . . He'd make someone a fine husband.

She'd certainly reacted strangely.

Jessie touched her index finger to her jaw. *Umm, I mustn't dwell on the handsome stranger.*

The mystery man had vanished quick as he'd appeared, but remained an enticing memory. It had been nice having someone defend her. No one had ever cared for Jessie's welfare before.

Bang!

A gent entered the car. "It's time, men," he shouted. Out the window as far as the eye could see buffalo grazed. Nearly every man aboard grabbed a rifle, selected a window and began firing.

Jessie put her head down, hands covering her ears, and cringed until finally the shots ceased. Her stomach soured and she felt life drain from her face at the spectacle. The train had passed the magnificent herd and left in its wake hundreds of wooly carcasses rotting in the sweltering sun.

Jessie patted the hidden compartment in her skirt, touched hard metal, and sighed; reassured her sidearm remained handy. She was clueless what else her epic adventure would bring, but ready for anything.

CHAPTER 3

The old man occupying the seat beside Jessie rose and strolled out of the car. A dirty leather pouch fell from his buckskin pants, landing on his seat.

Glancing around, no passengers seemed to be aware, so Jessie discretely retrieved the surprisingly heavy pouch. She shouldn't, but undid the stays, opened the bag and shook out a couple of nuggets. A silenced gasp escaped her lips.

Golden rocks shone, catching sunlight streaming in. Smooth, randomly shaped and sized nuggets lay in her hand. Only the brilliant color hinted at their value.

So this was what all the excitement was about. This explained the public's draw these last few years in search of wondrous pebbles.

Goodness, what to do now?

Sliding the yellow chunks into their pouch, pulling the cord tight, she rewrapped and concealed it on her lap beneath her hands. Glancing nervously around, it appeared no one witnessed.

Jessie dreaded the man's return. The old fellow's absence had been a welcomed reprieve. She'd avoided chewing the rag with the stranger, but couldn't avoid him any longer.

Finally making his way clumsily to the seat beside Jessie in the club car, he coughed--a hoarse, ragged, phlegmy sound.

Jessie cringed and breathed shallowly at the assault of foul breath and body odor penetrating his doeskin suit. He stunk to high heaven. Covering her nose stalled the scruffy stranger's scent.

Proper grooming appeared to be an alien concept to him. It must've been some time since he'd enjoyed the luxury of a bath. Ragged clothing in disarray, he appeared rude, crude and rough-and-tumble. With a gruff snort, he sniffed against his sleeve.

Knowing she shouldn't be involved with his sort, glancing about ensuring they weren't being watched, she tapped his arm.

Looking perplexed, their eyes met his from beneath fluffy, grey brows.

Jessie handed the pouch over whispering, "This is yours, sir."

His rough paw accepted it and his dark eyes went wide. His leathered forehead wrinkled as his brows tented, beginning to comprehend.

A broad grin exposed ragged teeth beneath a shaggy, grey beard. His hand trembled. Parched lips quivered. A lone tear escaped one eye leaving a damp trail on his dirty, wrinkled face.

"Goldang, lady, this is my life savin's, the whole shebang. It's all the gold I have to show for mining my Californi claim these last two brutal years. I monkeyed around and lost it. You found it fair and square. Why're you givin' it back ta me?"

"It isn't mine. I couldn't keep it and gyp you outta what's yourn. Excuse me, I mean yours. You dropped it when you walked away. So I held onto it for you."

What kind of woman kept a man's treasure? Not having much, only her honor, Jessie couldn't do such a horrible thing.

While he slept earlier, the old man's floppy, leather hat had fallen exposing a balding, dull dome lined with purple protruding veins that sprouted a singular strand of steel grey hair. A scraggly, thin ponytail dangled along his back like a snake escaping from beneath the lank, grungy hat that wagged comically with the train's motion.

His dull eyes filled with moisture, emphasizing yellowing spots in the whites. Greenish enamel covered his few remaining teeth as his arms flayed animatedly.

His rough, scratchy voice exhaled quietly directing his hideous odor in Jessie's direction. "I don't spend much time in good society. So I ain't got no idea how ta thank ya for your moral goodness, ma'am. I ain't used ta such displays. Most folks wouldn't return a fortune to its rightful owner. I'm in your debt."

"Please, sir, don't make big of it. The pouch is yours. I merely safeguarded it for you."

Would he burst into tears, or worse, attempt to hug her? Jessie gladly did the good deed when she picked the sack up, knowing it might put her in close contact with the stinky stranger.

"How can I repay your kindness? How about a gold nugget for ya compassion?"

His watery smile warmed her heart. "No need, I simply did right by you. Your gratitude is reward enough." Jessie turned away, but her peripheral vision showed that he dabbed at his eyes inconspicuously.

Later as the old codger snored loudly, his body rocked back and forth with the train's movement. A man in front excused himself to the woman seated beside him. After he left the car the woman cheerfully turned.

"You did an honorable thing. You're a fine woman, my dear." Her no-nonsense, olive-green dress and matching bonnet tied with a simple ribbon beneath a double chin, showed middle class status. Her blue eyes sparkled above pink, plump cheeks.

"Thank you, ma'am. I'm pleased to make your acquaintance. I'm Jessie Blackstone." She extended a gloved hand.

"I'm pleased to meet you, Mistress Blackwell. I'm Sara. My husband, Reverend Brown, and I are traveling to our new church in a township north of San Francisco."

"I'm pleased to meet you, Mistress Brown. I saw tub-thumpers preaching on the streets in Boston, but have never met a real gospel sharp before. Please call me Jessie."

"Thank you, Jessie, but only if you call me Sara." Sara blushed at the slang reference to her husband's profession. "Where do you hail from?"

"New Orleans, but I spent the last year in Boston. You?"

"St. Louis, the bustling gateway to the west. I hear New Orleans is an exciting city."

Jessie gazed upward reflecting. "Indeed, New Orleans is a melting pot of cultures with a life of its own. Its energy grabs your soul. People are passionate, living life to the fullest in the sweltering, humid weather and gulf sea breeze."

"It sounds exotic." Sara's shoulders rose and fell excitedly.

Jessie's mouth watered. "Absolutely. The cuisine is incredibly delicious. I miss spicy crawfish pie, seafood gumbo and beignets. Yum. The city is alive with rousing Cajun music, impossible to resist."

The body reacts unwittingly moving to the sultry beat, but a lady wouldn't admit that.

"What was Boston like, dear?"

"I only schooled there, but I slipped out without permission a couple of times to see the city."

"So brave, Jessie." Sara's hands went to her mouth--her eyes wide.

Jessie's cheeks burned shaking her head mischievously. "Sometimes I simply can't control my inquisitive nature. I enjoy learning and adventure. Something compels me when opportunity presents itself."

"What did you learn?" Sara laughed.

"Let's see. Boston pulses with power, politics and literary influence. Historical buildings reside alongside modern architecture on most every street, exploding outward into the bay atop dirt moved onto the ocean floor--such a marvelous idea. I understand there's crime and mob influence. As a student I wasn't exposed to it. Boston's seafood is good though--crab cakes and lobster."

Sara giggled. "It seems you enjoy food, Jessie. I've never eaten lobster. Are you destined for San Francisco?"

"Yes, I'm anxious to arrive. They say culture there is in league with New York and Chicago. It's a grand metropolis, with the best entertainment in the country. San Francisco is known as the Paris of the West and quite cosmopolitan. I can't wait to visit museums, ballets, symphonies, and stage shows."

As wife of a prominent San Franciscan Jessie would have access to those marvelous events. A hand lay on her tummy, flittering like a pit full of snakes. If she burped she'd probably spew venom.

"Delightful, I hope you enjoy it. I'm headed for a much less exciting life; though, we're having an adventure. We have a wee farm north of San Francisco. I'm anxious to settle there and hope the folks who invited us are welcoming."

"How interesting. So you're sod-busters?"

Sara smiled sweetly. "Indeed we are."

"Growing crops must be rewarding." Eager to leave her past behind and thrilled with the prospect of a happy marriage to Everett, who promised a luxurious lifestyle. No doubt, it would be an adventure, but Jessie longed for a simpler life and worried their mansion would be drab, pretentious, dull and stilted. Would she wither away in such an atmosphere?

Hopefully Jessie would be surprised and may actually like it. No matter what, she would never complain and could endure anything, determined to make Everett happy. After all Everett offered, it was the least she could do. Nothing could be as bad as her past.

Jessie strained to appear serene when her nerves were aflutter.

"I've read fearful tales about the wild west of thrilling frontiersmen and gunfighter escapades. I consume every exhilarating page. It's anyone's guess how much is real and what is conjecture to sell dime novels." Sara laughed.

"I've read similar stories." Unafraid, her past life had seen it all.

"Nice jawing with you, Jessie. I wish you well." Sara's attention focused on the returning reverend.

Casually tilting her head Sara rested on her husband's shoulder for the briefest second then raised it and smiled sweetly as their eyes met. The shared intimacy was a private moment, meant only for the married couple, unaware their love was so obvious to a stranger. Simple, pure, and easy, devotion played out in their lives. It seemed natural and rare.

Jessie had never witnessed such strong human connection before. Her eyes closed as breath caught in her throat. Would Everett treat her in such a sweet, loving way?

Patting her sea of skirts, Jessie's hand settled contentedly against hard metal hidden in the folds of fabric. Warm steel relieved the anxiety, breathing slowed, and her heart settled into a gentle beat. She adjusted deeper into her seat--at least as much as the corset allowed.

Jessie didn't attempt making friends and only observed other passengers. She had no idea what to expect. Notions rambled through her head. Filled with questions and a lot to consider, she remained quiet, attempting with difficulty to appear calm and composed while stilling the giddiness in her gut.

It was curious how Everett chose Jessie. There were more beautiful and experienced girls available. Why not one of them? It was baffling. She was nothing special.

I don't deserve this.

How would Everett react to Jessie's arrival? What did he remember of her? Was Everett as eager? Would her transformation please him? Could she pull it off and fit into Everett's world? Was Jessie smart enough to engage in stimulating conversation with Everett's friends? Or would they think Jessie stupid and backward? She mustn't embarrass her husband and would do whatever necessary to assure Everett had made a fair bargain.

It felt like a nest of hornets was loose in Jessie's body, wildly demanding attention and threatening to burst through her prickling skin. Laying a hand on her belly, closing her eyes, she breathed deeply and slowly to calm her raging pulse. Jessie's heartbeat slowed to almost normal.

Everett was an unattractive lubber who looked more plain and ordinary than he acted. His bulbous belly protruded emphasizing his short stature. Everett's temples were greying and his face was furrowed and rutted. The worst were his hands. Jessie detested Everett's probing wrinkled hands. She shivered, as though ice slid down her back.

Everett was a peculiar sort with an awkward, obvious discomfort around the fairer sex. She had heard that when a man was backward with women, it was inspired by his relationship with his mama. Was that true of Everett? Would his mama approve of Jessie?

Everett portrayed the gentleman. Prim, proper, and assertive in business, he was shrewd. Not a man to be toyed with. Everett wielded power like it was second nature to him.

He'd intimidated Mama. No man ever did that. But Everett had Mama eating out of his hands.

Everett seemed driven and on a mission, determined to have what he wanted. With resources and wealth he bought Jessie and made her his bride.

Why? Everett had meticulously handpicked and put Jessie through a long, humiliating inspection and riled her with impertinent questions before they quickly wed.

Puzzling.

Lips trembling, Jessie's gut went hollow like her heart. She dabbed an errant tear, as her shoulders and neck tightened. Arms clenched to her sides, she quivered from anger.

Jessie didn't deserve love, but pain and insult of rejection continued to wound her. She should be immune to Mama's callus heartlessness by now.

Everett struck a bargain for Jessie's hand in marriage and Mama had sold her. Mama was well compensated and had calmly negotiated as easily as if it were the sale of a case of liquor, instead of her only child. She cared so little.

Mama had noticed fear in Jessie's eyes. "Excuse us for a few moments, Mister Blackstone. I need a private word with my daughter."

Everett could've been the King of France, the way Mama beamed.

Everett left to enjoy free booze at the bar, while Mama told it how it was. "Jazz, now you listen good. Take this stud's deal. Go. Be a good wife. Do whatever it takes to please him. Be grateful, faithful and dedicated to Mister Blackstone. Honor your bargain. He's your savior. You don't deserve this. A plain, stupid wench like you ain't got no chance in this world. You ain't never gonna amount to nothin' without Mister Blackstone. You can't make it on your own. He's offering you a good life--a way outta this hell hole. So make the best of it."

Jessie had wiped a tear with the back of her hand. There was no choice. But her eyes must've appeared resistant.

"It's good business, Jazz. Girls like you are a dime a dozen." Mama had dismissed her. "No flak from you. Go get ready and I'll seal the deal with Mister Blackstone."

Mama had erased Jessie from her life, preferring the cash. No love lost.

That very day, Everett had made her his bride. They consummated the marriage that night. It was less than spectacular. They did the deed. Everett rolled over and started snoring.

The following day Jessie had been sent to Mistress Hatfield's Finishing Academy for Proper Young Ladies of Good Breeding and had spent the last year transforming into a proper lady.

She had worked hard, studied and practiced, determined to become the woman Everett wanted. Jessie learned to care for their home, entertain, and look the part of a blushing bride to please him.

Jessie forced back tears. She had no right to dream of life above her bend. Girls from her station didn't have such opportunities, not in a million years. Yet, Everett offered a dream. How could she resist with nothing to lose and everything to gain--respectability, a fine home and an exciting social life. More importantly, Everett promised a family.

Oh Lordy. Her heart soared with longing for someone to love--children.

If Everett treated her well, she would eventually learn to love him. She'd be a good wife, so maybe Everett could grow to love her, too. No one had ever loved Jessie.

Their children would never long for love. She'd see to it--be there for them, care for their needs, kiss their booboos and teach them to be responsible adults. She had watched mamas like that from afar with their children.

Jessie never had a proper home. Everett was wealthy and would own a magnificent home worthy of his status.

What kind of husband would Everett be? Would he be gentle with her?

Jessie understood nothing of man and women. What went on at the brothel had nothing to do with intimacy. And Jessie was a virgin when she and Everett wed, so she had commanded a good price. She was naïve when it came to relationships.

Far as Jessie could tell, sex was act of drudgery. Girls at the hog ranch said a woman could get something out of sex, like the man. How did this strange thing called an orgasm happen? How did one act? How did you know it occurred? This had never bothered Jessie before, not knowing. But now as Everett's bride . . . If they established a loving relationship, would that lead to such things? Perhaps she could achieve an orgasm.

Regardless, genuine affection would be enough to have a good life.

Closing her eyes she pictured Everett holding her hand strolling through a park with their four tiny ones, as a family--a real family.

Jessie wasn't good enough. *Hell no. Mama was right.* Coming from a despicable life she didn't deserve this.

But Jessie was proof life took strange turns. Marvelous changes occurred when you least expected them. *Don't dare question fate. Make the most of it.*

Almost swooning, she fanned her face and closed her eyes.

This was actually happening. Jessie had stepped head first into a wonderful, new world.

Her mind drifted to the sexy stranger. How nice it had felt having a man defend her. Jessie shouldn't dwell on him--only a pleasant diversion.

Everett was the future. He would care for Jessie--or see to her care. She assumed he would as part of their deal.

She sniffed back tears waving her fan and glancing around to be sure no one noticed.

At least Mama bothered to teach her one useful thing. A lady never went about without protection. Jessie had a few tricks up her sleeve. In this case, up her skirt.

She groped discreetly for the second compartment hidden within her flowing skirts. A solid lump provided another type of assurance. Her savings was securely hidden in the folds of her skirt. Surprisingly, Mama had allowed her to keep the funds Everett gave Jessie. Mama provided room and board, so Jessie figured Mama would take that money too. But she hadn't, so Jessie had socked it away. It amounted to a nice cushion.

Waving the fan to mask her satisfied grin, Jessie attempted to sit properly while the train jostled chaotically.

How would her adventure unfold?

Mystery was the future's appeal.

CHAPTER 4

The whistle startled and Jessie jumped in her seat. She gazed around at other passengers and shielded her nose from heady wood smoke as the train slowed.

Lilly's eyes went wide, focused on the windows. "We're finally here. It's been a long trip."

"It surely has. I'm exhausted and could use a bath." Jessie's insides wriggled in anticipation. Her skin prickled, and her heart skipped a beat, stealing her breath. She focused on controlling enthusiasm, remaining properly ladylike; and stayed sedately seated until the train screeched to a stop. One mustn't appear over-anxious, even as a miracle happened.

The conductor announced arrival, instructed them to disembark, and explained that luggage would be retrieved from the boardwalk.

Jessie and Lilly waited until most folks departed, quietly observing the anxious crowd pushing through. Finally, she stood and walked casually to the exit.

"Let's get a wiggle on, Lilly." Jessie took the few steps down to the boardwalk, holding her skirts gracefully with one gloved hand. The other gripped the railing. She moved toward the station to await their traps.

Jessie's heart sank to her stomach, looking around seeing no familiar face. A tremor of hysteria set in. Where was Everett?

Logan Pace exited the train and turned to help the old codger who'd been seated next to Jessie. Logan engulfed the older man in a bear hug.

Jessie shuddered. *What the hay?*

They were too far away to hear, but that conversation must have been a dilly. Jessie tried to not blatantly stare. However, Lilly caught her glimpse.

"Whoa, that boy's a looker. Do you know him?"

"No. We had a brief encounter on the train, nothing special." Jessie twisted, avoiding the sight, but longing to gape at Logan for one last time.

"Wonder what he's doing with the old mongrel who sat near you."

"It's none of our concern, Lilly."

* * *

Logan released the older man. "Glad to see you're well, Wilson. I wish I'd known you were aboard. We could've shared the journey."

"No worries, Logan, though I'm sorry I missed you. Well lookie yonder. There's that pretty piece of calico who sat next to me."

Following Wilson's train of vision to Mistress Blackstone and her maid, Logan snickered. They were a striking pair even though the tall, slim maid with blue eyes and golden braid dressed plainly. Jessie was shorter with a voluptuous figure, olive skin, glowing green eyes and copper curls. Each lady was lovely in her own way.

"Yep, she's a pretty tart."

"She ain't no tart, young man. That there's a real lady, a good woman. She's honest as the day is long, too. I'd a lost all my yeller hammer if t'weren't for her. That lovely returned my pouch of hard money intact when I dropped it. Now that's an honorable woman."

"Did she know what it was?" Logan's eyes were wide.

"Shore thang, she'd opened it. I could tell by the way t'was tied. Little missy knew t'was my pot of gold and gave it back anyway. If'n she'd a kept it, I wouldn't have a tail feather left. I'd a never knowed what come of it. I was a goner for sure."

Logan chuckled. "Little missy certainly is a piece of work. You should see the pig sticker concealed in her fan." The two laughed and hugged again. "Wilson, I hope to see you soon."

They went their separate ways. Logan strode purposefully toward Jessie carrying his leather satchel. His eyes locked on his target.

* * *

Jessie swallowed the lump in her throat. Logan removed his hat in a flourish as he approached--a magnificent sight. His smile engaged those delectable dimples. Logan's emerald eyes glistened roguishly as he bent into an abbreviated bow. Her belly flip-flopped.

"Good day, Mistress Blackstone. Do you require assistance? Is someone retrieving you?"

There was no avoiding Logan. Jessie attempted to hide her flummox and the urge to crawl beneath the boardwalk, by smiling congenially. She hoped Logan Pace wouldn't witness her shame.

How could Mister Pace look so tasty when Jessie was in a quandary? Clothing was plastered to her skin. Hair mussed from sweating like a sow. Everett seemed to have deserted her, when Logan stood here being sweetly accommodating. Mortified, she hid behind her fan.

"Indeed, Mister Pace, my husband will be around shortly. Thank you for asking. Good day to you." Jessie willed Logan Pace to leave.

Logan's brow rose at the dismissal. He nodded a salute, put his hat on and disappeared around the building.

Lilly eyed them suspiciously.

Jessie continued fanning.

Hell!

"It's hot out here. The temperature must be rising."

Why did the man have such an effect? Why'd he have to appear when her husband was tardy? No worries, Jessie had seen the last of Logan Pace.

Back to reality, Jazz.

"It's been a long time since I laid eyes on Everett. I hope I recognize him." A lump of trepidation formed in Jessie's throat. Her knuckles turned pale from exertion as she gripped her fan. Surely, Everett hadn't forgotten her.

"Of course you'll recognize him."

"Everett must be detained by something important. I'm sure he's only going to be late."

The steward deposited their trunks on the boardwalk, where Lilly claimed them. Then the women watched nervously as the boodle of travelers dispersed and thinned.

Finally an old, black gentleman in a dark suit made his way through the few passengers still milling about. Their eyes locked in acknowledgement. He walked toward Jessie, removed his black bowl hat and placed it under one arm. He bowed slightly.

"Mistress Blackstone?"

Jessie smiled gratefully. "Yes, I'm Mistress Blackstone. You are?"

"Madam, I'm Sebastian Dean." His broad smile revealed gleaming, white teeth and a warm welcome. "I'm Mister Everett's man, here to escort you home."

Jessie sighed relieved. "Thank you, Sebastian. I'm pleased to meet you. I expected Mister Blackstone. Is Everett all right?"

"Yes. Mister Blackstone was unable to come. He sent me to see you home. Mister Blackstone will join you at supper, Madam."

"All right, Sebastian. This is my maid, Lilly." Jessie nodded toward Lilly.

"I'm pleased to meet you, Miss Lilly." Sebastian bowed his head.

"It must be extremely important to keep Everett away." Jessie fidgeted and whispered to Lilly. Lilly nodded and turned pink avoiding eye contact.

Not daring to let on her disappointment, though anxiety at being delegated to Everett's man overshadowed her relief. It would be unseemly and Everett wouldn't appreciate Jessie questioning his actions.

"Yes, Madam." Sebastian scooped up their trunks, led the way then assisted the ladies into a lovely carriage.

"Everett enjoys good taste and quality." Jessie settled into cushy comfort of the velvet tufted seat, as they meandered through the streets.

"San Francisco's colorful hillsides surrounding the sparkling bay are breathtaking." Lilly's head spun from side to side.

"It's absolutely captivating. The harbor is lovely and the unique homes crowding curving streets take advantage of every possible plot of ground." On the edge of her seat, Jessie allowed the scenery to help distract and ease her frustration.

Everything will be fine.

Sebastian laughed. "Yes, San Francisco's a marvelous city."

"The blend of floral fragrance mixed with sea breeze is delightful." Jessie glanced around wanting to miss nothing.

"The brisk breeze is refreshing on this warm, sunny day." Gusts from the wide bay tested the stability of Jessie's hat. She checked the pinning to ensure it would hold.

"Without a hat, my hair would be flying wildly in this robust breeze." Jessie laughed gleefully.

"Bonnets might be better for this weather," Lilly suggested.

"Weather's pleasantly warm and sunny year round, with almost no cold or snow. The hardy breeze is consistent and strong off the ocean," Sebastian informed them.

Jessie whispered, "I wish I could unpin, fling my hat off, and free my curls to play in the wind." The women giggled. "San Francisco air smells clean." Trying to appear demure, she gaped curiously at the sights.

Sebastian chuckled. "Weather provides a unique agricultural environment. Abundant crops flourish in the fertile soil--some which are unsustainable elsewhere."

"How wonderful--I adore living near the ocean. I'm quickly falling in love with San Francisco."

"I understand you're from New Orleans." Sebastian turned toward the women.

"What is New Orleans like, Jessie?" Lilly gushed.

"Ah, New Orleans is passionate, smoldering, and seductively sensual with a hint of evil and mystery of voodoo." Jessie's brows rose. Her voice went dramatic and spooky, as if telling an eerie ghost story to an audience of children.

Lilly giggled and grabbed her hat in the wind. "You lived in Boston for a while?"

"Yes, Boston has an old world, dignified, almost imposing atmosphere of power."

"How does San Francisco fare against those two?" Lilly grinned enjoying the game.

"My first impression? San Francisco teems with alert activity. Vivid colors fill the air with intriguing aromas. The city boasts prosperity. Modern in every way, it's distinctive and charming. People are excited and happy, bustling from place to place."

"I can't wait to shop at those charming outdoor markets lining the streets hocking produce and fresh seafood."

"One can probably find anything in this active, pier-side market. I can't wait to be part of this captivating community-- to belong."

Sebastian drove the carriage up a steep, winding street lined with brilliant blossoms. The affluent area housed elaborate homes atop the peak.

"Many of San Francisco's wealthy reside here on Nob Hill."

They pulled through an ornate iron fence into a small, tree-lined courtyard. A striking home sat surrounded by a bed of roses and assorted flowers.

The awesome three-story, salmon-colored stucco mansion had thick columns supporting a second-story portico above a semi-circle stone veranda. Decorative railing crowned a huge ornately carved wooden door. Windows gleamed in the sunshine. Towering floral trees flanked the house.

"I'll never forget the scent of magnolia blossoms welcoming me home." Closing her eyes, she basked in glory.

Home.

A uniformed group lined the veranda steps standing to attention. Maids wore white aprons atop grey dresses with white collars. Tiny ruffled hats were pinned above severe buns.

Sebastian led Jessie and Lilly to the procession. "Mistress Blackstone, meet your staff. I'm Mister Blackstone's main man. I am your butler when you entertain, and I drive the carriage."

The hair on the back of Jessie's neck stood to attention encountering the stiff aura of the first woman. Probably in her fifties, the servant's plump, expressionless face held an air of formality. Something seemed amiss with this stern woman. Her cordial air felt forced and cold--a show for the others.

"Meet your house manager. Mable runs the household. The staff answers to Mable and me. Whatever you need, we will see to it."

"It's nice meeting you, Madam." Mable curtseyed smiling stiffly. "I look forward to working for you. Say the word if you need anything at all."

That's a lie. Mable doesn't want me here. I'll have to work on her.

Jessie nodded lacing her words with honey. "Thank you, Mable."

"This is Irma, your excellent chef." Irma was probably in her forties and pleasant. Her smile revealed a couple of missing teeth. On a heavy day, Irma wouldn't weigh a hundred pounds. A gust from the bay could blow Irma away.

"I'm pleased to meet you, Mistress Blackstone. I hope you're happy here."

Irma seemed hospitable, though glancing inconspicuously sideways, she seemed wary of the domineering Mable.

"Thank you Irma. I'm sure I will be." At least Irma didn't already hate Jessie.

"This is Lilly, Mistress Blackstone's maid," Sebastian introduced.

"Welcome, Lilly." Irma smiled extending her hand, which Lilly shook.

Mable appeared almost as wary of Lilly as she was of Jessie. Mable's words and expression didn't mesh. Mable wasn't fooling anyone. They weren't welcome.

"I've prepared a room for Lilly. Her required uniform's on the bed." Mable inspected Lilly up and down with an expression akin to distain. "I'll explain duties to Lilly once you're settled, Mistress." Mable's stern stare dared Lilly to argue.

Lilly nervously curtseyed, seemingly intimidated. "I'm pleased to meet you, Mable and Irma."

"It's good to meet you all. We'll get along splendidly." Smiling broadly at her staff, this rude domestic wasn't getting the upper hand. Jessie was the mistress here.

Thank goodness for Lilly. Jessie would be lost in a sea of old people.

A young man rushed from behind the house, drying his hands on his pants. Dressed for labor, he wore brown suspendered trousers and a tan shirt. His worn, floppy hat crushed beneath his arm, had seen better days.

"Cane is the stable man, gardener, and chops wood for the fireplaces and stoves."

Jessie suppressed a giggle at Cane's awkward attempt to bow. "It's pleasant to make your acquaintance, Cane. I'm sure this household is better for your service."

Cane blushed. "Thank you, Mistress. I'm happy for the job."

"Miss Lilly, this is Cane. Cane, this is Miss Lilly, Mistress Blackstone's maid," Sebastian explained.

Cane's eyes sparkled. He chewed his lower lip, not meeting Lilly's gaze.

Lilly held back a grin and batted her thick lashes. Her pink cheeks gave her interest away, as she nodded in Cane's direction.

Pleasure shot through her. This was a good sign. Love could live in this house. Jessie might find it here.

Mable approached, clearing her throat. "I'll see you to your room, Mistress Blackstone. If you need anything, tell Lilly." All business, Mable's temperament remained respectfully forced and frigid.

Sebastian held the imposing doors wide. "I'll bring your luggage up." Sebastian turned back to the carriage with Cane, hot on his heels.

"I like both men. They're welcoming and friendly. I'm not so sure about the women. Irma seems nice enough, but Mable obviously doesn't want me here. Mable seems to resent me for some reason." Jessie whispered for Lilly's ears only.

"Dinner's at six." Mable cleared her throat, following into the enormous foyer.

Irma scurried off and disappeared, presumably to the kitchen. Jessie gasped at the magnitude of the massive house.

"I'm finally home." Her voice caught, husky with emotion.

"The Mister will be home for dinner. You must be exhausted from your travel. You should rest before dressing to dine." Mable stiffly snorted.

"How peculiar, formality and pecking order govern the atmosphere. Mable rules the roost. My arrival seems to impose on her territory." Jessie whispered to Lilly.

"Irma seems nice but intimidated by Mable." Lilly whispered.

"I shall like Irma and can win her over." Jessie beamed. "My, this foyer's a splendid work of art."

The carved dome three floors above displayed a suspended glittering chandelier. Jessie's head jerked slightly backward to take in the vision.

The room smelled pleasantly of lemon. The wood shone in sunlight streaming through immaculate windows. Hand-carved railing crafted by a skilled artist graced the stairwell. White marble floors caught and reflected brilliant light.

Several sets of gigantic pocket-doors graced the foyer leading to rooms on either side. The long hallway ended at an archway where Irma had disappeared. The vast house shouted decorum and felt like it was filled with emptiness.

"It's lovely," Lilly spoke quietly, clearly intimidated by the enormous building.

"It certainly is," Jessie whispered. "Daunting--frozen in the hot California sunshine. I hoped it would be warm and cozy, and not so grand."

"It's huge."

"Babies will turn this monastery into a home. The sooner the better." They followed Mable upstairs.

"The Mister built this mansion for his mother." Mable snipped and glared at Jessie with one brow raised.

"He'll be happy sharing it with you." Lilly smiled.

Mable snorted then quickly regained her blank expression. She led them into a bedroom. "Your room, Madam."

Maybe Lilly was right. The thought gave hope.

"Thank you, Mable. The room is lovely." Jessie spun around in the center, beaming. "I adore the pastel yellows and greens with the splattering of lavender. These ruffled curtains are the sheerest silk. The whole boodle is delicate and feminine--absolutely beautiful. I'll enjoy the room immensely."

Mable didn't appear amused.

Would Everett sleep in such a room? Doubtful.

Jessie ran a finger across the gold trimmed, white dresser. Its triple mirror was perfect for applying makeup from the tufted seat. Jessie lifted the roll top of the dainty desk with its matching brocade lady-size chair. An elegant, hand-woven rug covered the immaculate wooden floor.

Jessie fingered the ruffled canopy of the oversized bed sporting a silk duvet and decorative pillows. Plopping atop the pale, green chaise, she eyed the matching over-stuffed chair in one corner.

"Wonderful . . . these cozy seats are heated by sunshine streaming through the window. It provides a perfect place to curl up with a good book."

"The city and bay views are breathtaking." Lilly stood in front of the window.

Jessie leaned on the marble sill and stared in awe of the splendor. She flung the window open and closed her eyes as the sea breeze cooled her face.

How had she fallen into such fortune? She must become worthy.

Mable's nose turned up sternly. "Ring the bell if you need anything. Lilly will unpack for you later. Come, Lilly, I'll show you your quarters." Mable spun and walked the length of the hallway. Her heels clicked as she almost ran. Lilly scurried to keep up.

At least Lilly wasn't a cold fish like Mabel.

Lying down, too excited to nap, her every nerve was alive and on edge like having swallowed jumping beans. Her innards did a dilly of a dance. Jessie's body craved exercise and jerked to attention. She must move about.

So many wonderful things were coming at her fast and furious. She welcomed them all. Jessie could hardly wait for Everett's return home.

Chapter 5

"Bees must be building a hive in my innards, they tremble so. Surely I'll spit honey." Jessie agonized, dressing for her first dinner with Everett. She must look perfect so Everett wouldn't regret their marriage.

Lilly insisted on unpacking and steaming Jessie's wardrobe, hovering about attempting to assist. After struggling to manage, Jessie pulled Lilly to the bed.

"Sit, dear Lilly. As much as I enjoy your company, I dislike being dressed. Help me with the damned corset and give your opinion on how I look. I can dress myself."

Lilly shook her head and shrugged.

"What do you think of this yellow satin? The narrow white pin-stripes and sky-blue piping give it an elegant charm. Don't you agree?" Jessie pranced in front of the full-length mirror with the dress draped across her front.

"It's lovely, Jessie. The heart-shaped neckline with its delicate lace trim shows the perfect amount of your ample cleavage. The cinched waistline accentuates your amazing figure. The Mister should enjoy you in the gown."

"Thank you, Lilly. You are a big help. I hope we'll become fast friends."

I've never had a friend.

"I'm touched. I would love being your friend, but the staff mustn't know. Their loyalty lies with the Mister. I doubt he'd approve of you befriending a servant." Lilly frowned. "They'd snitch, especially Mable. Mable has been with the Mister his whole life and his Mother before him. We mustn't anger your husband. I need this job."

"Mable raised Everett from a babe, which helps explain her resentment. Mable must think no woman's good enough." Jessie laid the gown on the bed and took Lilly's hands. "Don't worry, Lilly. We'll be discreet. I won't jeopardize your position. It'll be our secret." Jessie kissed Lilly's cheek.

Lilly smiled.

"It's settled. Help me on with this damned, Godforsaken torture device." Jessie scowled at the corset and they giggled.

"My, you have a gutter mouth." Lilly took the corset and opened the stays.

"That's one of our secrets, my friend." Jessie patted Lilly's cheek. "I must be a lady for everyone else. I can be myself with you."

Lilly blushed. "No one, especially someone with your rank in society, has ever trusted me before. As a servant most people look down their noses at me. Or they don't see me at all. You treat me like a real person." Lilly dabbed at moisture in her eye then helped with the constricting garment.

They laughed and joked as they secured the contraption's wicked stays. Finally Jessie was securely strapped into it within an inch of her life.

"No wonder women swoon at the slightest thing. I can't breathe in this damned thing."

Lilly repaired Jessie's cascade of curls then assessed her hairstyle with a hand mirror. "Lilly, you're quite talented. It's lovely how you placed sparkling butterfly pins strategically throughout the coif."

Lilly's face reddened as though unaccustomed to compliments.

Jessie squirted on imported Parisian perfume then stepped gracefully into the delicate gown that Lilly held open. Periwinkle toes of kid-leather ballet slippers peeked daintily from beneath the full skirt floating above multiple crinolines. She spun around, prancing giddily admiring her reflection.

"Will Everett like what he sees?"

"You're stunning. How could he not?"

As anticipation mounted and raw nerves trembled with expectation, Jessie's hands shook. She closed her eyes to focusing on slow breathing to control her rapid pulse.

"I'm trussed up like a turkey. Tonight must be perfect. It's the beginning of our lives together."

"How can it not? You have a marvelous life. Your wealthy husband is plum rich as possum gravy."

Jessie laughed nervously then descended the stairs and entered the dining room. Everett turned as she entered.

Candles glittered from a centerpiece of silver candelabra surrounded by fresh flowers. Two place settings of crystal, china and silver graced linen placemats with matching napkins. Everett reigned pretentiously from the head of the long mahogany table that could easily accommodate twelve, looking right at home in the copiousness.

She was thrown off kilter by the formality when Everett kissed her hand lightly and bowed, indicating the empty seat beside him.

"Good evening, my dear. I see you made it."

Unlike Mister Pace's intensely heated touch, no sparks flew from Everett's cool hand.

Disappointing. Jessie had hoped to enjoy a similar connection with Everett.

Everett helped Jessie get seated then took his place at the head of the table. Every move was properly executed, though they were completely alone.

"Thank you, Everett. The house is lovely. My room with its breathtaking view of your divine gardens is delightful. I'm happy to finally be home, here with you." Jessie spoke slowly and sweetly as a lady should.

Everett appeared satisfied without being moved by her arrival, as she had hoped. Everett placed a napkin on his lap and Jessie followed suit.

"That's wonderful, my dear." Everett rang a silver bell beside his plate. Mable appeared with a bottle of wine and showed him the label. He nodded. Mable uncorked it and poured a tad into Everett's goblet. He swirled the dark red liquid, eyed it curiously then sniffed and closed his eyes as he swallowed. Assured of its worthiness, Everett nodded. Mable filled his goblet and poured a glass for Jessie. Mable served fresh water from a pitcher then stood stiffly beside Everett.

"Thank you, Mable. I'll ring when we wish to be served." Dismissed, Mable left.

Jessie tasted the wine. "Umm, delightful."

"It's quite good, made from grapes grown in Napa, north of here by a gentleman named Charles Krug. His valley farm has the perfect climate and soil. I'm glad you like it."

"Thank you, Everett." Tension from Jessie's body slowly started to dissipate. She hoped Everett would relax too, because his stiff demeanor caused her skin to crawl.

"I want to discuss your duties." With careful measured movements Everett folded his hands on the table and stared at her.

Duties? This wasn't what Jessie had hoped to discuss first thing.

"All right. I'm eager to learn how you want things done."

How does a lady react?

Jessie folded her hands in her lap. Her insides quivered and the scent of roasted meat made her nauseous. Sun shone brightly through velvet-clad windows. However, Jessie shivered at the chill. Sweat--no glow--burst onto her forehead as she flashed from hot to cold and resisted the urge to wipe it away for fear of swooning.

This little get-acquainted chat wasn't going well. Everett was lock stock and barrel all about duties.

So be it.

"You'll manage the household With Mable as your right hand."

Oh, joy. I'm tickled and can't wait.

"Mable is devoted and will manage the house and staff. Mable will instruct Irma to cook meals with your direction." Everett turned a strange shade of grey. His eyes grew wide staring at the wall behind Jessie. And a quivering hand went to his chest as he appeared to have stopped breathing.

"Are you alright, Everett? What is wrong?"

Pausing for a couple of deep breaths, he shook his head as though clearing it then regained decorum and smiled. "Nothing to concern you, my dear. Only a bout of indigestion. Now where were we?" Everett went on as though nothing had happened. "Are you pleased with Lilly?"

"Indeed. Lilly's a blessing." *It didn't look like nothing to me.*

Everett nodded. "Very well. You may keep Lilly on. The garden is at your disposal. I expect you to make use of it when we entertain. Fill the house with fresh flowers. Cane is an expert in all things to do with the grounds. He can help. If Sebastian is busy, Cane can drive your carriage."

"That's topping good. I enjoy floral design."

I have my own carriage?

Everett must want to get details out of the way, so they'd be free to get acquainted. He was still a bit stand-offish. Jessie would soon remove his armor.

"We've a calendar of important social and business engagements posted on my desk. Avail yourself of it. Be prepared, prompt and dressed appropriately."

Alright already.

"Your wardrobe's extensive. However, purchase whatever you need to stay atop fashion trends. Appearance is important. Mable can direct you to purchase appropriate clothing."

Sure. I'll ask for her help.

"Thank you, Everett. That's very considerate." This explained the wardrobe full of gowns in her bedroom.

Jessie's job as Everett's arm candy was to impress his associates. Everett was fixated and a compulsive stickler for control. He didn't miss a thing.

Jessie could live with that. Perhaps Everett's obsessiveness was a blessing in disguise. Understanding expectations should allow her to surpass them.

Everett droned on and on about household expenses, handling merchants and Jessie's monthly stipend for spending money. Would it never end?

"That's very generous." Everything seemed covered. Jessie wasn't sure what she'd need cash for. But she could sock it away.

I must find a hiding spot for my stash.

"Don't go about town alone. It's too dangerous. Sebastian or Cane will accompany you."

"Thank you. I'm eager to explore this beautiful city." Jessie attempted to remain composed but her hands quivered. If she could unwind, perhaps Everett would be more at ease.

"San Francisco's a gem of a city with abundant culture and prosperous business. Unfortunately crime has become rampant, making it unsafe to wander about alone. Understand?" Everett glared pointedly.

"That's too bad, however, not entirely unexpected. Most cities experience a certain amount of unsavoriness. I'm not naïve about that. Cane and Sebastian will steer me to suitable areas to explore."

Everett cleared his throat. "My dear, I prefer to call you Jess. The short version of your name will sound like my pet name for you. It will indicate that our marriage is solid."

Opposed to real intimacy?

"We'll appear a loving couple finally reunited. How we met and your background must remain secret. Are we clear?"

"Yes, Everett, my fondest wish is for us to actually become a loving couple. What do you prefer I call you?"

Everett snorted unaffected. "Everett is fine. Anything flowing naturally off your tongue will do, as long as it is appropriate. We must keep appearances at all times."

"You're certainly formal, my dear husband. I understand you want to clear the air. I had hoped for a more intimate beginning to our relationship." Jessie swallowed and almost gagged on the knot growing steadily in her throat. Her trembling hands nearly splattered the wine.

Is this marriage to be a farce?

Everett's brow furrowed. His eyes glared with an unnerving look. Everett's critical wordlessness reminded Jessie of being at Mistress Hatfield's.

"We'll share a bedroom. Correct?" Though Jessie loved the perfectly feminine room as it was, Everett should be comfortable in their bedroom. He might wish to change the dainty decor.

"Shall we redecorate the bedroom to better suit your taste? I look forward to snuggling and enjoying your warmth beside me. We can chat about our hopes and dreams nestled under a soft comforter. Sleeping together shall provide familiarity. That will fortify our marriage bond."

Everett glared as though Jessie had spoken a foreign language. "I have no intention of sleeping with you. I have my own room. I prefer sleeping alone. I'm set in my ways and leave early for work. Cohabitation would destroy my routine."

Air sucked from the room. Jessie's face fell. Her stomach sunk to her lap. Rejected. She'd been too forward.

"I see." Jessie cleared her throat and met Everett's cool gaze. "I'm disappointed. How will we become emotionally intimate, if we don't share a bed?"

Everett raised his eyebrows. "I don't see the point." End of discussion. He hesitated a moment before getting on with business. "You will breakfast alone. I work long days. I will be home for dinner mostly. Mable will know if I'm expected. I'll occasionally spend nights at my gentleman's club. This should not concern you."

Great. Mable again.

"I see. You do still intend for us to have a family. Right?" Studying Everett closely, Jessie wondered what kind of marriage this would be.

Everett visibly stiffened, coughed and paused. "Sex is a touchy subject."

Surely we won't formally discuss our sex life. Please, let Everett soften on this subject.

Jessie's head flooded with questions and confusion. She fought tears filling her eyes.

"You do want a family. Don't you? I do. It's why I allowed myself to be coaxed into this unusual union."

Everett smirked. Allowing her to stew, Everett sipped wine before answering.

Strangely, it seemed Everett wanted Jessie at his mercy. She disliked the cruel game.

Was this marriage a grave mistake? Her mind raced frantically, stalling panic but attempting to appear calm and collected. Reaching her wits end, Everett finally spoke.

"Sex isn't a suitable topic. You must realize that. Since you brought it up, we'll discuss it. I'll join you in your bedroom on a regular basis when I want intercourse. As I please, you'll accommodate me. What we do in your bedroom will be a far cry from the facade we put before the public. We'll appear the proper couple and suitably affectionate. When alone you'll do whatever pleases me. What happens in your bedroom stays there. Understood?"

Jessie winced at the harshness of his commanding words. She would do most anything for Everett and didn't understand why he couldn't be sweet about it. Jessie would prefer teasing and lustful talk to this dictatorial attitude.

Everett leaned elbows on the table and linked his fingers together, eyeing her sternly. This seemed a maneuver appropriate for posing power and authority at a business discussion. Not in prelude to a loving relationship with one's wife.

Well, hell.

"Yes Everett. I understand. Your happiness and pleasure is important."

I'm his slut, Everett's fancy courtesan. At least I'm a high priced bed fagot. Mama would be proud.

So much for becoming lovers--this is a business deal for sex without attachment. I'm no more than a servant.

I must change Everett's mind. I won't give up hope.

Certain benefits came with being a rich man's wife. It beat the hell out of hooking in Mama's brothel.

Jessie got a nice home as a respected socialite in the community. And there would be babies.

"Thank you for bringing me here." She couldn't read his nod and glare. "Hopefully our union will soon result in a family."

It must be enough.

"Yes, you'll give me an heir." It was a command, not a hope or request. Everett's facial muscles eased and his hands dropped to his lap. His stiff demeanor appeared to be melting with the change of subject.

Everett wanted children.

His gaze finally settled on the painting above the buffet. Everett smirked.

The portrait of a lady with dark hair pulled into a severe bun atop her head. The stern looking woman wore a black dress with white collar. Its only adornment was a black bow tied at the collar. Her face would've been lovely had she smiled. She didn't appear the type who did.

Everett's haughty expression melted warmly.

Following Everett's musing the female appeared to evoke strong emotions in him.

"Is she your Mama?" Compassion filled Jessie's soft voice as hopefully she could reach Everett this way grew.

"Indeed. My deceased mother must be appalled. She should be tossing in her grave that I brought you here." Everett grinned wickedly.

Disturbing his mama's peaceful rest gave Everett pleasure. *Wow, this explains a lot.*

"Why'd you marry me instead of a debutante from your social circle?" Jessie wanted to understand.

Everett's hearty chuckle sent shivers skimming through her backbone.

"Those dry bitches never showed me the least morsel of humanity. They were clamoring for my money and position only. Besides, no proper woman is eager to distort her figure with birthing. Let alone waste time caring for children. Mama actually gave me the notion. She had no idea I would take it to the letter." Everett uttered a hoarse, guttural laugh.

Jessie shuddered on in the hot room. "How so?"

"Mama said I should pay for favors. She told me to satisfy my wicked urges without tarnishing a '*good woman*' with such ugly attentions. Well, I showed the old bat."

Everett stared at his mama's image. He appeared lost in a haze of painful recollection. Everett's words weren't meant for Jessie. They were for his dead mother. A stormy expression overtook Everett's face. His eyes glazed.

It must be a dark place, inside Everett's mind.

Trepidation seeped through Jessie's shivering bones. Goose bumps formed on her arms. Unexpected coolness filled the room like a window had flung opened.

This vindictive, evil side of Everett drove home his point, but there was no benefit to pursuing it. Better change the subject. Hopefully Everett would snap out of his ill mood.

"Darling Everett, I'm anxious. I can hardly wait to become a mother." Jessie's insides warmed. They shared this desire--a starting point they could build their marriage from.

Everett smiled, as though he hadn't left for a darker world of his own. Children seemed to be his favorite subject.

"You're young, healthy and will produce several children. I prefer a son first."

Jessie giggled. "We can't place an order to control the number and sex of our children. Though that would be wonderful."

Jessie heart warmed toward Everett like an injured bird, she could happily nurture so they could grow closer, and she placed her hand atop his. Everett jerked away awkwardly, as though unaccustomed to being touched and appeared flustered with his hand shaking when he rang the silver bell.

Flinching, familiar with rejection, the rebuff ended their brief, sweet discussion. But Jessie mustn't let it control her.

Breathe.

Mable entered with a tray and served dinner. All business, Everett explained their social circle, consisting of business associates.

Half listening while her mind roamed disappointed at the way things were going.

Everett dismissed Jessie after dinner without invitation to join him as he adjourned for libations alone.

Later he came to her bedroom filled with bottle courage. He uttered unsteadily tangle-footed, feeling his oats. Everett wore an embroidered smoking jacket and nightshirt. His stocky body was lightly coated with greying fluff. He smelled of cigars and bourbon.

Everett's presence filled the room. He dominated the air and ruled in Jessie's presence. She could hardly breathe.

Everett walked unceremoniously to Jessie's bed, indicating with a wave she should continue. He sat observing her unpinning and brushing curls from their bindings. Jessie draped hair alluringly about her shoulders attempting a sultry pose, hoping to tempt him and uncover the route to Everett's heart.

His glare sent shivers through her spine.

So be it. Two could play this game.

Everett moved behind fingering her curls then bent to smell the tendrils reverently and pushed the satin dressing gown to her waist, revealing a cotton chemise.

Jessie's shoulders stiffened nervously. She wanted their union to be better than their wedding night had been.

Clumsy, chubby hands stroked possessively. Everett buried his face in the curls, and she leaned into him observing in the mirror.

Everett sniffed her skin and kissed her neck and shoulders.

Goose bumps formed. Jessie's nipples stiffened as she shivered slightly. She placed her hands on Everett's hips.

Brushing her hands aside his dressing gown dropped unceremoniously revealing a dimpled, lumpy body.

Jessie gulped a breath of strangled air. *How could any man be so white?*

Everett pulled her to join him standing at the foot of the bed and kissed her forehead wetly. Tilting his head slightly he perused Jessie's face like surveying his territory. Everett's fingers slithered across her forehead and cheeks then stroked her lips softly at first then more firmly while chewing her lower lip, she feared what was to come

Everett buried his face in Jessie's ear. Nuzzling her neck leaving soft wet pecks in his wake, he moaned, as though eating a tasty treat.

His reaction pleased her. At least it was a human reaction, an intimate act, and something to work with.

Jessie tingled at his touch and wet breath on her skin, and her nipples hardened like marbles.

Soft hands unaccustomed to work explored her arms, belly and groped her breasts, as he gently squeezed the roundness through fabric. Then he pushed it down and lightly pinched the hard nubs, grinning, eyes wide.

"So sweet," Everett murmured to no one. His tongue trailed around Jessie's collar bone and between her breasts. He nudged the globes gently aside with his nose and snuggled amidst them.

"Umm, so soft. Mine. All mine."

Pleased, she moved into Everett pushing her hips forward as he gripped her. His *wanger* lying soft against her pantaloons he shoved her onto the bed, flipped her chemise over her head, and climbed on all fours above perusing Jessie's bare breasts with a wicked sneer. Everett bit one harder than necessary and squeezed the other uncomfortably.

Jessie wriggled, surprised at the discomfort.

Rising, Everett slowly pulled the pantaloons down. Her gaze locked on Everett's face as he exposed her womanhood. His mouth fell open and drool formed on his lip before he licked it and grunted.

Unimpressed with his puny erection, at least she had this effect on him. He might be human after all.

Everett tossed Jessie's undergarment, parted her legs and crawled atop her. His weight was substantial but not uncomfortable and long chest hairs tickled her breasts.

Jessie gripped his pudgy, white body with her legs. His tiny organ found its target and forcefully entered her not-quite-ready body.

Ouch!

Oh, well, she'd deal later with the torn, tender flesh ripped in the sudden invasion.

They rocked in a steady beat. Everett drooled and grunted in abandon pounding forth until a final grunt.

It was over.

Everett laid sweating heavily and gasping for breath. His face buried into her shoulder above one breast. Slobber dripped onto Jessie's skin, and she shivered. It beaded into a single blob before it slithered along her side.

Craving intimacy, emotional connection and a joining of spirits, she gently stroked Everett's hairy back, attempting to cuddle and bask in the afterglow that only he had enjoyed. Everett snorted loudly and rolled away.

Her heart fell and her eyes closed resolved to lie patiently until he slept it off.

It would be okay. The important thing was Everett's perception of their coming together. If he was happy, Jessie was happy--for the act meant nothing.

Eventually Everett woke. Jessie attempted to rub his bald head, hoping for some intimacy, she missed her target.

Everett rose quickly. Her hands fell empty, as he rejected comfort offered-- done with Jessie.

Everett didn't even speak but simply pulled on his smoking jacket then left the room without a word. Closing the door behind, he didn't bother to say goodnight. It couldn't hurt worse had he slapped Jessie's face.

Quivering, heart quaking, tears flooded her eyes and swarmed her cheeks, as she convulsed silently crying unheard.

"Goodnight, husband," Jessie whispered loudly then gagged sick at her stomach.

She had never felt so used before. The hoped for lovemaking desired hadn't transpired. Jessie cried for the loving husband and home she had dreamed of. Neither existed. Everett might be like Mama and not capable of caring or intimacy.

Their frigid house may ever be filled with love.

Everett needed a wife to impress the public and manage his home. He wanted a sex slave and broodmare for his children.

Jessie might turn Everett around, so his heart would soften, if she showed him love and devotion. She would please Everett tomorrow--another day. Another chance . . . to get it right, be a better wife and lover, and make Everett care for her.

It may prove difficult to love the cold, distant man, but she wanted to badly.

How did one grow to love a man? Jessie would figure it out.

CHAPTER 6

Lilly would keep her secret, so she confided.

"Our life is a sham. Everett doesn't love me. He only wants to fulfil his body's need for release. He wants us to appear to have a perfect marriage."

"Oh, Jessie, that's so sad." Lilly hugged her tight.

"Sex with Everett is good, because I'll soon be a mother. That's enough." Jessie shrugged. A baby would fill the gaping, wretched hole in her gut.

"At least your children shall lack for nothing. He can provide opportunity, a good life and a place in society befitting his family. The Mister can teach them to be productive to guarantee continued wealth." Lilly sewed a new garment.

"They'll have my undying devotion and love. I'll teach my babies to be good, honest people."

Hugging herself she spun around the room landing on the chaise beside Lilly.

"When I close my eyes, I hold the weight of a tiny being, snuggled securely in my arms--my warm baby. The sheer silkiness of his skin is so vividly ingrained. It's so real that I smell his soft whisper of breath." Jessie gazed out the window and dreamed of her lips touching her child's tender cheek.

"I'll hum a lullaby. I'll change my infant's nappies and tuck him in his cradle with a goodnight kiss. I'll sooth his fears and watch him bravely take his first steps. His first word shall be Mama." Jessie spoke wistfully.

"You'll be a wonderful mama, Jessie. Maybe your children will inherit your curly, copper hair. What color was Mister Blackstone's before it greyed?"

"I've no idea, Lilly. If they have my green eyes or his brown ones, it doesn't matter. As long as a boy comes first, I don't disappoint Everett. Happy and healthy children are all that matter to me." It was out of her control. Why worry.

Pleasing Everett wasn't easy. Jessie made every effort, as much as he allowed and managed every aspect and detail of home and comfort, daring not disappoint.

Jessie gladly gave Everett her body to be used as he pleased. She hoped it would result in her dreams coming true.

Those were the rules. Jessie played the game well and became Everett's arm candy--the perfect lady. Everett's friends admired her beauty, grace and wit.

Pulling it off easily, she laid it on thick, smiling, laughing and talking about appropriate subjects at suitable times. Jessie had them buffaloed, and they found her interesting and engaging. Everett seemed pleased and proud at the way she charmed his associates.

"This social life is exhausting. It's not my cup of tea. I do it for Everett. At least dinner conversation is stimulating. When we're in mixed company the men speak of business and politics. Everett doesn't approve. But I listen intently. I have learned a right smart amount from his partners."

"That's funny." Lilly glanced from her sewing. "Most women have no interest in business."

"I shouldn't be interested in such things. But I'm fascinated with issues of importance. I can't help listening."

"You enjoy the womenfolk and have made friends. Haven't you?"

"You'd figure so. But no. Not at all. Ladies in our circle are politely distant with no potential for friendship. They're all alike, shying away from intimacy and putting on airs. They are doing their wifely duty as expected. They are playing a role--the same as me."

"That's awful. Surely they have some saving grace." Lilly's mouth hung open at the concept new to her.

"I much prefer your company. You and I have stimulating conversations. Those women bore me to tears. They don't have an individual idea in their pretty heads." Jessie prepared for an evening out. "Thank goodness I have you, or I'd lose my mind."

"Unfortunate." Lilly shook her head.

"They make me cringe. Lawd Almighty, society women are gossips, talking terribly about one another behind their backs. They are spiteful and untrustworthy. When they aren't biting each other's backs, conversation drifts to boring subjects of no meaning. They incessantly discuss fashion as though lives depended on it. Entertainment debates are at least tolerable, but it's hard engaging in the importance of silk or satin, lace or piping. Fashion only concerns me when it pleases Everett."

Jessie spun in front of the mirror wearing Lilly's latest creation.

"He shall be pleased tonight. You look spectacular." Lilly beamed.

Her face heated at the rare compliment. Everett spared compliments as a waste of breath. His behavior showed she pleased Everett.

"It isn't all bad. Sometimes the ladies talk about children. I seize the opportunity to question and learn. But though they love their children, they don't enjoy the closeness I want with mine. Most contentedly direct their children's lives instead of participate in them. They allow Nannies or nursemaids to attend their babies."

"I suppose it's the way with the wealthy." Lilly continued sewing.

"Not me. I will be close to my family. I will be the one they turned to. Even if Everett insists on a nannie or nursemaid, I'll be the primary caregiver. It's non-negotiable. I'll stand for no less."

I'll defy Everett if necessary.

Lilly smiled sweetly continuing to sew. "Me too. I want the kind of relationship my parents had, with my husband and children."

"I can't say the same. I didn't starve. But Mama never cared much for me." Jessie wiped a tear with the back of her hand.

Damn! Rejection still stings. Don't dwell. Change the subject.

"I dread time alone with the ladies. They're not so bad in mixed company. After dinner women are sent to the parlor for embroidery, board games or charades. That is so mind-numbing and intolerable. I could pull my hair out. I wish I were a man. They adjourn to the library for cigars and tornado juice. Sometimes they enjoy a tad of twisting the tiger. That must be fun. I wonder what a cigar tastes like. Too bad the ladies aren't interested in poker." Jessie mimicked puffing a fat one.

"You're scandalous."

"Gents privately discuss important matters in depth. They argue about taboo subjects. Men wheel and deal to make important decisions about business and state matters, without having to be socially polite in their womenfolk's presence. They believe these things don't concern women in polite society."

"These things concern you?" Lilly stared quizzically.

"Of course, I'm interested in business, finance, politics and weighty matters. I wish I could join the men to learn how they rule, how decisions are made, and what's going on in the world. I'm smart enough to contribute, if only I were a man."

"You're a rare bird. You are as smart as a man. It'd be a waste of an amazing woman. Enjoy being female, Jessie." Lilly tweaked a curl, teasingly.

"Why torture myself? I'm doomed as a woman. It's my lot in life. The dutiful wife destined to stay a helpless outsider, without power to decide my fate. It's simply the way it is." Jessie shrugged.

Lilly laughed a dreamy expression on her face. "Being a woman is wonderful. You should try enjoying it and fitting in."

Suspicious!

"Is that right? Do tell. There's a sparkle in your eye lately. You're sweet on Cade. Aren't you? Are you keeping company? Do tell, Lilly." Jessie wagged her brows comically.

"Cade's nice. He treats me tenderly with consideration, like a grand lady. I may let him kiss me next time we're alone." Lilly blushed.

"Cade better be good to you, or he'll answer to me." Hands on hips, Jessie attempted a fierce appearance.

"You're changing the subject." Lilly tilting her head.

"I'll do my best when we adjourn for *'womanly'* entertainment in the parlor. While men drink brandy and smoke in the den I shall drown my sorrows in sherry. I will attempt embroidery, quilting or ridiculous games, and appear to pay attention to gossip. I'll even make an effort to participate."

"You may learn to like it, if you give yourself the chance."

"I don't fit in. I never will. I've endeavored to forge friendships with no luck. I no longer care that I'm on the outside looking in, existing on the fringes. I'll never belong. It doesn't matter because I can be myself with you."

"The string quartet entertaining tonight is in the parlor. Your floral arrangements smell marvelous throughout the house. Irma's dinner spread looks and smells scrumptious. You've managed every detail."

Jessie's smile didn't reach her eyes. "Everett's associates will be impressed. He has grown pleased with my hostess skills. It's my job, dear Lilly."

* * *

"Jessie, you aren't prone to napping. What's going on with you? Lately you're plum tuckered out."

"I'm not sure. My body craves a long restful afternoon sleep even when I'm not overly exerting myself. I can't keep my eyes open."

"Your appetite has dwindled."

"Some odors send my head and stomach spinning. Yesterday I barely made it to privacy before spiting bile swelling and gurgling from my stomach." Jessie screwed her face up.

Lilly found her few days later. Her head drooped above a slop jar, pale and sweating profusely. "You poor thing, here is a cool cloth for your head." Lilly held her curls out of the way. "Could you be pregnant?" Lilly whispered quietly lest other servants hear.

A slow smile filled her face. Lilly saw what Jessie hadn't been able to. "I certainly hope it's the case, so this misery results in something good."

"You've been sick for a fortnight now. May I send for the doctor?"

"Yes, it's time. Wait until the Mister leaves for work. Bring the doctor to my quarters. Keep it quiet."

"This house should warm up some with a child puttering around in it."

"I hope so." Jessie straightened her dress, checked her face and hair, making sure she was fit to be seen by the staff.

The doctor did an examination and asked questions, touched her belly, probed and made "hum" sounds. Finally he washed his hands in her basin.

"Mistress Blackstone, congratulations. You're with child." He preened proudly, as if he had something to do with the blessing.

She fought the urge to grab the short stocky man, hug him and do a jig.

Always remain the lady.

Demurely speaking, Jessie did her best to contain the herd of squirrely critters dancing in her belly. "Thank you Doctor."

"I'll see myself out." He left closing Jessie's door.

Lilly tapped, entered, and closed the door quietly. She leaned against it. "So?"

Feeling as though she glowed from inside, her grin spread from ear to ear, and her voice sounded elated. "I'm going to be a mommy."

Lilly threw her arms tightly around Jessie. Together they danced around gaily like two young girls.

"Everett will be thrilled."

Later, seated at the formal table for dinner, Everett smiled as his bride entered.

"How was your day, my dear?" Everett's cordial voice belied his formality. His manner put Jessie at ease. It was a good sign.

"Wonderful, Everett, I have exciting news and have been simply dying for you to get home to share it." Her voice sounded almost giddy.

Everett folded his hands in front of his plate, looking unamused with her unladylike demeanor. "Well, let's have it."

"We're having a baby. You'll soon be a daddy."

Everett gasped. His wide eyes radiating excitement, as much as Everett was capable of drumming up. He cleared his throat, as though swallowing emotion.

Overjoyed at Everett's reaction, Jessie touched his hand, and he didn't pull away. She could tell Everett was overcome, speechless and he looked pleased. But he wouldn't allow himself to show it.

"You've long wanted this. Now it's a reality." Jessie's heart flooded with a deep sense of satisfaction at having finally made Everett truly happy.

Everett's eyes watered. He smiled a real smile, fond and genuine for a change. "I'm grateful. I was right to choose you. You've come through for me."

You'd think Jessie was a stranger that executed a business deal. Her husband certainly was cold-hearted.

"Good. Pleasing you was my intention."

"I'm pleased. I want children very much. I've longed for an heir to carry my name and someday run my empire."

"If the first isn't a boy it isn't the end of the world. We'll have more children, I pray. We'll have as many as you wish. You'll love a girl the same. Won't you?" Jessie had an urge to hug Everett. She resisted, knowing he'd surely hate that.

"It will be a boy. However, a daughter will suffice."

Everett didn't appear too sure about the process, stammering more to him than to her. He carefully withdrew his hand from the grasp with a satisfied look.

Please don't let Everett hold the child's sex against her.

"I'm ecstatic and can hardly wait." Jessie wiggled unladylike in her chair, incapable of sitting still.

"This is delightful news, my dear. I trust you will care for yourself in a suitable manner. Nothing must happen to this child."

Jessie grimaced. "I've been sick in the mornings. I'm sensitive to odors. Some foods make me nauseous. It'll pass and is perfectly normal. I'm strong and healthy. The doctor said the baby should be fine. I'll take every precaution to safeguard our young one."

He leaned in, inspecting Jessie closely, gazing at her lap with an odd expression. "You're not showing yet. Until you do, this is our secret. The staff is aware of everything that happens in this house. We'll wait until we must to announcement this to our friends."

Jessie's eyes wide. "Okay. If it pleases you."

Perhaps this is how proper society handles pregnancy.

"Lilly has helped me, when I've taken ill. But I will be discreet."

"The staff gossips. The walls have ears. No secret is safe. There's no hiding your condition from the servants." Everett chuckled, proudly. He began eating his steak with gusto.

Jessie wanted to shout it from the rooftops. But she would do whatever pleased Everett.

Tender, lightly cooked filet mignon swam in its own juices on the plate. Gulping air, she cut the barely pink meat. Bloody juice oozed out. The scent assaulted her nostrils, making her head swim.

Damn Mable. She did this on purpose. Mable knows I can't tolerate blood swilling from my meat, especially now.

Jessie closed her eyes with a long, slow breath, and broke into a cold sweat.

"Are you ill, my dear? You look pale. You're glowing."

She sucked air slowly and dabbed at her clammy face with the napkin and sipped water to gain some control.

"I'll be fine. I only need a moment." Jessie's hand rose for an instant. She picked up her knife and sliced the meat into tiny pieces, playing with it.

"Take your time, Jess. You must eat. Meat is essential for your health and the child's."

Smiling, she speared a piece of steak. Closing her eyes, it slowly slid into her mouth, and she forced her lips to chew. Surprisingly it tasted delicious. Jessie ate another and took a bite of mashed potatoes with gravy. Better. Everett beamed watching her eat dinner without incident.

"I'll make an announcement at some strategic time in the future to proclaim the blessed event." Timing would result in a business benefit. Like everything in his life, Everett would use this birth to gain some advantage.

Soon morning sickness dissipated, and Jessie puttered around the house glowing with motherhood.

The servants seemed to notice a difference in their mistress. But of course, no one made a comment, but she could tell they knew by their protective treatment of her. Even Mable sported a new attitude.

* * *

Riding through town one day with Sebastian presented the perfect opportunity to learn more about Everett.

"Tell me about Everett's mother, Sebastian. I understand you worked for his parents since their marriage."

"Yes, Madam. I did. What do you want to know?" Sebastian smiled openly.

"Everett's daddy died when Everett was only five. It must've been hard on them."

"Yes, Madam. It was difficult. The Mistress became a widow with a young son, running a huge business. She was grieving her husband. She never fully recovered."

"How sad." Jessie hadn't considered Everett's mother as a grieving widow. She had only been the monster who'd verbally abused her son. Everett had complained about it more than once.

"Yes, Madam, very sad. The Mister doted on his boy. So when he died the Madam had big shoes to fill. She learned and managed the family business. At the same time she was mother and father for her son."

"What was the Mistress like? Was she loving and close to Everett?"

"The Madam provided a proper education. Master Everett enjoyed the best of everything. But I wouldn't say she was tender or affectionate. She was distant from the get-go. It was simply her way. Like most socialites, she left child rearing to professionals. She must've loved Master Everett. She did her best by him."

"Hard on him?"

"She had high expectations. She criticized and scolded. I suppose its difficult molding a boy into a strong man. Mister Everett strove for approval. I'm not sure he ever got it." Sebastian's tone grew nervous then quiet. Sebastian was probably wondering if he had overstepped and revealed too much.

Jessie treaded lightly. She dared not anger Everett by prying. She didn't want to get Sebastian in a peck of trouble with the Master, or make Sebastian afraid to talk with her.

"Thank you, Sebastian. I'm sorry to be so nosey. I only seek clarity, so I can be a good wife to Everett. It's my sole reason for inquiring. So please understand. I'll never mention you spoke with me."

"Yes, Madam. I've noticed that you're a good wife. The Mister is lucky to have you. It is why I've said this much."

"No worries, Sebastian. Let's forget this conversation took place."

Sebastian looked relieved.

Did Jessie make Everett happy, as she endeavored to?

Everett's relationship with his mama remained worrisome, however. The woman must've been a coldhearted bitch. Sometimes alone in her bed chamber Everett talked cynically about his mother and spoke as though their marriage was payback of some sort.

Everett's mama's berating and ridiculing Everett's sexual urges was instrumental in Everett's choosing Jessie for his wife. Not a lady-of-the-line, but she was raised in a house of ill repute.

Everett's mama would've preferred he marry a socialite and keep a mistress on the side. Everett had other ideas. He took his mama's words literally. Her voice still haunted Everett.

"You aren't much to look at. Your personality leaves a lot to be desired. But you're wealthy and well connected. So a multitude of prosperous debutantes scramble to be your wife. Don't expect them to do your bidding submitting to repulsive bed chamber escapades. No proper woman bothers with such repulsive activities."

Everett's mama's words proved true. Jessie had witnessed firsthand. Women in their social sphere were eager to marry well. Doubtful they were wildcats in the bedroom.

Everett didn't require a hot-to-trot lover. He did nothing special in the bedroom. Everett liked sex. From what Jessie gathered, but did nothing unusual.

Were those silly socialites too good for sex with their husbands? Strange.

The women they associated with resembled Everett's description of his mama. Undoubtedly they would've treated Everett with distain, as his mama had. Everett didn't need their money or social position for influence. He had all of that himself. So they offered Everett nothing. There was no point marrying one of them.

Inspired by his mama's words, Everett had gone to a strange city. In New Orleans Everett had searched for a wife and chosen Jessie.

What a shame, his mama's words had destroyed Everett's ability for intimacy with a woman. Jessie wanted that and could grow to love Everett if he'd allow it. It might not be as thrilling as emotions the handsome stranger on the train had caused. But it would be satisfying, nevertheless.

Jessie couldn't tell Lilly everything. But she shared what she could.

"Everett doesn't trust women--certainly not me. It's a shame. He has nothing to fear from me. I wish Everett realized that."

"From what you've told me, the Mister's mother was the root of his distrust."

"I'd never treat him badly like that. Surely he'll someday understand."

"Of course you wouldn't. I've seen you with the Mister. Though he's rather standoffish and formal, you try pleasing him. You don't have a vindictive bone in your body. It's obvious you want your marriage to work. He'll understand eventually."

"Thank you. I appreciate your confidence. I've never confided in anyone before."

"It goes both ways. You listen when things worry me."

Patting Lilly's hand she smiled.

Everett chose me. Someone who would be grateful, wouldn't interfere, question, berate, or criticize. Someone who would, willingly birth his children and give him the sex he wanted.

Ha! It's too bad the old bitch died before our marriage. Maybe she's livid in her grave. That would please Everett.

"Everett doesn't realize how much we have in common. He's been starved for love. As have I. Everett hates his mama." Jessie shrugged.

Lilly worked on Jessie's hair, preparing her for an evening at the ballet. "It seems everyone has personal problems, no matter how wealthy or prominent."

"I suppose station in life doesn't guarantee happiness. I don't know how to achieve the happy marriage I want so badly. We had barely met when we wed. Everett and I lived apart the first year. It's difficult getting through Everett's armor. Because of his mama he hates women. Everett believes we're all the same as her. It never entered Everett's mind that I might be capable of loving him. Or that he might love me back."

Everett called me an investment in his future, like a new suit of clothing.

"You married Everett. So surely there's potential for love."

"My dear Lilly, I wish it were so simple. Love isn't always present when the wealthy marry. Arranged marriages happen all the time for many reasons--influence, power, money or connections. I assumed my love would grow for Everett. I hoped Everett would someday love me. We share similar goals. We both want children. But it appears we have different expectations."

"Well you're having a baby. I'm glad you're stronger." Lilly shook her head. Concern showed on her face. She glanced at her still flat tummy.

"I'm good and blissfully happy." Jessie patted her belly, leaving her hand resting there protectively.

Lilly held the new dress in front of her mistress. It's higher than normal waistline was created in anticipation of blooming out with pregnancy.

"I'd best get downstairs. Everett doesn't like it when I dawdle."

As Jessie descended the stairs toward Everett, her husband watched from the foyer. Everett's eyes were glued on his wife.

Everett's greedy look was satisfying, like when he held her arm proudly while they entered a room together. A little thrill welled in her heart with growing affection for the strange stilted man she'd married.

Jessie wore Everett's favorite gown. The wine satin with a heart shaped waistline extended to a full skirt layered five times to the floor. The heart-shaped bodice trimmed in white lace, exquisitely displayed bulging cleavage. Apparently that was another perk of pregnancy.

Lilly had fashioned the gown to fit perfectly. It display a ruby pendant circled by glittering diamonds that nestled seductively between her breasts and matching ear rings dangled from Jessie's ears. Both were gifts from Everett.

"You're a vision, Jess." Everett breathed the words huskily. His smile created tiny crow's feet beside his eyes and warmed her heart. It skipped a beat at Everett's words and look of pleasure.

Shoulders erect, chin high, Jessie's chest filled with pride. Everett returned her smile from the foot of the stairs. She extended a gloved hand, which he accepted with a gallant bow and kiss atop it.

"Every man in the auditorium will have jealous eyes on you tonight. But you belong to me."

"Thank you, Everett. I'm delighted you're pleased." Jessie's cheeks heated slightly. Why must he refer to her as a possession?

Lilly observed from above, having arranged Jessie's unruly curls into a sophisticated chignon. Lilly had inserted a gleaming crystal comb beside the cascade of copper ringlets.

A slash of pain gripped Jessie's middle. Her eyes went wide as she felt blood drain from her head. Wobbling weakly clutching her belly she doubled over as horrific agony shot through. Her weak legs gave way refusing to hold her slight weight and sent her tumbling.

"Ev . . ."

Everett rushed grabbing Jessie, blocking her fall then scooped her up before she hit the floor. He laid her on the settee in the parlor.

Jessie screamed in misery and gasped. Another ghastly assault crashed through her like a blade slicing her open. Her eyes rolled back. Her head lolled limply unable to hold it erect. Everything went black.

Stirring awake startled and disoriented after what seemed only seconds, Lilly knelt at her side having rushed to Jessie when she'd swooned. Lilly held something bitter against Jessie's nose.

Jessie wrinkled her nose and sniffed, screwing her face up, flinching at the disgusting odor of smelling salts.

Mable sat a pan of water and cloth sat beside her. Lilly began bathing perspiration from Jessie's forehead, removed her gloves and bathed her wrists, arms, and neck.

"You'll be okay, Mistress." She cooed.

Everett stood aside helplessly. His face was white as a magnolia blossom. Mable stirred nervously beside Everett appearing flustered.

Another pain gripped and she grasped her stomach and writhed in torment, pulling her legs toward her belly. Jessie released a blood-curling scream that pierced the silence and contorted from torture. Hot, wet liquid gushed and flooded her gown. Blood dripped from the settee swelling into a pool on the wood floor.

Everett gasped. His face paled to ashy grey. Sweating profusely, Everett paced frantically and shouted, "Mable, go for the doctor."

"You'll be fine, Mistress. I'm sure of it," Lilly cooed soothingly as waterworks flooded Lilly's face.

Jessie's tears streamed freely as she trembled in terror.

"How can this happen? I did everything right. I took perfect care of myself, avoiding stress and strain. I can't lose my baby. I won't allow this. It simply can't happen." Jessie clung to Lilly's hand in a death grip.

"Stay calm, Mistress. The doctor will be here shortly," Lilly fretted.

Everett pushed Lilly aside, scooped his wife up and carried her upstairs. Jessie's head lolled and dropped helplessly against Everett's shoulder like a well-used dish rag.

Gently Everett laid Jessie atop the bed. Lilly followed closely and propped pillows beneath her head and knees.

Silently trembling, crying and sniffing Jessie acted completely unladylike as she seized her stomach afraid to breathe or move. Jessie shivered uncontrollably, so Lilly gently covered her.

Everett paced, not attempting to comfort and barely glancing Jessie's way, seeming bewildered and dazed, as tears filled his eyes.

Jessie sweated and panted, gasping for air. Gripping the blanket, each breath brought worse torment. Thrashing back and forth, weeping and whimpering torturing stabs came and went.

Time dragged endlessly until finally the doctor arrived. He banned everyone from the room, so he could examine Jessie.

Throbbing soreness began subsiding, leaving in its wake a dull throb in Jessie's center. Her heart thumped loudly in her temples and her ears rang a piercing echo while the world swam around.

Something had gone terribly wrong.

Jessie lay limply as the doctor examined her. He inspected the blood pool on her gown and sheet. He studied the puddle by the settee downstairs.

The doctor announced that Jessie had aborted the baby. The fetus appeared normal with no evidence explaining why. The doctor said these things simply happen without understanding or fault. It was just that way sometimes.

Jessie was left alone to rest. Hollow, empty and devastated, her whole body ached and muscles were depleted. The blessed sedatives the doctor left for her induced blissful nothingness as Jessie cried her to sleep.

Ordered to bed for a week, she never left her room or entertained guests. The exception was Lilly who kept vigil.

Everett didn't check on or try comforting Jessie. Nor did he seek comfort from her. So Jessie figured Everett didn't care. She had failed him.

Jessie was a worthless failure, like Mama said.

"Thank you for the fresh water, flowers and food." Despondently thanked Lilly Jessie didn't care one way or the other because her life was of no consequence.

"You must eat. Your weight has fallen rapidly. I'm concerned for your health."

Jessie stayed silently abed for the most part, rising only to relieve herself. She cried with abandon or stared off into the distance, seeing only visions in her head.

"Why bother?" Jessie should end it with the bottle of pills the doctor left. "No one would give a hoot. They may be relieved. It would be best for everyone. The pain would be gone. It would be easy falling into the long sleep."

"Jessie, don't talk so. Don't do this. Are you losing your mind? I love you. You must get better."

"How did this happen? Why me? I was so close to having the things I want most. Yet soon as they were within my grasp, they were cruelly wretched away. Mama was right. I'm not worthy."

"It's simply God's will with no rhyme or reason. You'll heal and have another baby."

"Why bother?" She didn't deserve happiness. Who did Jessie think she was anyway?

Panic filled Lilly's face. Lilly grabbed her cold hand with her warm ones. "I couldn't bear it if something happened to you. Please, grieve then go on with your life." Love seeped from Lilly's tight grasp bringing healing warmth into Jessie's body.

"Let's not discuss my depressing life. I'm miserable enough. Tell me. How are things with you and Cane? You've been keeping company for some time."

It was a turning point. Jessie wasn't a quitter.

Gads! It still hurts.

Lilly radiated happiness. Her eyes sparkled with promise. "Oh, Jessie, I'm so in love with Cane. He is the sweetest man I ever met. Cane is so good to me. He's a hard worker. He saves almost everything he makes to build a future for us."

"So has Cane asked for your hand?"

Lilly nodded gleefully blushing and twisting excitedly. "We're getting hitched. We are saving for a wee window-front shop in town. We'll live in the apartment above and our children will play in the yard out back."

Jessie swiped at a tear.

"Oh, I'm sorry. I didn't mean . . ."

Jessie reached for Lilly's hand. "Nonsense. You have the right to your dreams. So tell me what you'll do with a window-front building."

Lilly's dreams breathed a spark of hope back into Jessie's heart and it began opening to possibilities.

"I'll start a dress shop." Lilly blushed shyly. Lilly stared at her hands and avoided Jessie's gaze.

"That sounds delightful. You're an excellent designer and seamstress. Women in our circle have inquired about the gowns you made for me. They are jealous that you're my personal maid. With my recommendation, they'll bring you more business than you can handle."

"Thank you. That's extremely gracious. I don't want to leave you yet."

"When the time is right, do what you must. Live your life without worry about me. We'll always be friends." Jessie's hands went to her heart.

Lilly beamed. "When we save enough money and wed will you be my Maid of Honor?"

"It will be a pleasure. Thank you."

"Has the Mister been up to see you yet?"

"No. Regrettably he hasn't." Jessie dabbed at tears absent-mindedly. "Damn. Here I go with my raw nerves, blubbering like a baby again. I'm sorry."

"Mister Blackstone goes about his duties as normal. He warned the staff. He wants no rumor mill started from them. So folks won't hear about the miscarriage."

"It's Everett's way. Everett dares not show vulnerability. One's personal life doesn't interfere with business. Keeping your eyes on the prize and your mind firmly planted on goals no matter what's going on was Everett's motto. Business is the most important thing in Everett's life. To hell with me." Jessie's shrill voice trailed off.

Lilly scooped her into a hug. "You can still have a wonderful life with lots of children. You get another chance at happiness with Everett. Don't give up. I love you."

"And I love you, Lilly. Maybe you're right. I must start from the beginning, if I expect to win Everett's heart."

"Why would you say that? You're his wife. Surely he cares for you." Lilly looked perplexed. "Wealthy folks are a strange puzzle. I've never completely understood."

"Perception and public image are everything that defines Everett. These are lessons his mother instilled bone deep in Everett. He prefers solitude and won't let anyone in. Especially me." Jessie dabbed at moisture with a lace handkerchief.

The mirror reflected hair in disarray; skin dull and pale; swollen, glassy, bloodshot eyes accented with dark circles; a haggard, hollow face and listless frail body. Jessie didn't recognize the pathetic person in her mirror.

Lilly's eyes went wide. "That's so sad. I'll never understand rich folks. But I care for you."

Lilly's perception was spot on. "Rich folks are no different from the poor. With the same issues and problems, they deal with them differently. Everett was deprived of affection since his daddy died. His mama was a cold-hearted bitch. She beat an icy nature and distrust into Everett with verbal cruelty. It's no wonder Everett trusts no person at all. Why should he trust me?"

"When his father's ship sunk in that storm in the Gulf of Alaska and his mother became a bitter widow. She ruled with harsh, callous, heartless cruelty. It was Everett's undoing. It made

Everett the man he is today. As she threatened and browbeat him into a successful man, she scarred Everett forever."

"The Mister talks with you about his mother?" Lilly's mouth hung open.

"At times. And I learned from elsewhere." Jessie wouldn't betray Sebastian's trust. "She never failed belittling Everett in private. But she put on a proper show for society. She did unfathomable damage to Everett's psyche. He learned his lessons well. She's long dead but we still live by her rules. Everett considers all families should be strict and stern with their young, forcibly guiding them toward achievement. It isn't Everett's fault he's cold and bitter with a gaping hole in his heart. He is longing for fulfillment and seeking satisfaction siring children. I can relate. I understand."

"You're amazingly perceptive. I admire your compassion. But I couldn't feel that way in your shoes."

Jessie wiped a tear. "Mama was no different."

"You never speak of her."

"She's dead." *To me.*

Mustn't talk about Mama with Lilly. "Everett wants a son to teach the ropes to. He will guide our boy to greater success, and leave his empire to him. But I failed Everett."

"It isn't your fault. You can have other babies. You'll shield them from the Mister's meanness. Won't you?"

"Absolutely. I'll ensure they're loved. Poor Everett must be grieving alone and sick with loss, like me. He's avoiding me. I can't approach Everett. But if we talked, it might help heal us both and strengthen our marriage."

"If you wish for a happy marriage, you must make the effort regardless of your husband's standoffishness. Everett isn't going to."

Lilly's words held wisdom. So Jessie decided to reach out to Everett.

When she rejoined her husband for dinner, Everett acted as though nothing had happened. But he was more distant and formal. And his voice sounded cold and short.

"I am sorry about losing the baby, Everett." Jessie placed her hand atop his on the table.

Everett jerked away, as though the touch burned, and his glare threatened to set her afire.

"We share this loss. Let me help you." Jessie stammered the last of it, her voice quivering.

"You failed and disgust me in the worst way possible. We'll not speak of this matter again. Clear?" Everett's eyes steeled as he spat the words leaning into her.

Stabbing rejection bled Jessie's heart dry. "I'm sorry and understand. Know I'm here for you, if you wish. Pure and simple, fate and nature cruelly dangled our desire in front of us. Then she ripped it from our grasp. But we'll get through it. We'll rebuild and get on with our lives."

Everett's glare shot a fireball straight at Jessie reflecting deliberate betrayal. "Fate? You alone are responsible for killing my son. Forgiveness is beyond my grasp."

Air sucked from the frigid room. Frozen in place and unable to breathe, Jessie's mouth fell open, as bile rose in her throat. She shivered and her shoulders tensed at the oncoming assaulted--never having felt so scared.

Trembling, Jessie uttered, "Please don't blame me. It's not my fault. I wanted this child as much or more than you did. We'll have another child--an heir. We'll be parents. The doctor said there's nothing wrong with me. He assured me it wasn't anything I did. I'm not responsible. Yet my heart aches with guilt. My desire for a family remains steadfast. I hope you find forgiveness in your heart, so we can deal with this together."

Everett listened with a stern, braced expression as she rambled. Then he reminded Jessie of their next social commitment, as if nothing had happened.

"My associates mustn't learn of this. Understand?"

They eventually regained civility and conversed courteously. There was only politeness, and no warmth remained in their union. But in public they appeared a happily married couple.

Everett stopped referring to Jessie as my dear or darling, only Jess. He put no effort into their lifeless marriage, leaving her lonely and wrung out, like a worn-out mop.

After months of avoidance, Everett again began frequenting Jessie's bedroom. Only now, Everett remained distant and became rough. He never kissed her or brought affection to their unsatisfying physical joining. It was purely an act fulfilling a purpose.

"The Mister seems more himself lately." Lilly commented when they were alone.

"Soon we'll regain the easy companionship we previously shared. Everett comes to my bedroom. That gives me hope. It's enough for now."

"I guess it's a good thing." Lilly sounded doubtful.

"Everett was never warm and tender. But at least he was amiable and pleasant before. Our relations are no longer tender. Everett doesn't enjoy my body like before. But I'll get pregnant soon. Everett will forgive me when I bear his child, solving our marriage problems--the sooner the better."

CHAPTER 7

Tough subjects not proper for ladies were broached sparingly in the presence of womenfolk. Jessie continued paying keen attention, eavesdropping on the male discussions at dinner and social events. Unlike the other women, Jessie remained interested and curious. She listened intently hanging on every word eagerly and learned what she could about current events.

As tension mounted the men became intensely vocal, growing more and more opposed to the state of affairs in their fair city.

On one such occasion the Mayor expounded. "There's entirely too much unrest and crime in the streets. I'm vehement that we can't allow this continuing trend. California, San Francisco in particular, bears the brunt of riff-raft left now the gold rush has exhausted. This sad state of affairs affects everything we've worked to establish."

"The Gold Rush has petered out. We're left with a mess in our streets," Everett agreed. "Since James Wilson Marshall discovered gold, hordes of prospectors have rushed west searching for riches over-populating our territory. California has quickly gone from one thousand to more than one hundred thousand. All these men searched for a get-rich-quick proposition. Now it's over. Many are turning criminal. We must do something about this dire situation."

The Governor chimed in. "Funny how the most incidental things bring on drastic change. That carpenter at John Sutter's hydro-powered sawmill, found gold flakes at the foot of the Sierra Nevada Mountain range, in the American River base near Coloma. That's not far from San Francisco. Mistress Wimmer cleaned James find overnight in a bucket of lye soap. The muddy rock glistened and changed history. That third-ounce nugget appraised for five dollars and twelve cents. But old James placed it into a necklace as a gift for her. Sounds fishy to me. James must've been sweet on Mistress Wimmer. She was married, too—scandalous. But news spread, spurring prospectors in droves."

"There's been mass hysteria as thousands immigrated from far and wide at the news. Treasure lay about free for the taking in what they're calling Gold Country. I love this state and don't like what is happening." Another man sounded so angry he could swallow a horned toad backward.

The Governor sounded like somebody stole his rudder. "There have been discoveries daily since of immense deposits. So eager miners abandoned legitimate jobs searching for precious minerals."

The Mayor sounded mad as hell, like he could hunt bears with a hickory switch. "Prices are inflated with suppliers seeking to meet demand of eager prospectors. Many, like Everett here, have made their *Jack* supplying needs. So cost of living has risen drastically, making existence difficult. We've profited enormously, of course; but it's becoming an economic issue we must deal with." A rowdy round of agreement sounded.

Everett felt his oats. "These prospectors, or Forty-Niners if you will, are obsessed with striking it rich. It's completely ridiculous. It's been profitable for us, but has now become a problem."

Jessie's hands clasped and gazed at the table, as she listened raptly, hanging on every word. Everett glared, looking embarrassed at her attention to the conversation. The other dopy women were at least decent enough to pretend they didn't hear, as the men talked like mad, right in front of them.

"Only a few lucky prospectors struck it rich." One man *strung a whizzer*. "Some made a living but most were bitterly disappointed. Now the supply has dwindled to almost nothing. Thousands of broke, disillusioned miners have nothing to show for their efforts. They are looking for wages not there for the earning. Poverty and crime are a fact in this prosperous city we've worked so hard to build. We shall stand for this travesty no longer." His fist slammed onto the table and china bounced. The gent was mad enough to fight a rattler and give him first bite.

She jumped in her seat, startled by the vehemence and glancing around, was appalled at the women pretending oblivious. They didn't seem aware of what transpired in front of their eyes. Not one had a brain cavity large enough for a canary's drinking cup. Or they were the splendid actors.

"The sudden influx of leftovers from surrounding boomtowns and gold fields has become unreasonable. These yahoos are causing a strain on the economy, hurting our pocket books. Boys, our streets have become littered. Our city's infrastructure can't handle the rampant crime with our inadequate police force." The Mayor, at his wits end, could've bitten the sights off a six-gun.

The Governor put in his two cents worth. "This unacceptable situation isn't only a local problem. It is a national one. The United States has its eye on these western territories. The President himself told me about his annexation plans for California. He supports ridding the territory of these problems and has put money where his mouth is. He is whole-heartedly backing the consortium's plan to resolve this burning issue once and for all. We must follow through. I'm confident of success."

Plan . . . what plan, specifics and details? Jessie was bursting with intense curiosity and not above eavesdropping.

After dinner, in the parlor with the wives she feared death-by-boredom. She wanted to scream from the dull, lengthy discussion of the latest Parisian fashion.

What if Jessie tore her fashionable dress off and ran stark naked in the hallway? *Sakes alive!* She must get away from these mind-numbing trendsetters.

Luddy Mussy! They are dull as dishwater.

Unable to stand it anymore, she excused herself politely on the pretense of refreshing--lady code for *'she needed to pee.'*

Making sure servants weren't within ear shot alone in the hallway, Jessie sneaked to the library door.

Heated voices argued vehemently about *'the plan.'* Leaning her ear carefully against the door, eyes wide, mouth bowed, she feared to breathe lest they hear her pounding heart through thick mahogany.

The gentlemen weren't only venomously opposing the circumstances. These fellows were executing a plan in the near future.

The Governor spoke. "The time for talk and planning is over. It's time for action."

A round of applause, loud *'yeas'* sounded, making an ordinary discussion sound like a prayer meeting raring to go.

The bank President fed the fire. "Gold nuggets amassed in bulk await destiny. The three men we've hired are in place in the frozen north, awaiting the consortium's delivery of the gold. As decided, this shipment will change history ensuring Alaska is the next gold bonanza, boys." A rowdy roar sounded.

The Mayor declared. "The press will await the ship's scheduled arrival in Seattle in July. This year of 1887 is a year to remember, men. The blokes will profess finding enormous riches in the frozen Klondike. The only access to it is through Skagway, Alaska." Hearty laughter shook the room.

A greedy bunch of conniving, manipulative bastards.

"We've hired some of the best journalists today to ensure the press covers the news heavily. Newspapers will send word immediately across the continent chronicling the epic event. They will continue keeping it alive in the press as front page news nationally for six full weeks, or more. We've instructed they call it the Alaskan Gold Rush, when they write about it. The chain reaction shall forever be known by that name." Everett laughed that sickening, greedy laugh Jessie hated. He was behaving as crooked as a dog's hind leg. Another round of chuckles sounded.

"This news will trigger excitement across the continent, sending throngs of men flocking toward the rugged Alaskan wilderness. Tappan Adney, the seasoned outdoorsman and writer, shall accompany the *'Stampeders.'* That's a phrase Adney coined. I quite like it. Adney will chronicle the story, feeding the frenzy continually spreading the word, keeping excitement going on the mainland, and sending men northward."

Everett must be grinning from ear to ear.

Jessie pictured Everett drooling at the opportunity for riches resulting from their scheme. He likely had a big piece of the pie.

"Things are in place for the first heavy stream of prospector voyages north by late July, soon after our men profess their find. The journey is long, a minimum of two weeks to Skagway. So the first group should arrive around mid-August. California and surrounding territories currently house the bulk of the nation's treasure hunting enthusiasts. They should be the first jumping on the bandwagon. This news should send them scampering north, ridding California of its current problems. Of course, prospectors from all around will join in. Soon Alaska will be overrun with Americans." A round of hearty laughter sounded.

The Governor reported, "This coup fits perfectly into the nation's plans for expansion. With its abundant natural resources, inhabited by American citizens, will enable Alaska to someday be incorporated into the States"

The gall!

A hand to her chest attempting to still her pulse, her heartbeat pounded so fiercely loud in her eardrums, Jessie feared they'd heard it through the thick door.

These men are leaders of industry with steel running through their veins instead of blood. It's no wonder they make and shake the world. They'd steal the coin off a dead man's eyes and not bat an eye. Though Jessie admired them, she was stunned at their audacity.

Rejoining the women, her head spun consumed with thoughts of the excitement they were destined for. She could hardly wait to read the papers as this epic scheme unfolded. She was eager to learn how it changed their lives and to discover how deeply Everett was entrenched.

* * *

The following day descending the stairs, excited to enjoy the promise of a beautiful day with Everett off to the office already and the house quiet, Jessie paused frozen at the unexpected creak of Everett's study door opening.

What the hell?

"It's a deal." Everett's business voice dismissed the meeting. Jessie couldn't see the door from the staircase. She pictured them shaking on some proposal.

"Absolutely I look forward, Everett. This is the opportunity I've long searched for." Jessie froze afraid to breathe as the familiar sultry, sensual voice spoke.

"Well, let's get on with it. We have tons to do before departure. Sebastian will see you out, Mister Pace. Good day."

"Good day."

Sebastian led the tall, muscular man around the staircase toward the front door. Mister Pace ambled with confident ease. His delectable backside, slim hips and shoulders as wide as the sea came into view. Jessie's breath caught in her throat. She could gawk at that man walking all day and never grow bored.

Whew!

Logan accepted his hat from Sebastian then slowly turned as if sensing her presence. Or perhaps Mister Pace heard Jessie's pounding heart.

A perceptive smirk graced his beautiful face. It engaged those adorable dimples--impossible to exorcize from her dreams. Logan Pace leaned forward and swooped his hat in an exaggerated bow.

"Good day, Mistress Blackstone."

Trying to appear unscathed, her chin rose proudly. But Jessie's smiling eyes gave her true feelings away.

"Good day, Mister Pace." Her face heated. So did another strategic part of her anatomy.

Logan winked conspiratorially, then swung around and exited. Sebastian disappeared down the hallway.

She stomped her foot and shook her head as flames from her face shot out the top of her head

Damn him. He caught me eavesdropping. I should be embarrassed. To Hell with him. How dare Logan Pace make mockery of me? He's the one who should be embarrassed. Logan and Everett are obviously up to no good.

If Logan Pace was working with Everett, Logan wasn't the man Jessie had imagined. That was disappointing. Men were a dissatisfying lot.

At dinner Everett seemed distracted barely eating. He merely grunted answers when Jessie attempted conversation.

Everett rose after the meal. "Jess, we must discuss something of importance. Join me in the den."

"I'm delighted, Everett." A surprising turn of events, a command performance, but Jessie took a chair facing the hearth hoping for the best. Everett poured himself a tipple of whiskey and handed her a sherry.

"Thank you."

"Do you mind if I smoke?"

Jessie nodded, surprised Everett had bothered asking.

I wouldn't dare mind.

"Of course not, Darling, go ahead."

Taking the chair facing Jessie, Everett lit a cigar. It was a cool evening, so she tried to focus on the warmth of the roaring fire, dispelling trepidation seeping through her pores. Hands clasped in her lap to still them, she was nervous as a skunk in a house full of cats.

Everett looked pompous. He puffed and sipped fancy Kentucky bug juice while Jessie stewed, on edge.

"Jess, we're embarking upon an epic adventure the likes of which you've no comprehension."

Jessie tried reading Everett's eyes.

"We're moving to Skagway, Alaska."

Her mouth flew open and her face flared hot, struck mute, dumbfounded, and plumb weak north of her ears.

Everett puffed his fat stogie measuring Jessie's reaction. Sarcasm showed on Everett's face, as though expecting protest. Everett's mind was clearly made up. Any objection would be brushed aside as insignificant. Of course, his wife did his bidding unfailingly.

Why bother?

Jessie sat stiffly wringing her hands. She was surprised but not uncomfortable with the idea. Her innards flip-flopped, but she did her best to hide it.

So, Jessie would be at the center as Everett executed their controversial conspiracy. It was an elaborate deception of epic proportions. This was about to be an exciting adventure experienced firsthand.

Her mind raced and wondered, what Everett wanted from her? What reaction had he anticipated at this announcement, they were leaving their prosperous lifestyle and San Francisco?

He was wrong if he assumed Jessie would object. Telling Everett how thrilled she was would make the controlling beast way too happy.

Jessie smiled graciously and angled her head timidly. "Why? Isn't Alaska a brazen, uninhabited frontier?"

Amusement flashed in Everett's eyes. It was clear. The cynical, controlling bastard wanted his wife off-kilter.

Poo on him.

Having overheard the plan, this farce would happen with or without her. She might as well accept destiny and enjoy the ride. But Jessie must control her excitement.

What the hell?

"I own thousands of acres of Alaskan frontier. I will become filthy rich by extorting my businesses there. So it's decided."

Everett's high-falutin' air was amusing. He drew pleasure from springing this upheaval on his unsuspecting, stupid wife. Everett was willing Jessie to protest, so he could shut her down. He was in for a long wait, if that was what Everett wanted.

"But aren't you already wealthy?" She pretended innocence.

"Indeed. However, one cannot have too much money.

"Prepare to leave. Bring no more than two trunks of personal belongings, only clothing suitable for everyday wear. The weather's severe and cold, especially in winter. So pack appropriately. Don't worry if you have nothing warm enough. Once we arrive, we'll obtain outerwear suitable for the temperatures."

Jessie half listened as always while Everett droned on about details in a gleeful, enthusiastic voice, never considering she might be afraid, not up to the journey, or refuse to go.

Pompous ass.

Everett's voice was unusually chipper. While Jessie pretended to listen, her mind whirled with ideas bouncing around gaily.

"There's no social life. We won't entertain. So don't pack ball gowns. Bring only things suitable for work. We're there to amass a fortune." Everett grinned like a baked possum.

Did he expect Jessie to balk at leaving her fancy duds behind? *Not happening.*

He thinks I have no clue. Everett is eager to reap personal rewards. Let him gloat. He'll be easier to live with.

* * *

Jessie's last act of defiance was to stand up for Lilly as maid of honor. She would be damned if she would miss her best friend's wedding.

Jessie rode to the courthouse with Sebastian, who had promised to keep Jessie's secret and attended as Cane's best man.

After the ceremony, at the seamstress shop Cane had purchased for his bride, they celebrated with cookies and lemonade.

"Congratulations." Jessie hugged and kissed Lilly's blushing cheek. "You're lovely. My white gown was a perfect choice for your wedding.

"Thank you. I love Cade over the moon and back. I am hopeful about our future."

"You have a right, Lilly." Jessie stroked her friend's hand tenderly.

"Did you tell Everett?" Lilly licked her lips.

"Of course not . . . he wouldn't allow it." Jessie winked. "Everett prefers I remain isolated. That's why he chose to married me. I have no ties or family. I am a loner who exists only for him."

"I hoped things would get better. Perhaps once you're in Alaska with fewer social distractions, you'll become closer." Lilly patted Jessie's shoulder affectionately.

Doubtful.

"I sincerely hope so. Tell me about your plans."

"Cane's landscaping business is flourishing. He has contracts for several business and local mansions."

"That is wonderful news. You have a beautiful future to look forward to together. At least one of us has a happy marriage."

Jessie felt sick in the pit of her stomach at leaving her only friend, though they planned to stay in touch writing letters. Would there be others she could befriend in Alaska?

Before they left, Jessie gave Lilly much of her clothing. "Please rework some gowns for yourself." Leaving her only friend was a tearful, emotional upheaval for both of them.

"Thank you. That's very generous." Lilly wiped a tear as she helped pack.

"Sell most of the gowns. Use the money to start your business." Reality of saying goodbye was sickening. Jessie bit her lower lip to keep from crying.

Happiness continued to escape her, and she may never reach Everett.

With mixed emotions Jessie remained excited and anxious for the journey.

Everett and Jessie boarded a train to Seattle along with the bare necessities.

"I've never been on a boat. I understand the waters can be treacherous through the coastal waterway called the Inside Passage." Jessie knew how Everett hated being questioned. Apprehension combined with eagerness fought an internal unresolved battle. So Jessie stayed constantly queasy from the emotional upheaval.

"Yes, the weather's volatile. The current is unpredictable. Be wary. It can prove perilous in the best of conditions. You may experience sea sickness." Everett puffed the words in an exasperated manner and grinned, probably anticipating Jessie's potential illness.

Ass!

"Klondike territory is actually in Canada. It is only reachable through a hazardous passageway across a tremendous mountain range through the tiny coastal village of Skagway, Alaska."

"Why the Klondike?" Jessie timidly inquired with a husky voice allowing Everett to assume she didn't know.

"You'll soon learn why." A pretentious eyebrow wagged.

"Our train journey to Seattle was short." Ignoring Everett's audacity, smiling sweetly, playing the oblivious, meek wife, they walked the gangplank to the deck, far atop the vessel.

"Yes. But this ship will take us northward for about two weeks, to our destination. I've arranged for adjoining staterooms. They are the size of a closet in our mansion, with barely enough space for a trunk, a table for washing up, and bunk."

"Fine. I don't want to be cooped up. I don't intend to spend much time in my diggings anyway."

Jumping into this adventure feet-first, quivering with anticipation, Jessie made a conscious effort to contain her excitement.

Please don't let Everett ruin this.

Everett headed straight for a gentleman with smoldering, velvet-green eyes awaiting their arrival. Jessie's insides melted to mush, and she sucked in sizzling air hiding a scalding face behind her fan.

Everett seemed unaware of Jessie's surprise. But Logan's eyes on the fan suppressed a gleeful grin.

Thank goodness a sea breeze prevented Jessie from swooning. Electricity surged from head to toe. Her body sang with pleasure, recalling what this man's presence could do for it. This was an interesting surprise.

Oh well. It must be a hormonal thing. Too bad Everett didn't have that effect on Jessie. It was wasted.

"Logan, so glad you made it." Everett greeted the taller man with a hearty shake, clueless to the exchange between Logan and Jessie. "Let me introduce my wife, Jess. Jess, this is Logan Pace. Logan has agreed to become the manager of my logging company in Skagway."

Logan nodded politely, not letting on.

Ever the lady, Jessie extended a gloved hand. "Pleased to meet you, Mister Pace. It's convenient you're traveling with us. You and Everett will have time to discuss business."

Did he frown?

Logan cupped Jessie's hand in both of his eying it curiously. Logan kissed the top, as a gentleman would. As Logan's lips touched the glove he caught her eyes instantaneously before releasing it.

A rush of breath caught, and her head jerked. Her shoulders quickened as Logan's tantalizing mouth forced her stomach to knot. Jessie drew a deep breath and feared it might burst from her lungs.

Whoa! Doggies. Steady girl.

Gone quick as it jolted through it was over without Everett realizing what occurred. Jessie must watch out for this Mister Pace, who exuded danger. No worries. The man was Everett's business partner. Jessie had no intentions of becoming friends with the likes of Logan Pace.

She hadn't told Everett about her encounter with Wheezer.

No need alarming Everett. He would only be pissed.

Call me lily livered, Lawdy mercy!

"I am fortunate to have hired Logan away from his family's prosperous logging business. Logan and his brothers are experts in the field."

Everett's shoulders arched backward, his head held high, as if he were responsible for their success. Or like Everett had raised a prize pig at the fair.

"The business is in capable hands with my brothers. So I'm striking out on my own." Logan acted as if it were their first encounter. "This is an exciting opportunity to explore unknown territory in the Alaskan frontier. I hear no terrain can compare in beauty. They say magnificent scenery sparkles with glaciers surrounding imposing mountain ranges. It sounds amazing." Logan spoke easily, not intimidated.

Logan seemed unaffected by Everett's boasting. Logan's bulging muscles struggled to escape his business suit with every graceful movement. Jessie found it interesting a male could be so attractive. She'd never paid much mind to the looks of men before.

How would it feel to be cradled in strong arms like those? Too bad Everett wasn't built like that.

Logan's shaggy blonde hair was propelled by a coastal breeze and enticingly fluttered across Logan's forehead.

Too bad Everett is balding. It might be pleasant running fingers through such a mane.

Logan and Everett chatted amicably about their voyage, oblivious to Jessie's brain's ramblings. They discussed logging, machinery and equipment deliveries.

Logan's smiled warmly, and spoke pleasantly, without veneer--so different from her husband. Everett was brash, cunning, calculating, devious, and so full of his self. Everett evasively concealed his true nature from the world and used cruelty when it suited him.

It boggled her mind. Why the hay were these two together? Listening raptly observing, Logan followed her lead, not revealing they had met.

Thank goodness. Everett would be livid.

Logan interacted with the Captain, the crew and others, including Everett, genially calling everyone by name. People seemed drawn to Logan. They genuinely appeared to like him. No wonder. Logan was strong, confident, and gave the impression of honesty and openness.

That was a quandary. Why would an honest man be in cahoots with Everett?

Logan appeared to be sure of himself. He didn't seem to hide, but let the world see him. Remarkably at ease, Logan was pleasant, intelligent, and knowledgeable about his business, world affairs, and the region.

Fascinating.

Leadership flowed second natured and effortless from Logan. People flocked to Logan, naturally trusting and following. They seemingly respected Logan and wanted to be around him.

Logan graciously ignored Everett's dominant air.

Lord help me, I like this man.

Jessie was immensely drawn to Logan, like a cub to a mama bear. She must be careful not to upset Everett unduly.

There was something odd she was missing about Logan and Everett's partnership. She couldn't figure why Logan would throw in with Everett.

Everett's many acquaintances associated with him for benefit and power--nothing more. Cold and unapproachable, people didn't flock to Everett or befriend him without reason. So he had no real friends.

Stop this reverie. Panic? Of course.

Being aroused simply being around this male would scare the bejeezus out of anyone. Jessie mustn't drool for the gorgeous piece of manhood. Since when had she allowed bodily functions to rule her life?

Never!

Stop it.

Jessie must focus on making Everett happy and creating a good marriage. Luckily Everett didn't notice her despair. As usual, he was preoccupied, wrapped in his own world where he played his favorite role as top dog.

Thank goodness.

At departure the ship's horn signaled the beginning of the voyage. The trio waved to spectators as their vessel set sail. Passengers tossed confetti into the bay and giddy, excitement filled the air.

CHAPTER 8

"Oh, Everett, I am so excited about dining at the Captain's table. We'll have ample opportunity to meet other intriguing voyagers. It's gracious of the Captain. Don't you think?"

Half an hour underway, Jessie fumbled, arranging Everett's personal items in his stateroom, unable to contain enthusiasm.

"Jess, what on earth are you doing?" Everett grumbled from his bunk. Everett's face paled and his eyes glassed over.

"Unpacking, dear Everett, so your things will be easily accessed." Jessie stopped fiddling and eyed Everett. "You don't look good."

"Jess, leave my things alone. This damned ship's rocking is making my stomach rumble. Get the hell out, before I 'shoot the cat.'" Everett grabbed a bucket beside his bunk and dry heaved.

"You're green, Everett. I thought that was only an exaggeration. Guess not."

Everett's arm shot out pointing at the door. He snapped, "Out! Leave me to rest." Everett laid listlessly, a limp hand resting atop his closed eyes and trembled.

"Very well, if you insist. You'll be better after a nap." Jessie backed toward the door. "I'll take a deck chair close by. If you need me, shout."

Everett's stern look spoke better than words could. Jessie cringed and closed the door.

People-watching with a book on her lap, she was fascinated with the goings on. The crew bustled about, manning the ship.

Jessie became concerned by late afternoon and stopped by Everett's room.

A quivery voice begged entrance. Everett was pitiful. Having vomited continuously *'airin'-the-paunch'* into the bucket, Everett was *lookin' to die.*

"You're seriously ill, sweating profusely. Your pallor is bright green." Touching Everett's forehead backhandedly, he was cool and clammy. "You're not hot." Jessie filled a bowl and brought a cloth to bathe Everett's face.

"The motion of this friggin' boat has my *trolly-bags in a tither.* I am sick to my stomach." Reeking stench attested to it. "I barely get shed of one round of green bile. Another rolls up." Everett slapped at her ministering hands.

Jessie choked back a gag. "How awful, you seem so helpless." *Whoa . . .*

Regret came soon as the words exited her mouth.

Hating being seen as a helpless namby-pamby, Everett scowled. He groaned then lay carefully back down, unable to instigate the intended fight.

Jessie had never seen Everett so weak. Filling a pitcher, she placed it by his bed. "Please, try to drink."

Everett groaned again. She wet a hanky and wiped his forehead, face and neck, and this time Everett didn't resist. He looked like a sick puppy.

"You poor thing . . ."

"Leave me alone, woman." Everett bristled at her ministrations, weakly pushing her away.

"Can I get you anything?" Sitting on his bunk, hands folded in her lap. "Some fixings? Dinner smells delightful."

"Heavens no. The mere mention makes me nauseous, and whatever I drink comes back as bile." Everett's eyes closed. "Go. Leave me."

"If you insist . . . I'm happy staying with you. If you like, I can sit while you rest."

Everett needed her. Jessie wanted to help, hoping it might improve their relationship.

"Leave me, Jess. Don't hover. I don't want you here." Everett closed his eyes dismissing her.

Rising reluctantly, heart sinking, she paused at the door, needing to try. "I'll ask the Captain if there's anything to help you. The sea's not even rough yet. I understand we have a long journey, and it gets worse venturing northward."

"Stop talking, Woman." Everett gritted his teeth and spit words.

Jessie left fearing Everett would remain ill throughout the journey. She longed for Everett to trust her to care for him.

Captain Stuart's round table nightly hosted prestigious voyagers, including two businessmen, Logan, the first mate and Jessie. The perfect host, Captain Stuart encouraged conversation and ensured all participated. The Captain kept subject matter appropriate for ladies with discussions of travel, social events, latest headlines, books and cultural events. Wine and fascinating conversation flowed from salad through dessert.

"The food's scrumptious. Isn't it difficult preparing it on board ship?" Jessie enjoyed herself more than if Everett were present. She delighted at the stimulating talk and engaging company.

Especially impressed with Logan, she remained puzzled at why he befriended Everett.

"You hale from unsettled wilderness area. Yet you're highly educated, polished, cultured, and have charismatic manners. You are a skilled conversationalist."

Too bad you're a scoundrel helping perpetuate this scheme.

"Thank you, Mistress Blackstone. We may live in the backwoods of Oregon Territory, but my family believes in proper education. I'm fortunate to afford one. So I schooled in Chicago."

"That's nice for you."

Why are you with my devious husband?

Like the Captain, Logan made a point to draw her into discussion. Logan asked Jessie's opinions and listened intently. No man ever wanted her view before--on any subject. But to Logan, Jessie was worthy of attention.

He was an intriguing, beautiful puzzle that should remain at a distance. However, Jessie instinctively began relaxing, enjoying Logan immensely. She allowed her guard to begin crumbling, knowing Everett wouldn't approve.

Oh well! What harm could it do?

* * *

After dinner Logan strolled with her along the deck. "Look a shooting star--my first." Jessie jumped around, squealing and clapping gleefully.

Logan laughed. "You're delightful. Not the starchy, aristocratic matron more appropriate for my boss's wife."

"Thank you, Mister Pace. I think." Smiling, eyeing Logan curiously, Jessie's head shook. "You don't approve of me as Everett's wife, Mr. Pace?"

"I don't disapprove. However, no offence, but your charm seems wasted since Everett doesn't appreciate the remarkable woman you are. Please call me Logan. We'll be on this ship a couple of weeks. Formality would be tedious." Logan bowed.

Jessie grinned teasingly. "I take no offense. But I have to ask. What are you doing with Everett? I can't say you're wrong. Everett doesn't always approve of me or my instincts. I'm sometimes more emotional and inquisitive than suits his taste. I suppose we can drop the formalities if you'll call me Jessie--unless Everett disapproves when he soon joins us."

Her eyes sparkled in moonlight, pulling Logan like the magnet he'd avoided on the train. Logan didn't intend to avoid Jessie aboard ship. They were destined to be thrown together on the vessel, like it or not. Logan did. So he might as well enjoy it.

Logan couldn't very well leave the woman to her own resources. Everett would expect Logan to watch out for his wife's welfare, while Everett was indisposed.

There was no harm appreciating the woman's company, with her husband's approval, of course. Certainly by the end of the journey the three should become close enough. Stranger things had happened.

Jessie was easy to like. With luck, Everett might be more pleasant than he seemed. That too would be a welcome surprise.

"Make a wish. You should have whatever you ask for." Logan's tone remained friendly and casual.

Grinned like a young girl, chomping on her lower lip, her eyes rolled studying. Then closing her eyes she wished, and when she opened them spotted a fox drinking from a stream along the bank.

"Look, Logan." Jessie pointed at the lone animal. "He's so beautiful. I've never seen such a lovely creature."

Moonlight caught streaks in the critter's hair and shimmered like diamonds in the ship's wake.

Jessie appeared remarkably at ease--more so than she'd been with Everett. Though Logan barely knew her, he sensed a powerful connection unable to resist.

"He's a lovely creature. I've only seen red foxes before. This one's silver. It's funny how animals take on characteristic based on environment."

Jessie displayed one personality for her husband and showed Logan another. Logan couldn't wait to find out which was real.

"Will we change in our new environment?" Jessie asked timidly.

"That's an astute question." Would Logan become whole again?

Jessie gazed at the tree-lined bank. A finger to her mouth, and bit her lower lip, making Logan wonder what she thought.

"Would you mind explaining why you didn't tell Everett we had met?"

"You remember." Jessie's eyes brightened, twinkling in moonlight.

"How could I forget such a captivating woman?"

Her blush was quickly hidden behind her fan. "Why're you involved in this scandalous scheme? You don't seem the type to associate with the likes of Everett Blackstone?"

"What do you mean by scandalous scheme? I agree. Alaska doesn't seem a hot market for lumber. However, the territory has ample resources. Everett controls a good piece of woodland. Everett assured me there'll be a tremendous boon in Alaskan lumber. He offered me a ground floor opportunity."

Those delectable lips taunted, as her mouth curved into a bowed smile.

Logan's voice turned husky. "I won't belittle Everett. But you're correct. We're nothing alike. Everett and I aren't friends yet. We're only business partners. We made a deal I couldn't refuse. I'm looking to make a mark on the world. I'm seeking adventure, excitement, and opportunity to make my fortune. I long to make my own way." The night sky watched as Logan weighed his words carefully.

She nodded, seeming to understand. Logan took it as indication to continue.

"Everett needed my expertise to manage his Alaskan logging and lumber company. He offered me a home, good salary, and percentage of profits. It is an opportunity of a lifetime. Too good to pass up."

Jessie clamped down on her lip and nodded. "Does that explain why you were at our mansion?"

Logan's face heated. He grinned mischievously. "I came to seal the deal, not thinking I'd run into you. That was a pleasant surprise."

Jessie looked away. Her fan fluttered in front of her face, as color rose above her collar and across her cheeks.

"You could've knocked me over with a feather. I froze like a statue when I heard your voice, fearing you'd told Everett about our meeting."

Logan laughed. "I apologize, for my playful streak. I am sorry I startled you. Seeing you, even briefly gave me joy. We met on the train innocently enough. Why haven't you told Everett?"

"Nothing to do with you and me. The danger, your intervention, and the thing with Wheezer were an isolated incident. I didn't want to worry Everett because he's frazzled as it is. There was no reason to alarm him unnecessarily. It's well over. But I'm eternally grateful for your help." Jessie smiled pleasantly.

"You're welcome, dear Lady. I understand why you didn't tell Everett about Wheezer. But why didn't you tell him you and I met . . . so innocently?"

It seemed Jessie wasn't as affected as Logan had been. He hadn't been able to get the young bride out of his mind.

A sad look overtook her charming face. A single tear trickled along her olive cheek. She flung it off with a gloved hand before turning away. The air hung thick with scantly hidden emotion.

"We're recovering from rough patch. A devastating miscarriage has made Everett's nerves raw. You and Everett must forge a good working relationship. Telling him now would stand in the way of that. At this late a date it'd seem more significant than it was. Everett has a tendency toward jumping to conclusions. He's very protective."

"I'm sorry. I understand something of loss." Logan's heart panged at her revelation, and he glanced at the sea then back.

He didn't hide condolences on his face. Jessie nodded, looking away.

"Our meeting was significant to me. I've been unable to forget you. It felt as though I've known you from the first. You've lived in my dreams repeatedly since." Logan grinned sideways, wickedly teasing, his brows wagged comically.

Jessie's sweet smile could melt an iceberg. Those lovely eyes sucked Logan's soul into them. He wondered what secrets hid there.

"Maybe we met somewhere, maybe when we were children."

"You mustn't talk so, Logan. Possibly we knew each other in another lifetime."

"Could be. Not sure about that sort of thing. But it would explain the strange familiarity instantly connecting with you."

"Very funny. We're virtual strangers having barely met on the train. Nothing untold became of it or could. I am a married woman. So you mustn't flirt shamelessly." Jessie didn't appear offended--teasing perhaps.

"I apologize. You're safe with me. I've no intention of hurting you or your reputation. I admire your loyalty. Everett's a lucky man."

"He doesn't see it that way. Maybe this move will help Everett forgive me for losing the baby, so we can find happiness in Alaska."

Her sad face gouged craters into Logan's heart, and his mouth flew open. "What the hell? Everett blames you? Unbelievable . . . I am sorry, Jessie."

Compassion and something akin to anger churned wildly in his gut. Whether it was grief for her baby, worry, or arousal being so close to this tantalizing female, Logan felt unduly protective.

Everett--the cad . . .

"You speak with experience like you've lost a loved one." Jessie's brows tented.

"Indeed." Logan sought answers in the horizon as a scene played in his mind, a memory. Logan swiped a stray drop of moisture that trickled across his cheek and anchored.

"My fiancée, Amy, died of fever from the pox before we were to marry last summer, along with other villagers. After going in and out of delirium for days, in a final moment of clarity as I held her, Amy told me to be happy. Then she was gone." Logan wiped his jaw at the flow of tears. He gazed at the heavens, wishing Amy could reach from there and comfort him.

Jessie placed a hand on Logan's arm sending heat surging through his jacket and shirt, straight to his soul. Healing warmth was welcomed and embraced, eyeing the kindhearted woman.

"I don't discuss it. I have no clue why I talked about this with you. But it felt right and natural. So I guess it's a good thing. Thank you, for allowing me to vent on this night of confidences." Logan's laugh felt lighter than it had been in more than a year.

"Indeed. Thank you for keeping mine. I'll treasure yours in my heart." A gloved hand lay atop round, pert breasts.

Logan gulped at the knot forming in his throat, having nothing to do with Amy.

"No worries, your secret is safe and harmless enough. This voyage provides ample time to get acquainted and become friends."

Jessie emitted a lady-like laugh. "I can use a friend. My only friend was left behind in San Francisco."

"I'd have thought your life overflowed with friendships."

"I suppose I could've made more effort. But women in our social circle bored me to tears. I barely endured the dreary lot."

"And your friend?"

"Lilly was different, a real person, not simply my maid. She married our gardener. Lilly now owns a dress shop."

The joy in Jessie's voice warmed Logan on the chilly night. "I see." She was an unusual woman, who strangely had befriended her maid, instead of someone of her social rank. Logan found that admirable and confusing.

"Everett approved of friendship with staff?"

"He didn't know. Everett would never have approved. But there was no harm in it. So I didn't tell him." Jessie blushed, waving her fan. "I'm piling it on you today, Logan. I apologize for asking again. But please keep this quiet, also. Lilly and I intend staying in touch by writing. If he knew, Everett would forbid it."

"Certainly . . . how's Everett doing?"

"Not faring well. It seems he left his sea legs in Seattle."

Logan couldn't keep the smirk from escaping. "Too bad for Everett."

Logan tolerated Everett's absence well. Everett's pretentious personality would soon drive Logan to distraction once thrown together. But they needn't become friends to work together, though it would be good if they could.

* * *

Everett remained ill, rejecting Jessie's nursing attempts, sending her away cruelly every time. "Stop hovering, woman. Go. Leave me in peace."

Fretting about his health, daily checking in and encouraging him as much as possible, she ensured his care. But for the most part, Jessie left Everett to his misery.

"As you wish, please eat and drink. You need your strength. A bite of cold oatmeal should give you sustenance, if you can keep it down. You pleasantly surprised me by eating toasted bread yesterday. So I'll have the steward bring you a tray." Liquids did Everett no favor. So he struggled to stay hydrated.

"Out!" He groaned and shouted pointing to the door sending her away rudely. But she kept returning, faithfully devoted.

"Let's leave your door open a while so you can get some fresh air. The stench is palatable in here." Jessie stood by the open door one sunny afternoon, pleased to help.

"Shut the damned door. I can't stand the sight of ever-moving landscape."

Watching disappointed as he struggled for comfort on the bunk, she walked closer and supported Everett's arm.

"Let's get you upright so you can sit on the bunk. Or I can help you to the chair. That might settle your equilibrium. You may feel stronger upright."

Everett submitted, so Jessie kept him quiet company while he rested sitting on the cot. But Everett soon tired and insisted on lying down.

"Go, I've had enough company." He grasped his chest and all the pallor drained from his face. Everett's eyes went wide looking shocked. His right hand flew to his chest.

"What is it, Everett? What is wrong?" Fear ripped at Jessie.

Panting roughly Everett grumbled, closed his eyes then finally found his voice. Suddenly his eyes shot open. "Damn it, Jess. I'm sick." He gasped, turning bright green.

She rushed a pail in front of him as he spewed vile green.

When he finally stopped upchucking he muttered, "I can barely breathe. I feel like a mountain sits on my chest. My left arm aches with a strange numbness."

Jessie gasped and cupped his blanched cheeks. "Dear Everett, you sound direly ill. This is more than sea sickness. You need medical care. Shall I go for the Captain?"

Weakly Everett nodded as his head flopped backward exhausted.

Rushing from the room Jessie found the steward and sent him for the Captain then returned to Everett's side.

The captain inspected Everett with a solemn expression. You were right to worry, Mistress Blackstone. Mister Blackstone, you are gravely ill. You must have some underlying health issue. Have you ever had chest pains like this before?"

Everett nodded. "Occasionally, but they soon subsided with rest."

"Well, hopefully that will be the case again. I recommend you stay abed throughout the trip. Maybe rest will help. Try to eat and drink, but above all, avoid frustration."

Everett eyed the captain as though he'd said something ridiculous.

How could one avoid frustration, when worried for their life and sick as a dog?

The captain left them alone.

"Jess, if something happens and I don't make it, you must carry out my mission."

"Nonsense, Everett. You will be fine with some rest."

"But if I don't . . . promise me you will do as I say."

"Of course, Everett."

"Those two crates in the corner are meant for some men I am to meet in Skagway. When the ship arrives, stay aboard. Wait until passengers disembark. The men will expect to meet me. You must give them the crates. It is very important, Jess. I can't fail. If I cannot be there to follow through, you must do this for me."

"I would do anything you wish, Everett. You know that."

"Very well, then. You heard the captain, Jess. Leave me alone. You frustrate me. You aren't helping."

Against her wishes, Jessie complied and enlisted the steward to deliver food and drink to Everett. She watched over the process from a distance. She ensured Everett's bucket and room were cleaned, and he was freshened regularly. But nothing helped his mood. Everett continued refusing her help, too 'limsy' to venture out.

Finding solace in her budding innocent friendship with Logan, who was pleasant and easy to talk with and appreciated her company. Jessie was terrified Everett might not make it through this illness.

"We've traveled for long periods with no living soul along the coastline. There is nothing but spectacular scenery along this waterway. I'm spellbound by beauty of immense wilderness beyond my wildest imagination." They walked the deck one brisk evening three days out to sea.

"I adore the forest. My family depends on it for our livelihood. We're bent on protecting it in every way possible. It is God's incredible gift, to be treasured."

"What an astute observation. Your attitude is enchanting. I had no idea men held such deep appreciation for the world's natural resources."

"Not all. Many care nothing about depleting the land for gain. There's no good from that. It serves us well to protect and nourish what is provided abundantly, so future generations will thrive."

With every word Jessie became more impressed with the exquisite man who engaged and stimulated. She valued and respected his opinions and enjoyed conversing with Logan. They quickly grew into solid friends.

She felt valued and confidant in Logan's presence, like the lady she portrayed. They talked about business, family, and the future. Logan confided personal things, proving he trusted her.

"Won't you miss your brothers?" Bending her head sideways arching an eyebrow she grinned. "You aren't running from anything?" She laughed impishly.

"We're all running from our past in one way or another. I'm hoping the change of scenery will help me leave guilt behind that I survived when Amy died. Though my brothers don't need me, they didn't want me to go. But they'll do fine." The star-studded sky silently held their attention. "There's need for my skills in Alaska. I can make my mark there. I can't wait to get to work."

"I thought you were enjoying my company." Pouting her lower lip puffed out, playfully pretending insult.

"I didn't mean that I wasn't immensely enjoying your company." Logan swept into a low bow.

Jessie curtsied and they laughed.

"Everett assured me lumber will be a booming venture in Alaska. He didn't explain, only hinted he has the inside track, promising me a big piece of the pie. This is an adventure I've searched for a while now."

Understanding Everett's high hopes for profits in lumber, she couldn't jeopardize her husband's interests. But Logan wasn't aware of the scheme. Everett hadn't confided in her and apparently not in Logan either. Having discovered the truth on her own, leaving Everett oblivious to her knowledge of the conspiracy, divulging the plot would violate Everett's trust. So Jessie told Logan what she could, without being disloyal.

"Everett's associates are powerful people with the inside track on upcoming events. Certain things have been put into motion. Everett has reason to believe there'll be an explosion of development in Alaska. He's in on the ground floor of what will be a profitable venture. I'm pleased Everett extended you this opportunity and that we're on this voyage together." Jessie's cheeks fired at her honesty. She'd said enough.

"I see. So that's all you can tell me?"

Nodding she said no more. "Yes, I've perhaps said too much already. Women aren't supposed to pay attention to business matters. Rest assured. You made a good decision."

* * *

Logan laughed at the notice of her station in life. Logan doubted old Everett suspected Jessie's keen understanding of business.

She trusts and confides in me. I'm doubly fortunate on this amazing journey.

"You're very sweet and unimposing. That is odd for the wife of a pretentious tycoon. At the risk of belittling your husband--you must see Everett is a fuddy-duddy. But you're surprisingly down to earth. Your gentle nature is particularly pleasing."

"Thank you." Jessie blushed behind her fan.

"Your interest in our journey and excitement about the adventure are enchanting. Your appreciation of our magnificent surroundings is delightful. But aren't you afraid of the unsettled, lawless north and dangerous weather conditions?"

"Heavens no. I am thrilled we're moving there. But I wouldn't share that with Everett. For some reason, Everett prefers me leery. It pleases Everett seeing me in discomfort."

"That's not normal for a loving husband. It's very odd. Everett is a cold fish." Logan shook his head confounded.

She sniffed and shrugged.

"My dear fearless, Jessie, you're totally unafraid of the wilderness and sailing for the first time. That is admirable. But to live with a man who treats you so and remain unafraid? That is quite frankly daft."

"It does no good fearing anything. I'm going on this journey regardless. So I may as well enjoy it. I didn't like good society much. I prefer simplicity and peace. But I endured it for Everett. I can weather this for him as well. Seriously, however, this is more to my liking."

"You have remarkable sea legs. It's too bad Everett isn't fairing as well."

"Indeed. I wish he were able to enjoy it like we are. You and Everett could bond and become friends during the voyage. If only he were doing better."

"No worries. Everett and I'll be working together. We have time to get acquainted."

The conniving old devil won't make a good friend.

Jessie, on the other hand, is one of the most exotic and beautiful women I've ever met. The woman was surprisingly interesting and aware of current affairs. But her comments about women in business and Everett wanting her to be fearful explain a lot. Including her reluctance to express opinions and astonishment at being asked.

"You have an astute business sense, a keen wit and intelligent mind. Your questions about logging are insightful."

"Why thank you. Business is fascinating." Her blush endeared her to Logan. There was innocence about Jessie intriguing Logan. "Please, don't mention it to Everett."

Logan nodded silently.

Compassion filled her eyes. "Did you have reservations about leaving your folks?"

"Of course. I love my parents very much. My brothers and I were close. But it was time. What about you? Don't you miss family left behind?"

"I have no family, only Everett." Moisture filled her eyes and turning her head too late to hide, Logan pretended not to notice.

"I'm surprisingly comfortable around you."

"As am I with you, Logan."

It must be difficulty due to their loss that prevents letting her guard down around her husband. Surely Everett would get a handle on his grief by the time they arrived in Alaska, for Jessie's sake.

He's an ass.

It wasn't Logan's place to pry. It was none of his business. Logan mustn't read too much into it or let on to Everett he disapproves of his treatment of his wife.

"I'm grateful for your friendship. You're an amazing woman. You don't think Everett will object. Do you?"

"I hope not. He's very possessive."

Lovely by moonlight, Jessie was captivating. Logan couldn't get enough of her company. However, Logan couldn't go against or anger Everett. But she was fast becoming his best friend.

"Your man doesn't deserve you, but I won't interfere in your marriage. I respect you too much. I would never hurt you."

Logan couldn't quite put a finger on it. Jessie and Everett made a strange couple. They didn't fit. So why were they together?

A gorgeous, desirable woman, a lady head to toe, sweet, open, and completely unpretentious, she was sincere. Eagerly experiencing life, open to adventure, exceptionally smart, she was totally alluring. Who wouldn't want to be with Jessie? Why did she marry Everett of all people? A woman like her could have had anyone of her choosing.

Logan laughed at how Jessie's nose wrinkled when she tasted her first raw oyster. After swallowing she broke into an adorable grin, and the beaming approval melted a spot straight to Logan's heart.

"Delicious. I didn't expect to like the taste."

"Your child-like wonder is remarkable."

Everett was stern, proper, and full of himself. Expecting everyone to bow to his authority. He rudely proved to be more and more unbearable. Logan didn't take Everett too seriously. He could work for Everett, as long as it led to what Logan wanted from the deal. Logan tolerated the scoundrel. Logan didn't have to like Everett.

* * *

Early the fourth day out to sea Jessie checked in on Everett before breakfast. Stone cold on the bunk, Everett's fist gripped his shirt front and a look of agony was frozen on his still face. She rushed to his side.

"Oh, Everett, are you okay? Please be okay." Jessie touched the cold lifeless jaw of the man who had rescued her from hell on earth.

Everett had promised the moon and given her more hell. But he had also showed her there were other ways to live. He had turned her into a lady and exposed her to wonders she had not ventured to dream of. He offered this tremendous new adventure in Alaska. Now Everett had deserted Jessie when she needed him most.

Everett was dead. There was nothing she could do to change that. Saddened and terrified, what would become of her? As Everett died, so did Jessie's hopes of becoming a mother and having a happy married life.

Later that evening after the crew had prepared Everett's body, everyone on board stood on deck for a short ceremony. Logan stood close by Jessie's side fortifying her with his strength. Faces of passengers were filled with respect for her husband and sorry for the new widow.

"I am grateful for you taking charge, Captain. The offer to wrap Everett for the remainder of the journey, and hold him somewhere out of nose shot for burial in Skagway was gracious. However, as you pointed out, we still have a long voyage ahead of us. By the time we reach our destination, the corpse would stink to high heaven. So I'm glad I opted for burial sea. Thank you for everything you are doing."

Jessie wore the only black dress she had packed. "I feel awful that Everett's tortured life was cut short. I am consoled believing that Everett might be finally at peace."

If his soul ends up in the same place as his mama's, Everett went straight to hell.

Jessie lost her benefactor and protector, but also her punisher and imprisoner. Unsure if she was better or worse off, Everett was out of the picture.

She must've appeared properly grieving based on the way other passengers treated her. But Jessie had a hard time drumming up that spiritual feeling of grief.

Everett had never cared and had started treating her roughly without the merest consideration, so eventually Jessie had doubted being able to win Everett's love or love him back. But she had continued to harbor a glint of optimism.

"I am sorry for your loss." Logan meant it because he witnessed the distress losing Everett caused. Though Logan thought she might be better off without the cad, he hadn't wished Everett dead. And it appeared, neither did Jessie. "Thank you, Logan. I hoped our life would change once we reached Alaska, and we would have a long, happy marriage living there. I have never been on my own. I am scared, Logan. What will become of me?" That would never happen now.

Jessie had never been alone in the world. Someone always ruled her life. First it was Mama. Then it was Everett.

Logan stood protectively beside Jessie. "Don't worry. Everett has an attorney in Skagway who manages his legal affairs. You will find out once we arrived how your husband left his estate. With you the single heir, you are probably financially set."

Prior to that Everett had showered Jessie with lovely jewels and fabulous gowns. Of course those things were meant to impress his associates more than they were to pleasure her. After Jessie lost the baby, Everett had not been the most generous man. Had he considered her welfare in settling his estate?

"Thank you, Logan. But I will be worried until I know for sure. Then I will decide how to proceed with my life. But I can't think of that now. Now I must bury my husband."

Jessie listened patiently and contritely as the captain spoke words meant to comfort her. The only real comfort was Logan standing beside her in a watchful, shielding manner.

She laid a flower plucked from one of her fashionable hats onto Everett's wrapped, lifeless body.

"Goodbye, husband, rest in peace. May the demons that drove you, haunt you no more. We are both free."

* * *

As the days drifted on with the tide, Logan accompanied Jessie, and she seemed grateful to have him around. Logan did his best to convince her that she possessed the strength and confidence to make it without Everett. He didn't doubt Jessie was capable of taking care of herself. But for some reason she seemed unsure.

Days and evenings they walked the deck for exercise as brilliant landscape passed by.

"I'm fascinated with nature's bounty in this vast wilderness. I can hardly pry my eyes from scanning the water and coastline for wild animals and marine life. I'm never disappointed. Let's see, so far we spotted foxes, deer, elk, moose, wolves, endless eagles and caribou. And the ocean provides ample visitors as well."

She was the most remarkable creature Logan had ever met. Logan's eyes followed the long, slender arm pointing at her most recent find.

"There they are again. Orca whales bobbing their black and white heads beside the ship." Jessie squealed and pointed, laughing in another direction. "Oh, look. A whale's surfacing, spouting water from its air hole. He is creating quite a spectacle." Her feet shifted like a child barely containing the urge to jump around. "Last night a walrus family sunned on floating icebergs, scanning the surface for an unsuspecting seal meal."

"The farther north we venture, the shorter nights become. The sky remains grey, never getting completely dark." Logan gazed up.

"Yes, it's dusky most of the night, according to Captain Stuart. Sometimes in summer Alaska has no darkness at all. Plus sometimes in winter there's no daylight. It remains dark. It's an amazing phenomenon."

"Very odd, indeed."

"This is a great way to walk off that delectable meal. Do you think the crew and passengers consider me crass? I have not lost my voracious appetite with the loss of my husband."

"Not at all. You must eat to keep yourself healthy. You have a long journey ahead of you. It may not be an easy one."

"I realize that. I am wary of the future."

"You are not alone. I am there for you. I am your friend. But likely, I will also be your employee."

Her head cocked gazing at the sky. "Hmmm . . . I never considered I might have people depending on me now. I've never even been responsible for myself, let alone others. I know nothing much of Everett's vast affairs. He did mention there is an attorney in Skagway who handles his holdings, however."

"I am sure that lawyer will help you learn where you stand. I wouldn't worry too much about it. Everett was wealthy. I assume he left you well off. And don't doubt you are up to any task that comes your way."

Light from her eyes glowed inside Logan's heart and warmed him all over on the cool evening.

Suddenly the sky lit with magnificent color. Glimpsing the radiant display, Jessie unconsciously grabbed Logan's hand, stilling his heart. She pointed to the lights and startled. The heat of the touch warmed Logan's whole body. He sucked in a breath and held it.

"Oh look. I never expected to witness anything so beautiful. The sky is a living creature with bright greens and blues, purples and silver streaks filling the atmosphere. The glows are dancing in the night."

Spellbound, they oohed and awed at the spectacular production as Logan grew more enchanted by Jessie's charm by the moment.

Air sucked from Logan's lungs as her delicate hand rested trustingly in his palm naturally like it belonged there. The dainty fingers dwarfed in Levi's grasp. He breathed deeply and regained his bearings knowing that if his heart failed to beat again, he would die a happy man.

"I read about this. But I never figured I'd witness it." She reverently whispered as one might in in a gospel mill. "This brilliant phenomenon is one of nature's wonders, called the Aurora Borealis or the Northern Lights. These skies are frequently privy to this wondrous exhibition."

Logan reflexively stroked the silky palm with his thumb. Tenderly savoring the gift of her touch he wondered how her s kin would taste if he put his lips to it. But this was not the time or place.

Jessie's reaction was friendly and totally innocent. It was more about the lights. Not so, were the emotions pounding through Logan's veins, consuming his mind.

What was he thinking? He mustn't embarrass this lovely creature. So closing his eyes he took a deep, slow breath and finally dared to look.

Bewitched with nature's display, Jessie focused on the brilliant, colorful glimmer twirling merrily above them oblivious that she had reached out intimately.

"It's a sight to behold." Logan finally gambled to speak. Though the lights impressed, they paled compared to Jessie's glorious face.

Logan hadn't foreseen falling fast for this amazing woman who had unintentionally seized his heart.

Surprised at the emotions gripping him, Logan had never considered falling in love again or being capable.

He sure as hell didn't want to fall in love with a married woman. Logan hadn't intentionally pursued her and never would have, respecting Jessie and the sanctity of marriage. But she was widowed now--not a married woman. However, it was much too soon. She would be in mourning for a long while to come. Any advance he made now would be unseemly.

Logan would never cause her hardship. Exposing his emotions would only result in suffering. She had enough to handle.

Jessie seemed happy having Logan as a friend. Conversation and silence were easy between them. They enjoyed being together. Theirs must stay an innocent relationship.

* * *

Aboard ship almost two weeks, a sudden, bizarre roaring rumbled in the distance, startling them. Jessie jumped as massive chunks of snow-covered ice floated in the water and slammed against the bow.

"The farther we venture the more ice we see. They grow in size the longer the ship sails. The steward called them icebergs. Look, birds are floating atop some of the bergs."

"Seals are resting on those scanning the seawater spotting fish for dinner. They're curious creatures, bopping their heads surfacing for a look at the ship as we pass by."

Logan pointed out a chunk of ice. "Captain Stuart explained that icebergs are much deeper beneath the surface. They can do mortal damage if a vessel hits a large one. So he navigates the ship carefully avoiding collision."

"We're in the Captain's expert hands." Enthralled with the danger, she gasped eyes wide, scanning the water's surface near the ship.

"Of course."

Clinging to the rail leaning forward, she witnessed the exhibition. "It's mesmerizing."

The ship was nearing a gigantic wall of ice on the right side of the boat. The massive iceberg moved and roared, as though it were alive.

The Captain carefully maneuvered the area, providing not only safe voyage through the icebergs. He exposed a spectacular show for the voyagers.

Loud rumbling sounded. A soft roar broke the air, followed by, Crack! Bang! A shower of snow fell from a section of ice wall, forming a cloudy rush of softening snow floating toward the water's surface. Then a powerful splash rose. A huge slice of ice wall gave way and splattered into the frigid water. Silt shimmered covering the surface.

Jessie instinctively reached for Logan's hand. Shocked by her unexpected touch, his breathe stalled.

A mind-altering sensation surged through his veins. Rigidly still, eyes closed he memorized the touch of her soft skin. Warm and gentle, velvety smooth, Jessie's palm and delicate fingers wrapped around Logan's work-roughened hand. It felt so natural, as though it belonged there.

Logan opened his eyes and broke the spell. Jessie glanced away, realizing and probably embarrassed that she'd reached for him. Then she faced him, and their gaze hung in the thick, cool air. Silence spoke words not voiced.

She didn't blush but gently squeezed Logan's hand before withdrawing then grinned before returning to the display.

Passengers oohed and awed at nature's incredible show, with no idea how spectacular the moment actually was.

Logan would never forget her pulse churning in his hand. The brief interlude was guiltless. Their connection couldn't be broken. It was the beginning of something wonderful. No matter that anything more was forbidden.

Jessie needed someone. Logan was proud that she hadn't denied him the luxury of her friendship.

Logan's hand had never been so empty before. The absence of her warmth occupied Logan's mind.

Wanting redemption and escape from survivor's guilt, Logan sought to forget and heal, not looking for love. Powerless against Jessie's unintentional spell, he was done for.

A good thing Jessie wasn't available. There wasn't room in his life for a woman--not now. Logan came north seeking his fortune, importantly impacting territorial growth. So love was the last thing he needed.

But in their short voyage, Jessie had made an indelible mark on his soul. The charming widow had breathed new life into Logan's impervious existence and made him whole again. Jessie owned Logan's heart, but she had no place for it in her life. More than likely Jessie would return to her mansion in San Francisco.

Logan had no right to fall in love with Jessie. He should be remorseful. But why bother? How could Logan be guilty of something out of his hands? Logan's feelings for Jessie were beyond his control. It was too late. There was no turning back. What the hell should he do now?

Logan couldn't share his affection with Jessie and mustn't tell her. It would only burden her, and Logan couldn't have her. It was a pitiful shame, but it was what it was. Logan would deal with it . . . alone.

Jessie had enough on her plate. She meant no harm and hadn't meant for this to happen. Jessie had only been seeking companionship and friendship--nothing more.

She deserved better--the life of luxury her California life provided and a man capable of completely loving her.

He wasn't sure what he was capable of these days--not since Amy. But he cared for Jessie and would do right by her by being the friend she needed.

It was all Logan could do.

* * *

Jessie wasn't as clueless as she pretended. Her brain flooded with emotion. Logan's pulsating heartbeat pounded her hand. Its thudding throb casually melted a path straight to her heart and curled her toes.

How could she not compare the two men in her life? Logan was sweet and fun. Jessie felt capable and joyous with Logan. With Everett Jessie had been inadequate and apprehensive, always on guard, worried about displeasing him.

Why couldn't Everett have relaxed and been more like Logan? Why hadn't Everett caused her heart to race and blood to boil with pleasure the way Logan affected her? If only Everett had let Jessie get close to him.

Jessie refused to harbor guilt about their friendship, which was becoming tremendously important. She began to trust Logan, which was a rarity and didn't come easy. Not after everything Jessie had seen. But with Logan she relaxed and was herself, with no need to play a role. So their friendship became an oasis.

Jessie sure wasn't the New Orleans girl with a wag-tail mama any longer. She was not the ingenue she pretended to be in Boston, the ladylike product of Mistress Hatfield's Finishing Academy for Proper Young Ladies of Good Breeding. Nor was she the scared, young bride she'd been in San Francisco. Jessie's life was in flux and her world was changing. She was growing with it . . . but into what?

Jessie's sphere had expanded and she fast became part of it, growing into a new person formed out of experience. Good and satisfying, it felt right, like something wonderful was in store for the future. But it was terrifying as well.

Who would Jessie become in Alaska?

CHAPTER 9

The ship arrived in Skagway on a sunny morning as breakfast ended onboard. Eager but apprehensive for the voyage's end, every nerve in her body stood on high alert.

"Thank you, Captain. I've enjoyed your hospitality. You've been an impeccable host. And the funeral service for Everett was endearing. Thank you for that."

"My pleasure, Mistress Blackstone. I am sorry for your loss. I hope you enjoy your new home. And if you choose to return to the mainland, I hope you are able to sail home aboard my ship." The Captain kissed her gloved hand then went to say goodbye to other guests.

Jessie sought Logan out on deck. A twang of pain assaulted her chest stealing her breath. As she cupped Logan's rugged, work-worn hand in hers, Jessie resisted pulling it to her chest. She feared being away from the man who had been her rock throughout the voyage.

Jessie lifted her head and attempted a smile. Tears threatened as she met Logan's gaze. Unashamed of the intense sensations, she didn't bother concealing them. Only Logan was aware of her angst, since she had no need to disguise feelings or pretend with her dear friend.

"I can't explain what a blessing your company has been during this voyage. Your friendship means a lot to me."

"Skagway's a slight village. I understand our houses are both near the saw mill. So we'll be neighbors and see each other often. I would like nothing more." Logan bit his lower lip and stared at her mouth as she spoke.

Would those lips taste like honey? What thought put that peculiar look in Logan's eyes?

"Perhaps."

"I'm pleased we have bonded. Do you want me to see you safely to your home?" Logan's heart pulsed rapidly in the petite hand.

"No. That won't be necessary. I have a meeting onboard ship. I've contracted carriage for later today. The crew already loaded my cargo onto wagons that Everett had prearranged. My cargo will be delivered to my house and unpacked before I get there. Please take care of yourself. I hope to see you soon."

Logan's smile and the touch of his hand were unexpected gifts.

Logan's swallowed hard and glanced away as though sad.

Breakfast formed a rigid knot in the pit of her stomach. A heavy weight assaulted her chest, overcome with sadness. They wouldn't be spending as much time together now they had arrived. Impending separation left Jessie longing to pull Logan's hands to her lips and taste the firm flesh.

Stay focused on what must be done.

Logan's sad smile communicated more than words could. Their magical time alone ended.

Clearing his throat a few times, his head held high. "It's been a pleasure." He retrieved his valise, stepped lively along the gangplank, and put space between them. She gasped cool sea breeze and stilled the gripping excitement in her belly as moisture clouded her vision.

Everett hadn't been open-minded or understanding. He discouraged her forming personal bonds of any kind and wouldn't likely have approved of her befriending Logan any more than he would have her relationship with Lilly.

Well poo on Everett.

She needed friends, having so few successful relationships. Her friendship with Logan was good and precious. So Jessie kept silent determined to continue seeing Logan, as circumstances allowed. That is, if she stayed in Alaska. But she was feeling more and more certain she would.

Logan was in a vulnerable position--grieving Amy and starting a new life. Chances were he would be working for Jessie. The odd idea felt foreign and mixed emotions tore at Jessie as she waved goodbye.

The mesmerizing view of Logan's spectacular rump as he strode away gave Skagway females a treat. His swoon-worthy, slim waist and powerful, broad shoulders strained beneath his overcoat.

Logan was sure to become popular. That was none of her business and shouldn't concern Jessie. But whomever Logan took up with had better do well by him. Logan was a good man and deserved a good woman, someone pure with a flawless history. Not someone like Jessie. Logan had been hurt enough.

Damn it anyway.

Squaring her shoulders she walked toward Everett's room.

"Stop caterwauling." Jessie spoke to the walls of the room which was empty now except for the trunks in the corner. "You have a job to do." Her belly did a continual somersault of fear.

As suspected, she and Everett were the ones delivering the *"found gold"* to the impostors. It was no wonder Everett remained in his cabin during the trip to guard the gold.

Venturing outdoors she enjoyed the beautiful day while waiting for destiny.

Settled on deck studying cookbooks purchased in San Francisco, she hoped to distract from the terror of the coming confrontation. How would these men take meeting a woman instead of Everett? Would they listen or balk at what she had to say? She must find a way to manage them and complete the mission.

Clueless about housekeeping and cooking, she needed to learn to survive in the remote location with few resources. Jessie had proved to be a quick study in the past and was confident she'd learn.

Passengers lined the deck disembarking. Exciting, controlled chaos reigned as stevedores swiftly and efficiently moved crate after crate from the ship. They worked like a well-oiled machine, ensuring cargo delivered where it belonged.

Giddy with anticipation, eager to explore Skagway, Jessie had questioned the captain at length for juicy details during dinner the night before. Captain Stuart had held a captive audience elaborating about the city.

"The local Tlingit tribe of natives actually calls Skagway, Skagua, meaning 'Windy Place.' Chilkoot and Chilkat tribes hunt and fish, inhabiting areas nearby in more quiet locations like Smuggler's Cover, Nahku Bay and Dyea. Dyea is a centuries old Indian trading route popular with early prospectors heading to the Yukon."

Eyes wide she gave her full attention.

"Don't worry. Local tribes are peaceful, welcoming white men. The U. S. Navy and Army established a presence back in 1880. So they regularly patrol the area."

"I'm not afraid . . . after all, it is May, 1887. The United States is a world power."

"White men here are few," Captain Stuart humored, "with even fewer white women."

"Exploration is in full force. Is expansion expected?"

Do they know about the conspiracy?

"Earlier this year a prospector, Jim Skookum and his native Tlingit packer led Captain William Moore from the Canadian Ogilvie Survey Party across a valley along the Skaqua River. They named it White Pass. Moore, and his son Bernard, are building a town called Mooresville in the one hundred sixty acre valley. They are erecting a dock because they have big plans."

"My goodness, I had no idea. No wonder Everett wanted to come here."

Set in the distance from the port from the semi-circular cove lived the tiny town of Skagway. Its single, wide, dirt-filled main street consisted of ten to fifteen wooden structures. Boardwalks spanned along simple, single or two story store fronts, so pedestrians could avoid walking the muddy road unless they crossed the street. Impressive, imposing, snow-topped mountain ranges surrounded the town. Severely rugged terrain in the distance sported sparkling glaciers.

Skagway was the most adorable village ever. It was Jessie's home. Even the word *'home'* had a beautiful sound.

Warm seventy degree, summery weather blessed the lovely day. The morning had been much cooler. But as the day progressed, layers of clothing were removed for comfort. She contemplated severity of the winters, since hearing scary stories sighting fifty below zero temperatures and worse. Weather like that made surviving difficult.

Hopefully Everett understood what they were getting into and had prepared. He had assured their house was adequate. Their possessions had been delivered earlier, so everything should be unpacked, waiting arrival.

Finally late afternoon, Captain Stuart showed two surprisingly burley strangers to Everett's cabin. These brutish men were not the type Everett generally associated with. They were rough and rugged, wearing fur hats and dirty animal skin suits. Rutted faces sported long, greying beards draped atop ample guts. Their crude manners and gruff manner speaking with the Captain made Jessie wary. She would need to tread lightly with these men and demand respect. They wouldn't give it easily, her being a woman. It was essential they learn who was boss here. They mustn't realize how badly Jessie quaked inside with fear.

The captain opened the door and escorted the men inside the stateroom. They sat on the bunk and the captain stepped out. He spoke low so only Jessie heard.

"Are you sure you want me to leave you alone with these two?" Concern showed clearly on the captain's face.

"Not at all. But I must speak with them privately. It is of great urgency. Would you mind mulling around outside the door while we have a chat? That way, should I need assistance, you will be nearby." Jessie's heart fluttered and her breath gushed with relief as the captain agreed.

Patting her skirts to check on her weapon, she entered the small cabin. The lacy fan hung from her right wrist grasped in her hand. She was as ready as she would ever be.

The brutish fellows looked up surprised. They had obviously not expected a woman for this meeting.

"Good day, gentlemen." Jessie spoke slowly and succinctly watching their reactions.

"What do you want, woman? We are here for a business meeting." One scruffy man growled.

His voice sent warning sparks through Jessie's veins as she steeled herself hands on hips. "Your meeting is with me, gentlemen. I am the messenger sent here to finalize your deal."

"I ain't doin' business w' no split-tail." One man grumbled.

"We don't work for women." The other confirmed fidgeting in his seat about to rise and leave.

"Gentlemen, let's get one thing straight. You are in this up to your eyeballs. There is no way for you to back out now. You are not dealing with a woman. I am only the messenger. These are powerful men you have made a pact with. They mean business. They will not stand for shenanigans on your part. You will do as I say. You will carry out your bargain with the consortium or suffer dire consequences. So I suggest you calm down and listen. Then we can all part ways for good. And you will leave here very wealthy men."

The cads glanced at each other, their eyes wide. Then they took on a calmer demeanor.

"Spit it out, gal."

"Time's a wasting," shot the other.

"The two of you will accept payment as planned from me today. The gold is yours, as long as you carry out the plan. When I leave this ship, I leave the gold in your hands. Stay aboard until the ship sails in a few days. Say nothing until you arrive at the Port of Seattle. You'll be met by throngs of journalists who received leaked information about great news upon the ship's arrival. Speak with them all and tell the story as it was outlined previously to you. Claim convincingly that you found this gold in the far Klondike. It is important that these journalists hear and believe your tale."

"The Klondike can only be reached traveling on foot or horseback through Skagway then across treacherous mountain ranges in bitter weather conditions," one roughened voice argued.

"Exactly," Jessie laughed. "Your knowledge of the route will serve you well as you explain. Say that gold lies everywhere in the frozen Klondike for easy pickings. Talk with every reporter. Swear you found a multitude of rich veins. Once you've professed this to the last journalist, take your gold and disappear forever. You must become untraceable."

The men grumbled and quieted. "What if we take the gold from you now and just disappear?" They stood and made an attempt toward Jessie.

With a flick of her wrist the long, slim blade shot out of the lacy fan tines and glistened in the lamplight. Jessie's other hand pulled the revolver from her hidden skirt pocket and pointed it at one of the men.

"Sirs, you will take the gold when and if I choose to give it. And you cannot possibly run far enough or hide from the consortium. That band is made up of the most powerful men in the country, maybe the world. Should you not comply, or if you ever leak word about the conspiracy, you'll be hunted like dogs and killed. Understand?" Hoping her hands weren't shaking, she locked eyes with the ruffians.

They grumbled more. "We understand."

Jessie's tone became severe. Though her tummy was flip-flopping wildly, she didn't dare show weakness or quibble and broached no mercy.

Everett and his co-conspirators employed backing of local, state, and federal government plus businessmen with power to execute her threat. They could and would do it. So Jessie put the fear of God into the brutes.

"You've nothing to gain by leaking the truth. But you walk away with incredible wealth, going along with the plan."

"It's an easy choice that beats the hell out of digging frozen hard ground. We've done plenty of that the last couple years, with no success," a grizzled voice mumbled hoarsely.

"The threat's real. So are the riches. You made your choice before you boarded the ship. It's too late to back out now. So if you refuse at this point, you won't leave here alive." The men muttered but agreed.

Jessie pointed to the trunks in the corner. "Those are filled with nuggets amounting to approximately two thousand pounds of gold. I leave them with you. The group I work for is entrusting this dire task to you. I suggest you do it well."

Turning she opened the door, placed her weapons back in their hiding spots and left the shady men alone.

A huge burden had been lifted from her shoulders. Giddy inside, she greeted the waiting captain with a brilliant smile.

"Thank you Captain. It has been a pleasure sailing with you. I hope we meet again someday."

"My pleasure, Mistress Blackstone. Take care of yourself." His head bent to kiss her hand.

Shoulders braced back and head shot high, she strutted away feeling freer than ever. She took the gangplank to the waiting carriage.

Home at last. What adventures waits?

Chapter 10

The young man wearing a big grin, heavy-duty work pants and flannel shirt helped Jessie aboard the carriage he had brought to pick her up.

"Good afternoon, Mistress Blackstone. My name is Ben Carson. I work at the lumber mill. Your husband prearranged for me to pick the two of you up and take you home. I am sorry for your loss, Mistress Blackstone."

"Thank you, Mister Carson. I appreciate your service. Shall we go now?"

The fella clicked the reigns, and the two horses kept time taking the short ride to town through the solitary, badly rutted main street. The thoroughfare was a sloppy, loblolly mud path through town. Jessie's eyes were wide, and her head spun from side to side. She didn't want to miss a thing.

"Skagway is slight and quaint." Only a few people bustled about. Horses and wagons were sparsely scattered, with a few hitched to railings. Everett's saw mill inhabited the end of one of a couple of short side streets in the distant edge of town. Ben proudly pointed out construction, starting on a building in the town center. "It'll be your husband's grand hotel. Mister

Blackstone started building it before he died. I hope you will allow them to finish it." Ben's voice sounded hopeful.

The new elegant hotel would no doubt bring additional revenue into town. That sounded like a good thing.

"I suppose so. I know of no reason not to, at least at this point."

Ben appeared appeased.

"I counted four saloons. Considering how tiny the town is, it seems a bit excessive. But I like the names--the Pack Train, the Bonanza, the Grotto and the Nugget. They are bustling with customers in the middle of the afternoon."

Ben's young face pinked, avoiding Jessie's eyes. "I guess. But your husband owns part of at least one of them. I understand the Red Onion is quite profitable. It is the largest and has a brothel upstairs." Ben's face turned bright red, and sweat beaded on his forehead in the cool afternoon. "I apologize, Ma'am. I shouldn't speak of such things with a lady."

"That is fine, Ben. No harm done. I know of such things. As matter of fact, I may now be the owner, since Everett has passed on. I will need to ask my attorney." She hadn't considered she might end up as a madam. *Mama would be proud.*

"Locals fondly call this stretch of black mud Broadway Avenue. It is the commercial area of town." Ben appeared eager to change the subject.

"Skagway sure is a beautiful, sweet town."

"Hardly . . . it's dangerous, both day and night. The city is totally without rules or law." Ben grinned wickedly then appeared ashamed. "Sorry, Ma'am. It's been awhile since I've been in the company of a fine lady. My manners are off some."

Perfect for Everett's planned exploitation.

A man waved and grinned from the sidewalk. He looked like a dandy as he walked awkwardly through the muddy street. Approaching their carriage he blocked their way. The gent took his hat off as a courtesy, dramatically sweeping it forward then resting it beneath his arm. With no way of avoiding the intruder without running him down, Ben stopped, but was visibly irritated.

Ben whispered only to Jessie. "He wants to be taken for a serious, respected businessman." By his comments and inflection it was obvious Ben didn't respect this man.

The dude failed.

Jessie instantly disliked the fella. His strange demeanor gave her the willies. Unlike other locals, this character dressed in a fancy suit that was not at all appropriate for the muddy town.

"Mistress Blackstone, I'm so pleased you finally made it." The dolt bowed in a sweeping motion.

"You have brought us a lovely, sunny, summer day. I would like to introduce myself. I am Jefferson Randolph Smith. Most folks around here call me Soapy."

Jessie smiled deceivingly, not letting on her first impression. Ben sat silently hiding his dyed-in-the-wool attitude for Soapy. Soapy appeared satisfied with himself and oblivious to the slight.

The sap resembles a possum in a man's suit.

"I wish you condolences, Mistress Blackstone. I was shocked and saddened hearing about Everett's demise. And it was terrible timing, if timing ever comes into play in such things. Everett was my business partner. I suppose you will inherit everything he owned. I understand you are his soul heir and the only family Everett had. I'd be happy to take Everett's share of the establishment off your hands."

Jessie was surprised Soapy Smith knew so much about Everett and apparently her too. She would have to watch this one. He was a devil in disguise.

News travels fast around here. Or Soapy has the inside track.

"I'm pleased to meet you, Mister Smith. I'll take your offer under advisement. My attorney will be in touch, should I choose to sell to you." Ever the lady, Jessie smiled congenially, extending a gloved hand.

"Please, call me Soapy."

"We best be on our way. We have a lot to do. It was nice meeting you, Mister Smith. We will talk later, after I get settled." Jessie turned toward the road dismissing Soapy. Ben urged the horses forward.

Soapy reached the boardwalk and walked toward the Red Onion. Once out of ear shot Ben looked relieved.

"Avoid Soapy Smith at all cost. He's one of the most notorious con men in the west. After a run-in with Texas lawmen and again in Denver, Soapy moved north to Alaska seeking ill-gotten fortune. He has found success here. He is growing rich off the misery of others. He is unscrupulous and violent. Mistress Blackstone, you should keep your distance."

"It sounds like we may be business partners. I will need to find a way to manage that. Thanks for looking out for me, Ben. I appreciate it."

Ben looked embarrassed and blushed again. His shoulders hunched and he smiled silently to himself, as he drove the carriage.

Jessie hoped to avoid the unpleasant man, but likely Soapy was going to be a pain in her rear.

Growing more anxious to get settled, she fidgeted in her seat until finally they turned right.

"This is your home." Ben maneuvered the wagon around the bend and pointed across the street to the opposite corner. "That two-story on the right of the main street boardwalk is your mercantile. Mister Blackstone owned it.

"Impressive."

"Your house faces the side of the mercantile. To be safe, you should avoid the narrow alley lying behind the main street. Never go anywhere secluded. Much danger lurks about." Ben's stern glare was all the convincing needed.

"I have a direct view of the alleyway from my front door."

Ben pointed to a cottage beside the alley. "Logan Pace lives in the cottage. Mister Pace is the man your husband hired to run the lumber business and saw mill. Mister Pace was on the same voyage as you. He only just arrived today, too."

"Of course, I have met Mister Pace." "It's a darling bungalow. The house is right as rain for a single man and conveniently close to work and the town center."

Where is Logan now? She couldn't ask Ben. It would be unseemly.

Eyes wide, she studied the two story log house. "My home is grand. It is sizeable yet cozy with lovely shuttered windows flanking the bulky front door. It's convenient to town and the mill." Jessie clapped excitedly.

And Logan.

"So you approve?" Ben looked pleased.

"It's adorable. I look forward to sitting on the long front porch observing goings-on in town."

"The men and I from the saw mill built it to Mister Blackstone's specifications. It's a dandy, ain't it?" Ben looked pleased at the compliments, as his chest expanded proudly and he smiled.

"The sharp pitched roof will shed snow easily. The golden stained logs are thick and will contain warmth."

"It's delightful." She squealed.

Furniture and possessions had been placed where the crew had assumed they should go.

"There are three bedrooms, a living room, formal dining room and a huge kitchen. Behind that was a mud room. In winter you can hang overcoats along the wall and sit boots on the trays below to drain and dry, avoiding mess in the house." Ben pointed to the log bench and proudly bragged about features as though her approval meant something.

"Brilliant. This is perfect." Jessie's heart welled with hope.

"These rooms surround a central one, housing a water tank. It can be filled during warm weather. This cistern tank is in the middle of the house, so the water won't freeze. It will provide fresh water all winter long when the outside freezes around September. It doesn't thaw until late May or early June."

She clapped delighted. "What a luxury. I wondered how I'd manage when the world outside is turned to ice."

"A water pump in the mud room provides underground well water usable most of the year, but not during severely cold months."

"Each room has its own wood stove for heat. The kitchen has a huge, cast iron, wood-burning cook stove."

Jessie flinched. She must learn the art of cooking quickly.

Ben pointed out the back door to a building. "The shed's filled, brimming with firewood. It will remain dry and ready for winter. We will keep it continually stocked with excess scrap from the saw mill, providing an unlimited heat." Ben preened like a peacock and pointed out the back door. "Behind the house in the yard is a smokehouse for preserving game and fish. The door in the dirt mound is an underground root cellar for storing vegetables and canned food."

"Wonderful. I'll learn gardening and preserving. I'll plant a garden next to the smoke house."

"The growing season is short."

"No matter. I can still grow a fabulous garden." Having read everything she'd found about gardening.

"The ground is quite fertile." Ben pointed past her home at the end of the short street to the saw mill and lumber yard. "That's your lumber company and saw mill, where I work."

"I haven't gotten a handle on Everett's business holdings yet. But I hope for Logon to continue on to run the lumber business, as planned."

"Your hands are full, Mistress Blackstone. Your husband's fingers were in many businesses. He owns part of the only bank in town and part of the shipping company you sailed on."

Her fan flicked apprehensively, beginning to realize how large Everett's shoes were that needed to be filled.

"It's all so new and a bit intimidating, Ben. I appreciate your help today."

With wide eyes, Ben nodded. "It's a lot for one person to manage, especially a woman."

"Yes. I have no business experience. The whole thing is a bit overwhelming. Ben, do you know of any women in town needing domestic work? I will need help around here."

"I know just the person. I will send her around. Mister Pace told me that he will check in on you. He said to tell you to let him know if you need anything at all." Ben saluted with his cap as he headed out the door.

"Thank you, Ben." Her heart flittered with excitement at being alone in her home in a strange town.

Home? I like the sound of that word.

The next morning venturing to her back porch she leaned against the railing. Fog evaporated from the valley as an eagle soared overhead in search of prey for its breakfast.

A lone moose ambled awkwardly from the forest, through tall grass. He made his way to the clearing into the pond until his belly touched water. Dipping his antlers and most of his face in, he shook, spraying water across his backside. He leisurely drank before taking a slow stroll back into his forest home.

The awkward animal was one of nature's marvels. He didn't appear put together correctly. So huge and awkward--God must've taken spare parts and clumsily create the moose. He was a bizarre creature that adapted extremely well to his environment.

Could Jessie learn from that magnificent animal?

Her husband had been a cad who would have locked her in a dungeon, if he could have gotten away with it. It was scary being alone and uncertain of the future. But freer than with Everett, Jessie began realizing she might be better off.

Everett thought she'd be easy to please. And she was. Jessie was compliant, with low expectations. She had been grateful for anything offered. He hadn't cared if she was happy about their new life, and probably would've liked it better if she was miserable.

Jessie was thrilled to be in Skagway and at opportunity to start over. However, she was terrified of being responsible for herself and others.

"Oh, Lilly, I miss you. Of course, we will stay in touch. But I could use your counsel now. I can hardly wait to describe Skagway in a letter."

Lots of work would occupy her time, and a baby would make the house a real home. Jessie laid a hand on her flat stomach. She feared it might not be real, but had been queasy the last couple of mornings and suspected she was with child. She hoped so.

"Without Everett's influence you will grow up with unconditional love." Her hands caressed her belly.

Too soon to get my hopes up.

Love was an elusive emotion she had only read about, having never loved anyone or been loved.

"I know firsthand what it is like growing up in a loveless home. You shall never know that feeling. You will be loved, my little one." With closed eyes she dreamed of holding a wee one as it breathed life.

A sharp pain seared through her and a tear escaped, regretting not being able to hold her first baby before it died.

"This was a new beginning--a joyful time. I mustn't dwell the past."

"The future holds such promise."

Chapter 11

The next morning Lu showed up, a local Tingit woman. Lu's grown sons were married and away from home. So with just Lu and her fisherman husband at home, Lu was seeking work outside her home.

"Mister Ben say you need help in the house. Lu cook, clean, wash things, and garden for you. You hire Lu?"

Lu was an unexpected blessing. "I am happy you're here, Lu. I have a lot to learn from you."

Lu nodded her round head and her coarse, black head bobbed along. "Good. Mistress Jessie no lift heavy things until after baby girl come. Lu lift heavy."

"Baby girl? Lu, how did you know? So I really am pregnant. I thought so but was afraid to hope. I lost my last child. How can you be sure?" A thrill raced through Jessie, and goose bumps formed on her skin.

Lu shrugged, as though she hadn't thought about it. "Don't know how. Lu just know such things." Lu smiled broadly revealing a space between her front teeth.

Jessie felt a sudden kinship with the native woman. She could tell they were destined to be much more than merely master and servant. Lu felt more like family.

Family?

Jessie might finally have a loving family. She had Lu, and her baby girl was on the way. Jessie stroked her flat tummy, eager for the bump to grow and begin moving within.

* * *

Jessie strolled proudly along the main street to the office of Everett's attorney. Mister Simpson had sent word that he was expecting her. He had handled Everett's affairs, so was aware of Everett's demise.

Mister Simpson was the only law-book man in town. Jessie had no choice, but to deal with the gent. It was time she settled Everett's estate and sealed her fate.

After offering his condolences, Mister Simpson read the will.

"Having no other family, my worldly goods go to my widow, Jess Blackstone." Mister Simpson sheepishly stared. "Mistress Blackstone, you're a wealthy heiress. Your husband left you a fortune. I assume you'll want to return to San Francisco where the social life is better. So I'll handle your house sale here. I will arrange sale of your husband's various businesses on your behalf. And you can set sail on the next vessel heading to Seattle leaving Friday."

Mister Simpson leaned back in his leather chair. His suit coat fell to the side. His bulbous belly extended forward. He fingered the watch chain gracing his brocade vest, with a self-satisfied expression on his puffy face. Mister Simpson appeared oblivious to Jessie's angst.

Mister Simpson fidgeted, while Jessie let him stew. Quietly ruminating, she hoped the silence was deafening to the man.

She had dressed carefully for this meeting and dreaded the guaranteed confrontation. As suspected, Mister Simpson had made assumptions and interferences into her life that riled Jessie.

He needs a tight leash. Turn the tables. Show him who works for whom.

"Mister Simpson, you're incorrect. You are a pompous ass."

His feet hit the wooden floor. His chair sprung straight. He sat erect with his mouth agape, causing Jessie to laugh.

"I resent your haughty suppositions of how you'll handle my business. You take liberties to my disadvantage."

Fury fired Jessie's eyes. Her brows rose. Her head leaned slightly to the side. Steadfast she sat tall, shoulders back facing the flustered man. Determination clearly on her face, she spoke adamantly.

I wasn't wrong about him. He'll take me seriously, if he knows what's good for him.

Having spent the days since Everett's passing perusing every document in his baggage concerning his businesses and finances, Jessie was prepared.

"I'm ready and confident in my ability to make logical decisions. I don't need you thinking for me."

The arrogant old gent wouldn't influence Jessie. She was her own woman.

"Now, Madam Blackstone, I advise you don't make rash decisions in emotional circumstances. Your husband would want me to direct your course of action." Mister Simpson flipped his pocket watch back and forth, attempting to regain control.

"I assure you. I'm not motivated by emotion. I am clear-headed, confident and rational."

Jessie laid a stack of file folders on the edge of Simpson's impressive mahogany desk.

"Madam Blackstone, you're a lady of leisure, a socialite, not trained in business. I assure you, I'll make arrangements leaving you financially set for a comfortable life in San Francisco. You'll be much happier there."

"Let's get something straight. First of all, my husband's dead. I'm your boss. You work for me. I couldn't care less what Everett wanted. His wishes are of no consequence in the least. Second, I make my own decisions. You'll not do it for me. You are working for me. You execute my orders--not your own on my behalf. Third, Alaska is my home now. It is where I intend to remain. I've decided how to handle each of my businesses. So I will explain my plans in detail. You will execute my orders."

Jessie paused allowing her words to sink in then continued.

"Are we clear?" Leaning forward intimidatingly standing, hands placed on each side of the stack of files, Jessie glared at her shocked lawyer.

"Quite," he uttered looking taken aback by her assertiveness. Sitting tall in his chair Mister Simpson coughed clearing his throat. Then grasping a pen and pad Simpson prepared to take notes.

"I didn't anticipate your being so . . . determined. I certainly had no idea you'd be interested in business. I didn't mean to take liberties. I assure you. I have your best interest in mind. So please accept my apologies, Madam Blackstone."

"I do." Jessie calmly opened the top folder and began directing.

"We might as well get to it. I'll take notes and follow up." Simpson managed to appear newly respectful.

He must find their situation hilarious. Mister Simpson probably didn't suspect Old Everett had a wildcat living in his house, especially one done with being pushed around, and with a head on her shoulders. It was about time Jessie used it.

"First of all, I'll continue living in Skagway. I have no need for the house in San Francisco. Therefore, please sell it."

Mister Simpson wrote as dictated.

"I'll keep the saw mill and lumber business. It will continue with Logan Pace's supervision. There's nothing for you to do there. I'll keep the mercantile. I am satisfied with the current manager. I met with him this morning, and he is in agreement. So there's nothing for you to do there."

Mister Simpson continued taking notes.

"I have no wish to be associated with the brothel or saloon. However, I won't let go of them yet. They are profitable businesses and should bring a good price. But as long as Soapy Smith is involved, I will keep part ownership. Of course, I will leave the operation up to him and will try not to interfere."

"Mister Smith would like to buy them from you. He has already approached me."

"Tell him no. I will not sell to him."

Simpson nodded still taking notes, but looking distressed.

"I'll assume Everett's bank responsibilities keeping the partnership alive. I will soon meet with the manager to assure him. His job is safe there for now. I will also keep Everett's ocean freight partnership."

Mister Simpson appeared confused. He shook his head putting his pen down. Simpson linked his fingers together tenting them on the desk top. He propped his chin on them.

"Madam Blackstone, neither the bank nor shipping consortium will welcome a woman partner. Both require owners to sit on their boards. Since a woman sitting on the board would be unseemly, I assure you, this won't work."

"Honestly, I don't give a bear's ass what they welcome. Fact is I'm definitely a woman and absolutely a partner. Whether those old coots welcome me or not, is none of my concern. It's not by design. But I own Everett's portion of those companies. So I will sit on their boards and be their partner. They have no choice. They will learn to live with it."

Jessie sat back, folded her hands in her lap, and glared as he shivered like a chill shot along his spine.

"I've never dealt with a woman with such decisiveness or business sense. I have no idea how to 'handle,' I mean how to deal with all this, Mistress Blackstone."

He's out of his league and baffled.

"You best learn." Jessie calmly folded her hands in her lap.

"I'll advise your partners of your wishes. We'll see where it goes from there. But I wish you'd reconsider." Simpson pleaded hesitantly, yet failed to dissuade.

Resolve never faltered as she unwaveringly remained ever the lady.

"Yes, advise them. I understand these men and what they're capable of. So if they balk in the least, give them this message. Tell them I'm aware of the tremendous deception they perpetrated, the nationwide conspiracy they and my husband concocted. I am familiar with the depths of deceit they executed. I can identify business and government parties contributing to the conspiracy. I can easily have the ear of several of the nation's leading journalists. Should they attempt to oust me, I'll ensure the nation learns how the Alaskan Gold Rush came about, and who instigated it. So trust me. They DO NOT want that moose loose."

The lawyer appeared appalled at Jessie's language and gall at threatening powerful men. But he must carry out her wishes.

"There's nothing more to discuss. I have enough to take it from here." Simpson stood dismissing her, visibly worn out from confrontation.

He can't wait for me to get out the door. He keeps glancing at his desk drawer. He probably keeps his bottle of booze hidden there. The poor Mister Simpson needs a snort.

Jessie rose, took her files and extended a gloved hand. Simpson accepted and firmly shook it.

"Good day."

His mind must be racing. It's obviously awkward and he's not used to a woman giving orders. He must figure it is wrong on so many levels. We women have our places. Business isn't one of them.

"Good day to you, Madam Blackstone."

Lighter, she exited and a huge weight lifted from her shoulders.

* * *

The bank was not due to open to the public for another hour. Jessie strolled into the bank building. She was now part owners of it, and Everett had an office in the back room. Holding the key, she opened the door.

The bank president walked out from his office when he heard the door.

"Land sakes, Madam Blackstone, what are you doing?" He blocked her way when she started for Everett's office.

"Please move out of my way, Sir." Jessie showed him the key. "I have come to check on my late husband's business. This is the key to his office."

"I assure you, there is nothing of interest for you in there. Let me introduce myself. I am the manager, Mister Bentley." Bentley moved slightly, as she bullied her way toward Everett's office and slid the key in the lock.

"Mister Bentley, Sir, I shall have a look anyway." Jessie walked into the office and rifled through Everett's desk. The stunned manager stood watching from the door.

"Madam, I assure you that anything of importance will be handled by me or the person who assumes your husband's place as part owner of this establishment."

"That would be me." Jessie smiled serenely at the fidgeting balding manager.

A look akin to sympathy crossed Mister Bentley's face. He walked around the desk, pulled Jessie's chair back and put his arm reassuringly around her shoulders.

"Now, now, Mistress Blackstone, you must be distraught. That is expected in your situation. There's no need for you to be concerned. Let's get you a cup of coffee." Bentley led Jessie to the banking area.

The male teller had arrived and was stacking his drawer with cash for the day. The fellow watched them curiously.

"No, thank you. I've had plenty coffee. I am fine. So go about your business." Jessie shooed the manager away with her hand. "Open the bank. Help the cashier get ready for the day. Besides, there is nothing of importance in Everett's office, anyway. I will have no use for that space. Use it for other banking business."

"Of course you won't. Leave this nasty banking to us men."

The man must think me daft. I've had enough nonsense.

Jessie placed her gloved hands on her hips and braced her feet apart. "This nasty business is my concern, sir. I own at least half of this damned bank. I will do with it as I please. That means you work for me, Mister Bentley. So get the hell out of my way, if you want to keep your job." Glaring, she left no room for argument.

Visibly flustered, Bentley muttered and flubbed about. Likely he had never heard a lady swear, or seen one hell bent on managing commerce. Waving his arms Mister Bentley sheepishly walked behind the wall of bars separating tellers from customers. The cashier looked away pretending to focus on counting.

Jessie studied the room.

So this was what the fuss was all about.

She had never been in a bank before.

Surely there were other women who owned property, with all the widow makers in town killing prospectors left and right. Eyeing the services from a female customer perspective, an idea popped into her head. Jessie strolled to where the manager now sat at his desk.

"Continue running the bank as usual, at least for now. I will stop by weekly for updates. We shall discuss changes in policy and operation. Understood?"

With a flabbergasted look Bentley mumbled, "Changes? What changes?"

The young man was now poised behind one set of bars awaiting customers. He was the sole teller.

"This town is booming. With the growth, business will increase. We need a minimum of two tellers in this bank at all times. They can help with the normal exchange of monies. You as manager are busy enough. I suppose. You will do whatever bank managers do. What is that?" Jessie cocked her head.

Surely they didn't just sit on their asses all day.

"I handle mortgages, personal and business loans. I manage the finances and record keeping. I ensure the teller balances his books nightly and secure the funds. And I handle payroll."

"I see. It sounds like you have sufficient work to do. We shall hire someone to become the second teller. I'll select a suitable woman for the position and send her over." Jessie spun around to go. Her head rose high and her shoulders shot back.

"Woman . . . no woo . . ., woo . . . Women don't work in a bank. I ain't never . . . ," he argued ineffectually looking confounded.

Jessie turned around and smiled. "They do now." She spun and grinned proudly where he couldn't see and shut the door quietly, leaving the bank manager speechless.

Chapter 12

You're a big help and a great teacher. I sincerely care for you." Jessie pushed back a thick, ebony tendril from the shorter woman's forehead.

"I'm happy to have you to talk with."

"You fun, Mistress Jessie. I like work for you. You learn good." Lu giggled pointing to the garden they'd tilled, seeded and nurtured together.

"I'm proud of how our garden has taken off. The plants are producing fruit. So we'll soon be able to pick fresh vegetables for meals. And fragrant flowers will scent every room. It's been fun." Jessie clapped gleefully.

The women had hit it off immediately, becoming close. Lu took Jessie under her pudgy wing. She taught her to cook, keep house, do laundry, and grow a garden and how to preserve food. Jessie learned to can vegetables and fruits. A good student, she studied curing and smoking of meat and fish.

"You're the mother I always dreamed of."

"Jessie be like a daughter to Lu. Only have sons, all grown now and no need Lu. Jessie need Lu." Lu beamed broadly showing off thick molars missing a tooth.

"Indeed I do." With a hearty hug, Lu's smile warmed Jessie all over.

Lu had shown Jessie more love in their few months together than Mama had in the seventeen years she had lived with Mama.

"I adore the lovely, full-length coat your sister Sari sewed for me. It is made from soft deerskin with luxurious, fox trim around the hood, cuffs and around the bottom. It's warm and cozy. I love snuggling into it. It's the most beautiful thing I ever owned."

"Jessie funny. You rich. Wear beautiful ball gowns in other life." Lu laughed as they did laundry.

"That's true. Honestly, those elegant dresses don't compare to these gorgeous garments. Even the fur-lined mittens and warm, knee-high skin boots Sari crafted for me are perfection, and they are even water-resistant. I am lucky to have you and Sari. It's important ragging proper for the weather." Jessie needed the sturdy outerwear for her first frozen Alaskan winter.

"Sari be good seamstress. Lu glad you like." Lu grinned from one pudgy cheek to the other.

Chapter 13

The hoax succeeded when front page news traveled quickly as stories circulated nationally for six straight weeks.

The first prospectors followed that summer, rushing north to Alaska in July. By August a heavy stream of "Stampeders" started flowing northward.

Throngs of men arrived hungry and in need of supplies. Getting to the gold fields meant crossing the Canadian border and a long, arduous journey, requiring supplies to survive as they attempted the hazardous trek.

Logan stopped by one afternoon on his way back to the saw mill from the bank. In the yard beating a rug hung across the clothesline with a broom, Jessie smiled.

"Come visit, Logan. Have some lemonade with me. I could use a rest."

She sat the broom down and dusted dirt from her black mourning dress. After retrieving two tall glasses of sweet nectar from the kitchen, they settled into rockers on the porch.

"I'm giving the place a final cleaning before winter sets in."

"I see that. You seem to have taken to domestic life quickly." His smile was warm and friendly.

Jessie's heart sung in his praise. "I do love having a home of my own. I enjoy caring for it. I've learned a lot from Lu. She's a joy to have around. Gardening and canning are my favorite chores. My cellar is full of food for the winter. I hope you will partake of some of it. I have more than I will need. I'd be pleased to share with you."

"Thank you. It would be a treat."

"You're welcome to whatever you would like." She wiped sweat from her forehead with a hand. "It's exhausting keeping up with everything. Between the bank, the mercantile, shipping company, the saloons and completion of the hotel, I have little time for the pleasure of housework. Luckily Lu takes up the slack. And you manage the timber business well, taking that worry off my shoulders."

"I'm happy you decided to stay in Skagway. I'm also pleased you allow me to continue managing that business for you."

"It's the best decision I've ever made." Jessie had faith in Logan's integrity and capability. Her mill was in good hands. Having him so close was satisfying. She was lucky to have Logan in her life.

"Jessie, your mercantile is a gold mine. Miners are lined out the door, being as it is the sole source of equipment and supplies."

"You are right, Logan. Most prospectors are ill prepared, with no idea what a daunting journey they've partaken. They arrive on our muddy beach clueless how to survive brutal conditions."

"It is shocking being greeted by a wall of mountains. Needing to cross the jagged peaks seems like an overwhelming task." Logan shook his head wearily.

"They come here not read to meet the challenge of the savage landscape. Most have no idea how vast or heartless the wilderness is. It is unlike any environment they've been privy to." It broke her heart, but there was little she could do about it. "Many miners are discouraged by the insurmountably steep journey, climbing mountain after mountain to reach the Klondike gold fields. Many must make the trek several times to carry all of their gear. It's at least a year's passage."

"Some simply disappear, never to be seen again. They either die of exhaustion or face deadly scavengers bent on stealing funds and supplies."

Soapy and his gang of cutthroats and thieves were behind it, but there was no way of proving that.

"The magnificent landscape is savage and indifferent. Miners don't realize how common severe sixty-below winter temperatures are, proving deadly to many." Levi shivered.

Jessie's eyes went wide with horror. "Spring thaw brings its own set of unique dangers. Thick crusts of ice begin melting, creating powerful rushing water and deadly avalanches."

"With Skagway as the gateway to White Pass, they must take the crude trail through the gap in the narrow, twisting trail of obstacles through a sky-high mountain summit."

"They say it's deadly."

It exhausted Jessie thinking about it. Of course, she felt worn out most days now. Hopefully that would wane, and she'd regain energy. Soon her belly should start expanding and the baby would move.

Jessie was now sure she was pregnant. Even Lu thought so. She would tell Logan soon, when she started showing.

"It's not passable during winter. Even in summer it's a daunting journey in the best of conditions. So those flocking to Skagway late summer are stranded here until spring thaw." Logan gazed down the street at tents springing up, housing impatient fortune seekers eager to leave town for the gold fields.

"Our sleepy settlement has grown fast as greased lightning. There is no way of accommodating the furious mass. It has quickly become the enormous tent city it is today. They're even beginning to spread through side streets and outside the thoroughfare. These hoards arrive having traveled thousands of miles, only to find poor living conditions." Jessie shook her head concerned for the miners' plight.

Logan tented his fingers. "It's a wild lawless place without order, a society with no rules. Gunfights are a regular occurrence and street crime is rampant. Skagway is ruled by pilfering thieves. Jessie, please stick close to home, because it's too dangerous to venture far. I worry for your safety."

Had Everett uttered those same words, Jessie would've assumed he meant to keep her captive. The way Logan said them made her feel cared for and protected. Her friend watched over her from a distance. It was comforting knowing he was close by.

"I'll be careful, Logan. It breaks my heart. These miners are lucky if they live long enough to begin trekking to the promise land. Muggings are common. Bandits steal money miners brought with them, the gold they found, or their mining gear. It is a travesty."

"I fear deaths will be plentiful with winter approaching and bitter cold setting in." Logan's eyes were filled with sad compassion.

The prospect was disheartening. Impatience and sheer boredom are pitiless foes. "It's already September. As the reality of our Alaskan winter proves a dangerous season, miners are growing restless. They are overwhelmed, facing a daunting journey they can't yet begin. And now they face a long winter stewing about it. In the meantime, they must struggle to survive our lawless streets."

"We know Soapy Smith is behind the criminal element in this town. But no one has been able to do anything about it." Logan looked doubtful.

"Soapy's day will come. Mark my words. Folks will only stand for so much before they rebel. I ache for the many women left widowed. Their men are murdered. Penniless, without jobs those women are frequently forced into prostitution as a way to survive." Jessie dabbed a tear away.

"You would understand. You are a remarkable woman. Most women wouldn't give them a second thought." Logan beamed proudly.

"Some of those gals thrive in that career and like it. A few actually make it rich, mining the miners." She giggled. "Miners love '*ladies of the night*.' Those females provide essential diversion and entertainment. Men pay well for their services. The loose ladies perform on stage. Hooting and hollering miners toss coins and nuggets at the feet. Whores flip their skirts and show off their privates wearing no undergarments." Trying to shock Logan and throw him off base, she eyed him curiously. "Do you frequent such establishments?"

"I do not. I am here to make money. I don't have time for such nonsense. I do not bed women I don't care for. You shouldn't have to ask such a question. You know me better."

"I apologize, Logan. I just wanted to hear you say it." She smiled brilliantly.

"So how do you know all of this?" Logan cocked a brow.

Demurely Jessie blushed. "I hear things . . . around town."

She turned the subject away from herself. "The main street hums with activity day and night. Barrooms fill to over-flowing. Tent watering holes have sprung up all across town, along with dozens of doggeries and lush cribs. It's easy for men to find an establishment to hoist a bottle of brew or a shot of prairie dew. Though there's considerable competition, my saloon remains incredibly profitable."

Jessie sat back smugly, wanting to understand how Logan felt about her ownership of a tavern and brothel.

"I can see the entrance from my house. Your town center cat house, The Red Onion, remains the largest and most popular. A continual stream of eager miners goes in and out, at all hours to get laid and tangle-footed. That romping barroom of yours rocks continually with stage entertainment. The ragtime pianist tickles piano keys, while scantily clad floozies advertise their wares. They encourage miners to drink and spend hard earned money." Logan kept a stern face Jessie couldn't read.

Should she be embarrassed?

Why bother? It as a business, like any other--a fact of life.

"I stay out of the management of the Red Onion, and allow Soapy to do as he sees fit. I cannot for the life of me condone giving that place up, as long as Soapy is involved. Something inside tells me to keep Mister Smith close."

"Maybe it has to do with keeping enemies close so you can see what they are up to. The Red Onion is a good investment, housing the town's first brothel. Whores host guests in upstairs rooms." Logan's face pinked at the subject. Now she was getting somewhere.

"Don't be embarrassed to discuss it, Logan. You are my trusted friend. I don't like being in that business. But it is a sought after service that the miners appreciate. As long as it does no harm, I will stay out of it. Soapy has way too much mustard for my taste. He is a '*toff-dandy*' full of '*tara-diddles.*' His hell-fired thumpers bamboozle people to indulge their own greed. They

prey on the less fortunate. Soapy and his kind don't fool me."
Jessie concealed a smirk.

Soapy's pompousness and blusteration was tedious. He turned
her stomach and soured her trollybobs. She put a hand to her
mouth and swallowed the bitter taste rising. Jessie tried to appear
unscathed. Was it the topic or the baby doing this to her?

"Everett was every bit as bad."

"I'm sorry for your grief. But you are better off without the
high-bender." Logan put a hand on hers and her heart stilled.

Logan's embarrassment was sweet and thoughtful. Everest
wouldn't have given Jessie's discomfort consideration, discussing
painted cats, whores or ladies of the evening just to cause distress.
Everett enjoyed the advantage of talking about such things, since
she grew up around that life.

Chapter 14

Walking home from the fish market passing the Red Onion, a drunken miner fell out the swinging doors and landed against Jessie. As the man attempted to right himself she pushed him away. He groped her waist and slurred drunkenly, realizing he'd fallen onto a woman.

"Morning, Sweet Thang. How 'bout a kiss for old Daniel? There's a nugget in it for 'ya."

Assaulted by revolting whiskey stench from the snootful the fellow had enjoyed, Jessie backed quickly away and reached for her hidden pistol, since her fan weapon hung uselessly on the wrist carrying her purchase. But Daniel held Jessie tight and wrenched her arm pushing his unshaven face toward her.

From behind, a strong hand securely pulled Jessie backward. Her rescuer's other grabbed the miner's throat.

Startled, Daniel was lifted. The tanked gent came off his feet by the neck. The drunkard was forced to release Jessie by the tug.

She stepped quickly behind Logan, out of the way; while Daniel's face went white. Daniel's eyes bulged as they attempted to focus. His head lolled around, searching for who restrained him.

"Mister, you owe this woman an apology. So I suggest, "I am sorry, ma'am," be the next words from your sorry throat."

His face demanding, Logan's voice grew thick with emotion and barely controlled temper seeped from the huskily spoken words through clenched teeth.

Where did Logan come from?

Flannel sleeves rolled up exhibited enticing flexed arm muscles oozing strength. Logan's scantily buttoned shirt showed off a robust tan on his feathery-haired chest.

Logan plunked the drunk down and released him, not backing away. Stone still, Logan towered between Daniel and Jessie.

The shocked sap gasped for air with an intimidated look on his face. Daniel finally found his tongue. He was only able to utter, "Ma'am, I'm sorry. I meant no harm. I thought you was . . ."

Jessie interrupted before Daniel got into more trouble. "I accept your apology, sir. On the condition you think twice before accosting a lady again."

Indignantly raising a brow, trying to look fierce, she switched her bundle to the other arm. Jessie flicked the fan releasing the weapon, flashing its blade tauntingly in front of her sweetly smiling face.

Daniel got the message. Blood drained from his already ashen face, as he turned white as a glacier capped mountain. He gulped air, nodded and backed away quickly out of Logan's powerful grip and far from her dagger, obviously realizing he had insulted the wrong target. Not only could Logan have choked Daniel to death. Jessie would've stuck Daniel in the gut with her pig sticker. It was good that Daniel had been rescued.

"Yes Ma'am, I sure will." Daniel turned to Logan. "Thank you, sir." Daniel turned and ran along the boardwalk.

Jessie giggled uncontrollably, slid the blade back inside her fan, and lanced around. No one had seemed to notice.

"Thank you for your assistance, Logan. You're forever rescuing me."

A broad grin engaged Logan's whole face. Tiny wrinkles showed at the corner of Logan's glistening emerald eyes, engaging those adorable, deep dimples. As always, something magical happened when their eyes met. Words became unnecessary. Their hearts spoke through their senses.

"My pleasure, to continually rescue drunkards from you, my dear. It terrifies me that you walk these dangerous streets. You could hurt someone."

Zing! Lord.

Jessie could swoon at the sight of those dimples. Logan's smoldering eyes burned a trail directly to her heart. She wanted him to wrap her in those burly arms and scurry her to his home for safe keeping . . . or something better.

"I'm not a naïve youngster. I am a full grown, experienced woman who has lived in rough towns before. I'll survive. Skagway is simply going through growing pains." Her face heated as she got Logan's joke. "Oh, well, at least Daniel is safe from me now."

Logan winked adorably. "Still, I worry about you. Please be careful." Logan's rugged face beamed appreciation at her flirtatious smile.

Lord, help me.

Jessie enjoyed flirting with Logan. She had never learned the art of flirtation, but simply reacted instinctively this way to Logan--only Logan.

"Absolutely. You do the same."

Logan tipped his hat and went on his way. Jessie headed home.

She could handle herself and always had--with her blade and hidden sidearm. But it was nice not needing to. It was a marvelous novelty, having someone worrying about and defended her. Jessie felt safe with Logan nearby.

CHAPTER 15

1888

By spring about a thousand miners moved through town at any given time. The idyllic village grew drastically, springing from a handful of buildings to a full blown town.

Under Logan's supervision the lumber business remained the sole provider of a much needed natural resource. Her mercantile provided the only supply of gear. The saloons provided entertainment to the masses. Her bank boomed, as the safes filled with glistening nuggets. Jessie's shipping lines provided transportation to the land of plenty. It seemed she had cornered the market, thanks to her late husband.

Everett's and his band of conniving manipulators' plan continued working to her benefit. She stayed busy learning along the way. The bank partners had accepted Jessie and found her changes to their benefit as their profits grew.

The shipping consortium was slower to accept but they were forced to endure her attendance at their board meetings.

Jessie studied the shipping industry and looked for ways to benefit their company. She was determined to make a mark and force them to at least respect her as a partner. At first, the board men ignored Jessie. Then they slowly began to listen, when she had something to contribute. She could put up with their attitudes toward her. After all, she had put up with Everett. If she could do that, Jessie could do most anything.

Logan admitted, "I now understand what Everett had alluded to as, 'in on the ground floor of a tremendous opportunity.' Fast paced business continues growing."

"Yes, Logan. You are working long hours. I hope you are prospering along with your team of strong, hearty men. They seem eager for the work."

"I enjoy the work. I adore life in Alaska. I have fallen victim to the spell of my frontier home. I came to Alaska for only one reason, to make and sock away my earnings." Logan made a point to stop by regularly to check on her and chat.

* * *

On her knees that sunny afternoon, Jessie's dark cotton dress was tied between her legs. She crawled through her vegetable garden humming pulling weeds encouraging tender plants to healthy growth.

Sunshine glistened in curly copper locks escaping from the bonnet she'd worn to protect her delicate skin from the sun's warm rays.

Warm longing filled Logan's belly. He couldn't help but smile. "Well, well, well, this isn't your typical San Francisco elite, but a real woman engaged in meaningful chores. The surprising thing is you appear happy."

Jessie's stunning face appeared relaxed and at ease. She smiled obviously unaware and uncaring of the dirt streak across her forehead.

"Indeed I am." Wiping a stray tendril from her forehead left a ribbon of dirt in its wake.

It warmed Logan's heart seeing Jessie so serene, having appeared strained and on guard, when Everett had been alive.

"You're a natural wonder, a remarkable sight to behold." Something deep within stirred and his heart swelled, brimming full observing the exquisite creature.

The sort of ideal life partner men dream of.

"You're strong, unafraid of adversity and hard work. You are adventurous with good values and ethics. You are interesting and easy to be with. I've enjoy our talks."

"Why thank you, Logan. You flatter me. Careful, that might go to my head. But I enjoy your company also. I'm pleased you stopped by."

If she were his woman, Jessie would stand beside Logan no matter what path he took. She would warm his bed and set his senses afire with desire. Loving her would be ecstasy.

Logan's physique responded to his thoughts of her body beneath his. The notion sent goosebumps fluttering across Logan's skin. Logan's pants tightened as his masculinity responded in kind. Logan's eyes closed, relishing the idea of burying himself deep inside Jessie and touching her most inner depths.

She would make a fabulous mother, with his love seed growing within her body. Bearing Logan's children would fulfill him in the most masculine way possible.

The better Logan knew Jessie, the stronger his yearning grew. He wanted to be with her more each day; so hardly a day passed, that she didn't fill his mind. He couldn't resist the slightest glance and seized every rare opportunity to visit.

Logan dared only friendship with Jessie because she was in a vulnerable situation. She had a lot on her delicate shoulders. Many relied on Jessie for their livelihood, as she strove to manage her inherited empire. Still in mourning for her husband, she needed a friend. She didn't need Logan hankering after her.

Logan valued and respected Jessie because she was a good woman. He must be a good man, give what she needed, and not tell her what he longed for.

Logan's unfulfilled member relaxed. His pants loosened and his stomach soured, rolling with disgust. Logan swallowed the bitter taste in his mouth.

It was dangerous spending too much time with her, but he couldn't resist accepting and being happy for their innocent friendship. It was all he could have—for now.

Eventually Jessie would get a handle on her work. Her grieving period would end. She would be free.

He hoped to be the kind of man she needed. Would she then be open to a relationship with Logan?

Logan leaned against the porch rail, leisurely observing. Finally she finished and leaned back on her haunches smiling.

"It's a lovely day to tend your garden. Your crops are perking up nicely, thriving with this warmth and the love you bestow."

"It's my intention. I'm enjoying growing my first garden. I'm learning as I go. But Lu's my savior and teacher. I'm lucky for her guidance."

Jessie laughed aloud, a lyrical, delightful sound, and her happiness brought Logan immense pleasure.

"I quickly tired of eating burnt suppers. Though I did my best, I was a terrible cook. With Lu's wonderful help, I'm learning."

"Lu taught me vegetable gardening, since I only knew about flowers. In San Francisco I learned from our gardener. Cade happily answered my questions, but he found my curiosity unusual. Apparently, aristocrats aren't interested in the process of growing things. Cade didn't raise vegetables. So I learned some from books, and Lu taught me the rest."

"You're a natural."

"I hope you're right, and the crops come in abundantly. I'd be pleased to provide vegetables for your table. Please take some home."

Standing and straightening her cotton dress, copper tendrils fell loosely around her straight shoulders. Curls framed Jessie's face and escaping wisps fluttered in the slight breeze, urging Logan to reach out and stroke them.

"I'd be grateful for your vegetables. Thank you for the offer. I look forward to it. But if there's any way I can help, I hope you'll tell me. I know some about gardening. I assisted Mama with hers back home."

"You're welcome to them. There's nothing you can do. You've got enough on your plate already with the saw mill. However, I'm glad you stopped by. I enjoy your company while I work." Smiling shed removed her gloves, as she walked closer.

"I stopped by the port. Shipping lines appear to have resurrected every rusty steamer and retired vessel they could find to carry prospectors flocking to the area. They must've worked swiftly to make them as seaworthy as possible."

Jessie wiped her forehead with the back of her hand. "Indeed, they've responded to the urgency, feeding the tremendous flow of treasure seekers moving northward to the gold fields. It's appalling, but many an old rust bucket has set sail in precarious, unreliable conditions hardly fit for passage. It concerns me. It is an issue I continue to address with my shipping partners. I hope they soon listen and take better precautions. The liability could be devastating and tragic."

"You're right. It's a pity that eager miners put their lives at risk getting here, only to face worse peril."

"They seem to thrive on danger."

"As always, you're right on target with your keen eye for observation. Well, I best get to work, since the men await direction on a new load of lumber." Logan put his hat on and turned to go. "See you soon."

Jessie laid her hand on his forearm. The casual, friendly gesture sent goose bumps dancing rampant through Logan's body. Her heart beat against his skin making him wonder if she detected his trembling quake.

"Perhaps you can return soon for a glass of iced tea. Our time is precious. I enjoy your company."

Logan's body warmed from —her touch all the way from the top of his head to the tip of his toes. Jessie's soft voice fed him like a scorching fire blazing in his belly. Something came alive inside him in her presence. He smiled and reluctantly walked to the mill.

* * *

Something foreign and pleasant happened to Jessie only with Logan. He brought an essence of wellbeing and security to her life. And he set Jessie's senses ablaze with longing, though he remained forbidden fruit.

Jessie was still in a formal mourning pregnant with Everett's baby. And she didn't want to hinder Logan's dreams from coming true. In Alaska only for work, he sought to amass his fortune. She could not stand in his way by saddling him with her and Everett's child.

Jessie had never conjured lust with her husband. Everett had not ignited her passion--not like Logan. Her breath caught, and she didn't resume her tasks until Logan stepped into his office out of sight. She didn't want to miss any of the swaggers hinting at raw masculinity in his ambling pace striding purposefully down the street.

Such appetite and hunger were alien, having never lusted for intimacy. She did with Logan, however. The strange sensation yearned to satisfy desires Jessie hadn't realized her capacity for.

She craved Logan's bare skin, the taste of his kisses, his tongue, whether sweet or savory and whatever flavors his body possessed.

Jessie would enjoy exploring at leisure, doing evil things to and with Logan, driving him to ecstasy. She yearned to fill her body with his.

Jessie's desire became an unexpected pleasure. His physique and strength made an indelible impression, and Logan's mere presence tantalized Jessie's senses. She reveled in a dream she could never act upon. She cherished the secret sensations only Logan ignited--the innocent, guiltless sin.

It did no good harboring remorse or regret because she couldn't stop dreaming. Fantasies were the best she could do. Jessie came to grips with her situation long ago and decided to make the best of her lot.

But when they were apart Jessie yearned for Logan and the precious emotions his presence evoked. Their purely innocent bond brought absolute pleasure. She didn't understand why; and Logan remained unaware, but gave Jessie a remarkable gift. Women like Jessie settled for what they got.

Logan deserved better. He was honest and kind beyond comparison, with values and ethics consistently beyond reproach. The brilliant specimen of masculinity was the first person Jessie trusted completely.

Her body sang with longing for physical connection.

Lordy! Logan is sight to behold.

Closing her eyes, breathing slowed, and her pulse quickened. Visions of Logan's powerful arms surrounding her body filled her mind. Jessie's head swirled, dizzy at the impression of them lying nude body-to-body as his rough, work-worn hands caressed her.

Jessie shuddered and searing heat centered in her womanhood. Muscles quickened in her private place. Logan made her his alone, while she embraced his weight. Soft lips flamed on Jessie's naked skin searing flesh and branding her forever.

Jessie leaned against the railing. Lost in reverie, her insides quivered. Pulse quickened, and breathing came rapid and heavy.

Tasting Logan's delicious lips, Jessie imagined his flavor; and what texture and weight his cock possessed in her hand. Silky and firm, she stroked, bringing him to full erection. Logan trembled and she became alive with passion taking him inside.

Logan would make love to her. But he would want more than simply sex. He would initiate sensations and passion she had never experienced, so Jessie could achieve the mysterious orgasm. Logan would make her come, like a woman was meant to.

Shuddering, Jessie's private place burned with desire. Delicious heat throbbed in her womanhood. Logan's long, erect shaft filled her completely with its bulk. Her eyelids twitched as she convulsed. Her rear clenched as sheer instinct took over. Jessie gasped for air. Contractions from her core shook her being, with Logan buried deep inside filling her body and mind.

Jessie didn't recognize what was happening. It gripped her like a huge ocean wave, rolling, surging and pounding. She rode the swell and her heated dreams forced toward climax. A whisper in a voice she didn't recognize uttered, "Logan."

Wave after wave rolled Jessie. Convulsing and throbbing again and again, her breath caught ruggedly. Her eyes twitched, and she finished.

"Logan," she whispered to herself. "Forgive me for using you scandalously. You deserve better from me as a friend. I must never offend you by letting on how I fanaticize about you this way. I care too much to hurt you so."

Thank goodness for the post supporting Jessie's spent body. Her knees were too weak for her weight.

A knowing smile spread across Jessie's satisfied face, having experienced her first orgasm. The wondrous event had occurred, and she wanted more.

This visionary experience with Logan was so different from what Jessie had experienced in real life. With Everett sex had been all business and about his pleasure alone. Sometimes his pleasure included cruelty.

During their last encounter Everett had screamed as he came, "You stupid bitch, it is your fault I hit you. You need a lesson. You make me do it, you pathetic, useless, disappointment. Where's my son, my heir?"

Jessie had endeavored to appease Everett, but it never worked. Nothing helped. This had become the only way Everett could reach climax.

Wouldn't he be shocked knowing his last miserable inter-course had finally produced the longed for child?

Jessie hadn't dared cry in front of Everett, because he got off on tears. It would have only spurred more violence.

She had been a bad wife despite her efforts unable to satisfy her husband.

Jessie had tried hard, but hadn't become pregnant again. So Everett remained ashamed, regardless what she'd learned and had done to become a lady he could be proud of.

Mama was right. Jessie was a failure at the one thing that meant the most. She had failed to produce Everett's heirs and failed them both.

Too bad, Everett hadn't lived to meet the tiny being now carried in her womb.

Chapter 16

Work took a welcome break when she ran into Samuel Steel at the bank. Jessie invited Superintendent Steel of the North-West Mounted Police for a home cooked meal. She asked Logan to join them. The Mountie had crossed the border visiting Skagway after hearing so much about it.

Samuel arrived, dressed in full uniform, a striking gentleman sporting a bouquet of flowers for Jessie and a bottle of Canadian wine for Logan.

"Thank you for having me." Sam spoke as they ate. "Dinner's delicious. It is a pleasure being graced with such loveliness at the dinner table. I appreciate your hospitality. I spend much of my time in the wilderness, and rarely have opportunity for a home cooked meal or the company of a fine woman." Samuel took another bite of savory pot roast, gravy and mashed potatoes.

Jessie's face heated at the rare praise. Sam's taffy mustn't get to her. Sam was only being pleasant. Logan didn't seem to be bothered by Sam's praise. Everett would've been livid hearing such compliments for his wife.

Jessie had outdone herself by serving homemade biscuits, roast, and freshly baked blueberry pie from berries she'd picked in the forest. She enjoyed cooking Logan's favorites and loved pleasing him.

"I am pleased to have you and Mister Pace at my table, Superintendent Steele. I haven't entertained since my husband died, and I arrived in Skagway. I'm glad you made time to join us. What brings you to Skagway?"

"I came to see what all the fuss was about. Men are flocking into the Canadian Yukon in search of gold. Word has gotten out in the States that gold is easy pickings in our frozen wilderness. Last time I visited this sleepy village there were a few private dwellings. Now it's a bustling metropolis as the gateway to my country."

She smiled at the handsome, older gentleman. "So seeing for yourself out of curiosity, how do you find our town?"

"Honestly," Sam put his napkin onto his lap, as though seeking a tactful way to say it. "This is about the roughest place in the world. Last night bullets ripped through the walls of my cabin. Roaring gunfights went on all night long. Mortally wounded victims were left lying in the streets. Folks went about their business. This town is littered with gunmen, schemers, dreamers and prospectors ill-fitted to their task. I believe Skagway quite frankly, is hell on earth."

Logan rubbed his chin. "I can't argue with you there, Samuel. You hit it on the nail-head. Are you staying long?"

"Absolutely not. I leave tomorrow. I have had enough of Skagway for a lifetime. One night here is like an eternity in hell. I don't envy you this city." Sympathy oozed from his eyes. "Aren't you scared, Jessie? This is no doubt a terrifying town for a genteel lady?"

"Not in the least, Sam. I love this chaotic town. I am happy that Skagway's my home."

Sam shook his head dubiously. "My compliments, Ma'am. You are braver than I. You are gracious, kind and quite a looker. Aren't you concerned about safety?" Sam eyed her curiously.

Sam said bluntly what came to mind. His words would have pissed Everett off, had he been there. Jessie imagined smoke would have been billowing from Everett's ears about now. Logan however, had a beaming look of pride on his face.

Logan answered with a glint in his eye. "I assure you, Mistress Blackstone is capable of defending herself. She is one of the bravest women I've ever met. As long as Jessie is happy here, I will keep an eye out for her safety. There is something about this crazy town that just feels like home. So we stay."

Sam looked doubtful. "I personally don't see it. I applaud your guts, though. It takes hearty folks to weather the hurricane that has hit this sleepy village. More power to you."

After the guests left and she cleaned up, Jessie retired. *Will I always be alone?*

Jessie grasped her belly. Her back had ached all day as she cooked and prepared for entertaining. Now an odd tingle in the pit of her middle left her feeling wary as she drifted off to sleep.

CHAPTER 17

Jessie came awake with a start somewhere near morning. A sharp pain split her body. She cried out. Shocked to alert, she realized no one could help her.

Jessie attempted to get up, but a splitting pain knocked the strength from her. Her legs gave way, and she crumbled to the floor. It felt cool, soothing and supportive. So as pain eased enjoying it for a while longer, swooning in and out of consciousness, she convulsed and throbbed in unending, unbearable misery.

In a dream-like daze, Jessie finally came completely awake. She felt somewhat stronger and more clear-headed. But when she attempted to rise, she was unable to sit. The pains eased allowing her to cry until sleep returned.

Soon another sharp pain split Jessie. She cried out. Piercing agony ripped her abdomen sending convulsions heaving, swelling, and stabbing with gut-wrenching sharpness. A continual flow seared through her. Sweating, surrounded by drenched night clothes, Jessie swooned in and out of consciousness in unending, unbearable misery combined with an exhausted dream state.

Something sticky wet and cold oozed around Jessie's legs. Lifting her gown, a puddle of dark red gore lay beneath. Swimming in the pool of blood laid a child's form.

My baby. . .

Crying in agony, holding the tiny dead being in her hand, tears flowed for hours. Finally exhausted, unable to cry more, Jessie placed the remains on a clean town. She washed herself then cleaned the mess on the floor.

Placing the wrapped corpse reverently in a cigar box tied with a pink ribbon, she took it out back and dug a hole beside the apple tree. Jessie buried her young then lay on the grass and wept until blessed sleep came.

Lu found Jessie that way in the morning. She instinctively understood, since the story lay right in front of her. The shovel and newly filled hole were damning evidence of a grave.

Lu spotted Logan stepping out his front door heading to work. Lu ran to him.

"Come, Mister Logan. Mistress Jessie needs help." Lu didn't wait for an answer, but ran immediately toward Jessie's back yard.

Logan was shocked and terrified, as he took long running strides following Lu. Beneath the apple tree, Jessie lay sleeping atop what appeared to be a newly dug grave. It was a small mound of freshly tilled dirt that told the story breaking Logan's heart.

Jessie had been with child—-Everett's child. She hadn't confided her secret in Logan, though she must've known. It was three months now since Everett's death, so she must've been aware of her pregnancy.

Logan scooped Jessie up and carried her sleeping body to bed. He left her to Lu's care. Lu brought in a pan of warm water.

"I bath and let Jessie sleep." Lu shooed Logan from the room. He reluctantly left his love in Lu's capable hands.

* * *

Jessie may've heard banging around in the kitchen and dining room. She wasn't sure. It could've easily been her scattered, tortured dreams.

Finally awaking around noon and calling for Lu, Lu tottered in with a tray. Sitting it on the bed, she wiped a stray tendril from Jessie's forehead.

"You be well now, my Jessie." Sadness ruled Lu's face.

Not trying to hide the sorrow in her voice. "I'm not sure I will ever be well, Lu. I'm such a failure. I've lost another baby. Everett would probably kill me, if he were alive."

"Poo on Mister Everett. He sounds like the devil."

Jessie's sad smirk was spontaneous. "You aren't far off, Lu. I've failed myself as well. I wanted this baby girl so badly. My body just couldn't hold onto her." She swiped tears running down her cheeks.

"Not always Mommy's fault. You lose another baby. Yes?"

"Yes. I lost our first child in San Francisco."

Lu took her hand. "Baby not die because of Jessie. Something wrong with Mister's seed. Bad seed not make good baby. Not your fault. Eat and rest. Lu take care of work today. Tomorrow soon enough for Jessie to get up."

"How did I get to bed? I last recall lying on the grave."

"Mister Logan carry you. He very worried."

Logan knows. Jessie wasn't sure how to feel about that.

Lu stood as though the discussion was over. It was a fact, as far as Lu was concerned. Lu had a strange sense and seemed to simply know things.

Jessie had not found Lu to be wrong so far. Maybe Lu was correct now.

She had people who cared. Lu was the closest thing Jessie had to family, like the mother Jessie never had but always wanted. And there was Logan's friendship. But her baby was dead.

Sadly, Jessie had grown used to loss.

But she was alive.

Life went on.

* * *

The following day, Lu and Jessie ventured out to the garden. An ornate metal cross had been erected at the head of the tiny grave. Grateful tears streamed unchecked down Jessie's face.

"Who?" Lu's dark eyes filled with tears busting loose beneath her furrowed brow as she pointed to the marker.

Jessie dropped her hoe and hugged Lu as her heart soared with love for the sweet woman.

"It had to be Logan. He is the only person who would do something like this."

Lu nodded. "Mister Logan be good man."

"Yes he's extremely kind. This is a beautiful gift. I appreciate it more than I can say." Jessie picked her hoe up, filled with joy.

"Gift of love," Lu nodded, as though it were the most natural thing in the world. "Mister Logan a good man and love Jessie." Lu nodded repeatedly, like the more she nodded the clearer understanding would be.

"It's a generous deed. I'll never forget Logan's compassion." Jessie blushed.

Working in the garden, she joyfully sang the hymn recently learned written by someone named George Doane. Lu sang along.

Softly now the light of day
Fades upon my sight away;
Free from care, from labor free,
Lord, I would commune with Thee.
Thou, whose all-pervading eye
Naught escapes, without, within,
Pardon each infirmity,
Open fault, and secret sin.
Soon for me the light of day
Shall forever pass away;
Then, from sin and sorrow free,
Take me, Lord, to dwell with Thee.
Thou who, sinless, yet hast known
All of man's infirmity;
Then, from Thine eternal throne,
Jesus, look with pitying eye
(1)

CHAPTER 18

On Sunday Jessie attended the new church in town and was surprised when Reverend Brown and his wife Sara greeted her at the door. They recognized Jessie from their train trek westward to San Francisco.

"Jessie Blackstone, right?" Sara beamed.

"Indeed, Sara. I'm happy you and Reverend Brown have taken charge of our new church." Jessie released her hand and shook the Reverend's large paw.

"Call me Richard, Mistress Blackstone." The Reverend's friendly smile beckoned.

Jessie warmed to Reverend Brown right away. "Call me Jessie, Richard. I'm so happy you and Sara are here. I hope you like Skagway."

"Indeed we will." Sara led her to the front pew.

"Sara," Jessie whispered, "I've never been in a church before. I don't know how this works or what to do."

"Just relax, Jessie. Do what the others do. It will come to you." Sara patted her hand and took her place.

Jessie enjoyed the service listening aptly to the sermon and joyously singing hymns with the parishioners.

Saying a silent prayer for her dead children, she hoped she'd done it right. Being new at this Bible thing, Jessie wasn't sure of the process.

Sara noted the tear escaping Jessie's face. Silently Sara held her hand providing support without being asked. The service gave comfort to Jessie's aching heart and helped fill its gaping hole.

Maybe there is something to this faith thing. It was worth a shot.

CHAPTER 19

All was tranquil at Jessie's house. Home had become a place of peace helping heal her bruised heart.

Hoeing her precious garden rows, she enjoyed seeing them grow tall and green. The plants provided much needed solace. Sorrow and rage Jessie had felt at her loss slowly melted, as her hoe slapped the ground harder than necessary, unearthing offending weeds. She appreciated the exhausting exertion. Enjoying the warm, sunny weather and glorious day, she worked in her zone, happily engaged in the beloved chore.

Having gone to the bank attending to the mill's accounts, Logan passed and spotted Jessie. He strolled over.

They enjoyed chatting from time to time, but Logan worked long, hard hours, so had little time of his own. He hadn't seen Jessie since he had helped Lu get her to bed that fated morning.

Jessie always seemed thrilled when he showed up. Logan felt awful for her loss, and regretted business keeping him away. He had missed Jessie and was eager to see her, even for a few minutes.

"Good afternoon." Logan smiled and approached admiring the rows of lush greenery. Vegetables hung proudly on healthy vines.

Jessie wiped a wild curl from her sweating forehead. Copper curls caught the sunlight as she adjusted her bonnet. Logan's chest tightened so it was hard to breath.

"Good morning, Logan. It's good to see you."

"Your garden's flourishing. You certainly have a green thumb."

"Thank you, I was hankering for a break. Join me while I rest a spell. Let's enjoy a glass of lemonade."

Jessie stumbled and lost her balance. Logan grabbed her arm preventing the fall. Wordlessly tears glistened, filling her forest green eyes. She rolled her shoulder as though releasing a cramp and appeared exhausted.

Logan relaxed his grip and smiled. Their eyes met and pity flowed from his as his hand gently cupped Jessie's jaw. His thumb tenderly stroked her skin, and he ached for her loss.

Logan's blood boiled in his veins with longing, and lightning flashed scorching his brain.

Jessie turned and closed her eyes, sniffing back tears. She visibly struggled to remain calm and breathe normally. Holding her head high, shoulders straight she acted rattled. Having obviously not planned on sharing her distress, she hugged her body, controlling quaking muscles and trembling hands. But Logan knew her well and saw it all.

Jessie's tears had branded Logan's heart. He ached to comfort Jessie, as she avoided his eyes. Straightening her skirts, she righted her appearance, and tried to appear brave pretending nothing was wrong.

"Are you all right?" Logan cringed with grief for her loss. His hands on hips, Logan's body tensed. He was distraught with longing to ease Jessie's pain.

"I'm fine. Thank you."

Logan's arms were never as empty, as when he had released Jessie. He barely resisted pulling her into them, to comfort her and fill the void in his burning heart.

Logan's face grew hot as though touched with a scalding iron. His neck muscles tensed supporting scorching blood surging through bulging veins. Logan gulped breath while his gut rumbled, and acid churned wildly. Nothing Logan did could bring Jessie's baby back or protect her from the sadness. Sickened he saw grief blatantly on her sweet face.

"Something more valuable than vegetables has grown in my garden. I assume you are responsible for that work of art." Jessie pointed to the lovely marker beneath the apple tree. "Thank you for that, Logan. I treasure it." She swiped a tear with the back of her soiled hand, unaware of the dirt streak it left on her cheek.

"It was the least I could do. I'm so sorry for your loss. I didn't realize you were carrying a child. Had I known, I would've encouraged you to do less hearty work." The guilt he felt couldn't be hidden in his eyes.

"Logan, you couldn't have helped this. I couldn't either. Nothing I did should have hurt my baby. Lu wouldn't let me do any hard manual labor. She is very protective. It was simply not meant to be. It was nature's way. I must accept the loss and go on."

"I'm sure you did everything possible to ensure the baby's safety. You would have been a good mother. Maybe someday you will have another child."

"Doubtful. I can't imagine marrying again. My life with Everett was not the best. I don't think anyone would actually want me. I've been a failure as a wife and mother. I'm no big catch." She disappeared inside returning with two tall glasses of sweet nectar.

"You would make anyone a worthy wife. Don't talk yourself down so. Any man would be lucky to have you."

Jessie shook her head adamantly. "No. You are wrong. Some men might want the money Everett left me. But I am not the sophisticated, blushing bride you assumed me to be when we met. I am not worthy of a good man. Besides, I have way too much on my hands to be tied to a house and husband. I'm better off alone." Jessie looked resolved.

"I find that hard to believe. But I do agree that you are better off alone, than you were with your late husband." At least there was that.

Jessie was safer with Everett out of the picture, even in lawless Skagway.

Logan's heart filled with longing for the woman in front of him, having loved Jessie since they arrived together. She had been forbidden fruit. Respecting the sanctity of marriage, Logan never would have pursued her while Everett was alive. After his death, Logan honored Jessie's right to her formal mourning period. Then she had become consumed with learning how to handle her vast empire and worked long hours. Now it seems Jessie had decided she didn't want any man. It was her prerogative, but it saddened Logan.

Grateful for the responsibility of his job, long days of heavy labor kept him from constantly pushing himself on Jessie. She didn't need that—not with everything else she had to bear.

Geez!

Jessie had no idea how much Logan desired her. And he couldn't tell her, because it would only hurt her worse.

Logan faced her and held her hand.

Jessie shivered, visibly shaken. Her eyes filled with moisture, and her hand posed between them stalling Logan's action.

"Jessie, my dearest friend, I feel your pain in my heart, your grief in my soul. I despised Everett. But I would have loved your child with him, as much as if it were my own. I'm sorry you lost the baby. If I could make it better, I would. This isn't your fault. You mustn't blame yourself. I hate hearing you talk badly about yourself and wish you would value you as I do." Logan ran a distraught hand through his mane. His voice growled, fighting emotions surging through him. Speaking was difficult.

"You have no idea what I deserve, or who I really am. Everett isn't all to blame. He was a tortured soul. But he was right to blame me." She turned, staring at the mountains.

"Nonsense, there's no excuse for the way Everett treated you."

Jessie slightly shrugged, looking to the horizon. "He was not always that way. He was kind to me at first. Everett became frustrated and disappointed when I failed him. I never produced a child honoring our bargain"

"What the hell? You were the cad's wife, not a punching bag. You can't control nature. You didn't deserve him berating you because you hadn't produced Everett's precious heir." Logan stomped and paced. "It's intolerable, that your husband convinced you that you are of such a low worth. Don't you see? You have grown into an amazing, incredible woman." Logan shook his head frustrated, struggling with the idea.

Jessie squared her shoulders. Her chin held high, sternly and squarely. She stared into Logan's eyes and spoke slowly, deliberately.

"Leave it be. You don't understand. But thank you for caring and for the cross."

"My pleasure, Jessie," Logan spat at the sky, closed his eyes and attempted to still his pounding brain.

Jessie wanted to ignore the elephant squarely between them, pretending nothing was amiss. Failing bitterly, she sniffed and wiped her tears.

What was she afraid of?

She dusted her apron and skirts then put her gardening gloves in her pocket. Chin held high, Jessie casually walked toward the door and turned to hide her tears. But Logan spotted them.

Logan understood Jessie better than she realized. She needed propriety, as a proud woman and a lady. Logan couldn't cause her more pain. She had been hurt too much already.

"Go now. I need time alone." She disappeared into the house.

If only things had been different. Circumstances were against them. In another life, they might've been able to be together. The sad truth was that Jessie didn't want Logan.

No matter what his gut told him, or how much he cared, Logan couldn't do anything to harm Jessie. He couldn't push himself on a woman who didn't desire him. Logan respected Jessie too much.

They could only have friendship. He mustn't forget his desire for her and keep a distance.

Logan couldn't give in to his yearning to hold and kiss Jessie or understand her loyalty defending her late husband. He couldn't fathom why her self-worth was questionable in her mind.

It was probably Everett. Everett had demeaned her and beat her down, so her self-esteem was non-existent. Logan wished he could help Jessie see how worthy she was. But that would mean being with her, and Logan wasn't sure his heart could stand that. The more he was with Jessie, the more he desired her.

Oh Lord Almighty.

* * *

Jessie watched Logan's broad shoulders slump, as he walked slowly toward the mill. She spoke to Logan's backside, once he'd gone well out of earshot.

"Thank you, Logan for caring. No matter how lusty my fantasies are about you, I'll never come between you and your dreams."

Jessie had been denied a loving relationship with her husband. She could at least fortify her soul with harmless intimate fantasies. She should be ashamed . . . but wasn't. Instead Jessie enjoyed how Logan made her feel.

Flushed as sensations overwhelmed, she allowed the dream of making passionate love with Logan to play out, for Jessie's enjoyment alone. At least she had this . . . the delusion . . . and Logan's friendship. Surely no harm would come of it. No one would ever know.

Jessie stared into the woodlands behind her cabin. Lost in musing, eyes closed, she focused on visions in her mind. Hunger couldn't be fed in reality--only in whimsy. Her eyes closed and the vision flowed . . .

Logan wrapped his strong arms around her. Her head rested easily supported by Logan's firm muscled chest. Logan's heart pounded against her cheek through soft flannel. His warmth seeped into her through the embrace, and her skin fired with need. Her core sprang to life, pulsing with appetite. Jessie wriggled in her seat.

The visual felt strong and real. Logan's touch was a physical reality in her mind.

His scent of pine and wood shavings filled Jessie's nostrils and clung to her body. Logan's heart beat fervently, explosively.

Her mind wandered freely. Intimate visions of behavior unbecoming a lady controlled her.

Logan's magnificent nude body pressed to Jessie's skin, bringing magical responses all the way to her secret gift. A surge of moisture dampened between her legs, and she squirmed--the instinctive response. Her buttocks tightened, relishing delicious sensations.

Logan's distinctive aroma flowed across Jessie's willing tongue. She licked her lips, at his slightly salty taste. Swallowing, savoring his tantalizing flavor, Jessie's palate eagerly begged for more.

Intoxicated anticipation of outrageous abandonment provoked her to do scandalous things to Logan. Intimacy electrified her senses; and her pulse raced, as her heart nearly beat its way from her chest.

Dreaming, Jessie's eyes closed. Logan's naked body filled her mind, inducing shivers through her spine. Heat flooded Jessie's belly, and she panted rapidly.

Sweat beaded her chest, tingling eager breasts. They begged to be touched, longing for Logan's hot wet mouth to engulf the hard tips, sucking, and licking. His rough, work-worn fingers touched Jessie there, scorching her skin, branding her heart. Arching she gave her imaginary lover better access.

Her legs separated, begging for fulfillment.

Unaware, Logan cast his spell that had become as much a part of her, as her own heart and soul. Jessie's dreary, tormented world filled with enchanting pictures of lusting for Logan, generating pure torture and incredible release. The fantasy left her sated, wanting more.

Though her lurid dreams were wrong, and Logan would be appalled if he knew, it was pointless trying to stop. And Jessie didn't want to stop.

Dreams of Logan reverently loving Jessie kept her sane in her insane world. It was a disgraceful preoccupation, yet Jessie lacked shame where Logan was concerned.

Wishing Logan was her husband didn't matter, because wishes didn't come true--at least not in Jessie's world.

He was her only friend. So Jessie mustn't allow her bad choices to destroy his life. She wouldn't let her scandalous past shame him.

Jessie had made her bed and it was hers alone.

Coming reluctantly to earth straightening her skirts she went inside to cook supper.

"Mister Logan leave?" Lu glanced across her shoulder. "He be a fine man and need a good woman." Lu grabbed her apron and tied it.

"Logan would be a wonderful husband." *He'd never lay a hand on his wife.* "He'd be warm, loving and would cherish his wife."

"He nothing like your Mister? Your mister not a good man? Right?"

Jessie shrugged. Lu shook her head and went to finish dusting.

Lu sure had it right. Logan was perfection in male form. So completely masculine, yet so tender, Logan's endearing charm came natural.

What woman wouldn't want him? Jessie felt her stomach ache and sink low, at the thought of Logan doing the things she fantasized about with another woman.

When they were together Logan treated her as though she were precious. She felt like the center of his world and that she mattered to him.

"You precious . . . you important, you no realize?"

Had Lu heard her thoughts? Jessie certainly hadn't spoken aloud.

Lu shook her beautiful round head.

Surely not

Dreams don't come true for undeserving people like me. There's always a catch.

"Lu no understand. Jessie be good woman." Lu stood hands on stocky hips.

Everett chose her, like anything else he'd purchased. Mama had save her for just such a bargain and was pleased to sell Jessie for cash, making out like a bandit. Jessie went from one hell to another, as was fitting.

"Everett married me, gave me a home, security, respectability and promised me a family. He never loved me. I was only a possession to him, a means to have a family. I never produced a child for him. I failed Everett as a wife. Even my own mother didn't love me."

She couldn't tell Lu everything, because no decent person would understand Jessie being bought and paid for.

Gazing into the distance, Logan's face flashed in her mind, and she cringed.

Jessie had been birthed into Mama's New Orleans brothel and hated it there but had no other options. Mama's possession, same as to Everett's, she was cheap.

Jessie's father was an unidentified gambler passing through town. Or at least Mama said so. He knew nothing of Jessie and wouldn't have cared if he had known. Jessie had no desire to know the man.

That life seemed far away, like a long ago dream Jessie would never return to. But the disgrace was part of her and gnawed at her gut continually.

"I was fed, clothed and provided shelter. But love was withheld and foreign. Mama didn't have a clue how to love.

Mama only took care of responsibilities. I was a burden and nothing more."

Lu frowned, clearly concerned and saddened.

"I've usually got good instincts about people. It is a skill I learned watching people. I wish I'd read Everett better. But I had never met anyone like him before. He was gallant, elegant and took an interest in me. So I was fooled. I'd seen happy families playing together in the parks and wanted that. When Everett offered marriage, I accepted it. I made a bargain to be a good wife and birth his children."

And I stepped into the lion's den.

"Everett provided for me. He opened new horizons for me. Everett gave me hope, though reality isn't as he promised. Some has been worse. Much of my life is also better than it ever could've been without him."

Shrugging she surveyed her home then hugged Lu again.

"This is a good home and a good life."

Lu embraced her tenderly.

Under Lu's tender care, Jessie had healed from the miscarriage and grew stronger than ever--physically.

Could Lu provide a cure for Jessie's broken heart?

CHAPTER 20

Jessie believed that God wasn't willing to trust a baby to the likes of her. Or was it this town? Did God not want to bring a child into this wild, dangerous place?

No, God blessed the location abundantly. So it was Jessie who was undeserving.

She and Everett had been a perfect match. He was a tortured soul with fury in his heart. Jessie was of questionable heritage, and a whore's bastard child. No wonder--the Lord hadn't blessed them with children. They didn't deserve happiness.

Life went on relentlessly, however.

Doing laundry Jessie and Lu talked with an easy companionship.

"Soapy donated money to build a gospel mill. I went Sunday to put in an appearance. But I enjoyed it. I had never attended church before."

"Husband and Lu will attend services, too." Lu nodded, folding sheets.

"It's surprising because Soapy's such a scoundrel. Who would've thought he'd be so generous to the town?"

"Peoples no taken in by Soapy's gift. Everybody knows he buys affection." Lu laughed, placing pudgy hands on her ample hips. "Peoples understand what Soapy about--bad, like your mister was."

"Oh sure, it's a ploy to improve public image. Perception is everything. Soapy cares what the town thinks, especially business owners and politicians. Soapy likes being the big man in town. You're right. Everett was the same."

"Soapy very bad." Lu glared out the window.

"Yes. It's common knowledge. Soapy and his band of thieves and cutthroats are the roots of evil here. Soapy rules with an iron fist figuring he owns the town, which he does in a way. Folks let Soapy Smith get away with it." Jessie rolled her eyes.

Lu nodded and shook her coarse, spiky head.

"Soapy is a charlatan who loves the game, taking with a knife or persuader what he can't swindle from miners other ways, slaughtering men daily for gold, cash and gear. Most Stampeders are easy pickings who bring money for mining gear and to buy a stake in the gold fields. Prospectors are gamblers, looking to get rich quick. They want more money with less effort. But relentlessly they work to strike it rich. Most are gullible, prime targets for Soapy's schemes and clever confidence games. Sadly there's nothing done about it, because Soapy's is the only law in Skagway."

"It a shame. Peoples need to band together. Do something." Lu shook her head.

It wasn't surprising how gullible the stampeders were, since they fell for the conspiracy Everett and his friends cooked up.

"More prospectors and willing victims arrive weekly."

"Your Mister Everett like Soapy. They cut from same cloth." Again, Lu had read Jessie's mind. The woman was an enigma. Lu stared straight into her eyes, as though daring argument.

Jessie couldn't.

"I am sure Everett was aware of Soapy's illegal activities and condoned it." Jessie bit her lip. "He was a partner in crime and a criminal in the worst way . . . as bad as Soapy."

The newspaper arrived with each ship from Seattle. Jessie devoured it cover-to-cover. It spoke of the first ever video film shot of the Sheath, a ship leaving for Alaska loaded to the gills. Like every other ship, it headed to the frozen north, it brought a boatload of fresh prospectors flocking to seek their fortune in the gold fields.

After reading the newspaper, Jessie set about her morning chores, lamming rugs on a clothesline with a broom. She glanced across the muddy street, along the alley running behind the business district.

Jessie spotted a pile of clothing lying motionless. Dropping her broom she rushed to check it out, disobeying Ben's warning to stay out of the alley.

The pile was a man lying face in the mud, positioned awkwardly and not moving. Squatting, Jessie rolled him over. The gent's cold, stiff body appeared he'd '*gone up the flume*.' Her heart sank low in her belly viewing the snow-white face. Air rushed from her lungs as she spotted the ugly, jagged line slitting his throat.

He had bled out into the muddy soil. Jessie held fingers to his neck checking for a pulse and found none. Sadly brushing hair from his face, Jessie examined further.

The bloke was only a boy, not more than sixteen or seventeen years old. Jessie cradled the youth's head in her arms crying for the poor lad who'd '*taken the big jump*' alone. Likely, no one else in town would cry for him.

Closing his lifeless grey eyes, Jessie gently laid him back down. She picked up his hat sitting beside him in the mud and covered his face with it.

Something shiny stuck in the earth where the hat had lain. The thieves who had '*dry-gulched*' the poor soul had missed it in their rush under darkness, as they had killed the young man.

Jessie pulled a nugget from the mud. It must've fallen from the tiny, drawstring bag lying beside it. As she opened the sack several stones toppled out. The boy owned a considerable bag of gold, probably hidden in his hat. The thieves probably hadn't looked there. Jessie slipped the pouch into her pocket and wiped her tears.

She understood being alone in the world, being targeted, and becoming a victim. But the boy's death was a waste. He was young and could've led a long life. But Soapy's band of villains stole it.

A shame. Something must be done about the law in this town.

Jessie walked to the undertaker's shop, one of the most profitable businesses in town, boasting a steady flow of customers. She instructed the undertaker to take care of the boy paying with a nugget.

"Please make every attempt to identify the boy. If you discover who he is, report to me and only me. If anyone traveled with him, I must make contact with that person." She dabbed a tear with her hanky.

The undertaker tilted his head quizzically. "Don't take on so, Mistress Blackstone. He's merely another fagged out miner who *hung up the fiddle*. Why do you need to meet his buddies or kin?"

"How dare you, sir! This was no guttersnipe. This is a young boy with living to do. His whole life lay ahead of him. Whoever robbed and bed this young one down should be prosecuted and hanged. And it is no concern of yours why I choose to learn who the boy was." Jessie's nose flew into the air making tracks out of the shop before saying something she'd regret.

Jessie didn't tell him about the gold. She hoped to learn the identity of the boy. If the youth had family or friends in town, she planned to turn his treasure over to them. Otherwise, she would hold onto it. She didn't want Soapy's gang to get wind that she had it. They would be angry and after it—for sure.

It was minutely satisfying, knowing Soapy's band of crooks didn't get the boy's gold. They must've taken everything else of value.

Jessie walked past the saloon and glanced in the window. A couple of men were playing faro. Another two sat at a table sharing a bottle. Shock froze her feet in place. She could hardly believe her eyes. Logan was sharing a drink congenially talking with Soapy.

What the hell?

A few minutes passed. They shook on something, making a deal then Logan stood to go. Jessie snapped out of her stupor and quickly made her way home.

How could Logan have deceived her this way? Flabbergasted, hardly believing what she had witnessed, her eyes didn't lie. Jessie never would've suspected Logan was involved with Soapy.

Logan and Soapy were working together. So Logan had been in on the scheme. He was a party to the evil Soapy and Everett perpetrated all along.

Jessie had been a fool.

Her stomach went sour, and bile rose in her throat. She felt physically sick. There was something very wrong with her judgement where men were concerned. First she had been taken in by Everett's smooth promises. Then Logan had played the part of an upstanding, trustworthy friend. Jessie was no friends with the likes of Soapy Smith. If Logan was in with him, she had judged Logan way too kindly.

It was a tear squeezer when the undertaker sent word the next morning. He hadn't identified the youth. The young man would be buried without anyone grieving him. He would be forever one of the many John Doe's buried in the bone orchard.

Someone needed to mourn the boy. Following the undertaker's wagon, walking slowly to the outskirts of town she paid her respects. Jessie stood quietly beside the open grave as the only bereaved.

The grave diggers lowered the wooden box and shoveled dirt atop the grave. They placed a rock at the top and a smaller one at the bottom, marking the grave without words etched upon the poor lad's stone.

Jessie knelt beside the fresh mound and said a prayer for the boy's soul. New at this praying thing, she hoped God, if he existed, would forgive her inexperience and hears her prayer anyway. Jessie asked him to welcome the lad into heaven. Then she placed a wild flower bouquet upon the cold dirt.

"It's a sad travesty that this wasn't the gold mine or motherlode you ventured to Skagway to find. However, it is your stake in Alaska. You own this tiny plot of ground—bought and paid for."

Sickened with grief for the nameless child, Jessie left him alone in the cold earth. She blamed Everett, Soapy, herself and Logan for his death. They were all responsible, being at the root of this tremendous scam. As the instigator, Everett had started the gold rush conspiracy in the first place. Jessie carried out the start of it in Everett's stead. Soapy continued preying on those taken in by the rouse.

How the hell did Logan fit into the madness?

Jessie walked slowly home feeling like she was the devil's puppet, sick at heart. The poor lad frequently came to mind during the next few weeks.

Will I end like him?

CHAPTER 21

Aching inside, learning the ugly truth that Logan deceived her, was almost more than Jessie could bear.

She couldn't face him. So she avoided Logan the next few weeks, staying indoors when he might pass her cabin.

Jessie admired the four jars of blueberry jam on the table and two pies that cooled alongside them. The previous day she had trekked into the woods and picked the berries. Lu was not as eager for Jessie's woodland ventures.

"I love the abundant forest surrounding my home. I adore wandering freely through its well-worn paths created by forest creatures, admiring flora and fauna. I find it curious so many varieties of ferns, herbs and flowers grow in the deep, shaded woods. The forest provides a welcome retreat from the hot summer sun. Being alone in the woods is a special freedom. Don't you agree, Lu?"

"Be careful picking fruit. Bears eat berries and they eat nosey white women, too." Lu swatted Jessie's behind giggling.

"I'm careful. But I enjoy the forest so much. It seems something wonderful is at work in the glorious, remote space. It elicits a spiritual sensation touching me as I become one with nature. I am a creature roaming the forest splendor."

"Predators live in woodlands. They fiercely protect territory, food, and young. Kodiak or brown bear attack when close to cubs. But grizzly no need reason or hesitate. Only charge, protecting or not." Lu wagged her finger.

Jessie laughed. "It's worth the risk. Inside those timbers I become part of the food chain. I must remain on high alert. But the forest is splendid. Lush undergrowth is rich with fruit. Many trees provide nuts. I adore harvesting nature's bounty, scooping handfuls from thick bushes into my bucket to make delicious, nourishing meals. Yesterday I was lucky and discovered a treasure trove of blueberries. You love blueberry pies."

Lu shook her head. "You a sweet one, Mistress Jessie."

Carefully, Jessie removed the last two pies from the oven wearing thick mitts. She carried them gingerly out the door and placed them on the wide porch rail to cool.

Back inside, Jessie carefully packed jars of blueberry preserves into a tote cushioned with dish towels, so they wouldn't clang together. She made certain the jars sealed properly before carrying them out to the root cellar.

Passing her garden, Jessie admired the lusty plants. Zucchini hung thick on strong vines where her garden thrived.

"I'll pick zucchini for supper and fry some strips tonight. It's my favorite way to eat it. I'll enjoy fat, juicy tomatoes, since they are plentiful." Jessie happily talked to herself.

She sat her bag at the mound of firm dirt past her garden beside the smoke house and slipped open the root cellar lock. Entering the cool darkness she felt gingerly for the lantern on the nearest shelf then lifted the glass globe. Locating dry matches kept in a tin next to the lantern Jessie struck one, lighting the kerosene lantern.

The room sparked to life, fully illuminated and glowed soft yellow. Jars gleamed in the light. Jessie swelled with pride and satisfaction having filled shelves with blackberry, blueberry and raspberry preserves, fresh honey from a local bee keeper, green beans, corn, sauerkraut and beets lined three walls from floor to ceiling. Dirt floor bins on each side were filled with potatoes and sweet onions.

Retrieving a clean cloth from her bag she dusted the jars that she had delighted in preparing. Jessie discovered satisfaction and fulfillment feeding her and others, canning, smoking meat and fish, caring for her home and cooking.

She had come a long way from a New Orleans street urchin. Jessie had become a real lady, a devoted wife and a self-sufficient home maker. No matter the drawbacks, Jessie had built a good life. With everything in order in the root cellar, she lifted the globe and blew out the light. She clutched her empty tote and stepped into the stunning, sunlit day. Catching an odd, putrid scent filling the air, Jessie halted.

Yuck! What in tarnation?

She swallowed the sour taste sliding across her tongue, secured the door, and turned toward the house. After only a couple of steps a shriek of terror shot out and was instantly stifled. Jessie stood statue still, frozen in her tracks, afraid to breathe, and every nerve in her body sparked.

A huge brown bear turned observing the unwanted intrusion. Standing beside the back porch the massive animal helped himself to her pies. Munching away he pinned one with an enormous piercing claw. His paw looked as big as Jessie's head. He had knocked the second pie to the ground to be eaten next.

The critter didn't want to be disturbed. Happily enjoying his snack focused on the oozing sweet purple filling, he shook his burly head warning her off. He was letting Jessie know she wasn't getting his pies. Baring dangerously piercing yellow fangs he roared a deep, guttural threat. His incisors dripped a slimy combination of pie filling and saliva.

His fangs were at least as long as Jessie's hand. Her whole head would fit into his drooling mouth. Purple filling and slobber dribbled from his sloppy red tongue when he shook his shaggy head. He emitted a threatening roar, reverberating in clear, crisp air that sent shivers through Jessie's spine.

She cringed, not wanting to tangle with the beast. Afraid to breathe the air because it might anger him, she conceded. He was welcome to the pies.

The beast could kill with one swat of a massive arm. Connection with one of those severe claws would slit her throat or chest, causing mortal injury. Or he could sink those extended fangs into skin. Mauling by a bear was terrifying and would be a horrible way to die.

Jessie was petrified and surprised she didn't wet her pants. Her head swam. She controlled her trembling, so as not to scare the bear into attacking. Any movement might send the mighty predator into frenzy.

Jessie wished she could reach for the gun hidden in her petticoats. Movement could rouse the great bear to charge. A bullet from her pistol would provide only a bee sting of pain to the tough predator. So she stood deathly still as blood drained from her face and the world turned surreal.

A sudden loud clanging combined with a shrill whistling rang from the front of her house. Mister Bear startled at the warning sounding beyond the line of vision, as someone banged on metal and fiercely blew a whistle.

The bear couldn't see its origin either, but searched around for the invisible threat. Shaking his bulky head back and forth, the bear watched Jessie as she stood like a stature. Still afraid to move or breathe, she somehow remained calm. There was no time for panic.

"Run you son of a bitch. Get outta here." An angry voice shrieked from somewhere unseen.

A brash uproar of metal against metal and piercing whistling persisted. Moving closer and closer to the back of the house the threat remained invisible.

The creature seemed perplexed. Should he risk losing his bounty by confronting an unseen adversary, stay and fight for his pies, or run? His big head went from Jessie to the scary noise and returned. He glanced to the woods as though pondering what to do. He decided not to risk losing his treasure by confronting the invisible menace. He was not interested in tangling with Jessie, who presented no real threat. The true hazard was the invisible, blood-curling disturbance coming toward him.

The alarmed bear seized the remaining pie with his fangs and made a run for it taking the pie with him. He bound awkwardly and swiftly high tailed it into his timberland home.

Once the pillager was completely out of sight Jessie turned to her rescuer. A brave woman ran still beating on metal toward the back of the house. She shouted furiously at the huge creature until he loped out of sight.

"Get out of here, you brute."

He never turned to view his predator. Jessie stood paralyzed in awe, as the scene unfolded.

The audaciously costumed woman wearing heavy makeup on her lovely face had a red feathered plume springing from the back of her bright, orange hair. Her green and black striped satin skirt was cut shamelessly short exposing layers of ruffled crinolines. Long legs were covered with black, silk stockings. High-heeled shoes brazenly exposed slim ankles. Her heart-shaped bodice displayed ample cleavage and creamy, white skin with a hint of freckles. She wore a whistle on a ribbon around her neck. Her adorable face broadly grinned. Thick red lips bared gleaming white teeth.

The woman was a cheerful sight to behold. Jessie liked her instantly.

The outlandish female carried a galvanized bucket and a steel pipe. The gloriously heroic woman flamboyantly and vulgarly struck the bucket with the pipe creating a horrendous racket and saved Jessie's life.

Eyes met and locked, suspended in the moment, while they acknowledged each other. Each realized they knew the other but not personally. Their lives were different but in this they were the same. They were joined in this experience, one with nature. Something deep and personal exchanged between them.

Suddenly both women burst into rambunctious laughter so hard tears flooded their faces. They bent forward, slapping their legs hysterically. The cheekily dressed woman timidly approached. Jessie threw her arms out in welcome, and her hero melted into them. Clinging together, they supported each other until finally, after laughing and crying exhausted, they drew apart. The gals studied each other curiously. The red headed stranger grinned from ear to ear and slapped her leg.

"That was the damned, funniest, scariest thing I ever witnessed."

"It sure was. Thank you. I was a goner if you hadn't shown up. The bear could've killed me. I never want to encounter a beast so close again. I am forever in your debt. Your bravery saved my life. You're the pluckiest woman I ever met, my champion, my hero."

"You're welcome, Mistress Blackstone. Twas my pleasure." Her broad smile exposed straight white molars.

Jessie figured them to be similar in age.

"Where are my manners?" Flustered Jessie took the woman's elbow and steered her toward the back porch.

"Come in for a glass of cool lemonade and some blackberry pie." Jessie's shoulders shuddered still laughing.

"Are you sure? The bear ate the two on the porch?" The redhead laughed, slapping her thigh.

"He didn't get the first two I baked this morning. Yesterday in the same woods he escaped to hide in, I picked blackberries until my fingers were stained. Thank God I didn't run into Mister Bear then."

Stopping at the door the redhead pulled away. "I appreciate the invitation, but couldn't possibly."

"Are you off your nut? You saved my life. The least I can do is share pie and lemonade with you." Jessie pulled the woman along by the hand, accepting no argument.

"Ma'am, taint proper, me entering your home."

"Ridiculous!" Jessie pushed her through the opened screen door into her kitchen to the table.

"Mistress Blackstone, you know what I am. Don't 'cha?"

Mistress Blackstone shouldn't disgrace herself keeping company with her sort? Though Jessie had become a good actress in all this time, she wasn't naïve.

"I certainly do. You're a lovely woman who saved my life. You are my hero and a conqueror of bears." Jessie's giggles were contagious as her fist shot into the air, sending the two of them into unbridled laughter.

When Jessie could finally speak without cracking up again, she assured her new friend.

"This is my home, you're my friend. I'm forever indebted to you. But I am also proud to call you friend. And my friends are welcome in my home."

Jessie poured cool glasses of lemonade. She cut slices of scrumptious blackberry pie then sat across from the woman. Taking the strange lady's hand, she smiled at her surprised face.

"I understand what you do and how you live. So let's get past that nonsense, because I appreciate you more than you can possibly glean. So what's your name and tell me about yourself?"

Jessie released the stunned prostitute's hand leaving no room for argument.

The woman sat quietly for a moment sipping the cool drink, her face blank. Then she took a bite of the delectable pie and smiled, relenting.

How could she not?

"Thank you, Mistress Blackstone. You're a remarkable woman. No one's ever treated me wi' such kindness. Thank ya for your hospitality. Your pie's the best I ever ate. I don't blame the damned bear for stealing 'em." She blushed at her curse. "Forgive my speech. I apologize."

"Poppy-cock, I've heard the word before and spoken much worse myself." Jessie winked.

"I'm Rosie, Rosie Donovan. I work above the Red Onion."

Jessie didn't flinch. "Nice meeting you, Rosie, I'm Jessie. No more, Mistress Blackstone."

Rosie nodded. "As ya wish, thank ya, Jessie. I'll call ya by your given name in private. But should we meet on the street, I'll look t'other way. Tis only right and respectful." Her Irish lilt crooned endearing lyrics as she fumbled the language in her own special way.

"Should we meet on the street, I'll call you Rosie. You may call me Mistress Blackstone, if you wish. I'd prefer Jessie. I won't tolerate you looking away, politely avoiding me in public. I'll respect you in public, as I do in private. I prefer you do the same." Jessie folded her hands in her lap.

To hell with convention. I won't deny this lovely woman.

"Thank you, Jessie. I appreciate it. But I don't want ta bring ya disgrace. I won't be the cause of gossip 'round town 'bout cha. The town might react poorly." Rosie appeared troubled.

"I don't give a fig about what this town thinks. I'm nothing to them. Use your own judgment. I'll follow your lead. I don't wish to harm you or your position. I wouldn't want you to lose your job or for Soapy to take it out on you."

"Let's not worry. Let us spend this precious time getting acquainted."

Rosie nodded meekly.

"Would it be too personal, if I inquired how you found your way to the Red Onion? If you don't want to discuss it, I understand. You have the blarney in your accent. I suspect you're from Ireland."

Jessie set about enjoying her pie, allowing Rosie time to relax and decide how much to share. Jessie was thrilled at the company of another white woman. She adored Lu, but Lu was older and more like a mother. Rosie was closer in age and would be a good friend. Or at least, she hoped so.

Jessie hadn't realized how alone and separated from the community she had been until now. Busy learning survival skills and business, she had allowed herself to become a recluse with no social life. A bitter taste filled her mouth.

Everett had thrived on control. Jessie was his pet to be paraded in front of those he wanted to impress. She had been more a slave who bared the brunt of Everett's fists. But he was gone now.

Logan had betrayed Jessie. Everett's treatment had been unforgivable, but Logan's lies had injured far worse.

"Why yes, I'm Irish. I hale from County Cork. My man, Kurt, and I moved ta the States together. Kurt twas a restless one seekin' his fortune. He called me his Rambling Rose. But he was the one with wandering britches."

Rosie's smiling eyes went damp and glistened. Rosie settled into a wistful smile. "I'd a followed Kurt anywhere. We were dirt poor. Kurt was always striving fer more. So we worked our way west too late fer riches of the California Gold Rush. Kurt learned of abundant strikes ta be had in Alaska. So we worked for wages and a stake ta prospect here. Kurt and I made it as far as Skagway."

Rosie stared at the wall, wiping a solitary tear with her hand. "Our first night Kurt left me alone in our tent. Kurt went ta the saloon fer a cup seeking ta get the lay of the land from other miners. My loving man never came home. Kurt had been bush-wacked in an alley and left fer dead. He took two bullet holes to his chest. Our money was stolen off his dead body."

Rosie swiped a tear with the back of her hand. Jessie passed her a dry dish towel.

"Twas more'n a year ago, I buried my sweet Kurt in the cold Alaskan ground."

"I'm sorry, Rosie. Unfortunately, it's the norm around here. It has become a way of life in this lawless town."

"Surely 'tis. Anyway, I'd no money ta live on, no prospects or cash for passage back ta the continent. So I became stuck here.

I tried ta find work in town, but twas none. Finally, I gave up. I visited the Red Onion, and they were happy ta have me."

"Yes, Rosie. I'm sure they are. You're lovely underneath all the makeup." Jessie brushed a radiant, red tress from Rosie's cheek.

Rosie blushed. "Thank ya. Me Kurt always told me I was a looker. But it doesn't matter ta these men what I look like. Long as I got the right equipment and lay for 'em, they're happy."

"I understand." Jessie patted Rosie's hand.

"Thank you. I appreciate it, and thank ya for not looking down on me. 'Tis been a long time since I've had a woman ta talk with." Rosie finished the pie and drank the last of the lemonade. "I best go now. I'll be careful leaving the back door, so no one sees. I don't want 'ta tarnish your reputation. It mustn't get around that ya entertained a floozy in your kitchen."

"Don't worry, Rosie. But I appreciate your consideration. Please come back again soon. I want us to be longtime friends." Jessie liked Rosie's daring, plucky spirit enormously. And Rosie had been a good woman until she became a victim of circumstances. Jessie understood like no one else could, how Rosie chose prostitution as a last resort.

Jessie hadn't been a hooker, but she grew up in a cat house and had been a victim of circumstances, too. Raised into the sinful life Jessie had thought it normal. She knew no better, until she married Everett, so understood that Rosie had no choice.

Regardless, Jessie harbored extreme shame and guilt about her past. It gnawed at her soul. The bastard child of a slut, she had punished herself for her history her whole life, regardless that it was not her fault. Meeting Rosie gave Jessie new perspective and realization; she had been a victim also.

But the guilt remained, though as years passed the sting had diminished some.

Could Jessie forgive herself? She'd never considered the possibility.

CHAPTER 22

Rosie frequently visited, careful to not be seen by the towns-people. Jessie eagerly anticipated their talks.

Rosie often helped with whatever chores Jessie did. They washed clothes in a galvanized tub on the porch, scrubbed them on a washboard and hung them on the clothesline.

Chores were a welcome reprieve from Rosie's normal day, giving her a semblance of a normal life. So while the laundry was drying, Rosie helped can food.

"Today I am canning apples from my tree. They are abundant. So I put some in your bag. When they ripen I can't eat them all fresh. You might as well enjoy some of them. The rest are perfect for canning. I can make pies throughout the year."

Jessie built a fire in the rock fire pit she'd erected in the yard. She suspended a galvanized tub above it, on a cast iron tripod. Rosie filled the tub with water. When it came to a full boil, Jessie used a special gripper to carefully place filled jars into the water.

"They must boil long enough to cook the filling and kill germs."

When they were done, Jessie used the tool and removed the jars. She then placed the hot containers carefully on a towel.

When they cooled, the metal tops popped downward slightly, sealing precious nourishment inside.

"This ensures the jars are air tight. It keeps bacteria out, which allows them to be stored for later use. I'm not sure what a bacteria is. However, it spoils food, makes you sick and can kill a person. So this method ensures food is fit to eat."

They placed the canned products gently on shelving in the root cellar.

"Thanks for your help. No matter the task, you always help when you show up. I appreciate that. And I enjoy your company. You make any arduous task much sweeter."

"I like it too. I used ta help Ma can vittles back home in Ireland. Besides, compared ta my days at the Red Onion, house-work is a pleasure."

The women got on perfectly, having a lot in common. They easily understood each other. Jessie had confided about her past, confident her secret was safe with Rosie.

"The arshole hit ya. I don't fathom why the hell, ya were so damned loyal ta him. I don't see why ya don't hate your dead man's guts." Rosie was livid. "He didn't deserve ya."

"I needed him." Tears filled Jessie's eyes.

"I understand, to a point. But his brutality would have surely escalated had he not gone up the flume. You're better off without that bastard."

"There was no alternative. I made a bargain. I owed Everett everything. Look what happened to you when Kurt died. Everett was a major influence, so I couldn't easily leave him. I couldn't do what you do and go into hooking. I left that life behind me for good. I swore I never would."

"You didn't owe the ill-tempered scoundrel your life. Everett would a kill ya."

"If I left Everett, he would have made my life miserable or killed me. I couldn't have run far enough to escape Everett's reach."

"Jessie, he'd a killed ya stayed with him as well. That's how it happens with abused women. The abuser's compelling need becomes worse and worse, escalating many times into murder."

"But Everett is gone now. I'm safe and making a good life here in my blessed home. I'm a very lucky woman."

Tears filled Jessie's eyes. They weren't tears of joy, though she was joyous about finally having a real home of her own. They were tears of regret—for the loss she felt about Logan. Jessie's heart felt as though part of it was missing some essential part of her being, gone with the gust of Logan's lies.

Logon circled around behind the house, finding Jessie and Rosie deep in a serious discussion sitting on the back porch where shade concealed them from prying eyes.

Jessie lit up joyfully as she spotted Logan. An instant smile flashed on her face. Her expression was impossible to miss. Soon as she realized her instinctive reaction, she forced it away. Her heart flip-flopped and sank to her gut bringing a heaving sensation with it.

"Ladies, I hate to interrupt." Jessie popped from her seat and secured her sewing on the table.

Logan strolled toward them, unaware of Jessie's disappointment in him.

"Logan, how are you?" Jessie didn't offer but Logan took the third chair on the porch.

Having noticed, Rosie's face filled with concern. Rosie couldn't possibly miss the strained tension happening between them.

Jessie tried being polite, as Logan expected, but the words came out sharp and clipped.

"Rosie, this is Logan Pace. Mister Pace works for me. He runs the saw mill. Logan, meet my friend, Rosie Donovan."

"I'm pleased ta meet ya, Mister Pace."

Rosie fumbled as though unsure what to do. But Logan extended his hand and smiled. So Rosie placed hers in his. Logan bowed to kiss Rosie's hand before releasing his hold. Logan's smile looked genuine.

"I'm pleased to make your acquaintance, Miss Donovan."

Logan had to know Rosie's identity. Surely he had noticed Rosie around town. Everyone knew who the painted ladies were. However, Logan treated Rosie with respect, so Rosie beamed.

"I'm happy Jessie has a lady friend. It's important to have someone to talk with."

"Thank you, sir," Rosie stammered fidgeting worse than a cat in a room filled with rockers. "Jessie, I must leave. You and Mister Pace have a nice visit."

"Please, don't go on my account. I didn't mean to chase you away." Logan stood respectfully.

"Yes, Rosie, please stay awhile." Jessie pleaded as she panicked.

"I must go, but thank you. I enjoyed your company and the lemonade. Take care of yourself."

Rosie kissed Jessie's cheek and whispered in her ear, "Be easy on the man."

She glared questioningly. Rosie must've picked up on Jessie's angst, knowing her well. Rosie slipped quietly away skirting the edge of the woods invisible to onlookers.

My life's filled with secrets and shadows.

"Please go." Jessie stood to excuse Logan. She timidly whispered wringing her apron nervously. "I don't want you here, Logan Pace."

Logan's face reddened to the color of the apples Jessie had canned. His brows rose and his mouth hung open looking stunned.

"Please sit with me. Explain why've you been avoiding me, and what's got your bloomers in an uproar."

"I'm busy. It's not a good time. So go."

"Are you all right? Did something happen? I couldn't bear it if anything happened to you."

Jessie was touched but mistrusted Logan's earnestness, now doubting everything about him. He was a good actor.

"My problems are my own." Trying to sound adamant, she stormed inside, letting the screen door slam.

Waiting, her back against the wall, Logan's footfall descended the steps. She held back a curtain enough to peek out and caught saw his painful expression. The look of sadness on his handsome face shredded her heart. Even with anger and distrust, Logan cast his spell.

"Goodbye, My Love.

* * *

He searched the sky for answers, confused and hurt by Jessie's dismissal. A massive weight lay heavy in his chest overcome with sparking emotions barely able to breathe.

Logan's grief over Amy had dissipated into fresh Alaskan air over the period he had lived there. He would forever love Amy in his heart, but memories of Amy no longer held the same horrific pain. That searing ache was because Logan's heart was now filled with Jessie.

The widow Blackstone consumed Logan's mind and haunted his dreams. But she was learning to thrive in Alaska, building a new life and mourning her dead man—-without Logan. Logan shouldn't burden Jessie with his longing for her and had been consoled with being her friend. But now she seemed to be dismissing their friendship.

Something had happened that was coming between them. Something was eating at Jessie. She seemed angry with Logan, but he had no idea why. She hadn't even given Logan the opportunity to question her.

* * *

It was killing Jessie being so close, wanting Logan and knowing she couldn't trust him. The range of emotions was vastly different. The emotional part of her wanted to say. "What the hell?" Grab Logan and make him hers. The logical part of her wanted to forget he existed.

All her life men had meant nothing to Jessie. She never wanted one before.

With Everett sex was a means to an end and not a primal urge. But she desired Logan and craved sex with him.

Jessie had fallen in love. God help her. She craved an intimacy of souls. How could she achieve such a status with the lowlife Logan had turned out to be?

Jessie shivered.

Chapter 23

Jessie had spent the day with the mercantile manager helping him reconfigure the store.

"Thank you for your insight, Mistress Blackstone. I believe our new layout for the store will make shopping more convenient for customers and encourage larger sales."

Jessie smiled proudly at their achievement. "I am pleased. I am happy you like it, Vincent. I reviewed the books. New stock items have already resulted in increased orders. Those products seem to be more in demand as Skagway has grown. New folks making the town their homes have different needs than gold prospectors do."

"For sure. Many men have begun bringing their womenfolk to live here. They require items not sought out by our previous customers. It is impressive how you have stayed on top of trends."

"Thank you, Vincent. It seems to be working. Business continues to boom."

On the way home from the mercantile she glimpsed a heap of red fabric behind the saloon. Curiously, Jessie stealthily skirted the building, making sure no one observed her slipping into the alleyway back of the whorehouse.

The red and black fabric pile turned out to be a shiny satin dress atop a ruffled white crinoline. Rosie lay unconscious and motionless encased in the heap of cloth. Blood that had trickled across her face dried around her swollen eye.

"Oh, Lawdy! What in tarnation happened?"

Jessie knelt beside her friend. Tears filled her eyes. She brushed Rosie's hair aside, getting a better look at a cut on Rosie's forehead. The wound puffed up beneath crusty blood.

Jessie took Rosie's pulse and sighed with relief. It was weak but Rosie's heart beat steadily.

Comprehension set in that someone had heartlessly brutalized Rosie and left her to die. Tears stained Jessie's face, and her heart ached like it had made contact with a serrated edge.

"Who did this?"

Jessie rolled Rosie's unconscious body onto her back. Rosie's dress was torn at the bust, exposing bruises forming on Rosie's shoulders and chest. Her skirts were ripped and muddy from lying on the ground. Rose wore no undergarments, only the ragged crinoline. Her pantaloons were lying in a muddy pile nearby, ripped to shreds.

Jessie spotted Logan on the street corner leaving the bank for the mill. Frantically she ran to him.

"Help me. Rosie's hurt. I must get her home. Rosie needs medical attention."

Not waiting for an answer, Jessie made a mad dash toward the back of the saloon. Logan followed without question to where she knelt, cradling Rosie's head.

"Help me get her to my house."

"Is that wise? I can take Rosie to her room in the brothel. Someone there can care for her." Logan swiped his hair back with his hand.

Jessie stared at him as though he were daft and shook her head vehemently.

"She's my friend. I'll care for her. Are you helping me? Or not?" Jessie spat the words, so Logan would understand there was no swaying her decision.

"Of course." Logan knelt and scooped the limp woman up. "Whoa, I'm surprised how little she weighs. Rosie appears heavier in this get-up."

Logan carried unconscious Rosie to Jessie's house, following her determined footsteps. They rounded the end of the street and entered through the back door, avoiding unnecessary gossip.

Jessie held the door. Lu stood silently, eyes wide and mouth open. Logan brought Rosie in following to the bedroom.

"Put Rosie on my bed. Thank you, Logan. I appreciate your assistance." Jessie nodded toward the door excusing Logan.

"Should I go for the doctor?" Logan fidgeted, not backing away.

"No, she'll be fine once she wakes. If Rosie needs the doctor I'll send Lu."

"What if town folks learn of this?" Logan's brows tented and his face filled with concern. Rosie was well known. "I like Rosie, and she's a decent person. Rosie is good to you, and earned my respect when she braved the bear for you. But the public may not see it that way."

"I don't care what these people think. I owe them nothing. I owe Rosie my life."

Logan beamed. "I'm worried about how this might turn out. But I have never respected you more. I admire your steeled resolve and loyalty."

"Thank you for your help. I can take it from here."

Jessie couldn't wait for Logan to leave. Being around him melted her insides with longing. Her skin crawled because her body betrayed her as Logan had.

Jessie had no choice but to ask for his help. But she needed Logan to leave, before her reserve was completely gone.

Thank goodness Logan left with a hang-dog expression on his face. His shoulders slumped, and he appeared confused, hesitating. Finally he did as asked.

With Logan gone, she could again think straight and focus on nursing Rosie. Jessie filled a water pitcher, and Lu brought clean towels then bathed Rosie's bloody face. As Rosie woke with weakly drooping eyes, Jessie smiled reassuringly at the disoriented woman.

"I am glad you're awake. I have been frantic with worry. You will be okay now, Rosie."

"Thank you, but where am I?" Rosie winced and grabbed her head then lay still on the soft pillow.

"My bedroom. Where do you hurt? What happened to you?"

Rosie spoke softly through tears. "I went to the outhouse to pee. Walking back to the brothel, some dude grabbed me. He shoved me against the building. I fought. But he was a lot bigger and overpowered me. He kept hitting my face, wearing a ring of some sort that cut my forehead." Rosie touched her swollen forehead gingerly, flinching at the contact.

"He kept punching me in the belly until finally, I simply stopped fighting. The monster raped me. When he finished, he threw me on the ground, kicked me a couple times in the side and belly, before he left me like a worn out old shoe. He probably figured I'd lay there and die."

Rosie swiped the tears flowing rapidly from her swollen eyes.

"I lay there for a spell, thinking I'd gain strength to rise and go in. I must've passed out."

"You were out cold when I found you. You must've lain there all night. You could've died alone and cold."

Jess's eyes flashed like lightning from fury welling. She wished to go guns-loaded and avenge Rosie. Rosie's health remained Jessie's top priority. She would likely never learn who gave Rosie a licking anyway.

Jessie's manner turned soft and affectionate, holding Rosie's frail hand. Jessie gently caressed the top with her thumb.

"How'd I get here? I can't stay in your house. I must go." Rosie attempted to rise. Rosie's breath caught, and she stilled suddenly, grasping her ribcage. "Golly Moses. That was a mighty searing pain. My sides ache something fierce."

"You're staying put. Logan carried you here. No argument from you, Rosie. I'd wager your ribs are broken."

"Logan knows better. Is he off his chump?" Rosie shook her head and winced. Jessie pushed Rosie gently back on the plush down pillows. Rosie lay limp on the feather mattress while Jessie pulled the thick comforter over her.

"I'm nursing you back to health. Lie still while I'll wash you, if it's okay with you. Then I will slip on one of my gowns. If you've the strength you can sip some chicken soup. Lu's making a pot for you. You can fill your belly and take a nice nap." Jessie spoke quietly and calmly in a determined manner.

Rosie relaxed and stopped resisting. It was no use arguing with Jessie in control.

"How can you keep me here knowing this will ruin your reputation?" Rosie's ineffective argument and weak voice convinced no one. "I should rise and leave. But I simply don't have the strength.

If you'll summon Logan, he can help me home to the brothel." Rosie lay limply and closed her eyes.

"Nonsense." Jessie unbuttoned Rosie's dress and slid it gently off her bruised, battered body. Then Jessie giggled and winked. "Rosie dear, just think. If Everett were alive he would be all beer and skittles learning about this." Giggle, giggle. "No worries, Sweetie. The devil no longer owns this house. I do. I say what happens in these walls now. You stay put. You're on the dodge and 'all-stoved-up.' You are remaining with me as long as it takes to get you back on your feet."

"Won't Lu spread word around town? Gossip would ruin your reputation."

"Absolutely not, Lu can be trusted. Lu would never do anything to endanger me because. She's family. Besides, I don't give a damn what people think of me. Since I took over Everett's businesses, they all think me daft anyway."

Jessie washed Rosie with a soft cloth. The warm water laced with fragrant soap was soothingly pleasant. Rosie began relaxing drifting in and out. Jessie continued cooing softly until Rosie's quivering settled and relaxed more. When Jessie finished bathing Rosie, she pulled out a soft, cotton gown and dressed Rosie in it.

Lu brought fragrant, soothing chicken soup. Lu's face held sympathy for the battered woman.

"Miss Rosie, eat." Lu handed the bowl to Jessie. Then Lu left them alone while Jessie spoon fed the healing broth.

After Rosie's meal Jessie quietly shut the door as Rosie drifted off to sleep

Having suffered internal injuries, for several days Rosie had difficulty going to the bathroom and bled when she peed. Her ribs were clearly broken, so Jessie bound her tightly, providing some relief. Rosie refused involving the doctor, because word would get out that a languid lady was living under Jessie's roof.

After a week with Jessie's help, Rosie could sit and eat at the table. Lu made comfort food for meals, accommodating Rosie's condition. Gradually Rosie's appetite returned.

So did her strength. Within a couple weeks, Rosie walked slowly, holding on to things. By the third week, Rosie insisted on returning to the brothel.

The box herder was surprised at Rosie's return. "You disappeared into thin air. I assumed you were dead, you took up with a miner, or you boarded the ship to Seattle. I'm pleased you're back. I haven't given your room to another girl yet. But you still look ragged."

"Thanks, Joe." Rosie never told him where she'd been. Only that she'd been battered by a John, who obviously didn't want to pay for her services.

After a few days Rosie stopped by for a visit.

Jessie looked up from where she scrubbed laundry on a washboard in a galvanized tub. "How're you doing?"

"Better, thanks to you. I appreciate everything ya done for me."

"You can always count on me."

Rosie sat on the steps watching Jessie work. Rosie would normally help, but wasn't yet up to the task.

"I'm considering leaving." Rosie measured her friend's reaction.

Jessie's demeanor remained quiet, patiently waiting.

"The beating made me wonder if Skagway is the right place for me. I might join the Daughters of Joy. Do you know of 'em?"

Jessie shook her head, but would hear her friend out. Jessie owed Rosie that much respect. Used to losing things and people she cared for, they moved in and out of Jessie's life. Though Jessie's heart ached, she would miss Rosie's visits terribly. But Jessie wouldn't hold Rosie back.

"This woman, Margaret Vera Dorval, runs a busy house in Dawson City. Maggie owns nanny shops in other exotic places too, like Shanghai. The Daughters of Joy work outta the Dawson City house. They are a band of entertainers and prostitutes doin' well. They're short a couple 'a girls according ta Wendy Wong. Wendy is one of Margaret's girls. I met Wendy awhile back. Wendy said I could sing, dance and make a fortune. Dawson City's a booming place in the heart of the gold mines. I'd have a better chance 'a getting gold from the miners there where 'tis fresh in their hands. Margaret might help me set up my own 'cigar shop.' That's what they call a one-nanny brothel. One whore in Dawson city got extremely rich and she's as ugly as a mud fence. But the miners loved her. She sang, danced and tossed her crinolines high givin' 'em a free shot. She never wore bloomers. So they got a good look at her privates. Them old boys were grateful for the exhibition and tossed thousands of dollars her way. She amassed a fortune and high tailed it back ta the states, with some fancy man."

Jessie continued listening quietly, no expression on her face.

"Come with me."

Jessie stood, straightened her skirt and crossed her arms smiling sweetly. "Rosie, do what you have to do. I understand if you leave for Dawson City. But, please remember, I love you. I will desperately miss you. But I can't go. I've worked hard making this my home. I have responsibilities here—people who depend on me. I won't leave Skagway."

"Thank ya, Jessie for everything. I'm not sure yet. I want time to ponder on it. If I go, twill be before winter sets in. It's still a long and dangerous journey, even with better established routes. I wanted your opinion in case I decide ta lite out. I been scared ever since the beatin'."

Jessie placed gentle hands on Rosie's shoulders. "Rosie, do what's right for you. I support you, no matter what. But understand. Bad men beat defenseless woman most everywhere. Dawson City's no safer. However, I owe you my life, so if you need a friend, I'm here for you no matter what. We're family." A tear trickled undisturbed down Jessie's face.

Tears rolled heavily down Rosie's, too.

"Thank you. You've no idea how comfortin' 'tis, knowing that. The feelin' is mutual. I love you, Jessie." Rosie wiped tears with the back of her hand and left quietly skirting the forest with discretion.

So much suffering . . . so many secrets.

Chapter 24

Jessie took the steamer to Seattle for a yearly board meeting with the shipping conglomerate. Upon return she shared what happened with Rosie.

"They are starting to accept me as one of their board. However, as good old boys tend to do, they generally come to the meeting with their minds made up from discussions they''ve had previously over a game of twisting the tiger and a few glasses of fancy fire water."

"Naturally. So did you get them to listen to reason?"

Jessie put hands to hips. "Indeed I did. It wasn't easy. But they are gentlemen, so they listened when I had something to say. I figured they would simply discount my words. But at times they even agreed to use my ideas for improvement. I made it difficult to argue when I sited data I gleaned from studying the shipping industry."

Rosie laughed bawdily. "You are difficult to overlook, my sweet friend. So all your hard work was worth it."

"Absolutely. And the trip was a welcome diversion."

"It couldn't have come at a better time. It took you out of Logan's pathway for a short while."

"Yes, and I was grateful for the time away. Did my being away give you time to determine the future course of your own life without my influence?"

Rosie's smile was brilliant and her red curls bounced excitedly. "There is no better place for me than Skagway. I have people here who care about me—you, Logan, Lu and my friend from the mill, Ben. I don't want to start over in Dawson City."

"That is wonderful news, Rosie." Jessie hugged her friend tight and allowed tears of joy to flow.

"You seem to enjoy working on the shipping line's issues." Rosie commented helping fold laundry fresh from the line.

"I do. Everett is likely turning over in his grave at his wife's shenanigans." Jessie laughed as she helped Rosie.

"You are no longer the meek, quiet-spoken woman whose whole world revolved around Everett."

"That was the way Everett liked it, and I never thought to defy him."

"Jessie, you have become self-sufficient, confident, and grown into an independent woman, since you came to Skagway."

"Thank you, Rosie. My world looks different now. However, if Everett had been good to me, even civil I never would have questioned our life together. Now I question everything about it. My loyalty to Everett's memory has waned. I realized now, I never owed him my life."

"The old bag was not a husband anyone could love. You tried but he made it impossible. Everett was abusive. There is no way to condone that."

"I suppose so. At any rate, I stand alone now and am learning to be responsible for myself. I have people who support and love me. I am trying to learn to love myself. That was the hardest thing."

"Keep at it. Someday you will see the Jessie I know and love. You are worthy, Sweetie."

* * *

Spring 1898

Jessie met some interesting folks on the cruise back to Skagway. Two well-known journalists, who had been taxed with keeping the Alaskan Gold Rush hot in the press back in the States, were aboard. Tappan Adney and Jack London were comparing notes, and they asked Jessie if they could interview her and some other locals while in town. Robert Service, a well-known poet also aboard ship, had decided to linger in Skagway for a couple of days. So Jessie invited them to her house for a dinner party.

In order to provide the writers ample fuel for their pens, Jessie included her friend Harriet Pullen. Harriet was quite a character—the kind of woman legends sprung from.

Jessie was in a quandary about spending such time with Logan. But the authors were interested in learning about the lumber business. So Jessie invited Logan Pace for their benefit. She could surely handle Logan for one evening in the company of all those people.

Jessie and Lu prepared a scrumptious meal of venison stew, fresh vegetables from her garden, potatoes with freshly churned butter, and yeast rolls and for dessert, baked blueberry cobbler, served hot with sweetened cream.

Having company provided a welcome diversion. She tried to relax and enjoy herself, no longer having to worry about how Everett would act at social events. He had been forever unpredictable showing off his young wife wanting the envying of other men with Jessie on his arm. However, Everett had also been prone to outrageously jealous with violent rages and beatings.

Jessie was especially impressed by Robert Service, having read his poetry. She felt a kinship, keenly understanding his work.

"Robert, you perfectly captured the chaotic Alaskan gold fields. You clearly exploited your experiences on paper with precise tales of crazy suicidal tendencies of miners in your poem 'Cremation of Sam McGee.'"

"Thank you. It's true. Many a good man has gone off his rocker, cashed in his chips, never hitting pay dirt. But it's rare a woman understands my work as well as you."

Jessie was familiar with the desire to commit suicide, having briefly considered it after her first miscarriage. She had been desperate for a baby. Everett's blame and subsequent abuse devastated her spirit. It took years to totally discount the notion, but Jessie would never have acted on it. She finally came to grips with the sadness and became determined to live. Suicide wasn't the answer. Nevertheless, Jessie understood the inclination.

"Thank you, Robert. I will treasure the books you gave me forever. I enjoy reading and love your writing."

"You are welcome, Jessie. Enjoy them with my blessings. Thank you for being a wonderful hostess."

"Jessie, you've outdone yourself. These're some mighty good doings you served. I'm a fair-to-middlin' cook myself." Harriet Pullen sipped her glass of whiskey.

"Thank you, Harriet. I'm glad you enjoyed it. I like cooking for company. I am pleased you were able to come tonight. These gentlemen were anxious to meet you. And I rarely enjoy the opportunity to spend time with another white woman, since there aren't many who stay in town. You're a shrewd business woman, and I admire you so."

Logan boasted proudly, apparently also being in awe of Harriet. "Harriet seized opportunities during the mad rush for gold, realizing the key to riches is servicing the masses."

"Indeed, I arrived in Skagway last fall, broke, optimistic but ambitious. I quickly learned survival." Harriet was a corker, sipping whiskey like a man and puffing a cigar the same as the fellows, while Jessie enjoyed a small glass of wine.

"So, Harriet, tell me how you thrive in the circus-like environment." Robert toasted Harriet with his glass.

Jessie had taken an instant liking to the strong, earthy and pleasant woman. It appeared the men did as well. They were anxious to learn all about Harriet's adventures.

"I had seven dollars to my name. I didn't know a soul in Alaska. I had no place to go when I stood on the beach in the rain. The tented city shouted, cursed, and surged around me. I had a revelation. I had no choice but survival for myself and my family."

"That's an accurate description of the town, saying volumes in only a few words." Logan applauded.

"What about your husband?" Tappan sought to understand how a woman could make it without a man in the hostile land.

"Sadly, I'm a widow. My sweet husband died a few years ago, long before I set sail to Alaska." Harriet wasn't insulted by the assumption that only a fool woman would venture here without a man.

"How exceptionally brave of you. You made a fortune from meager beginnings." Jack toasted Harriet.

"I enjoy talking about my escapades." Turning to Jessie, Harriet continued, "As you well know, this frontier is difficult for women. Regardless, I've become quite wealthy." Harriet smiled sweetly patting her hand reassuringly.

"I admire your spunk, Harriet. Sometimes we women are forced to step up and do whatever is necessary in this man's world." The two women seemed to have a lot in common.

Jessie and Harriet had discussed her late husband at length in the past. Harriet had known Everett previously. She saw right through Everett, and read him as the pompous ass he was. She knew how he treated folks and had suspected he was less than gracious to his wife as well. But those words were unspoken. Harriet told Jessie once she didn't think much of Everett portraying the biggest toad in the puddle.

Some folks thought she and Everett had been an odd match. Everett was such a peacock and Jessie was straight from a vaulting house, even if she wasn't a prostitute herself. She had bamboozling folks into believing her a proper lady. But Harriet, like everyone else except for Rosie, didn't know about Jessie's past.

"Some men think women like the two of you have high-handed ideas. Personally I see you as the gutsy, hearty folk that make this new frontier great." Robert cleared his throat.

"Oh land sakes, there ain't no call bein' all biggity." Harriet glowered.

She gulped her gut-warmer like it was water instead of expensive Kentucky bourbon, shipped all the way from the bottomlands. Harriett certainly wasn't a boot-licker. She told it like it was, and laughed bawdily, joking and slapping her leg as she spoke.

The men were no fools and had no choice but to laugh along. They did seem to enjoy Harriet's tales, however--as did Jessie.

She sipped wine, enjoying the lively exchange, intrigued by Harriet's handling of the men's questions. Jessie could learn a trick or two from Harriet. Harriet had struck out penniless on her own, raised her children and built a fortune in business, all at the same time. Like Harriet, she was learning to take care of herself, stand on her own two feet and survive without Everett.

Something to ponder . . .

Thrilled to have company, Jessie hoped to learn more about the goings-on outside of Skagway. Stimulating table conversation was a rarity in her house, especially since she had been in formal mourning.

Jessie could barely be civil to Logan. But he was her guest, so she strived to be cordial. She caught him staring during lulls in conversation, but diverted her eyes concentrating on her other guests who hadn't done her wrong.

Jessie portrayed the perfect hostess, as a lady should. She shared bottles of rare wines shipped in from California. After dinner she opened a jug of bourbon all the way from Kentucky.

Logan told funny stories about quirky happenings in town and adventurous tales of exploring Jessie's vast land holdings for the lumber business. He spoke about his family's lumberjacking business. Her guests roared with laughter at the escapades of Logan and his brothers as youngsters.

"Jessie owns thousands of acres of timber. We frequently venture into the wilderness selecting and marking those for harvest. My lumberjack crew cut mighty trees then load them on wagons and bring them to the mill to be cut for usable lumber." Logan's eyes went wide. "It is hazardous work, and a fella had best know what he's doing."

"There seems to be an endless supply of lumber in Alaska's wilderness," Jack observed.

"It appears so. However, we're selective and take only trees which need clearing so others might grow as tall." Logan's shoulders were back and he sat tall and proud of the work he and his men did.

Robert pompously boasted of his experiences and the hardships in the mining fields. Robert's lofty view from the pulpit seemed to separate him from human suffering.

"These men are a rare breed, with fortitude and nothing more. Many are clueless how to mine for gold, fumbling through the process. But they all share confidence that the Mother Lode awaits them if they humbly keep at it. They are certain they'll be lucky enough to hit the jackpot. But fortune is fickle, and the nature of a prospector is that of a gambler living on luck."

"It's appalling. But who am I to complain about such foolishness?"" Logan looked ashamed as he admitted it. "The mill makes money supplying the huge demand caused by the gold rush. I in turn profit, as does Jessie."

"Of course, we're making a fortune from their exploits. However, I find these miners remarkable. Not many get rich, and it's a shame." Jessie smoothed her skirts in her lap feeling disheartened and full of compassion for her fellow man.

"You're right. Those who find anything at all believe abundance to be endless. What they harvest they gamble away in barrooms, losing fortunes." Robert shook his head sadly.

"I've witnessed prospectors lose as much as fifty thousand dollars in one poker hand." Tappan explained.

"It is a phenomenon I'm in awe of." Robert laughed heartily, slapping his leg. "Mining is a difficult venture. If one is lucky enough to stake a claim, there's no certainty. So they struggle to find gold with minimal likelihood of success. It's difficult making a living." Robert learned this from firsthand experience.

"It's back-breaking work in difficult circumstances. Bitter weather conditions make it harder and harder profiting, while they dig in frozen tundra searching for glistening rock. And for what?" Robert shook his head dubiously.

"Many give up, selling or deserting claims, while some stay going into more practical, profitable ventures." Jessie poured her guests more whiskey and topped off Harriet's glass. Harriet already slurred her words, feeling her oats, but she remained friendly and joyful. So Jessie didn't mind.

"They've discovered a new route to the gold fields, calling it the Chilicoot Trail. It doesn't sound any less hazardous or shorter, since some miners must make fifteen trips getting everything across the mountains." Tappan puffed his cigar.

Jessie listened raptly, eager for news. "Why bother if it isn't better or easier?"

"It's a shorter trip, about five hundred miles to the gold fields and Dawson City, where they're home free. So the trip takes months," Jack explained.

"There is no easy way to get to the promise land." Harriet snorted as she puffed her big cigar.

"Dawson City's the boomtown nearest the gold fields." Sipping coffee she viewed Logan in her peripheral vision. It was impossible missing the question in his eyes. Jessie would have to confront Logan with what she had discovered soon enough. Tonight wasn't the time or place.

"Yep, it is a daunting journey through uncharted wilderness. Most of the time miners have no vague idea where they are or where they are going. There are no maps or directions for the new route. Many never live to tell about it." Logan sipped his bourbon sparingly. His green eyes twinkled like a pond reflecting tall pines.

God help me. I wish I didn't love those eyes.

Jessie straightened turning away from Logan. She hadn't meant to look at him anyway and mustn't do it again. The sight of him weakened Jessie's resolve. "Terrifying."

"Miners thrive on the thrill of the unknown, enjoying adventure and excitement of most any kind," Jack explained. "Once they get past the mountains, they must float gear on the river. That's a difficult task in itself. They must survive the treacherous, wild White Horse Rapids. Many have died, and many who made it lost everything they owned in the attempt. But if they survive the rapids, it's an easy float the rest of the way to Dawson City."

"Getting there is only part of the problem," Tappan argued. "There are so many people on the journey, getting there before the crowd is important. So miners line up on the mountain pass like a pilgrimage disappearing into blue sky as they trek upward toward white mountain peaks."

"Yes," Andrew agreed. "There are so many miners. It is first pig to the troth. The early bird gets the worm."

"Once they arrive at the gold fields, they must pick a plot and stake a claim, if they can find one available. Most start digging immediately. It's hard work, digging by hand with crude pitch forks, chopping slowly through frozen ground. Most finds are at least in thirty to fifty feet of rocky frozen earth," Jack explained.

Jessie's eyes were wide with wonder, and she shook her head.

Logan nodded. "Bitter winds and high altitude make it hard breathing. So the process is extremely difficult labor. These men move by hand tons of gravel and earth. No matter how hard forestry and the lumber business is, it's nothing compared to the brutal work of miners." Logan sounded grateful for his profession.

Jessie's wide eyes put a smile on Jack's amused face. "It's changing the territory. Dawson City's fast growing into a metropolis similar to cities miners rushed north to escape. Disillusionment and dissatisfaction are setting in, as the adventurers are looking for the next big find. Some folks returned to live in Skagway." Jessie smiled broadly.

"Yes, they're helping build the town. Stores, offices and saloons opened by miners, line the muddy streets of our fair city." Logan glanced sideways at her and she quickly turned her head, not acknowledging his smile. Jessie grabbed the bottle and topped off her guests' bourbon. "Mining certainly is a difficult life. So, Harriet, tell us how you amassed your fortune." Jessie smiled sweetly at her welcomed guest, enjoying the spirited discussion.

"It was challenging. But I gave it my all, figuring all you can do is all you can do. I drove a freight outfit during the day. I made tin pans from scrap food cans and at night, baked apple pies in 'em. I owned a herd of horses in Washington Territory. So when I earned enough dough, I sent for 'em. I started a freight hauling business with my horses. It proved profitable, since I knew the route like the back of my hand."

Harriet sipped whiskey and filled a blanket then licking the paper. She stuck it in her mouth, lit a match against the table and puffed the cigar she'd rolled.

"That is a perilous job. It is impressive that a member of the weaker sex could manage such a remarkable feat." Jack coughed, straightening in his chair. "And now you're one of Skagway's most illustrious citizens."

Jessie wasn't sure if Jack meant that as a fact or if he was trying to put Harriet in her place.

Harriet attempted a blush but it was beyond her. Harriet was past embarrassment or intimidation. She was exceptionally pleased at what she'd accomplished. And she should be. Harriet would never let any flea of a man diminish her efforts. Harriet's smile was as sweet as honey.

Jack cleared his throat, looking flustered. "I didn't mean that derogatorily, Harriet. I apologize if it sounded that way. It's just that Alaska breeds a unique sort of female. Women with the wherewithal to do what is necessarily, like you, seem to thrive here.

"Jack, Alaska brings out strength in the weaker sex, like Jessie for instance. She works in a man's business world and excels. Jessie is one awesome woman. Don't you agree?" Harriet grinned and Jessie wanted to wrap her in a bear hug. But all she did was smile gratefully at Harriet.

"I'm honored to be considered in league with you, Harriet. I admire everything you have done."

"Harriett, do you know Joe Brooks?" Logan asked.

"Old Joe is a good friend and a competitor in the freight business. Joe became a successful packer with more than three hundred mules. He earned in excess of five thousand dollars a day renting out his animals." Harriet sipped her whiskey.

"So I've heard." Tappin lit a cigar and cleared his throat. He puffed his cigar and smoke blew in Harriet's direction. He waved it away with a hand. "Joe Brooks is unscrupulous. Joe can't be trusted to ensure goods get where they're supposed to go. If a better offer happens on the table, Old Joe has no remorse about dropping his freight wherever it is and serving the more profitable customer."

Harriet bristled at his implication of her involvement in unseemly business affairs. "Yes, indeed Old Joe does. Fortunately for me, Joe's reputation makes my business more profitable. People trust me where they can't trust Old Joe." Harriet laughed heartedly and slapped her leg.

"What have you learned of the railroad expansion?" Jessie felt embarrassed at the implication and hoped Harriet wasn't angered. Harriet seemed to let it slide off her shoulders.

"White Pass Railroad supposedly winds through the mountains, climbing to elevations of nearly three thousand feet in a mere twenty miles. I don't envy builders the challenge. Hazardous terrain seems insurmountable, yet they'll soon complete the task." Andrew leaned forward appearing happy to have a change in subject.

"It sounds overwhelming, all right. They blasted through mountains creating tunnels where going around would be more hazardous. It's an expensive venture costing ten million dollars. So some call it the 'railway of gold.'" Logan laughed.

"WP&YR has cliff-hanging turns, many bridges and trestles to raise the hair of travelers. It has the tallest steel bridge in the world." Jack's eyebrows rose as he spoke proudly.

"I'm not sure I'd travel the rail, though it goes all the way from here to Whitehorse. That's a town in the Yukon of Canada. So it's certainly a time saver." Harriet slapped her thigh and scratched her leg.

It tickled Jessie that Harriet hadn't attempted to appear the lady. Harriet arrived at dinner in men's workpants with suspenders, not bothered to dress for dinner. How would Everett have reacted to such garb on a woman?

"Fascinating--technology sure is something. Alaskan ingenuity is inspiring." Andrew's hand curled at his chin, a curious expression on his face. His index finger supported his tilted head with a questioning expression as his brows rose.

"How will the new rail affect your business, Harriet?" Logan tented his hands between his knees leaning toward Harriet.

"Freight hauling operations are destined to peter out eventually, especially with the rail putting a crimp in my operation." Harriet didn't look worried. "A person must strike while the iron's hot. Fortunately I got in on the ground floor and amassed a substantial fortune. When it's over, it's over. Exactly like anything else, hauling has a temporary lifespan. That is to be expected.

Nothing lasts forever. But no worries--I've enough money to support myself and my family for the rest of my days." A distinctive glint flashed in Harriet's eyes.

"In the meantime, you're making a ton of money hauling cargo for miners across White Pass Trail." Jessie clapped her hands gleefully.

There is truth in Harriet's words.

Everett's time of control had ended. What of Soapy's reign of Skagway? Would that also run its course?

"You have braved those treacherous trails many times. That takes grit and stamina." Jack eyed Harriet's with admiration in his eyes.

"I certainly have. It's a rough journey every time. There's no wonder folks nicknamed it Dead Horse Trail. It's a brutal route for sure. I've lost many a horse on that trail." Harriet sipped her tongue oil with a self-satisfied look on her face.

Jessie admired how at peace with her world Harriet seemed. Harriet's relaxed attitude toward change was inspiring. Jessie had always been able to drum up excitement for adventure, yet had also feared change. She wished she could find serenity like Harriet for the unknown future and develop confidence in her ability to make it alone no matter what. If Harriet could feel that way why not Jessie?

"Skagway's grown from a tiny burg to a well-populated city with about eight thousand folks living here." Robert glanced to Logan for confirmation.

"About a thousand miners a week pass through. Skagway has blossomed into the largest city in Alaska." Logan sat back in his chair and crossed those long legs.

Jessie sighed quietly. "Dawson City is in chaos much like Skagway. The circus-like atmosphere is euphoric. The air smells of gold fever intoxicating prospectors finally reaching their destination. Packed muddy streets are highly animated with activity. Masses of prospectors and animals swarm the town in a carnival-like way. Some call Dawson City the Paris of the North," Jack shared.

"I'm satisfied with life here. Lumberjacking is fine by me. I have no desire to mine for gold or visit Dawson City, with all its fuss." Logan shook his head looking disgusted.

Logan's essence warmed the cool room. Jessie didn't like it but couldn't help her attraction to Logan.

If only he were the man I thought him to be.

"I agree. This town is wild enough for me. I love it here. Skagway is my home. Besides, the draw of digging in cold dirt for gold holds no appeal to me." Meaning it, Jessie sat pensively silent for a while, fumbling with her fingers and trying to exorcize Logan from her mind.

Robert Service shared news learned onboard ship. "Gold has been discovered in barren, northern Alaska, near a tiny village called Nome. It is rugged and sparse, a new frontier, so many prospectors are trekking to the far region in search of gold. Especially now that Dawson City has become a metropolis, similar to towns they came north to escape."

"How will Skagway be affected? As a sea port, surely we'll continue experiencing constant traffic moving through on the journey north. I can't imagine going through the struggle they'll face." Jessie's eyes were wide with sincere concern. "Nome is way, way north."

"You're correct, dear Jessie." Logan avoided her eyes, smiling congenially at her guests. "Traffic should continue flowing through Skagway." "Prospectors thrive on struggle and look forward to it. It has become their way of life. They'll survive the pilgrimage to Nome. Or they won't. It's simple," Robert predicted, not appearing surprised.

Turning to Logan Jack sipped his drink. "Logan have you ever considered prospecting?"

"Never."

"What about you, Jessie. You have no inclination toward digging in the dirt for shiny rocks. Do you?" Jack gave her a friendly grin.

"The only digging I do is in my garden. I guess you could say I'm a prospector of sorts, however. I providing what miners need." Jessie laughed and glanced at Logan. A blond curl fell across his forehead escaping his unruly mane. Her urge to touch it and gently push it back into place then run her hand through his thick tresses, filled Jessie with longing and sadness.

Damn it!

She still lusted for Logan.

What the hell?

Her previous opinion had been a delusional fantasy anyway. The real Logan turned out to be a disappointment. Jessie was a fool Logan had toyed with for pleasure--a chump falling head first for his deceit.

Jessie had hoped someday she and Logan would be together. Bad idea! That would have been like jumping from the bear to the mountain lion. Which was worse?

Damn it!

Why did a woman need a man in this worrisome life? Why did Jessie still desire Logan?

"Ever find gold on Mistress Blackstone's property?" Jack asked causing Logan to laugh.

"I haven't wasted time looking for the mysterious yellow rock. And Besides, Jessie wouldn't want me to." Logan glanced her way for confirmation.

"No. I don't want miners working on my land. We strive to preserve the forests and protect the natural environment as much as possible. Logan knows how to do that with the lumber business. Besides, in a way I'm a different sort of miner. Thanks to my deceased entrepreneurial husband, Everett, who had insight and a keen mind for commerce, I am in the business of 'mining the miners.' Supplying their needs is a much more profitable venture. It's a sure thing." Jessie held her chin high.

"Another avalanche hit this last week on White Mountain Pass. Several miners were killed. Some have not been recovered." Andrew shared the latest information he'd learned.

"Unfortunately, it's one of the hazards of the trail, especially in spring. The thaw comes and tragedies occur. Recovery efforts aren't always successful." Tappan put his cigar out in a crystal ashtray. "I came to Alaska with the Stampeders and seen many good men die in such disasters." Putting his cigar out in a crystal ashtray, Tappan Adney, a seasoned outdoorsman, shook his head sadly.

Jessie was profoundly interested in Tappan's work. "I've read your stories. You're quite successful. You must be making a fortune, chronicling the Alaskan Gold Rush."

"Indeed, it is a profitable adventure for me." Tappan smiled.

Jessie turned her attention to the captivating Jack London. "You also came to Alaska as the gold rush began. Jack, you have become world famous for writing about the search for the Mother Lode."

"Indeed, during the last couple of years my craft has made me the best paid writer in the United States." Jack London slurred his words charmingly and smiled at Jessie, enjoying too much Kentucky bourbon.

"Quite an achievement." Jessie admired Jack's work.

"I'm proud of my accomplishments. I ventured north in my early twenties with stampeders, writing of their exploits and experiences." Jack London's rugged individualism and striking vitality were engaging. He was a fun-loving gentleman, an adventurer at heart, and a fetching young man with a fascinating colorful character. Jack London brought laughter and enjoyable table conversation to Jessie's party.

"You're an eloquent speaker with incredible tales to tell. I've enjoyed your stories" Logan agreed.

"I appreciate your opinions and am impressed with your ethics and good morals. It is rare finding a man of principles in Alaska these days." Jessie avoided Logan's glance. Though she felt the heat searing through the fabric of her frock as he flinched at her words. They must've hit home, and rightfully so.

Logan was guiltier than most, but he didn't realize she was aware of his involvement. He should be ashamed. She had considered Logan above it all. But he had proved to be as bad as Everett and Soapy--one of them. And she was a dope he had fooled.

"You're admirably quick siding against injustice, Jack. I noticed you're with the underdog in most instances. You certainly aren't a supporter of Soapy Smith." Andrew cocked a brow at his fellow writer.

Jessie flinched,

"The man's pure evil." Jack raised an eyebrow and declared--plainly outspoken. Logan's eyes went wide, looking surprised. His brows arched and his head tilted back, his chin high. Jessie tried reading Logan's thoughts about the turn of conversation, wondering what he was thinking. Since Logan and Soapy were two of a kind.

"I'm writing a book about the frozen north. It is a new venture for me, having never written a novel before. I figure it'll take a few years finishing and publishing," Jack confided.

"Fascinating." Logan seemed more relaxed with the change in subject. "Does this work of fiction have a name yet?"

"Indeed it does. My book will be titled '*The Call of the Wild*.' I'm telling the tale drawing on my personal Alaskan experiences. I am excited about it."

"I hope to read it when it's completed." Jessie's pulse beat with anticipation.

"I'll mail you a copy, my dear Jessie," Jack promised gallantly then turned his attention to Tappan Adney. "You're an explorer of the trails leading northward through Alaska."

"Yes, I arrived, among the first reaching remote destinations, at the core of the gold rush."

"I read about your exploits in Harper's Weekly," Jessie noted.

"Tappan, you're famous worldwide for articles chronicling the Klondike Stampede." Andrew joined the conversation.

"Tappan quickly became one of the most famous, longest running journalists writing about the gold rush. Mister Adney is uniquely suited to journal the exploits. Tappan, your skills as a rugged outdoorsman and explorer are unsurpassed." Logan sat his whiskey glass down, still half full.

"Because of Tappan's writing expertise, he endured when other journalists fell from popularity. Not only writing about his experience, Tappan also brought along a camera and recorded the gold rush in photography," Jack explained. Tappan took a picture of the dinner party. "Jessie, I'd like you to have this photo as a gift. Please accept it as a thank you for graciousness hosting dinner for us."

Jessie was thrilled at such a unique keepsake. Perched on the edge of her chair, she studied the visual on paper, curious about the new technology. "I've never seen a photograph before, let alone owned one, Thank you so much, Tappan."

Jack changed the subject. "I met Jim Skookum recently. I understand you are friends. Jim Skookum, George Carmack and Dawson Charlie discovered gold on Rabbit Creek, off the Klondike River. That is a treacherous six hundred mile journey from Skagway. Having arrived at Rabbit Creek after releasing the Henderson claim for good, washing dishes in the creek they unearthed a thumb-sized gold nugget. It convinced them to stay and stake their claim on Rabbit Creek."

"John Lindt also found a fortune in gold on Rabbit Creek. So they got in on the ground floor and were lucky. Most never find anything." Jessie sat back laying the shot of her new friends on a side table.

"Rabbit Creek is being renamed Bonanza Creek, suiting the location of such rich gold strikes." Logan's relaxed hands lay in his lap. He appeared at ease with these men.

"They hardly found anything for a long time. Most of the clan exhausted their efforts and abandoned their shares. Finally they discovered opulent gold veins described as 'thick as bread loaves.' The Carmack family claimed most of the land on Banyon Creek before other prospectors arrived in Alaska. Brothers Charlie, George and George's wife Kate staked four flourishing claims. Kate's brother, Skookum Jim, and George's nephew, Dawson Charlie, also struck a rich bonanza," Tappan explained.

"Wow! It is a rare find. I'm happy for them. Kate Carmack is a wonderful woman and a good friend." Sincere happiness filled Jessie's voice.

"Let's hope they don't piss away their windfall. Many do on drink and women in countless saloons that have sprung to life. Dawson City now has as many as Skagway. Miners are extravagant in their gifts to ladies of the night. They toss gold nuggets at their feet as they dance. Many believe their wealthy finds will last forever." Jack leaned back, a smirk on his face.

"It's unlikely they'll lose their fortune. I met Kate when they traveled through Skagway. Kate is focused and driven, keeping her eye on the prize. Kate does whatever is necessary to secure her family's well-being. She'll keep her men on the straight and narrow." Jessie patted her lap, happy for her friend's fortune.

"Kate's a strong, hard-working woman. Alaska attracts this kind of person, especially the women." Harriet sipped her drink. "Kate Carmack isn't a white woman. Kate is a native Tagish. Kate was born one of eight children from an arranged marriage between the Tagish and Tlingit people, forming a trading partnership. After losing her first child and husband, Kate married her deceased sister's husband, George. Kate works the claim alongside her husband." Avoiding Logan's direct gaze Jessie timidly glanced at him out of the corner of her eye.

Heavens he's so handsome! He takes my breath away.

"What other news have you heard?" Ever the journalist, Tappan must be considering another story on his belt.

"They barely existed until the family discovered gold. Kate kept house and cared for their daughter while doing laundry for people, sewing miners' winter clothing and making moccasins. She picked berries, trapped rabbits and other critters feeding her family. Kate Carmack is an inspiration, a hearty woman, for certain. I'm happy they finally struck it rich. If anyone deserves wealth, Kate Carmack has earned it." Jessie clapped proudly. The evening had proved to be a rare treat. She was enjoying it while it lasted.

Jack chimed in, "The gold rush spurred a people bonanza with palatable excitement. It's easy to become swept into its magic."

Logan bragged. "We're becoming quite metropolitan. Skagway established its first post office and has its own newspaper, the Skaguay News."

The men appeared dually impressed.

Jack change the subject. "Canadian Mounties have begun guarding the pass, establishing a post. They are stopping prospectors from entering their country unless properly supplied. So they don't arrive and perish from being ill prepared."

Tappan sipped his drink. "George Brackett established a toll road to White Pass City, about fifteen miles into the valley."

"I'm not familiar with White Pass City." Jessie was eager for any news.

"The tent city sprung to life on the Klondike trail, as another example of 'mining the miners.'" Tappan explained. They all knew the only ones getting rich were supplying the miners' needs. "How is it, Jessie, being one of the few white women in Alaska?"

Oh, Lordy, would Tappan write about her? Everett would've been furious. But then, Everett no longer ruled Jessie's world.

"The winter is unforgiving. Company is sparse. Skagway is an unlawful community. Yet, I absolutely love it here." Jessie's voice was wistful with emotion. "Alaska is amazing. There is with something completely real and alive about its rugged vitality. It's the most beautiful place I could imagine." Everyone laughed when Jessie told of the bear stealing her pies. Of course, she left out the part about being rescued by a prostitute. "Well," Jack noticed, "you're among the minority of unique women enjoying it here."

"Awhile back a cheerful woman worked at a restaurant in town. Her name is Mollie Walsh. I liked Mollie very much and hoped we'd become longtime friends. But Mollie only stayed a year. She saved everything she earned to buy supplies, hired a packer to transport her across the Canadian border about thirty miles away and opened a primitive restaurant or 'grub tent.' Mollie now serves hearty meals for freighters passing through in her own establishment. Mollie's customers adore her for what she does for them. Mollie Walsh is another example of a new age of brave Alaskan women." Maybe Jessie could steer Jack's literary interest toward Mollie, so he wouldn't write about her.

"I've heard of Mollie Walsh." Jack acknowledged with a slight nod.

"Life in the frontier is a challenge, especially to a woman. You're no exception." Logan smiled exposing those irresistible dimples.

Lord, not back to me again. Still not immune to Logan's charm, her chest swelled with warmth as his powerful eyes bore a hole through her defenses. Jessie wouldn't be taken in again, now that she understood what Logan was about. Though she loved the scoundrel, she must keep her distance.

"I'm fortunate having a real house, in a real town. My late husband had it built before we arrived." Jessie smiled with sincere gratitude for what Everett had provided her. "The town is wild, rowdy, and everywhere you look there's some form of danger. But it's simply the way it is." Jessie's voice was calm and matter-of-fact.

"Well that's definitely a frontier woman's attitude. You're remarkable, Jessie." Robert smiled.

Her guests weren't aware if the miseries of her past marriage.

Far as the public continued to believe, she and Everett had been a loving couple. Jessie saw no need to malign Everett's good name or change the public's perception. That was all in the past.

Jessie didn't want Tappan writing about her, digging into her history. Writers were good at removing exterior layers looking for accuracy, and digging for the golden nugget of truth buried in the depths, when things weren't as they appeared. That was what they did as journalists. It would not serve her well, if she were their subject. Jessie's life was filled with illusion, regret and scandal. Oh well, they probably didn't realize that and thought they read her like a book.

Hopefully!

Swigging back more bourbon, Harriet belched and her words slurred as she apologized. They all laughed and Harriet laughed at herself along with them.

Later, they said goodnight. Logan hesitated, but shook her hand like the rest and left with the others. Jessie cleaned the mess and retired, brushing her unruly mop of curls until they shone in her reflection in the mirror.

Jessie was pleased with her first dinner party. She had learned a lot about current events from her visitors. The male visitors had been a joy and gleaned enough information to stoke their journalist muses. The evening turned out to be a delight.

Jessie was thrilled to have invited Harriet. Like Harriet, she had changed and was a product of her experience. She was beginning to like it that way. Jessie had grown even fonder of the bold woman who turned out to be the icing on the cake.

Staring into space soul searching she considering her relationship with Logan. He had seemed a good friend in the past and had supported Jessie's decisions and work she was doing. He had managed her mill successfully, bringing in an impressive profit.

But things weren't always as they seemed. The problem-- Logan had stolen her heart. Her love for him had grown into something deeply entrenched in Jessie's soul. Learning he was in cahoots with Soapy, she no longer trusted Logan. But she couldn't stop the love that lived for him in her heart. Neither could she stall the longing for Logan. He was like a chronic disease that kept returning to cause her agony.

Why did Logan have to be so damned irresistible?

CHAPTER 25

Logan went away for a couple weeks foraging for lumber. He had been happy putting distance between himself and Jessie. Something was going on with her that he didn't understand. She seemed angry with him for some unknown reason. She had been cordial enough during the dinner party, but kept a distinct distance. It made Logan feel sad and he worried continually about Jessie. Being away for a while should help Logan regain perspective and focus on work, instead of that woman who consumed his dreams and filled his heart with longing. By the time Logan returned, he had almost convinced himself it had been in his mind. Logan longed to ask Jessie to marry him, but worried it might be too soon. She was starting to handle her business with flair and understanding. She had become quite capable over the last year. Her mourning period was nearing its end, as evidenced by her throwing the dinner party Logan had attended before leaving town. Maybe soon, she would be ready to hear him out.

But first Logan needed to find out what was needling her. That is, unless Logan had read something into it that wasn't there. Logan had accumulated enough money so he and Jessie could live well for the rest of their lives. Of course, she had Everett's estate and had grown that fortune into an even larger one.

Jessie might never consider marrying Logan. She didn't need a man to take care of her. She had said she didn't want another man and was financially set. How could he win her heart?

Logan would have to tread lightly considering Jessie was stubborn as hell. But Logan loved her. He even admired her loyalty to Everett and his memory. He was proud of the way she had handled herself in the precarious position she found herself in.

Logan wanted more from Jessie. He wanted her for his own, and decided he would his damnedest to make her fall in love with him. If only she could learn to love him as he did her.

Logan couldn't help loving Jessie. He would until the day he died, whether she would eventually have him or not. But he had never told her how he felt.

The time had come for leveling. There was no point hiding any longer. Maybe knowing, she would accept him as a lover.

If Logan did nothing, soon another man would speak up and take Jessie's love. Logan wasn't the jealous type. But he had witnessed admiration in the eyes of Jessie's male guests at her dinner party. Those adoring looks had caused a bitter rumbling inside Logan that he still couldn't dispel.

Maybe Jessie would marry Logan even though she didn't love him. After all, Jessie had married the ass, Everett, without loving him. Jessie had tried to make that marriage work. Jessie had been the kind of wife Logan would've adored if she were his. She had attempted to care for Everett, even though he was the sorriest excuse for a man on earth. That blasted fool had been blind and only treasured money.

She must like Logan. They had been friends since they sailed to Skagway and had gone through a lot together.

Logan was in a quandary. Jessie had acted peculiar, distant and unusually cool when he'd carried Rosie to her house. She had spoken with a curt manner and eyed Logan with cold detachment instead of her normal, casual manner. Of course, Rosie's condition had been paramount and Jessie's prime concern.

Had she been distracted? Or was it something more? Had Logan offended Jessie in some way?

Missing her filled Logan's heart with fiery coals. Heavy and hot they stoked an internal potbelly stove, as he burned to be with Jessie. Logan longed to hold her, to kiss every inch of the woman he desired like no other. To peel her clothing off revealing the wonders of the woman he craved to bury himself inside.

Logan's passion ached. Jessie's smile would make it all better when he stopped by her cabin the day he returned home.

* * *

"Good day to you, Logan." Jessie behaved cordially and relaxed. She was not exactly friendly, but cautiously looked at Logan's glorious, beaming, emerald eyes and studied her face.

"I missed you, Jessie. It's good seeing you healthy. Something has changed. You look stronger, more confident." Logan's jaw twisted. "There's no light in your eyes. Something's missing." Logan appeared to be trying to look right through her as corners of his brilliant eyes wrinkled delightfully. He reached to brush a stray tendril from her forehead. The contact caused Jessie to flinch, sending shivers through her spine, searing her skin leaving a mark. So she backed away putting distance between them and turned her back.

"I'm fine. So no worries."

Logan walked around forcing Jessie to face him. Arms crossed, grim-faced, his muscles visibly tensed. Logan squared his feet readying for battle.

"Something is wrong. You are blue, like a prevailing sadness overshadows you. What's going on? Please trust me. You can tell me anything." Blood drained from Logan's face leaving him pale as a glacier beneath his deep golden tan. Those glorious green eyes were hard to resist, imploring her trust. Her heart swelled filling with love. She reminded herself that though she may love Logan, she couldn't trust him. Jessie squared herself, feet parted; arms crossed, chin high and met him face on. Having had enough of being the victim, Jessie was unwilling to take guff from men no longer.

"It's not your concern."

Logan's head jerked backward as though she's physically stuck him. His eyes went wide and his mouth gaped open. "I thought you trusted me. Have I offended you? Tell me, please, what's the matter?" Logan's beautiful forehead displayed a quilt of wrinkles. His brows tented. Logan's eyes drooped and filled with what appeared to be sincere concern.

He's a good actor. Back away.

"Why should I trust you? You're one of them. You are no better than the rest."

"One of whom? I'm the same old Logan you've always known. I am your loyal friend who would do anything for you. Truly. Why turn on me?"

"You're not the man I thought. You misled me." Jessie stood ready to do battle with her finger wagging in Logan's face.

"What in tarnation are you talking about?" Logan shook his head. His mouth opened. Confusion in his eyes glanced around until his gaze locked on Jessie's for a long moment. Logan looked stricken by the accusation.

"Enough!"

Logan spun around. His hand anxiously raked through his hair. He gazed at mountainsides surrounding them for answers as he twisted. Turning back, Logan gently took Jessie's wrists, untangling them from her sides. Slipping them into his calloused ones, Logan tenderly caressed her hands resting dwarfed in his massive mitts. Shocked by the sensation of him, Jessie couldn't withdraw and refuse him. Her hands lay limply accepting the support and warmth radiated, forcing its way to her arms, filling the void in her chest. Logan's heat surrounded her like a warm Tlingit blanket.

Jessie curiously eyed him wishing she could deny him. Tears flowed unabated onto her cheeks. Rejecting Logan was beyond Jessie's power.

Without releasing her, Logan wiped a tear from her face. His ever so light touch with the back of a gentle finger raised goose bumps on her arms. Jessie quivered reacting to the tingle zipping through every vertebra.

Even angered and knowing the kind of man Logan was, his powerful influence on Jessie's senses had not diminished.

Jessie's nose lifted and her shoulders held high. "Very well, if you must know, I've learned the truth about you."

"What did you learn?" Logan's face screwed up, perplexed.

"Don't try to molly coddle me. My eyes don't lie. You were drinking and chewing the rag with Soapy in the barroom, laughing and talking like old chums shaking on a deal. There's no need pretending any longer. I know you're part of the debacle Soapy and Everett have inflicted on this town. You are no better than them. You have been in cahoots with them all along. I only saw what I wanted to see in you." Jessie glared defiantly hands on hips.

"In cahoots about what? I detest Soapy. Soapy Smith is the last man I'd be in dealings with. I am not trying to soft-soap you." Logan appeared perplexed.

"The two of you were together. I'm wise to you. I don't trust you because you betrayed me. So what else did you lie about?"

A light bulb went on in Logan's eyes. "My, dear sweet Jessie, you're mistaken. I did meet with Soapy. Yes. But am in no way working with him. You see, I took issue with Soapy's attempting to lure my men away from the mill to work for him. I had heard about it before the trip here. Word gets around about such things in the industry. I complained to Everett the day I met him at your house. Everett told me to handle it."

"And?" Jessie rose sternly.

"After Everett died, I couldn't bother you with such a trivial thing. You had enough on your plate. And you were mourning your husband. So I met with Soapy to make him understand that you being his partner, it wasn't in Soapy's best interest to anger you. You have enough power you could buy and sell Soapy Smith a dozen or more times. I have a business to run and need my men working. Soapy would be wise recruiting thieves elsewhere. And Smith isn't stupid. He understood the wisdom in my words. We shook on it then I left. That's all there was to it."

Jessie didn't doubt Logan's words. He spoke the truth.

Mesmerized, she listened intently. With each word the weight on her heart lifted a speck. The ache in her gut dissolved like icy mountains thawing in springtime.

"Oh, Logan, I doubted you. I'm an awful friend." Blood rushed from Jessie's head. She wiped a tear from her eye. "I've missed you so."

"I've missed you as well."

Her face lit with a huge grin, and her shoulders rose. She closed her eyes then opening them. Jessie smiled because everything was brighter.

"Okay if I ask you something?"

"Of course, ask away."

"Rosie is a good friend, hum?"

"Indeed, I trust her completely."

"And you're tolerant of her profession?"

Their eyes locked as Jessie gleaned what sped through Logan's mind. "Rosie didn't go into hooking because she wanted to. Rosie needed to survive when her husband became bushwhacked and killed, soon after arrival in Skagway. Whoring turned out to be the only work Rosie could get."

"I see. Still it seems odd, Everett Blackstone's widow befriending a prostitute."

"Indeed. Everett would have been livid. But he is gone now. And you wonder why I can be tolerant of prostitutes."

Logan held a hand up. "Your friendship and reputation is safe with me. It still surprises me that a lady like you would take up with a lady of the evening like Rosie is now." Logan's eyes were wide, questioning.

Jessie took a deep breath, put her hands on hips and squared her feet. Holding her head high, she spoke staring squarely into Logan's eyes then sucked in a fortifying breath. She tried reading Logan's reaction as she let it all out.

"I was the bastard child of a New Orleans madam. I was never a prostitute, because Mama saved me for just such a bargain. That is where Everett found me. I was but a child at seventeen. Everett bought and paid for me. Then he sent me to finishing school for a year to become a lady. Mama took money from Everett, and Everett got me as his bride. So you see. I come from a life where men paid for sex. It was all I knew when we met. So I didn't balk because life with Everett was better than the one I knew." Jessie shrugged and peering into Logan's mind, attempting to understand how Logan was handling the shocking revelation. But his eyes were thoughtful, remaining compassionate and filled with kindness as he listened quietly.

"Everett chose me. He took me out of the life, taught me to be a lady and the wife he wanted. So I understand Rosie. At least Rosie was a lady before becoming a tramp. I'm an imposter pretending to be a lady all this time for Everett's sake. I was pretty arm candy for Everett. I was never his wife. I was his slave and personal whore, bought and paid for. I have no right to look down my nose at Rosie, or anyone else. I am the worst."

"This explains much I've wondered about." Logan rubbed his face looking away remaining silently mulling it over. His broad shoulders heaved and he breathed hard. She didn't dare interrupt.

Finally Logan turned. "Jessie, please don't speak ill of you. It pains me hearing you say those words. You don't pretend, because you are a real lady. Don't you realize that?"

Jessie shrugged. "You mean a lot to me, Logan. So I can't lie any longer. I owe you the truth. Especially since I accused you of deceit, when I deceived you all long. I understand if you walk away. I ask only one thing. Please, don't share this information. I've only told you and Rosie."

Logan's eyes filled with moisture. His cheeks fell as his brow furrowed.

"My sweet, Jessie, I could stop breathing easier than I could turn away from you. You're as much a part of me as my limbs. My heart aches for what you've endured. You have nothing to be ashamed of. You were an innocent victim--a child. You weren't at fault. But your mother, on the other hand, should be drawn and quartered."

Jessie swiped the streaming tears--a tide she couldn't control. Her shoulders heaved roughly, and her breathing huffed on the verge of hyperventilating.

"Never be less than the gracious lady you are. Where you've been is past and over. Each step since has helped you become who you are. So live in the present as the fine woman you are and be proud." Logan smiled broadly, wiping tears with his cuff. "I love who you are."

Jessie blushed, flustered, turned and escaped indoors. She needed a few minutes alone where she cried heartily, leaning her hands on the kitchen table. Once spent, Jessie's chest ached from sobbing. She doused her face with cool water and brushed her hair.

She put together a snack tray and returned with tall icy glasses of lemonade and freshly baked cookies. The friends sat comfortably together enjoying the silence. They sipped the sweet liquid before discussing the elephant on the porch with them.

* * *

Logan locked on Jessie's face the whole time they talked as a shadow masked her usual sparkling personality. Her eyes had lost their normal depth. Something had stolen joy from her having nothing to do with him or her past.

"You make the best lemonade ever, so thank you."

She nodded silently, wringing her hands in her lap.

Logan stared without seeing the forest behind the house as visions of them together ruled his imagination. An invisible blade twisted back and forth, sawing at his gut until surely his intestines would spill onto the porch. What would he do if Jessie knew of his love for her and still yet refused him? He had to risk it. The thought brought bitter bile rising in his mouth.

"This cannot go on." He slammed a palm against the rail.

"What is wrong, Logan?" Jessie spoke calmly. Her voice and demeanor were soft. Standing her ground, legs firmly planted apart, hands on hips, head held high, and a warrior ready for battle.

"To hell with it."

"What has your drawers in a bind, Logan?" His gaze held hers steadfast, mesmerized, and unable to look away.

"Another time." Logan's eyes looked like shimmering pools of emeralds as they filled with moisture. "Thank you, Logan for not making me feel worse about my past. I appreciate you keeping it to yourself. I'm trying to live with it and get on with life."

"I understand. You are safe with me, Jessie. I must go now, but if you need anything at all, you know I am here." Logan's head hung and shoulders slumped, feeling defeated. This was not the time to declare his love. This was a time to let hurt feelings settle.

For now Jessie was lost to him. But with time, hopefully, things would settle down. Then maybe he would have a chance with her.

* * *

A finger fell to Jessie's lips, gently hushing her words. Logan pursed his own uttering, "Sshhhhh."

She scrutinized Logan curiously, mesmerized by the spell those emerald eyes cast and quietly waited.

"Oh, Logan, I behaved unfairly. I wronged you. I am such a lunk head jumping to conclusions and throwing you to the wolves.

I wrote you off as a schemer the likes of those scoundrels. I don't deserve a friend like you. Could you ever forgive me?"

Logan pulled Jessie to his chest holding her tight. She relaxed resting her cheek against his soft flannel shirt, listening gratefully to the sweet pounding of his strong heart. Her arms slipped easily around his slim waist. Her eyes closed and tension she hadn't been aware of melted. Breathing slowed, and the world came into balance settling gently onto its axis.

Jessie breathed Logan's unique scent. Her one true love, his intoxicating essence was a sensual odor combined with pine. It was a delightful fragrance she could get lost in.

But he mustn't do that. It would ruin everything if she revealed her feelings. Speaking it aloud could destroy Logan. If Logan knew Jessie loved him, it would be the last straw.

Logan could never love a woman like her, not after knowing the life she had led. It was a miracle he still wanted to be her friend.

He was here to work and was her employee. If she told him, things would become even more strained between them. Jessie wouldn't do that to Logan. She loved him too much. It wasn't fair to this gentle giant. So she decided to simply enjoy his company and keep her trap shut.

"Why're you so sad?" Logan leaned back facing her without releasing Jessie. She pulled away, straightening her skirts and glanced around.

"I never thanked you for the marker for my baby's grave. That was the nicest thing anyone ever did for me."

Logan pulled Jessie tightly against his chest and the heat through his work-worn flannel shirt comforted her. She sobbed for the loss of her children, for the loss of her innocence, for her misery with Everett, for missing Lilly and for how she had and continued to hurt Logan. The steady rhythm of Logan's heart as he cradled her in his firm grasp kept Jessie from shattering into a million tiny bits and blowing away in the strong Alaskan gusts of wind.

She let it all out and let it go. But nothing said or unsaid could make it better. Logan's strength was enough.

HIs tears fell on Jessie's curls as he cried with her. She gazed up into his moist emerald eyes. His unashamed trusting smile showed that Logan shared in her loss.

"Jessie, you are loved so much. If I could make this right for you, l would."

"Thank you. I appreciate your sympathy, support and listening. Talking helps and grieving alone is exhausting."

"It's more than sympathy. Your baby was part of you. So it is precious to me. It makes no difference that it wasn't my own."

"Oh, Logan, you've such a loving heart. I adore you. You are the best sort of friend." She wiped a tear from Logan's cheek, bringing her hand to her mouth tasting the salt.

"Logan," Jessie backed a step. .

"I don't expect anything from you. I just want you to be happy."

She stroked his arm and he pulled her tight to his chest so her breasts pressed against his belly. Logan kissed the top of Jessie's head, holding her against his torso.

His lips lowered to gently take hers. Sweet and tender, they kissed long and lingering. Each drew something essential from the other, lost in the moment, willing it to last.

Logan's tongue dipped leisurely into the soft moisture of Jessie's honey sweet mouth licking, sucking until she did the same. Slowly, gently, indulging and exploring the taste and texture of true love.

Lingering, neither wanted it to end. But finally they drew apart. Neither worried about who might see. They simply didn't care any longer

Jessie whispered against Logan's lips. "Lu will arrive soon."

"I must go. Goodbye for now." Logan kissed the top of Jessie's head then left her sitting on the porch. He blew one last kiss.

At her lowest point Logan brought a ray of sunshine into Jessie's world. Unable to hide passion for him any longer, having never been in love before, Jessie felt amazing.

She needed to tell him. But she hadn't yet, not in words anyway.

Jessie's lustful fantasy she'd thought as an idle pastime had helped her survive trials of a life in flux. Maybe it hadn't been lust after all, but love that Jessie shared with Logan. He deserved to know—even if he could never be completely hers.

She was in love. For real—not a fantasy—not lust. Jessie loved Logan. Too bad she wasn't good enough for him. But loving Logan was a splendid thing.

It was the most incredible feeling of freedom that she had ever experienced. It was good and true, even though they couldn't act on it. Its power and greatness couldn't be diminished, like a silken thread of hope worth living for. Cherishing her love for Logan would sustain her and make her stronger.

Jessie felt like a winner in a no-win situation. She had discovered something precious. By loving Logan she had hit the mother lode. Knowing this changed Jessie and love ruled supreme in her singing heart.

Jessie tried explaining to Rosie. "All my life I have tried to be worthy, tried to be good enough and searched in the wrong places for love. I tried to love the unlovable Everett and strived long and hard to make Everett love me. Everett remained incapable of giving or receiving love."

"The fool," Rosie's eyes were filled with compassion.

"Our baby might've breathed love into our lives, but that was not to be. I was doomed to never have a family. And love remained an unknown quantity until now."

"And now?" Rosie cocked her head and an orange curl flopped sideways.

"Loving Logan is something I can cling to in this dismal world. It is the only love I shall ever have, but it is forbidden love. I am not worthy of Logan. He needs a good woman, someone he can be proud to call wife."

Of course, Jessie wouldn't act on her feelings for Logan. Their kiss had been the end of it. She would never forget, having memorized every millisecond of their joining. That one kiss must sustain her.

"That sounds like a bunch of blarney to me. That man needs a warm woman in his bed. I think he fancies you, Jessie."

"Maybe, but I'm not a wise choice for him. My background has tainted me. I could never saddle Logan with the likes of me. Logan is a fine, upstanding man. He deserves a good clean woman, someone he could be proud of as his wife. Logan has been grieving the death of his sweetheart and the guilt of surviving his Amy is what drove him here. He is here for one reason only—to make his fortune. If Logan ever gets over grieving Amy, maybe he will find someone worthy to love. Logan is a handsome, virile man and a good catch. Someday a fine lady will stroll into Skagway and sweep Logan off his feet."

And Jessie would want to die.

CHAPTER 26

1898

Rosie helped hang clothes on the line in her back yard one sunny morning. "Your fine hotel is finally opened. The golden dome topping the corner cupola must've cost a pretty penny."

"It did and I love the way it glistens in the sunshine. The hotel is a fitting tribute to Everett's genius in the business word." Jessie picked another shirt from the basket. "Everett would have been so proud he probably would have crowed. The Golden North Hotel was his masterpiece and one more feather in his cap. It has only been opened a short while and is already bringing in extreme profits despite the exorbitant cost of accommodations. It stays booked to capacity with heavy traffic of prospectors. Someone told me about ten thousand per day come through town. That is a lot of people, especially given the town was a simple village of less than a hundred when we arrived a few years back."

Rosie laughed shaking her head. "What a shame Soapy continues to rule, fleecing unsuspecting prospectors."

Jessie hung up the wet sheets. "The community resents it and with Skagway's growth the public's is calling for law and order.

I read in our new newspaper, The Daily Alaskan, the town has formed a Chamber of Commerce."

"Yep, and a volunteer fire department, so we're coming up in the world. The White Pass & Yukon Route Railroad is nearing completion." Rosie hung another towel.

"Yes the paper said we're being called Skagwayans. Our new post office has finally opened. Our chaotic town's a changing." Jessie put hands on her hips.

Rosie's hand went to her lip. "Honest citizens are angered at Soapy's exploits. They want the end of Soapy's evil ventures. They've formed the Committee of 101, vigilantes opposing Soapy's reign of terror. People are trying to establish law and order by riding Soapy out on a rail."

Jessie stopped and stretched her aching back. "In retaliation Soapy's formed his own gang called the Committee of 303. They've declared war."

"Soapy is a complicated man who can be surprisingly generous and charitable. He named himself a self-styled patriot." Rosie wiped a stray curl from her forehead.

Jessie lifted the basket settling it on her hip. "Peers and enemies alike tout his bravery. He's loyal to his gang but unscrupulous and a scoundrel with the motto, 'Get it while the getting's good.'"

Jessie led Rosie toward the house. In the kitchen Rosie helped Lu make lunch for the three of them. Jessie went to dust the living room.

Joyous voices streamed in through the window from the street, so she glanced outside.

Logan stood in his doorway, a broad grin on his face, stepping out to greet two visitors. Strangers far as Jessie could tell, but obviously not strangers to Logan. Logan beamed at them as his massive arms were thrown around the petite blonde woman. Gripping her in a bear hug Logan lifted the startled, giggling female, swinging her round and round, and hugging her tightly.

The air rushed from Jessie's lungs. She felt weak in the legs and her head felt like it was in a vice. The adorable, tiny female chuckled with delight. Her voice told something of her age. She was young enough to giggle. The strange gal kissed Logan's cheek with a familiarity that gored Jessie's heart like a roaring steer's horns.

From the back the aged man with her wore a long, scraggly, silver ponytail hanging from beneath a bowl hat. It lay against his suit coat as he laughed in a deep, gruff voice that sounded oddly familiar. But Jessie couldn't quite place him.

Finally setting the tickled female down, Logan grabbed the older gent in a bawdy hug. The men laughed heartily, as if one had told a real corker. Stepping behind the couple, Logan wrapped an arm around each of them and pushed them into his house, while the woman chortled adorably.

Craning her neck Jessie eavesdropping unsuccessfully. Only distant muffled voices chatting gaily gave the gist of the conversation. But it was clear that Logan was delighted and welcomed them into his home as though they were intimately close, especially the female.

Jessie's heart ached and she felt the flood of blood deserting her head. The world spun and blurred, while she sank into a chair unable to force air into her starving lungs. Having held her breath for so long, her lungs refused the intake. Swallowing her heart back into place with difficulty, her body went limp. Her head ached, and her ears rang a high pitched sound she focused on in a daze. The dusting rag fell by Jessie's feet as she stared blindly dumbfounded.

"What's wrong?" Rosie squatted in front of her, having found Jessie in the mystifying state. Fanning her face, Rosie brought Jessie around.

"I'm fine." She mustered a slight smile and rose, straightened her skirt. She snatched her dusting rag. "Really."

After explaining what she'd witnessed, Rosie looked doubtful. "Are you sure? I find it hard believing Logan has a sweetheart he didn't tell you about."

It was sad but he deserved a good woman. "Absolutely, I witnessed them with my own eyes. They must've arrived on the ship today. Before they went inside Logan said something about them staying with him. But I didn't catch it all, though Logan acted over-the-moon happy. You should've seen them carrying on. And on the front porch, too. So clearly Logan is enamored with that exquisite creature, as she is with him. It was obvious that woman was tickled pink finally being with Logan. But of course she was. Who wouldn't be? And the older gentleman must be her father, bringing her to Logan. So I figure they're betrothed." Jessie tried busying herself dusting but found it difficult concentrating.

"How could this be? Why hasn't he told you? He's your best friend. I'd have sworn Logan was in love with you." Rosie shook her head, hands on her hips.

Jessie blushed. So the cat was out of the bag. "We're friends. I love Logan. But he only thinks of me as a friend. That doesn't mean Logan tells me everything. Though I thought he'd tell me something of such great importance as this. Logan deserves happiness and family. I can't give him what he needs. But I want him to be happy."

"How generous of you." Rosie's stern brow indicated she saw right through Jessie's veneer.

Dabbing at tears, her face filled with pain. "I trust you won't speak a word of this. I can't be with Logan and give him a family. Logan deserves someone better than me." Jessie straightened her neck, her head held high. "I love Logan enough to want him to be happy, so if this woman can give him that, more power to her. I'll never begrudge him happiness."

Tears in full bloom now, Jessie sniffed and dabbed. But they kept flowing. When they finally stopped she blew her nose and smiled dismally, thankful Rosie didn't judge her or argue. Rosie could never convince Jessie differently.

Rosie held her at arms' length. "Life sure is a 'hummer.' Ain't it? Just look at the two of us, living proof."

Jessie grinned back and Rosie giggled. Then Jessie giggled back. Before long they were in a hysterical fit of frustrated laughter.

"We sure as hell are. I love you, my sweet friend."

"And I love you."

A few days later on July 8, Governor John Brady arrived for Skagway's first ever Independence Day celebration. Soapy Smith, being a prominent citizen, stood on the podium with the Governor. Jessie stood beside Reverend Brown and Sara on stage. With Soapy as Grand Marshal in the parade townspeople became further angered, seeing it as a political slap in the face.

A boodle of folks showed for the festivities. The streets were lined with proud citizens eager for the community dinner and street dancing following the starchy speeches. Logan, his lady friend and the man assumed to be her father, attended the event. The trio listened to the speeches and milled around the crowd stopping frequently chatting with Logan's friends. Logan introducing the couple to everyone they met. Jessie successfully evaded them in the crowd.

The older gentleman, like Logan, dressed formally. From the distance, Jessie didn't get a good look at him. She still couldn't place him, though something was strangely familiar about him.

The young woman wore a lovely baby-blue gown layered with lace and trimmed in white. Her tiny blue hat crowned atop golden curls, tucked into an attractive chignon. Long finger curls bounced as she walked. One arm remained possessively tucked into Logan's. The other graciously sported an opened parasol protecting her fair skin from the sun. They made a striking couple. The sight of them together soured Jessie's stomach.

Why's she such a damned lovely creature? Logan was much taller. His blond mane was tamed into submission for the time being. The lady's fair skin and blonde hair were the perfect complement to Logan's ruggedly tanned, features. Her gown emphasized a slim waist, perky bosom and petite figure. The gal radiated blissful happiness, possessively clinging to Logan, while Logan escorted her around. Occasionally she rested her head against Logan's arm affectionately, as she beamed into his face.

Jessie was chilled to the bone, despite the warm sunny weather. She couldn't stand much more torture or she would surely die from jealousy.

Logan glanced congenially toward Jessie on stage, smiled sweetly and briefly nodded his handsome head. Then Logan eased his group closer to the stage. *Sakes alive, he's headed our way!*

It appeared Logan intended to introduce his lady love and her companion to the folks milling around on stage.

I've got to get out of here.

Jessie helplessly stewed.

Lawdy! Mercy! I must escape.

Riddled with jealousy and pain, Jessie's insides were 'twistical' eating their way out. They would surely burst through her skin soon. Though Jessie wished Logan happiness, she felt tremendous loss. Watching Logan spark with the adorable female who could make beautiful babies with him was more than Jessie could bear. *Skittles!*

She reached for Sara's wrist whispering into her ear. "I'm not well." Clutching her belly, she lied to the minister's wife. Would God damn her for that?

Sara nodded, clearly sympathetic and patted Jessie's hand as she released her. She was glad the Governor was distracted as he jovially mused with Soapy. There was a chance she wouldn't be missed.

"Lookie there will you. Our Logan has found himself a young lovely. They make quite a couple."

Jessie didn't wait for Soapy's response. His words would likely be offensive anyway. As dull as dishwater, she sidled away from the crowd and headed home before she tossed her oats. Pining for Logan when he was clearly in love with another left her limsy feeling like her belly had taken a lambasting.

So Jessie slipped away unnoticed. Sara would say she was ailing if anyone even bothered asking where she had gotten off to. Likely no one would care.

Lands sakes, if I were a man, I'd head to the nearest saloon and get loaded to the gunwales on bug juice. A gut warmer would taste right nice about now. I've had all I can tolerate of men for the time being.

* * *

Four days later, Jessie sat mending shirts when an urgent banging sounded on her door. She jumped and flung it wide. Logan's face was pale as he danced in place wringing his hands.

Her heart fell silent, afraid to beat. Her belly had taken on a swarm of bumble bees.

"What on earth?" Jessie gasped noticing Logan's labored breath.

Logan's eyes darted from side to side as he assembled words carefully. "We must go immediately to the wharf. There's a peck of trouble. One of my men came to get me. You and I are needed. So come, quick and get a wiggle on. We've got to stop this."

"Why, what's the disturbance about?" Jessie led Logan inside, grabbed her wrap and followed him.

"I'm not exactly sure. You've met Frank Reid, the leader of the vigilantes."

Jessie nodded vaguely beginning to understand.

"They're hell bent on ousting Soapy of control. From what I gather, Frank is leading an angry mob determined to ride Soapy out on a rail and get rid of Soapy once and for all."

"So? He deserves it, as crooked as a dog's hind legs. Why do we care? Let them at him. I say." Jessie rushed following Logan's pace and he hoisted her into his wagon.

"Soapy and some other men are penned in by the mob. Innocent men are in the wrong place at the wrong time. Association with Soapy is likely to get them hurt, or worse. Something bad is going down. We've got to get there. Maybe we can stop it. People like and respect you, Jessie. They might listen if you *can get the opportunity to talk.*"

Really?

Jessie nodded. She fell silent, praying for the town's people. Visions swarmed through her aching head. Wringing her hands in her lap, her mind raced. Gloom swept Jessie into an abyss.

Silent, Logan left her to worrying. He maneuvered the wagon quickly along the bumpy, washboard-rutted thoroughfare through town toward the wharf. The air smelled like a mildewed saddle blanket after it'd been ridden on a sore-back horse in the middle of August. The atmosphere felt palatable filled with the odor of smoke. The angry crowd in full force shouted and screamed obscenities.

Frank, Soapy, a handful of others argued on a platform. The angry mob shouted, urging the fight onward.

Soapy grinning like a baked possum, attempted one last time to convince them he wasn't a threat. His voice sounded so shrill it was like someone forgot to grease the wagon wheels.

The angry mob wasn't buying it, knowing Soapy for the weasel in the hen house he was. Soapy had underestimated their contempt. Things quickly went from bad to worse.

Jessie and Logan pushed through throngs of revelers. She moved in slow motion like a crippled turtle, making slight progress toward a bug dinner.

A terrific gun battle ensued. Mass hysteria broke out. Shots rang out. Screams, gasps and someone cried loudly. The air filled with the stench of gunpowder and doom. Logan shoved Jessie behind him, shielding her from stray bullets with his body. Pushing and shoving the mob flocked the street. Noise loud enough to wake snakes roared from the masses out on the shoot. The wrathy crowd roared, mad as hornets.

Finally gunfire ceased. The hullabaloo quieted to a dull roar. Logan and Jessie made their way through a quieted, suddenly passive crowd. People silently observed remaining fallout and backed away, making room for the injured lying about the wharf.

When they arrived at the front, Frank and Soapy lay on the ground bleeding heavily, having been shot during the battle. Several injured lying nearby.

She shouted to Logan above the rumble of the crowd. "There's Frank. He has been hurt." Jessie rushed to Frank's aide. "Land sakes, someone get the doctor." She screamed to the crowd, kneeling beside Frank.

Turning Frank's body over, a heavy stream of blood gushed onto the wooden platform. A thick, bloody puddle lay beside him.

"Be still, you are bleeding badly. We'll get medical care and you'll be okay."

Ripping her petticoat, Jessie wadded the strip and pressed the wound hard, hoping to stop the gushing blood. Frank screamed then passed out.

Jessie kept pressure on the wound and instructed men standing around. "You there, help us get Frank to the wagon."

The men complied wordlessly, looks of shame on their faces as they loaded Frank. The doctor arrived and examined Frank first.

"It's a gusher. He's gone up the flume. I'm sorry, Ma'am. This sometimes happens when you've gotta' be the biggest toad in the puddle." The doctor turned to check on the injured.

Logan flicked the whip and made tracks back to her house. She sat silently beside him. Her hands trembled.

"You want me to stay with you?" Logan asked when they arrived.

"No, thank you. Go see if anyone else needs your help. And you've got guests to attend to." Jessie shouldn't keep Logan from his love.

Truthfully, she could barely stand looking at him since he'd finally found a woman of his own. Sure as shoot, it hurt too damned much. But Jessie shrugged and hid her agony, glad when Logan finally left.

Lu brought word that the U. S. Army had stepped in and restored order to town. Frank Reid had died immediately in Jessie's arms of his gunshot wound. She attended Frank's hero's funeral at the bone yard on the outskirts of town the day following the riot.

Two weeks later Jessie spoke with Rosie, "Soapy died today of his gunshot, after lingering these past twelve days. Though Soapy was complicated in life, not so much in death."

"What a waste." Rosie shook her head. "However, the town is safer without Soapy Smith in it. Now maybe law and order can be established."

Jessie nodded. "Soapy and Everett were two of a kind, cut from the same cloth. It is fitting that they both died the same way--sad and alone. Soapy is labeled in death as a criminal and an outlaw. Everett at least had been respected, which was of paramount importance to him."

"Soapy's funeral is tomorrow." Rosie gazed out the window. "I will not attend."

CHAPTER 27

No sign of Logan's woman or her father.

She sat in her living room dazed as though dreaming. The world appeared oddly soft, not solid. Everything swam in a misty haze engulfed in an odd dimension parallel to the world Jessie lived in. She must be dreaming. Ever since Logan's woman came to town, she felt as though simply going through the motions as expected. Fragile as a piece of fine china, she might shatter at the least vibration.

Something would snap soon. Jessie's world would resume familiarity. But it never happened.

I'd best continue this odd dream in bed where it belongs.

Jessie woke the next day full of vitality. She had a revelation and felt happier than she had in weeks about a decision she had made.

Jessie walked the short distance to the Red Onion. She closed her eyes and breathed deeply gathering strength.

"Be still my heart." Jessie swung the doors wide as her heart gushed full. She held her breath at gasps from inside and entered the saloon going straight to the center of the room.

Piano music halted. Dancers on stage froze in place. Raucous laughter and chatter ceased as the rowdy tavern hushed to a sudden eerie quiet. The barkeep circled from behind the bar, rushing to Jessie's side. "Madam, you can't be here. 'Cause this ain't no place for a proper women. You gotta go." He pointed to the doors.

Jessie stared with determination. "Sir, I beg your pardon, but I'll stay as long as I see fit. I own this establishment."

The stunned bartender's eyes went wide. His mouth hung open, speechless. Rosie sprinted down the steps from the stage where she'd been performing and rushed to Jessie's side.

"Mistress Blackstone, you mustn't be here." Rosie must've figured she had lost her mind. Jessie had in a way.

She rocked her head one way and another then gently touched Rosie's flushed cheek.

"I came for you, sweet Rosie. You're coming with me. So gather anything of importance. You're not coming back to this awful place. You are moving into my house. And hell, Honey, don't call me Mistress Blackstone. Call me Jessie."

"Have you lost your senses? I can't do that. I belong here." Rosie whispered, her shoulders sinking hard, making her smaller.

"You absolutely don't belong here, my dear friend. You're done with this place. So do as I say." Jessie pointed toward the doorway to the stairs. "Go get your stuff or you're leaving without it."

Hands on hips, Jessie slanted her head meaning business, not to be deterred. Rosie shrugged and went upstairs doing her bidding. The men in the bar continued staring. With Jessie standing in the center of the barroom without a care in the world like she had spent every day being ogled by miners in a brothel barroom, they whispered quietly among themselves.

Rosie returned with a carpetbag, her coat across her arm, and followed. Jessie swung the doors wide then turned to the tavern interior.

"As you were, gentlemen," Jessie smiled sweetly and followed her friend out.

"What the hell's going on? Have you lost your mind?" Rosie walked swiftly, as they strode toward home.

"You're done with that life. You're living with me."

"I can't live with you. It would be unseemly since I'm a whore and you're a lady. It would destroy your status in town."

"Pfffttt, poppycock. I've no standing in town. People barely realize I exist. I don't care for their ruminations because they don't care about me. But I care about you, my friend. You're a lady. Your whoring days are over."

"I'd love living with ya. It don't matter a smidgen. Because I can't depend on ya supporting me. I ain't no slacker. I gotta earn my own way."

Jessie stopped in front of her door and put hands to hips.

"Very well. I need your help. I trust you. Most of my life I depended on someone else to take care of me, never figuring I could make it on my own. That's what Mama and Everett wanted me to believe. Like it or not, I'm on my own now. I have been for some time. I've been taking care of myself and seeing to the security of those employed by my businesses. Let me take care of you. I want to hire you, Rosie. It's high time I get some help. You can be my assistant." Jessie blushed. "As you may know, many people depend on me for their livelihood. I can't bear letting them down. But it is a huge job and I can use your help. Please say yes."

"Yeah the uppity old schmuck you married was successful. Everett's hands were in every profitable venture around. You've done a right fine job continuing to build those businesses, though it is a taxing task." Rosie's eyes glistened with moisture.

"That Everett did. Now all those people need me for their means of getting by. I've got to take care of them. But it's a lot to manage. I need help. Please help me, Rosie."

Rosie gaped proudly. "Of course but what can I do?"

"I need someone I trust managing the books. I am an extremely wealthy woman. I could own this whole damn town if I'd a mind to. I've a lot of paperwork to keep track of. So help with that if you will. I'll provide you home, food and salary. Please do it . . . for me."

Rosie threw her arms around her friend. "I absolutely can and will. I can write, read and got me some numbers learning in school. I can help ya with all 'o it."

"Good. It's settled. We'll convert the extra bedroom into an office to share. Go pick out which bedroom you want." Jessie swatted Rosie's behind and they both giggled.

CHAPTER 28

Early on a cool spring morning, Rosie delivered mail to the ship sailing for Dawson City. Lu hadn't yet arrived. Chatter sounded out front of Jessie's house.

Logan, his woman and her pa approached the porch. Jessie froze beside her upstairs office window, silently listening to conversation below. She sneaked a peak from behind sheer curtains. Her heart pounded in her ears. Blood in Jessie's veins turned to ice water.

"We're gonna be late for the ship," the young lovely argued impatiently.

"Nonsense, this won't take long. Jessie is my friend. I want you to meet her before settling in at Dawson City. It's been such a hullabaloo since you arrived, I've had no opportunity to introduce you."

"Yes, there's been a lot going on in Mistress Blackstone's life since we arrived. There was the riot and that Frank fellow's funeral. I also heard that Mistress Blackstone arranged to sell her share of the Red Onion this week." The blonde cooed in a purring voice capable of sweetening the harshest coffee better than honey. Even though it was difficult hating the woman, Jessie was inclined to.

It appeared the town rumor mill had gone out about liquidation of the tavern. With Soapy out of the picture, Jessie had no more qualms about selling it. Being a profitable venture, it was snapped up quickly by another business man in town.

"The woman has been through the mill, for sure." The older gent spoke in a familiar voice Jessie still couldn't place. "I've been looking forward to seein' her again." The gravelly voice growled.

So I should know him. Clearly he knows me.

Logan knocked loudly. "I hate leaving town without saying goodbye. Jessie has been consumed with work. I've been overloaded at the mill since the riot. But I don't want her thinking I've deserted or slighted her."

"Nonsense, I'm sure Mistress Blackstone is capable of handling things in your absence. You have made sure he mill is covered. Mistress Blackstone doesn't need you for anything other than that." The young lady's argument sounded petty as she gripped Logan's arm with a gloved hand and patting his bicep with the other. Her actions brought home once again what a striking couple they made. The female's silver blue traveling dress with matching hat were a perfect match for Logan in his best suit. Logan's muscles bulged against the well-tailored jacket. When no answer came to their knocking, the older gentleman patted Logan's back. "We must go. The ship is almost ready to set sail. We can't be late."

Logan hesitated until the lady tugged on his arm playfully. The familiarly proved they knew each other well. But of course they did. Lovers would.

"Come on, sweetie. The Mistress is either out or asleep. We must get going." She teasingly giggled patting Logan's firm jaw. "I can hardly wait to get to Dawson City and complete wedding arrangements."

Jessie slapped a hand across her mouth as she coughed, gasping for breath. A lump lodged securely blocking her windpipe. She leaned against the wall for support. Her knees threatened to drop her weight being too much for them to hold. Frozen, she focused on breathing as the group chattered.

I mustn't be discovered snooping.

Finally Logan gave up and they left.

It's true.

Tears streaked along her face. Logan was preparing to marry his woman and settle in Dawson City. But at least with them living in Dawson City, Jessie wouldn't be forced to befriend Logan's bride and endure them flaunting their love in front of her every day.

CHAPTER 29

Over breakfast one cool May morning Rosie's head shook as she read the paper. "Dawson City has exploded to twenty thousand citizens. It's easy getting there by the newly established waterway."

"Yep, and I'm happy you decided not to move there."

"Me too. I'd miss you too much. This article says that tourists have begun flocking here to learn what the fuss is about and explore this new frontier. These travelers have no inclination to dig for gold. They are simply curious about our environment and come to enjoy what Alaska offers."

"Can you imagine . . . tourists no less?" She giggled impressed that their itty-bitty part of the vast world had become worth attracting tourism.

"I wondered if law and order would ever reach us here in the wilds. It came quickly, once Soapy was out of the picture." Rosie sat a plate of biscuits and caribou gravy in front of her.

"Indeed. Civilization is now firmly established in our neck of the woods." Jessie's satisfied grin went straight to her eyes as she poured coffee.

Rosie eyed her reaction. "I hear Logan accompanied his guests to Dawson City."

Jessie hesitated measuring her words. "Indeed. It seems he had made arrangements to take the young woman and her pa to Dawson City. Logan trained and put Ben in charge of the mill. I met with Ben. He is quite capable of handling things, at least until Logan returns. Though I doubt Logan will stay for long. Considering his woman is in Dawson City, Logan will be eager to go back permanently to be with her." Jessie tried smiling and appearing upbeat but inside her heart was withering like a tomato left on the vine after a thick frost.

"So Logan and his sweetheart won't live here? That is good. It would be too difficult for you." Rosie's brow tented and her eyes filled with sympathy as she cut through the façade.

Jessie blushed. "Logan will likely stay here only long enough to teach Ben whatever he must learn to manage the saw mill permanently. Logan promised Ben it would be in time for the next wilderness venture for lumber."

Jessie sipped coffee trying to manage her erratic aching heart. She ignored Rosie's implication that she would be hurt by witnessing Logan with his woman.

Change the subject, before I blubber like a baby.

"Skagway is settled nicely into a thriving metropolis. Soapy's gang has been eliminated. I'm happy it's more peaceful and no longer afraid to venture out exploring." Jessie had taken a newfound interest in her thriving city. "I love everything about Alaska."

Rosie patted Jessie's hand then dug into her breakfast. "You thrive on the town's energy."

"I admire all the resilient, vibrant characters inhabiting this land of dreams. These are people with true grit who bravely set out into the unknown exploring a fantasy. Whether it resulted in the form of gold nuggets or a thriving business, they're strong enough to endure, persist, prosper and flourish. These hearty people handle brutal weather conditions and enjoy whatever nature throws in their paths."

Jessie's old enthusiastic spark came alive. Her child-like spirit was born again.

"A land of dreams 'tis, indeed." Rosie laughed.

"I've grown slowly with the town. I have melded into its core. Skagway is as much a part of me as I am of it."

After finishing, they stepped outdoors and Jessie inhaled clean, fresh air. A salty ocean breeze combined with pine from the vast valley. Contentment filled Jessie's soul.

"Isn't this the most idyllic setting for our quaint, picturesque town? The broad beach lines one side and the spectacular mountains span the other, surrounding us like arms of a loving parent."

"It certainly is heaven on earth, at least to me." Rosie slipped an arm around her friend.

"'Trampousing' about town is a luxury; now the streets are safe, being absorbed in the smells and sounds of our lively wilderness community."

Rosie giggled. "You talk like you're describing a lover."

"It's all I've got. This town and my friends like you and Lu. You are my family. You are my love."

"What about Logan? Logan is your friend. You're young enough to remarry and have a family."

"Yes, Logan is my friend. But I'll never remarry nor have children. I have relinquished hope for such things."

"Why? You might find someone else."

"I'm afraid to consider it. I feel old in a way, having lived so much. My sordid past haunts me. Having been married, lost two children, become widowed, fallen in love, and lost the one man I'd even consider being tied to again--I don't have it in me."

"That's too bad. You're too young to give up the ghost. I'd adore finding, loving and growing old with a man. It takes a certain kind of fellow to forgive what I've done, however." Rosie's face saddened.

"Yes, Rosie. Don't I know it? But you're a good woman. Surely there's a good male out there who will understand that."

Rosie looked doubtful.

* * *

As the town became nonviolent, Jessie ventured out more. Finally free, she strolled along streets in town. Frequently she stopped to talk with shop owners and chatted with people she encountered.

Jessie began recognizing residents, discovering she enjoyed their company. Frequenting local cafés and restaurants for tea or a slice of pie, she swapped recipes with the cooks. Pleasant and friendly, Jessie became known in town, building a reputation as a good neighbor and generous friend.

She tried explaining to Rosie. "I am Everett's widow, an elusive oddity in town. I present a curiosity to many. But Skagway is busy with people moving in and out quickly. So many residents never gave me any weight."

"Most people have embraced you and you have finally integrated into the community. Your friendly nature puts people at ease allowing friendships to form."

Thank you, Rosie. That is sweet of you to say. For the first time ever, feel a sense of belonging."

Logan had been absent from Jessie's life for a while. "Rosie, you should have seen me hiding from Logan and his people. My cowardice was shameful. But I'm glad I managed to avoid meeting Logan's woman before they'd taken the new waterway to Dawson City. I simply couldn't bear her giving me that sugary smile of hers."

"Logan returned sooner than we anticipated." Rosie reminded Jessie.

"That is true, Rose. However, since then Logan has been consumed with work. He took a team of men venturing into the forest for lumber. And Logan has been teaching Ben, I assume to take over when he's gone for good. He's probably anxious to return to his lady love." Jessie had avoided the lumber mill completely.

Instead, she immersed herself in managing her businesses.

"It has been a long, uphill road making your way in a man's world." Rosie spoke proudly. "You have worked diligently. You are finally earning tolerance and respect from some of your male peers. "

"Yes, and it has been all-consuming."

"Don't you miss having Logan around?" Rosie cocked a brow eyeing Jessie skeptically. The sad pit of her stomach rumbled in answer. "I do. But Logan and I are still friends, if distant ones. I don't doubt Logan's friendship. I could count on him if need be. But I couldn't bear being around Logan with his woman. So I am glad he is moving with her to Dawson City." Jessie's heart broke. "It hurts too badly picturing Logan with that woman." Logan would leave soon to go marry his lady love.

Skittles! No . . .

* * *

On Jessie's way home from the wharf a sassy, young woman attempted rescue of her skirts from the muddy street, disembarking from a wagon. The gal politely instructed hotel staff where to take her trunks that had been deposited onto the wooden sidewalk. The lovely woman spoke English with a hint of Irish brogue. Her glistening, green eyes and pale skin were set in a crown of flashy, red hair. Flaming curls were topped by a feathered hat that matched her merlot colored, velvet wrap. The vivacious woman provided a curiosity Jessie couldn't ignore.

"Hello, you must be new in town."

The beauty beamed surprised. "Hello." She smiled taking Jessie's hand and giving her a sideways assessment.

"I'm Belinda LaRooney. It's nice meeting another American woman here."

"Welcome, Belinda. I'm Jessie Blackstone. You're right about women, though numbers are growing steadily. Menfolk are finally bringing their ladies here to live." Jessie shook Belinda's gloved hand.

"Blackstone, are you related to Everett Blackstone, the owner of this hotel? He's quite the entrepreneur. They say his hand is in almost every profitable venture in town. So he's my inspiration."

Jessie laughed at the fairly accurate description of the scalawag who committed the travesty of a gold rush. If Everett and his cohorts hadn't propagated the rumor of a tremendous gold find in the Klondike, all this never would've happened.

Their conspiracy did the trick. California had been ridden of the unpopular element left from the spent California Gold Rush. And Alaska was populated with thousands of American citizens. All the while Everett's and now Jessie's wealth boomed amassing an incredible fortune. Yes. Everett's scan had left Jessie set for life. And his associates had profited likewise.

"You could say that." Jessie grinned guardedly, not about to share everything with this lovely Irish-American woman. "He's gone now. As Everett's widow I own the hotel. It was only started when I arrived in Skagway. So I took over finalizing construction."

"I'm sorry for your loss. May I invite ya ta lunch at the hotel restaurant? I'd enjoy getting acquainted. You're a true pioneer. I want ta hear how you, as a white woman, survived."

"Welcome to our fair city, Belinda. I'd be honored to lunch with you. We can eat at the restaurant or I can cook you something at my house."

"Wonderful." Belinda beamed decisively. "Tis settled." Belinda flew off to get checked into the hotel, calling across her shoulder as she entered. "Meet me in half an hour in the hotel restaurant. Lunch's on me."

"I look forward to it."

Over lunch, Belinda confided, "I'm destined for Dawson City. Skagway is merely a stopover on me journey. Darlin, I plan ta become the wealthiest woman in Alaska. Me intention is ta be ta Dawson City what Everett was ta Skagway. I'll own the town."

"It's an extremely treacherous journey, taking a minimum of six weeks if you go across land."

"Yes. We're traveling across the mountains. I'm prepared for the trek. We'll be there before cold weather."

"How will you earn a living?" Jessie leaned on her palm curiously.

"I designed long, lightweight tubes. We'll pull 'em behind us o'er the mountains. They're full a things rare and luxurious. Women a Dawson City will line in the streets ta buy me fine merchandise I bring in me tubes. Since the contents are light weight, they are worth a hundred times their weight in gold. Gals will pay whatever I ask ta purchase me goods. These tubes will set me up immediately with working capital ta start other businesses."

"What on earth is inside them?" Jessie shook her head confounded.

Leaning on the table and whispering, Belinda warned, "Promise you'll not tell a soul." Jessie nodded and leaned forward. *What could be so hush-hush?*

"Your secret's safe with me." Jessie would never betray a confidence or jeopardize Belinda's plans and friendship.

"My tubes are stuffed full of filmy stockings and silky lingerie. I'll sell these scandalous, glamorous garments at exorbitant prices. Ladies of Dawson City are starved for feminine apparel and will adore me lacy treasures."

Belinda giggled with glee at the prospect, clapping her dainty hands. Her broad grin exposed gleaming, glacier-white teeth.

"I'm sure they will." Jessie snickered at the idea of females standing in a long row waiting for the opportunity to purchase naughty goods.

"What an ingenious plan. It takes a woman of insight to recognize such a delightful opportunity."

"Absolutely," Belinda toasted with iced tea. "The sale of these frilly items should net several thousand dollars. I'll parlay that into much more. I brought cooking gear and a tent to open a restaurant. All I need are food supplies, which I can purchase from locals. Next, I plan ta establish an outfitter shop and a construction company. I've established a deal in the works ta purchase forest land supplying me saw mill and lumber company, and supporting me construction business with wood. Dawson City's booming and needin' my services. I'll leverage the growth and make a fortune." Belinda chuckled heartily as red curls bounced when she animatedly spoke.

"I'm sure you'll be successful. You're ambitious, fearless and industrious, with a well-honed plan and a shrewd mind. You'll no doubt achieve your goal." Jessie saluted. "As much as I hoped you'd stay in Skagway, I wish you well."

"Tell me about your escapades. It must be some mission, takin on your husband's estate."

"Let's say the shipping consortium had a hard time getting used to my presence. Those old coots fought tooth and nail and balked, until they realized I wasn't surrendering my shares. I listened respectfully as they discussed matters at meetings. I learned best I could, until finally, they began lowering their guards. I proposed purchase of new ships and those we set standards for existing ones, making our valuable cargos safer, protecting our investment and contributing to the bottom line, which of course, is their main concern. I'm proud of my achievements. It gave me a feeling of empowerment and immeasurable fulfillment."

"So true, men don't like a woman thinking for herself, much less telling them what they should do. The way to their hearts is definitely through their wallets." Belinda spiked a big piece of steak and chewed. "I quoted facts and provided data that other companies are expanding. They listened. Because of steel the size of the prize is enormous. The shipping industry is booming off the Pacific Coast. We simply can't afford being left behind by competition like the W. H. Mitchell Company from San Francisco. In the last ten years sixty nine vessels have shipped a hundred ninety eight thousand tons in this region, with three hundred vessels. Most make round trips full of cargo, shipping not only natural resources, but also salmon and other items like furs from the frozen north. So as a result of my argument, we ordered four new ships."

The woman clapped in glee. "You proposed a way ta manage the vessels in disrepair?"

"Indeed, I did. My argument about cost proved helpful. There's also the safety factor. Our ships are costly and expensive. But cargo is high valued. So our ships must be top notch and in good operation to be in on the ground floor of booming tourism in the northwest. We can't afford for one of them to go down."

"So what're ya doing?"

"We selected ten of our best engineers and two board members to devise a check list. Whenever a ship comes into port, before it's reloaded with passengers or cargo it goes through an extensive safety check."

"That's brilliant." Belinda took Jessie's hand. She capped Belinda's with hers, making the connection with her new friend and warming Jessie's heart.

"Thank you, Belinda." Belinda's eyes gleamed with moisture. "I understand the rail opens soon. The post will carry mail frequently between our towns. So let's exchange letters and stay in touch. It'd mean the world to me. It is rare meeting a woman who thinks like I do. Most aren't interested in business at all. Ain't it fortunate we met?" Belinda recognized that Jessie was smart and capable. But not used to such esteem, Jessie's insides tingled in glee hearing this brilliant woman considered her a peer.

"That would be wonderful. I'll never forget you, Belinda. Plus I'm excited about your venture. I understand what you're doing and why. I can't wait to learn of your exploits. I look forward to your letters." Enthusiasm filled Jessie's voice.

"I'll certainly share them with you. Please keep me informed of the latest Skagway gossip." Belinda winked.

It was a joy being out in public fearlessly meeting people. Jessie was grateful for this blessing and felt her soul healing. She had much to consider.

Belinda seemed eagerly meeting the devil head-on. She was conquering Alaska, bravely reaching out. Belinda grabbed life by the balls. Could she be as brave and true to herself? Could Jessie act powerful and courageous for the first time ever?

She had done right by Everett. She had shown proper respect playing the grieving widow, as expected by custom. That was enough.

It was Jessie's time to shine.

But what did she want from life? In the back of her mind, Jessie had assumed Logan would play a large part in her future. But like everything she loved, Logan had come and gone with the brutal Alaskan wind.

What now?

Later Jessie tried explaining to Rosie. "I have learned business and survival in this frontier town. I'm no longer the naïve girl bought and sold by Mama in New Orleans. I am not the young woman who became a willing victim as Everett's abused wife. When Everett married me, I understood nothing of life, because in my miniscule world women, sex and life were cheap. I was convinced I was cheap and worthless like Mama said. I believed her. So Everett continued devaluing me and convinced me I wasn't worthy, even as I matured and learned to be a lady. So I remained a victim blinded by his lies. But now I've grown beyond that. It's clear now. I'm smarter, more resilient, self-sufficient and capable."

"I agree. You're growing more independent. You have proved yourself a shrewd businesswoman and a force to be reckoned with. It seems something wounded inside you has finally healed." Rosie smiled proudly. "You even act and look different."

"It's a pity that I wasted so much time fearing Everett. I was terrified to challenge his authority, afraid he would toss me out on the street. That seems so long ago. I feel like a different person now. I never had a real home. But I do now. This is my home. I am a part of it. The townspeople, the writers, the Mountie, and all the others who've visited these walls are my friends."

"You're easy to be friends with. I love you like the sister I never had."

"And I love you, Rosie. I want people in my life, people like you, Lu and Logan who bolster my strength and keep me sane. I never had a proper family. You are my family, even though we weren't born to it."

"You're fitting in right nicely with the town folks."

"I'm enjoying it immensely. I am building the life Everett promised me, despite him. However, you know I did everything in my power to create a happy home with Everett. But he refused to try. Everett only wanted me only to bear his children. When I failed him, Everett made our lives pure hell."

"The bastard gave you respectability and not much else. The SOB made you his slave and personal mistress." Hatred burned in Rosie's eyes. "I guess, from desperation and fear, I believed I couldn't make it on my own. Something inside me died with our daughter. I no longer cared whether I lived or died. Everett was gone and so I wasn't afraid of him any longer. But the miscarriage felt like it ripped my spirit out from my body, so nothing remained worth losing. Ain't it funny how one has to hit rock bottom before she can finally grow strong enough to survive?" Jessie chuckled soundlessly as her chest heaved then she cried on Rosie's shoulder.

"You understand me like no one else can." Jessie smiled through happy tears. "We share a common bond. I'd give my life for you."

Rosie brushed a stray tendril from Jessie's forehead. "As I would for you." The two women held each other at arm's length. "So what'll you do now?"

"Go on living, I guess." Jessie eyed Rosie curiously. "What do you mean?"

"Somehow I always figured you and Logan would be together."

"That ain't to be. Logan has a woman. They're planning a future, talking wedding plans. He'll go to her for good before long."

"Won't you fight for him?" Rosie placed her hands on hips defiantly.

Jessie glanced at the ceiling then back. "I never cheated with Logan. We were only friends when Everett was alive. I enjoyed his company, but that was all there was to it. Make no mistake. Logan's the love of my life, though I have no right to a man such as him. Loving Logan is like stopping an unrelenting avalanche. I couldn't help loving him."

"You were faithful to the end. You honored Everett in life and death. You were a good wife to that arsshole. Everett didn't deserve you."

"Yeah and look what that loyalty got me. I'm a widow and alone. Logan has fallen in love with another. So I've lost him for good. She will be a better woman for Logan, more the kind of wife he deserves. Logan is happy. That's what matters." Jessie tried looking peaceful with her decision, but doubt and sorrow were clearly written on her face. She could see it reflected in Rosie's eyes.

Rosie's brow rose suspiciously and her head shook. "Wow, that's a load of stupidity."

Jessie wiped and laughed through her tears. It was just like Rosie to call her on her crap. "I'd do anything for Logan."

"That is the dumbest thing I've ever heard. You should fight for Logan, if you love him so much." Rosie laughed.

"You're right. It physically pains me, but I want Logan's happiness. He deserves it." Jessie wiped a tear and took a deep breath.

"Well, he ain't married yet. The poor man's sleeping alone. So it ain't over. If you love Logan, fight for him." Rosie glared, hands on hips, her eyes holding a dare.

Jessie laughed out loud at the bold thought she hadn't considered. "I won't come between Logan and his woman. I wouldn't have let Logan break up my marriage. So I can't do that to him. Besides Logan knows I'm free and has made his choice."

"You won't leave town if Logan moves his wife here?"

"I'll never leave. I love this bustling town full of spunky people. This beautiful place, the delightful sea air and tremendous forest walls surrounding the town sustain me." Jessie leaned on the window sill. "I respect the big 'ole, hungry bear who stole my pies. I am fascinated by the distant wolves skulking along the tree line. A killer whale cresting icy water's surface in the bay spewing magically from its spout makes my heart sing. Eagles spreading majestic wings scouting for prey soar over my home, blessing it. The enchanting, rangy awkward bull-moose drinks from my pond living at peace with me. All these things Alaskan are a part of me. I can't give it up."

Rosie grinned from ear to ear. "I know how much you cherish your home."

"Skagway is my home in every sense. I finally have a real home."

Jessie glanced around the perimeter where wilderness surrounded her like a warm hug. Glaciers and snow-topped mountains reigned in the distance. Majestic backwoods and wildlife within it demanded respect. The ocean breeze blew from crystal clear water in the sterling cove, surrounded by sandy beach bay.

Home.

"What happened to you today? You're different?"

"Nothing to worry about. I simply came to a realization. I met a fascinating woman whose gumption inspired me. I faced the devil I knew, haunting me even after his death. He's no longer a threat ruling me. I have let the past go." Jessie beamed.

Rosie nodded, putting her hands to hips. "Hon, personally, I'm happy the bastard's gone. By letting the past go, are you willing to forgive yourself your heritage? You owe yourself the respect you show others, Jessie. You must learn to love yourself."

"I forgave Everett for the way he treated me. Harboring anger against him only hurt me. Everett feels no pain from it. Everett lived in a hell of his own creation. He tried quelling his demons by hurting me. But Everett only punished himself more by living a miserable life."

"You don't hate him?" Rosie's brows flew up, eyes wide, mouth open.

"No and I never wished him dead. Everett hated himself enough as it was. Everett is free from the devils haunting him. So am I. Forgiving lifted a tremendous weight from my shoulders. For the first time I'm truly free."

"You're an exceptional person. Not many would be so merciful. I couldn't do it."

Jessie felt as though an aura of light surrounded her. Her excitement was contagious.

"I was convinced I couldn't make it on my own. I believed I owed Everett my life and needed him. I don't. I'm grateful for what Everett brought to my life. But I've punished myself for my sinful past. It's high time I forgave myself."

CHAPTER 30

Jessie woke startled by pounding on her door. Sleepy eyed, she jumped from bed, stepped into slippers and grabbed her dressing gown. Lu hadn't arrived yet for the day, but would let herself in through the kitchen. So it couldn't be Lu. It was still too early for the sun to crest the mountain tops. The bay lay foggy beyond the house. So blurry-eyed, Jessie met Rosie in the sitting room wrapping her robe tightly.

"Who in tarnation could be in such a hurry so early?" Rosie lit a lantern.

Jessie rushed to the door, unbolting it. One of Logan's lumberjacks stood on her porch. Recognizing him, she couldn't recall his name. He was young, about eighteen, tall and lanky with arms well-muscled from work. His snug shirt displayed a firm chest and flat belly. Then he removed his cap, holding it to his chest fidgeting nervously. He frantically panted like he'd run a long ways.

"I apologize for waking you, Ma'am. I am Richard Smith. I work at the mill. I wouldn't impose if it weren't an emergency. I came to fetch you. There's been an accident. Please come to the mill. We need your help."

Jessie laid a gentle hand to the desperate boy's chest, hoping to calm him. He attempted a weak smile as he gulped air.

"Please, come quick. I'm fetching the doctor now. Mister Logan needs you, and we . . . we . . . all do."

Richard whirled to leave then glanced back, making sure she understood. So Jessie nodded, a dazed expression on her face, and he fled the porch in a flat run toward the main street. Jessie closed the door turning to Rosie, who'd stood behind her listening with worry on her face. Neither spoke, but ran to their rooms to dress. Quickly slipping off her robe and gown, she grabbed the first dress found, not bothering with all the undergarments convention required. She slipped it on then having slept in wool socks, Jessie stepped into mukluks and sprinted out the door. Rosie followed in in her footsteps.

Jessie absentmindedly ran a hand through her tousled hair. Her appearance didn't matter. Logan needed her quickly. So the women sprinted the short distance to the mill.

Men zipped to and fro with purpose. The air filled with trepidation. Jessie consciously made herself breathe, hoping she wasn't swallowing the scent of doom surrounding the frantic men. They had been in the wilderness downing trees and weren't expected back for a few days.

What emergency could possibly require Jessie's help? Where in the hay was Logan?

Nervous men noticed the women standing in the door. Their eyes filled with concern. Sudden quiet enveloped the room as Jessie stepped into the office she had rarely set foot in there before, having left it to Logan's management.

Jessie looked for Logan's familiar face. Her head darted around with no success. A sense of tragedy overwhelmed her.

A combination of frantic disorder and mourning prevailed. The crew avoided looking directly at Jessie, causing more concern. With eyes were down-trod, sadness on their faces, a few surrounded several tables.

Finally, a man turned greeting them. The rest went about helping injured friends. "Mistress Blackstone, thank you for coming. We need all the help we can get."

The air had been stolen, sucked from the room. Her lungs went on strike, refusing air. She closed her eyes and struggled for calm as her head spun. She leaned back and sucked her lower lip in biting it, waiting for her world to stop whirling. Jessie wobbled as though fainting. So she focusing on breathing, and steadily composed herself.

Get ahold of yourself, Girl.

Rosie saw Jessie was consumed with panic, grabbed her and slipping an arm around her shoulders forced a smile. Opening her eyes, Jessie's false bravado fooled no one. She bit her lip, not finding her voice. Her hands shook.

Breathe . . . you can do it, in, out, slowly. Finally Jessie felt better.

"Where's Logan?" A scratchy voice quietly crackled. Was that her voice? Would her weak, wobbly legs hold her weight? Her shoulders slumped and her eyes locked on two tables. Feet stuck out from beneath blankets. Men parted, giving Jessie a view of two injured men, lying there. The two other tables held men completely covered except for their boots. So staring at the boots, she tried recognizing them, but didn't. However that meant nothing.

Dropping Rosie's hand, Jessie walked to where Ben, Logan's close friend, lay with his eyes squinted closed. Ben's face squirrelled oddly, withstanding pain. Jessie picked Ben's hand up, and he opened his eyes barely attempting to sit. Her firm hand gently pushed Ben back down.

"Lay still, Ben. Please rest until Doctor Adams gets here."

Ben sighed relieved and his hand trembled in Jessie's. His heart pulsed--a strong, steady rhythm into her palm.

"Where's Logan?" Jessie's eyes clouded with fear.

Ben shook his head, doubtfully. "They rushed the four of us here. We filled the wagon. The first escaping massive snow drifts." Ben winced. "The search party's looking for survivors. They'll find him, Mistress Blackstone. I'm sure of it." Ben's expression looked grim.

Her gasp startled men around her.

"Please, Ben, call me Jessie. So there's hope. That's good. They'll find Logan."

Please let him be alive.

In the meantime, these men needed her. The hope Logan was still alive must help her remain unruffled. She was responsible for this crew as her employees. With Logan out of the picture, Jessie was all they had. That left no time to fall apart.

There was work to do. Concern filled her face. Her brow furrowed, and she sighed before speaking softly to the injured lumberjack. Jessie hadn't been aware of holding her breath until she gasped for air.

"Where do you hurt, Ben?"

"My arm's broke. I'm sure. I have a bum leg that I hope isn't broke, too. My head hurts something awful, but my vision is fine."

"That doesn't sound too bad. Your injuries should heal good as new. Doc will be here shortly." Jessie grinned as Ben's sullen, damaged face swelled where he would soon have a beauty of a shiner.

"There's no easy way saying it. Some didn't make it." Ben's eyes filled with moisture he was trying to restrain. He trembled. "It was awful. We're lucky to be alive. Four at least are dead. We were caught in an avalanche--a freak accident."

Slam! Jessie's heartbeat shut down. Logan could easily be one of them.

Dead.

NO! Stop.

"I don't understand how this can be. What happened? Logan will be here soon and fine. He must be." Jessie refused to consider anything less. Ever so gently, she examined Ben's damage. One worker brought a chunk of ice wrapped in a handkerchief. Ben applied it gingerly to his swollen forehead.

"Tell us the whole story, Ben." Rosie cooed softly, standing close.

"We were camped at the foothills of a mountain; sleeping in tents, when a loud crack . . . a roar filled the air. We woke to rumbling, like thunder. It was too late to escape the avalanche since the mass of snow and debris rushed down the mountainside. We scrambled for the closest cover. John and I rushed to the base of a boulder, with a couple of others. We sought shelter beneath the rock, hoping it'd create blockage shielding us from the mass rushing toward us. We dove beneath the rock as a tall pine downed by the rushing flood of snow fell across the boulder top, forming a protective tent effect atop us. The avalanche continued piling on top burying us beneath about four foot of snow."

"It took hours, but we dug our way out with hands and pocket knives. It was a long, difficult battle, but finally, we reached air. We expanded the hole until we could crawl out." Ben's face grew grim. "We're grateful we survived. There were four of us beneath the snow-covered tree. Three survived. One appears badly hurt. And Jake and I sustained minor injuries."

"Doc will be here soon." Rosie brushed a strand of perspiration-soaked hair from Ben's forehead reassuringly.

Slowly as though in a trance, despair in her heart, Jessie glanced at the blanket-covered bodies. Ben followed her train of vision.

"John's dead. The tree hit him in the head as it landed across the stone. John must've died instantly. Of course we didn't realize until we opened the hole and let in enough light. In the dark, we couldn't be sure what condition any of us was in. The other body is Jason, who was hit by a rock that crashed down along with snow, tree trunks and all sorts of stuff." Ben hesitated. "There are others, Mistress Blackstone. I mean, Jessie. The search party is still digging for missing men. I pray they find 'em alive."

"No sign of Logan?"

"I didn't see him, but they'll find him. I'm sure of it, because he's resourceful and strong. Chances are he survived." Ben tried being convincing and failed.

Jessie stared in a trance at two dead bodies occupying tables beside Ben. Melancholy filled her heart. Sorrow engulfed Jessie realizing Logan may soon lie there on the table, a blanket covering everything except his grotesquely exposed boots. So speechless, she simply stared in a stupor with her eyes glazed over until a pain in her gut jolted her alert.

Whew . . . breathe . . .

This wasn't the time to collapse and act helpless. Her men needed her. So she shook her head clearing it, stood, smoothed her skirt and jolted blood back into her hands. Gaining self-control, with resolve Jessie moved forward.

"Lord, let them find him alive."

Nature didn't give a hoot what Jessie wanted. The brutality of Alaskan reality had once again taken its toll.

Ben's eyes were locked on Jessie.

"We weren't aware how bad it was until it ended. We were cramped together, frantically digging our way out hoping for survival. So when Jake climbed out, we tied our belts around Damon to get him out. Next we tied our belts around John and forced his body clear. Then they pulled me out." Tears filled Ben's eyes.

"I'm glad you're alive, Ben." Jessie glanced at Rosie, who understood and moved closer to Ben's table to administer to Ben. Men parted so she could stand beside Jake. Jessie avoided John's body, though she clearly viewed it out of the corner of her eye.

"Jake, I'm glad you're safe. We will do what we can to make you and Ben comfortable."

Someone set a bowl of fresh water on the table along with a few clean rags. The women dipped rags and cared for their charges. Jessie tenderly bathed Jake's sweating face and neck, brushing back wet hair. She unbuttoned Jake's shirt and washed dried blood from his chest. Jake weakly smiled, grateful but too exhausted to move or speak.

Rosie did the same for Ben. The women worked diligently, using gentle touches on tender skin. They cooed softly, calming fears of the men.

Helping the injured, provided therapy Jessie needed to calm her spirit. She could make a difference and care for this fellow. She couldn't help John.

But Ben and Jake were her charges now. God willing, they'd become friends. So Jessie vowed to learn the names of her men and get to know those who survived.

Thud!

The image slammed heavy into her belly.

Shake it off. Breathe . . . don't lose hope.

"Mistress Blackstone, you don't need to do this." Jake whispered weakly.

"Nonsense, call me Jessie. Certainly I must help you. Besides, it's good being useful. At least I can make you comfortable until Doc gets here." She gently wiped blood from Jake's forehead. Jake allowed her to administer to him.

Finally Doc Adams and the undertaker burst into the room at the same time, followed by a cold blast of spring air. Jessie moved aside, allowing them access. The undertaker went straight to the covered lifeless bodies.

"Thank you, Mistress Blackstone. I'll take it from here." Doctor Adams reassured the room.

Jake uttered, "Thank you, Jessie." Jake's eyes filled with gratitude and discomfort.

"You're welcome." Jessie smiled sweetly, pushing hair from Jake's forehead before backing out of the way. She surveyed the room full of men milling around.

My men, my responsibility.

She spoke calmly in a quiet, comforting voice. "Please everyone, call me Jessie." Most men smiled and some nodded going about their business. "If you need anything, please come to me."

Jessie and Rosie took seats, hands clasped in their laps awaiting the doctor's prognosis. The undertaker helped a couple of men load their fatally wounded friends onto his wagon, saying he'd be back later if there were other bodies to be buried.

Doc administered to the injured and set Ben's leg. He put splints on it. Doc checked their eyes and bandaged their wounds.

Then Doc announced to the room. "These men will be fine with recuperation. Their injuries should heal."

Everyone in the room breathed a loud sigh of relief. Having taken Rosie's hand in a death grip, Jessie's fingernail prints had embedded in Rosie's palm. She patted it gently and smiled.

"I'm sorry."

Rosie shook her head and whispered. "No worries."

They strode home silently, eager be useful as their minds spun. No words were necessary. The women entered Jessie's house forcefully with a lot of responsibility on their shoulders.

Jessie remained terrified for Logan and the rest, but this wasn't the time for giving into fear. So she buzzed with vitality. Work needed doing and she must come through for her men.

Since Jessie was part of something. She belonged here where she felt needed and loved.

Wow! What a revelation.

She'd finally found her place in life. So glaring at her wardrobe of black she donned a yellow dress with a white apron. Jessie was done with drab mourning clothing. She pinned her hair into a back twisted knot then did her morning ablutions.

Rosie and Lu joined Jessie in the kitchen where they explained the situation to Lu. The three women fried caribou sausage and made gravy, while she baked fluffy biscuits and Rosie fried potatoes and eggs. Then they packed everything into baskets that she and Rosie carried out the door.

"See you later, Lu." Jessie kissed Lu's cheek. Lu blushed, a broad grin exposed jagged teeth.

"Mistress Jessie, you look lovely today."

"Thank you. If you need me, I'll be at the mill." Jessie took the steps and strolled to the lumber mill.

"I no need you. Take care of your men. Lu have lots to do here. Take your time and stay long as you like." Shaking her round head, Lu went back to work.

Jessie had been going through the motions since Everett's death. She had hesitated getting on with life. With business and work as the balm curing what ailed her. It had also provided an excuse for avoiding moving forward.

Jessie had taken a steep path up a slippery slope in the past. But no longer abandoned, scared and alone, she had family, people she cared about and those who needed her. So now Jessie was finally fully engaged in living.

When they arrived at the mill, men continued milling around caring for the injured. Some prepared to join the search party. The women stayed out of their way as they worked, and found an unused table along one wall where they placed the food.

"Come and eat. You must be starving. No one goes back into the wilderness without a good meal in them. So, come and get it." Jessie's order came with a brilliant smile. If she could keep her spirits up, they would as well. And they needed her hopeful and positive.

Bustling about the office the ladies served food and made plates for the injured. Jessie helped Jake with his meal while Rosie fed Ben.

Shouting outside and wagon wheels sounded. They rushed toward the mill office. Everyone turned toward the windows curious about all the commotion outside. As her heart stopped beating, she gasped and sat Jake's plate on his belly. Jake waved her on signaling he could handle it. Jessie was free to go find out what was happening.

A wagon loaded with men stopped at the office steps. Jessie rushed toward the door, followed by the men and Rosie. Flipping it open, she took the few steps to the rutted, muddy ground. Her dress yanked high in an unladylike fashion. Not only were her booted feet exposed, but also much of her lower legs.

Jessie didn't give a hoot.

The men didn't notice.

Jessie focused on one face in the group. Her heart beat so rapidly and strong, it might burst through her clothing.

CHAPTER 31

Logan climbed from the front of the wagon, an injured arm closely held against his stomach. Logan's eyes locked on the vision before him, as the two of them revolved in a world alone. They were unaware and uncaring what transpired around them. Jessie rushed at Logan as though her life depended on it, because it did. Careful not to bump his damaged limb, Logan accepted her with his strong, uninjured arm and circled her shoulders. She leaned into Logan. Her face cradled against his torn, soggy jacket. Tears mixed with the dampness from melted snow.

Jessie's hand lay against Logan's soft, wet shirt. Logan gripped her trembling body tight against him, as though she were his life line.

Six others exited the wagon with the assistance of friends and co-workers. The group glanced at the couple. Most smiled and some blushed in embarrassment at invading such a tender moment.

They made their way into the office where their injuries would be treated by Doc Adams. A few were wet and cold, but all were exhausted.

Jessie expelled a gush of air, grateful at the sight of the empty wagon. There were no dead in this load, only survivors.

For the moment only one man existed in Jessie's eyes. She breathed in his fragrance, having come so close to never seeing those mesmerizing green eyes again, never having those powerful arms around her again, never smelling the intoxicating scent of Logan again. Jessie memorized the moment she'd never forget.

Eventually able to stand on her own, Jessie pulled back gazing into those brilliant pools of emerald shaded by lush, thick lashes. They smiled back at her, telling her Logan still cared. The man she adored was alive.

Logan lit Jessie's world like the northern lights.

"I feared you were '*gone coon.*' I have never been so scared in my life." Through tears of joy, Jessie happily

Grinned.

Logan's hand caressed Jessie's unruly curls and slid around to cup her chin tenderly.

"I wouldn't dare do such a thing. I have way too much to live for."

Time froze, and then Logan showed those adorable dimples. Jessie's insides did a jig.

"I'm sorry I embarrassed you in front of your men." Jessie attempted to pull away. But Logan resisted, keeping her breasts firmly pressed to his belly. Logan's amused smirk puzzled Jessie.

"You could never embarrass me. Don't you know by now how much I adore you? I could shout it to the world. I have bided my time until you were ready. Besides, these are our men, not mine."

"But, Logan, what about your woman?" Jessie tilted her head, furrowing her brow.

"What in tarnation are you talking about? You're my woman and the only one I want. I have no other. I wouldn't consider another." Logan muttered looking completely baffled.

Jessie frowned. "The lovey, young blonde and her father who lived with you last winter, before you took them to Dawson City. I overheard her making marriage plans. You'll be going to her before long, or bringing her back here, once you are married."

Logan threw his head back. His shaggy, damp mane flew in the breeze as he laughed loudly. "Oh Jessie, you are so mistaken, sweetheart."

Logan released Jessie as she pulled away, bracing her feet apart and hands on hips. When he finally stopped laughing Logan placed his big mitts gently on Jessie's shoulders, staring into her distraught, confused face.

"You, my love, are the one woman in this world for me. Long ago in another life I loved Amy. She's gone. Since Amy I haven't looked at another woman . . . after meeting you."

"But, Logan, I . . ." Jessie stammered.

"You're right. The lovely, blonde woman and her daddy stayed at my cabin. I tried introducing you more than once. But you were either ill or not around, so I never got the opportunity. Had you gotten a better look at the man or met them, you probably would've recognized the old gent. My Uncle Wilson Pace was fortunate enough to be seated beside you on the train to San Francisco. Do you remember him? You rescued his pouch of gold."

All smiles, still confused the light began to dawn. "So the woman . . . ?"

Logan laughed heartily nodding. "My cousin Etta Mae--she and Wilson were on their way to Dawson City. Wilson's business partner happens to be Etta Mae's fiancé. He went ahead of them and opened a restaurant in Dawson City. Etta Mae and Wilson were heading there meeting him and have the wedding Etta Mae spoke of. By now Etta Mae has happily married her Justin.

She was as anxious as a long-tailed cat in a room full of rocking chairs to be with him."

All tension melted from her body, and Jessie felt light as a feather. The fog had rolled off, and the sun shone more brightly. Air felt cooler and crisper, more vital and alive. Birds sang love songs in the trees.

"Logan, I've been such a fool. I suspected you loved me as I loved you. But I couldn't allow myself to hope we could be together. I used my situation to avoid finding out. I wasn't ready for another heart break. I insisted on honoring Everett properly and focused on the businesses. I've been such a coward. I should be ashamed. I did all that to avoid trying to claim the one thing in life I truly wanted. I had grown so used to loss and rejection. Everything I desire rips from my grasp, usually at the last minute. I was afraid to want a life with you. I was unable to face the possibility of you rejecting me. I knew I wasn't good enough for you. I wanted the best for you, my love. When the avalanche hit and you weren't in the first wagon, I tried hard being positive. But no matter. I expected the worst. It's what I'm used to."

"No more, my dear Jessie. Those days are over. The past is the past. You and I are alive. We have survived against all odds. This is a new world. You are the only woman for me. I'm never letting you out of my grasp again. You are my woman from this day forward. Got that?" Logan stared sternly.

"So the old gentleman was that stinky prospector on the train? My goodness, he cleans up well. I didn't recognize him all duded up. I sensed something vaguely familiar about him but never suspecting him to be the old miner." She laughed gaily, shaking her head.

"Indeed he does. Wilson is a dreamer, an adventurer at heart. I'm glad he's finally settling down with his daughter in Dawson

City. But there's potential Wilson will get his hands dirty there searching for the mother lode." Logan laughed slapping his leg.

"I'm so sorry. I avoided you and your family on purpose. I spied you hugging and kissing the young woman. Jealousy got the better of me. I couldn't bear meeting your lover. I'm a fool."

"You are my fool, my love. I shall never love another." Logan kissed Jessie's nose and pulled her tighter.

Her smile could've lit the night sky. "Come inside, you need Doctor Adams."

Jessie took Logan's hand and circled it around her waist then led him inside. He possessively kept her close.

She continued leaning into his embrace when Logan took a chair along the wall awaiting his turn. Jessie sat beside her man, their thighs meeting, both needing the other's touch.

She ran her finger reverently along tender skin beneath Logan's black eye. Downward, softly it scanned across his lips, barely touching the sweet skin. An almost wicked grin materialized on Jessie's face.

"You're hurt. Your face is gloriously colorful. Are you sure your head is all right? There's a bump on your handsome forehead that doesn't mar your appearance in the least. It is turning a peculiar shade of green. You have a marvelous black eye." Jessie bolstered Logan's spirits with teasing.

"I'll be fine. The doctor can check me when he's done with the others. I'll heal from my minor injuries. The broken arm will take the longest." Logan leaned his cheek into Jessie's loving hand, which she hadn't removed. She stroked Logan's arm tenderly then reached for his good one and held it gently caressing the palm with her thumb.

If the men were shocked, they didn't show it. Everyone went about their business, as though Jessie and Logan sitting intimately together holding hands was completely normal.

"Do Ben and Jake have family who'll care for them?"

"Ben's sister lives in Dawson City. Don't worry about Ben. I'll take care of him. Ben can stay with me until he recovers."

The room wasn't big enough for privacy. Several men were crammed into the tight space. So every word spoken was heard by all.

Rosie turned her attention from Ben to Jessie. "Jake's wife is on her way here. She'll take care of Jake."

Rosie helped Ben sit up. The two acted comfortable together, friendly, familiar even. How had Jessie missed this?

"That's good. You're a good man. If you and Ben need anything at all, say the word. I'd be pleased to help in any way. As a matter of fact, I'll cook for you. Rosie, Lu and I will bring meals to your cabin until you and Ben recover."

"Thank you. That will be wonderful." Logan broke into a broad smile. "I'm looking forward to it. Your mourning duds are gone. You look lovely, Jessie. There is a glorious spark in your eyes. Something subtle has changed in you. Whatever it is, I like it." Logan hugged Jessie tightly.

The undertaker entered to speak with Jessie.

"Mistress Blackstone, you have my condolences. I'm sorry for the men you've lost." All business, no genuine remorse, he had already taken three additional men brought in dead in another wagon. That made five so far.

No more!

Jessie's heart felt heavy. "Thank you, Mister Forester. I appreciate your service. Please take care of my men. I will pay for everything."

"Yes Ma'am." Undertaker Forester grinned. "Given the warm weather we're having this spring, I recommend quick funerals."

"Thank you, but it's the choice of the men's families. Please clear arrangements with them. Bring me the bills. I will make any decisions necessary for those without families."

"Very well. Bye now. It's still early. Graves need digging." Forester's voice sounded way too chipper for the situation. He took the steps in a sprint.

"He's downright excited at the opportunity. I think there were dollar signs in his eyes." "It's the business he's in. One, undoubtedly, hardens against death in such a profession. So don't take offense." Logan winced adjusting his broken arm.

"We've prepared a meal." Jessie faced the workers. "Those who recently arrived, please eat. You must be famished. May I make you a plate, Logan?"

"That's considerate. I'll eat after the doctor examines me." Logan glowed proudly. "We appreciate your kindness. Thank you, Jessie."

"It's the least I can do. You and these men are my responsibility. I don't take it lightly."

Logan winked. "And I figured you were taken with my charm."

"Well, there is that." Jessie grinned, smoothing hair back from Logan's forehead, taking pleasure in touching him. The sensation of Logan's mane sliding between Jessie's fingers felt better than any gold prospectors could possibly find. It was a pure luxury.

* * *

Correct about his injuries, Logan was released by the doctor. Logan took Ben home with him. The next few days Jessie and

Logan attended funerals for the dead. Three were married. John had a brother, who also worked at the mill. A fifth deceased turned out to be a loner with no family. Jessie met individually afterward with each family, figuring out how best to help them. Two widows moved to the mainland wishing to raise their children near family. She booked passage to the continent. One, a native, stayed at the home she and her husband had built in Skagway. Jessie made sure they all wanted for nothing.

"It's bad enough they lost a loved one. They shouldn't suffer financially, too. These women won't be forced into work in a brothel like you and I did, dear Rosie. They'll be able to feed their children." Jessie caressed Rosie's hand tenderly. "In my charge no woman will suffer as we have."

Logan drew near encircling them both in a hug. "I'm proud of you both. You are a couple of fine women." Logan beamed with pride. Rosie's eyes filled with moisture radiating happiness.

The women delivered meals to Logan's house daily as promised. Ben and Logan seemed to enjoy them immensely and acted happy for the company.

Jessie was over the moon that Logan had survived and came home. Her world had suddenly taken on a new shine that had nothing to do with the brilliant summer sunlight.

Jessie took the opportunity to learn from Ben and Logan. She asked question after question about logging, absorbing whatever knowledge she could.

"Profitability is impressive. I'm glad I kept the operation. I've assured the crew their jobs are secure. The mill will continue as always, under your expert supervision." Jessie gave Logan the smile that came right from her heart.

Logan winked proudly and possessively. He gave Jessie the adorable, sideways intimate grin that always melted her insides to mush. Her face went hot, red blush.

In a rare moment alone Jessie leaned into Logan and whispered. "Logan, I love you with all my heart."

Logan's emerald eyes twinkled with delight. He brought Jessie in for a quick kiss. "I adore you. I want you for my wife. Marry me. Soon."

"There's nothing I want more." Jessie grinned, squirreling her nose and raising her shoulders. "Soon as you're well enough, we can talk seriously about it."

"Talk, hell, I've held off asking you for the past few months, giving you needed time to firmly plant your feet on the ground. I'm done with talking, woman. Let's jump the broom and get it done." Shaking her head, Jessie's curly tresses bounced freely. She now wore them unrestricted about her shoulders, the way Logan liked it. Jessie laughed gleefully. Logan reached for a tress and measured its texture in his fingers.

"My Darling Logan, you understand me too well. You are right. I had something to prove. I had lots to learn. And I discovered I can stand on my own two feet."

"I had no doubt. But you've proven yourself. I'm proud of you. You've done well with your businesses. Not many women could rise in a man's world and be productive. You've honored Everett. You have proved to yourself that you are strong and capable."

"You're right. I believed myself worthless. I needed to know I could make it without letting you assume responsibility for me when Everett died. I wanted you with all my being. I couldn't become your responsibility without finding myself first. Then I believed you'd found another woman, so I was devastated. Thank you for understanding me better than I understood myself. Thank you for being patient, giving me the precious time I needed."

"Things are different now. You're different." Logan's fingers slipped into Jessie's hair, cradling her head.

Jessie kissed Logan's wrist as he held her. Being open with Logan, touching him this way, gave her pure pleasure.

"Yes, they are. I'm optimistic about the future. For the first time ever, I'm confident. I'm on the right path--my path--not one designed by others. I'm on a path of my own choosing. This is my life. Skagway is my home. You are my man."

"Skagway has embraced you too, my dear Jessie. You are an important citizen. I'm impressed that the mayor invited you to help christen the Golden Spike Ceremony tomorrow."

"Indeed, it's quite an honor being invited. The whole town will celebrate the opening of the WP&YR. The rail is finally completed from Skagway to Whitehorse. So the Yukon is now easily accessed." Jessie shook her head in wonder.

"Who else would the mayor have wanted? Too bad the gold rush is beginning to peter out. Many prospectors are rushing north toward Nome to the next big find."

Jessie still hadn't told Logan about the sordid conspiracy Everett had perpetrated, starting the Alaskan Gold Rush in the first place.

"You are coming to the new depot at Second and Broadway when we're cutting the ribbon. We will celebrate with music and food at the new hospital built by the railroad."

"You still haven't answered my proposal. Will you have me?"

How could she resist the twinkle in those glorious eyes? "Of course, Logan. I will be honored to be your wife."

Logan cupped Jessie's face in his hands and kissed her nose. An impish grin took her face. She perked upward so their lips met in a sweet, tender caress neither wanted to break from.

CHAPTER 32

1900

"It's commendable how you've become adept at forecasting and development. You do a great job staying aware of what the public wants and providing plenty of it."

"I couldn't do this without you, Rosie." The women worked companionably in their shared office in Jessie's cabin.

"I'm sure you could. But am glad you didn't want to. I enjoy working with you. Who'd have thought a few years ago that you and I would be trusted with such massive responsibility? Things sure have changed around here the last couple of years. The Skagway of the past is gone forever. More than three thousand people live in our village."

"Time has flown by. Can you believe we've become the first incorporated Alaskan city? That allows property owners voting rights. But of course, being a woman I can't vote . . . yet. Though I own property and businesses. But considering where our town came from, it is remarkable."

Like many women who came to Alaska during this time, they were a breed unto themselves. Incredibly determined, bold, unfettered, and fearless, they lacked inhibition. They catered to no societal restraints. Many having been languished lilies, downtrodden women with invincible spirits.

"Women of Alaska do whatever is necessary." Jessie winked.

"Yes, and generally thrive here more easily than men."

"You and I certainly have. We've accomplished a lot together. I owe a lot to you, Rosie. You're good at what you do. You keep me honest and on top of things."

"Do you ever get lonely, Jessie? There must be more to life than work?" Rosie rested her chin on her hands atop the desk.

"Honestly, I was too busy the last couple years. I never gave it much thought. After the avalanche I realized life is too short and uncertain. Losing those poor men and almost losing Logan scared the bejeezus out of me. Tragedy brought home clearly that I cannot bear life without Logan. It's time I fished or cut bait. Logan is my man. I want him in my life for good."

"Logan and Ben are doing well now and working. But Logan is still sleeping alone. So are you. What are you doing about it?" Rosie's hands went to her hips in a dare stance, glaring at Jessie with a 'get-off-your-butt' look.

"Yep. I've had enough. It's high time I fixed that situation. I'll do it tonight when the men come for dinner. Though Logan proposed and I accepted, we made no specific plans, but agreed to discuss it once they healed."

"It is time you got off your rump. Grab Logan by his 'wanger' and make him yours." Rosie clapped gleefully and grabbed Jessie's shoulders. They danced round like silly children.

Later that sweltering, seventy two degree evening of July, soon after the spring avalanche Jessie, Logan, Rosie and Ben rocked on Jessie's back porch. Filled with a scrumptious meal they leisurely sipped goblets of locally-made wine.

"You two have healed nicely." Jessie topped their glasses off. "Thanks, to you ladies." Ben toasted the blushing women. Ben winked at Rosie.

Ben?

Rosie acted lighter, more carefree, stealing glances at Ben whenever she could. Rosie's eyes held a special spark lately, especially when Ben was around. Rosie frequently watched Ben when he wasn't aware. Sometimes their gaze locked like they communicated without words.

Rosie's was in love. *I should've known.*

Ben invited Rosie for a stroll. Holding hands, the couple walked toward Jessie's favorite forest pathway.

"They look like lovebirds. It's wonderful that Rosie has found a man who respects and loves her as she deserves." Jessie put a finger to her chin, tilted her head and squinted watching the lovers disappear.

"They've spent considerable time together since the avalanche. Ben is smitten. Being a decent, upstanding man and good friend, I'm sure Ben will make a worthy mate for Rosie." Logan followed Jessie's gaze.

"You two beware the big brown bear." Jessie called after their friends.

"We'll be careful." Rosie and Ben waved and laughed.

"I'm happy for them." Jessie settled into her rocker.

"I'm not surprised. Ben used to be one of Rosie's regulars. So Ben is aware of Rosie's past. Rosie is the only reason Ben frequented The Red Onion. He hasn't gone there since Rosie left the life."

"Ben understands how Rosie ended up there. He doesn't hold it against her?" Jessie's eyes filled with concern.

Logan nodded, taking Jessie's chin in his hands. "Ben is a wise young man. Ben spends his free time with Rosie. They have bonded while you ladies nursed us back to health." Logan grinned and wagged his brows lecherously.

The couple was swallowed up by the majestic forest. Her heart overflowed with happiness for her friend.

"They make a lovely couple."

"Are you happy, Jessie?" Logan stared deep into her eyes. He viewed her soul and read her innermost secrets. Then he drew Jessie toward him.

A familiar spark flickered at the contact, surging along Jessie's arm and straight to her heart . . . then lower. She leaned toward Logan like a moth to a flame, indulging in sensations Logan's touch produced.

"I'm happy with you, deliriously happy." Jessie melted into the sensual, deep green eyes she adored. Her future reflected there. "Only one thing could make me happier." She grinned wickedly as the delicious flame shot to her belly and flared directly south. As dew pooled between her thighs, Jessie quivered.

"And what would it be?" Logan smirked.

She leaned more and their bodies fused together. Her lips parted slightly as she swallowed. Jessie's breasts rested enticingly against Logan's lower chest. Her belly lay flat against his midriff. She wiggled wantonly, their eyes never losing contact.

Logan stiffened, welling against the intimacy of Jessie's warm belly. She squirmed, thrilled as the hard heat of Logan responded and grew quickly. She giggled and pressed harder against Logan's rigid erection.

"Um . . . I've made a decision." Jessie's voice was thick and deep, almost a growl. She grinned mischievously biting the side of her lip.

"What would that be, my love?" Logan played along, fondling a curly tress. "I enjoy the way you've started wearing your hair down, free alluring and sexy. I can run my fingers through it and lock them there, never letting you go."

Early evening light caught the golden flakes in Logan's unruly mane. Jessie's fingers raked through it, gently gripping a handful.

"That's precisely why. My goal is bewitching you and never allowing you to regain your senses."

"You've succeeded. Honestly, I'd never resist or stray. So tell me what you've decided." Logan bent sniffing the scent of her hair, kissing her head, drawing back and gazing into Jessie's eyes.

"I've decided I want a man in my life and in my bed." Jessie whispered softly so her breath sent goose bumps welling around Logan's neck. He shivered, holding her tight. His reaction delighted and spurred her on. She wiggled against Logan's jerking manhood wantonly.

"A man, any man in particular?" White teeth sparkled, as Logan chuckled. Logan's throaty laughter vibrated against Jessie's body as her heart skipped a beat. She wagged a brow lustfully.

"There's only one for me, a real man in every sense of the word, the only one who can satisfy me. I'll have no other." Jessie's nose wrinkled.

"Are you sure there is such a man?" Logan played along, tilted his head sideways, furrowed his brow and pretended to consider it.

At arms' length Jessie shamelessly appraised Logan, scrutinizing her prey up and down like a prized pig. Then she pursed her lips and nodded. "One specimen meets my needs right here in Skagway."

"So what are your intentions? Are they pure?" Logan's erection pressed against Jessie demandingly. She wiggled with abandon, quickening Logan's pulse. Logan's breath shallowed to a low pant. Her eyes grew smoky and her voice sounded audaciously sexy. "My intentions are scandalous and indecent. I shall have my way with him. He'll be mine, only mine. He will pleasure me endlessly, faithfully submitting to my insatiable, randy needs. Filling me with his seed, he will take pleasure in my physique, submitting to my every fantasy. He shall enjoy it as much as I, while he makes me laugh and plays with me. He shall work beside me as my partner in all things."

Jessie laughed a guttural sound deep in her throat, lustfully unashamed. She pressed against Logan's rock-hard shaft while their eyes held captive. Involuntary she squirmed in anticipation.

Logan's manhood reacted, hardening until they could stand it no more. Jessie's words inspired lusty visions held at bay for too long. No longer restraining, she was finally ready. Logan could have her and make Jessie his.

"We best go find this man for you. You have an immediate need of him." Logan's composure lost, searing need in his groin reached an unbearable peak. Taking Logan all in, Jessie's looking of longing spoke volumes. Her mouth opened provocatively and she licked her bottom lip. Tingles surged through her spine and she shivered, swooned and floated in a sea of yearning desire. "I do have an urgent need. Take me to my bedroom, my darling Logan." Begging for fulfillment, Jessie's lips reached upward accepting Logan's, as they consumed her.

Logan scooped her into his arms and lunged toward the door. Jessie flipped it open as she had her heart.

About time!

Their lovemaking began gentle at first, exploring and curious. The lovers were learning each other's bodies and needs. As each gave and received, grateful for the opportunity, their loving was unhindered without guilt or shame. It developed into a magical coming together reaching their peak simultaneously. Jessie's eyes rolled back into her head and twitched through the sensation. Her body convulsing as she rolled with it.

When the tumultuous sensation settled into a low hum in Jessie's body, a look of shock remained on her face. Lying spent in each other's arms her curled around Logan's side and her leg lay casually thrown across his manhood. One arm curled across Logan's chest as Jessie's hand caressed his jaw and fingered his mussed mane. She smiled wickedly.

"You adorable minx, what's going on with you?"

"Only surprised, that's all." Jessie's blush expanded all the way to her chest. Heat spread throughout out her being. Logan gently fingered a pink crest, coaxing it again to firm.

"You're the essence of a blushing bride. Why is that? You've been with another. You were married for years."

"Yes. I've tolerated sex. But I never made love before." Jessie corrected Logan with a grin. She sucked an earlobe into her mouth, breathing moisture seductively into Logan's ear. As she spoke, her breath sent shivers along his spine. Goose bumps formed on Logan's arms.

"I never realized it could be this incredible." She stroked Logan's face, running a finger across his lips. With her eye on Logan's mouth, Jessie licked her own.

"Are you telling me you've never climaxed before? You have never enjoyed an orgasm?" Logan's brow scrunched, perplexed.

"Never, my love--only with you." Jessie bit her lower lip. "I confess. I had orgasms fantasizing about you in the past. I realize that was a shameful indulgence. But I couldn't help myself."

"Wow! I'm shocked and flattered. But I'm not disappointed." Logan's head shook. Jessie saw in Logan's eyes that Logan realized the importance of her confession.

"My fantasies about you were delightful and wonderful. But you're better in reality." Jessie whispered. Her finger ran across Logan's damp cheek, gently crossing the crest of his strong jaw.

"You wantonly begged me to make love to you." Logan suckled Jessie's finger. His eyes teased as he nibbled, holding it between his pearly white teeth. Then Logan grinned, Jessie's finger still captive.

"Absolutely, I wanted you inside me since I first realized my true feelings for you." She observed Logan curiously as her pulse skipped a beat.

"I wanted you as well, my love. But I dared not let on how badly I hungered to be inside you. You were forbidden fruit." Logan gently brushed a tendril from Jessie's forehead.

"Honoring my marriage was important. I gave my word to be faithful. So I resisted feeling anything but friendship toward you. Then after Everett died, I wanted to shamelessly throwing myself at you. But I was afraid you wouldn't want the likes of me. I had to show Everett the respect he deserved. It was the honorable thing to do. Without honor, I would've been nothing."

"I understand. I am a man of my word. I respect your determination. I too value the sanctity of marriage, as a sacred union. I respected your decision. Everett was not an honorable man. You were better than he ever could've been. You needed time to grow and learn to be on your own. You needed to find a way to face down whatever devil from your past haunts you. If I had convinced you to come to me right away, you would never have learned how strong and capable you really are."

"No longer. I'm free. I love you with all my heart and soul. I want you in my bed each and every night and beside me as we grow old together."

"So are you asking for my hand in marriage?" Logan teased haughtily.

Jessie's head tilted. Smiling she winked. "Yes,

Will you marry me, Logan?" Jessie was lost in those dreamy eyes she lived in.

"It would make me whole and the happiest man alive."

They kissed softly, long, slowly savoring the taste. Her pulse went into overdrive and the kiss deepened. Heat flared between them radiating sheer bliss.

"Let's marry right away. But first, make me do that thing again, please, Logan." Jessie felt her cheeks go hot. Logan didn't need asking twice. He knew exactly what she wanted and was eager to give it to her.

Their lovemaking took on a frenzied, steamy need hell bent on exhaustion. Racing pulses consumed them with pleasure paramount, giving and receiving. When Jessie opened, taking Logan in without restraint nothing held them back any longer. Her eyes fluttered of their own accord. Her climax began tightening, flexing around Logan. Logan let himself go as Jessie's pulsing insides gripped his shaft. Two hearts beat as one and convulsed in ecstasy.

* * *

The next day they wed in a small ceremony. The house filled with people she cared for who returned her love. Jessie's heart welled with gratitude.

More than two hundred white women now lived in Skagway. But only three attended the exclusive ritual while Reverend Brown officiated. The Reverend was accompanied by his wife, Sara. Rosie and Ben witnessed the nuptials. Lu and her husband Cable were the only other guests.

Celebrating with a supper of fresh salmon Cable caught in the bay, steamed asparagus and baked potatoes from Jessie's garden, the newlyweds were toasted with locally made wine. The festive celebration was everything she wanted.

"Our wedding is perfect." Jessie whispered blowing seductively into her husband's ear and giggled at Logan's response, wiggling in his seat.

Later, giving privacy for the newlyweds' wedding night, Rosie stayed at Ben's cabin. As Ben and Rosie left, Rosie blushed and kissed Jessie.

"Congratulations. You finally have the man of your dreams." Then Rosie walked back to Ben, who wore a promising twinkle in his eye.

"Mark my words. Those two will be next." Jessie whispered to Logan.

"They make a fine couple. I suspect they'll soon be sharing news." Logan nodded.

Finally alone, Logan took his bride's hands. Logan gazed longingly into Jessie's eyes. "Forever, my love--we have forever together."

"Forever and you're my life, my only true love, the only genuine man I've ever met. All others pale in your wake." Jessie gazed into the emerald eyes holding her heart and soul.

There were no secrets between them. Logan understood Jessie's past. Their history didn't matter, except that it had made them who they were today. She was enough. Jessie was Logan's everything, and he was hers.

Forever together--a promise.

CHAPTER 33

1901

The Alaskan Gold Rush, an outright lie, a conspiracy was brought about by a sinister hoax. The scheme was perpetrated by powerful men bent on eliminating the western U. S. of an unwanted element. They put into play the elaborate plot that was bold and audacious in execution. From their perspective, it was a huge success.

Not for others. Approximately thirty thousand prospectors survived long enough to arrive at the Yukon gold fields. But only about two thousand discovered gold. Among those discovering gold, only about two hundred found significant amounts. Gold didn't lay waiting for miners to simply scoop nuggets and fill their pockets, as they'd been told. The treasure was hard found and difficultly excavated in brutal weather and horrific working conditions. The enormously expensive, hazardous venture required horrendous drudgery. Still most efforts proved unprofitable. So many wisely called it quits.

It was a treacherous time and place with unscrupulous, savage elements everywhere. Not only brutal weather and perilous terrain, but also the human element devastated the mining population.

So only a handful of successful miners actually made it out alive with their gold.

Jessie, among the frontiersmen and women, accepted the incredible challenge. She not only survived but thrived in the Alaskan frontier.

"I struck gold of a different sort. My search for love and family netted what I pursued my whole life. Logan, you and my friends in Skagway are the mother lode I long sought after. This year since we wed has passed quickly. I can hardly believe it's already summer."

"Indeed, my darling wife, time passes quickly when one is as happy. You're everything I ever wanted in life." Logan pulled Jessie onto his lap, nuzzled her neck and sniffed her essence.

"And you are my dream come true, my amazing husband." Jessie kissed Logan long and luxuriously before they pulled apart so he could leave for work. "My love for you blossoms like a flower growing stronger each day. It has been a magical year." When they weren't working, they were inseparable.

"My whole life, I longed for the type relationship my parents and brothers enjoyed with their womenfolk. When Amy died I settled for adventure and career." Logan anxiously leaned on the door jamb stalling.

"I too settled for home and respectability, not finding belonging and love--until I met you, my sweet Logan."

She brushed a curl from Logan's forehead. Sliding her fingers into his mane, Jessie pulled Logan toward her. She could barely stand being separated from Logan, though he worked close by.

"You are the woman I dreamed of. Strong, adventurous, unafraid of hard work, you are honorable and devoted. I never believed you'd ever be mine. I fell head-first for you, but you were married, so forbidden. I became resigned to living a bachelor's life.

I abandoned the dream of a partner and house full of children. I couldn't have you and wanted no other."

"I knew you'd make a wonderful husband. But the idea of you with another woman tore my insides to shreds. Though females have been few and far between here in Alaska, sooner or later you would have found a lover. I wanted your happiness, knowing it would cause me pain. I figured I wasn't good enough for you."

"My sweet Jessie, you are everything I ever wanted. I have desire for no other. I couldn't comprehend another gal in my bed. In my heart we were tied together, so I had no choice but to settle for your friendship. I'm so very happy you're my wife. You are my one true love, and much, much more. We're partners in every sense."

"We are that, my love." Jessie nodded then kissed Logan's chest beneath the collarbone where slight wisps curled above his shirt.

Logan's brow tented. "I hate that your life has been such a struggle." Logan quivered slightly at what Jessie was doing to his neck.

"Indeed it has. Everett provided opportunity to escape the hell Mama put me in. Everett brought a different hell into my life. But my experiences have made me the woman I am. So I can't regret a minute." Jessie cupped Logan's chin in her dainty hands.

"Everett was a damaged soul for sure."

"He was but I can't hold that against him. Everett expanded my horizons. The glamour and culture of San Francisco with the mansion and servants was fun for a while. But it meant nothing because in Everett's world I was but a fixture on his arm. I didn't participate in his life. I only decorated it. I merely existing in that world. Things are different here in Alaska."

"Yes, you've certainly flourished here, my woman."

"Alaska is exhilarating and vibrant with boundless possibilities. I'm at one with nature here. I can't imagine living elsewhere."

"It's a unique life suiting you well. You've achieved success in your own right. Our life together is gratifying and fulfilling. It is more than I ever hoped for." They kissed long and tenderly.

Logan eventually broke them apart hesitantly, his breathing husky with longing. "I could stand here and kiss you all day. But it wouldn't be wise. A fresh load of timber needs unloading. The men await direction. Will you be okay?" Logan held her at arm's length.

Jessie glowed with health and happiness. "Absolutely. Later, my husband." She handed Logan his lunch box. With another quick peck, Logan took off for work.

Unusually energetic, Jessie cleaned the kitchen, having already done a load of laundry while Logan ate breakfast. Then she hung rugs on the clothesline beating dust from them with her broom.

* * *

At the saw mill Logan helped unload timber with the crew sorting logs depending on how they'd be used. The commotion sounded loud and rowdy as the lumberjacks toiled. The gloriously clear spring day brought shining heat to a balmy seventy eight degrees. Logan wore bib-overalls atop a work-worn, red flannel. The sleeves rolled up revealed powerful biceps and an Alaskan tan. Sweat beaded Logan's brow. Wet tendrils clung to Logan's forehead as he did a good days work.

Lu ran frantically into the lumber yard and rushed to Logan, holding her long skirts up in her haste. "Mister Logan, come quickly. Mistress Jessie need you."

Logan loved Jessie with all his being. Logan's fantasies had come true. Strong and smart yet she was so gentle and giving. Jessie was compassionate and loving. And Logan couldn't live without her. So Logan silently prayed as he ran fast as lightning toward home.

Lord, let Jessie be okay.

She had become a real hellcat in the bedroom. Logan blushed at visions coming to mind, having never imagined Jessie as such a woman. But Logan sure as hell liked her that way. And sex in her past had only been physical acts Everett enjoyed.

Jessie never did. With no love involved it had meant nothing.

Between Logan and Jessie sex wasn't scandalous. There were no phony displays of caring or lecherous, sleazy side tainting the ultimate act. It was not tarnished by demons but robust and pure.

Logan couldn't get enough of his exquisite wife. Jessie had learned to enjoy as well as give. She reveled in her desire, insatiable and spirited. She was unashamed in her curiosity, enthusiastic delighting in Logan's body as her personal playground. Jessie had grown ravenous, tantalizingly wanton leaving Logan intoxicated and addicted.

He was the only man she ever loved. Logan was the only man Jessie ever would love.

Please don't take Jessie.

CHAPTER 34

Jessie's life had been fulfilled with Logan in it. Alone in her bed she awaited her man, needing Logan more than ever. She controlled her breathing, attempting to still the pain. Jessie focused on her lover, distracting from the agony.

Their loving was pure, intimate and satisfying. It was romantic and reverent but exhilarating. With sultry abandon their need would forever be magical, growing daily as a force of nature, without reservation. Serenity came with their joining, along with completion and wholeness. Together they were perfection.

Where the hell is Logan?

Their life together had been blissful. Logan's presence illuminated Jessie's world. Logan gave her everything she could've imagined and more. They would get through this together.

Please help us. But if I die today, I die a happy woman.

Well ahead of Lu, Logan busted through the kitchen door never slowing his pace until he reached their bedroom.

On the bed, sweat beaded her face. Curls clung to Jessie's damp forehead. Eyes dazed in a trance of sorts, she mentally focused on breathing as writhing daggers shot through ripping her apart.

Jessie absently held a death grip on Rosie's hand. As Logan entered, Rosie peeled her fingers from her hand. Logan replaced Rosie at the bedside, noting whitening of Jessie's knuckles as she gripped him hard. Her nails dug into Logan's palm.

Another horrific slice blasted through her agonized body. Jessie flinched enduring it. Moaning horrifically, writhing and arching stiffly, Jessie excruciatingly suffered and brutally squeezed Logan's hand.

Logan soothingly caressed Jessie's arm. He softly cooed serene words as her helpless torture showed on his sorrowful face, shattered his heart and filled his eyes with moisture.

"I swore to protect you. This's my fault. How could I have done this to the woman I love?" Logan's voice was but a whisper, Jessie was incapable of answering.

Doctor Adams entered calmly smiling. "How's my patient doing?"

Jessie's guttural squall pierced their eardrums. The scream must have shattered the window panes, a fitting answer to the ludicrous question.

All business, Doc Adams prepared for the chore. He assessed the situation then gave Lu and Rosie orders to boil water and bring clean sheets. The women retreated to carry out their orders.

Doc Adams placed a hand reassuringly on Logan's shoulder. "You must leave, Son. I'll care for your wife. You can wait in the parlor."

Logan stood. Jessie's hand still gripped his. Her eyes locked with a haunting expression and desperately begged.

"Sorry, Doc. I understand it's unconventional. But I'm staying. I can't shield Jessie from this agony. But I'll not disappoint her."

"Logan, your objection opposes convention. Personally it is indecent in my experience." The old doctor appeared taken aback.

What the hay? This is a new world. Life in Alaska is certainly not orthodox. I've learned to live with strange oddities. I realize I cannot dissuade you. You best not pass out on me though." Doc shook a finger in Logan's direction.

Logan nodded and grinned.

The doctor shrugged and let out a guttural, "Humph!"

Jessie shrieked as a furious contraction slashed through her. Her hand crushed Logan's. As the pain dissipated deceptively she relaxed. But immediately, another explosion racked Jessie's body. Unwavering they came with urgency erupting fiercely one after another, leaving her exhausted and delirious.

Logan stared in horror, looking terrified at the intensity as he clung to her. Jessie focused in a trance governed by her goal and misery. In another realm, she was nearly oblivious to her surroundings, as the doctor prepared the bed and attended Jessie's body. Her muscles taunt, she fought the raging, suffering rolling through her being and panted profusely. Her forehead grew slick with sweat. Hair stuck to her face and neck.

Logan whispered, "Breathe," and stroked Jessie's forehead. Rasping sounds emitted from her as each stab surfaced. She squirmed and writhed, unrestrained. Another piercing shriek.

Finally, Doc Adams grinned in satisfaction. He squatted between Jessie's legs, arms extended, and palms poised and ready.

"Come on, Jessie. One more. It's almost over. You can do it now. Push hard." Doc's command was calm and eased Jessie's fear. She arched. Her head fell backward. Her fists tightened. Heels dug into the mattress. Jessie's face grew red and purple with exertion. Her eyes squeezed shut. She focused on her chore. Commanding a powerful thrust, she screamed long and loud. A blood-curling sound shook the room. Jessie gasped for air heartily with relief as it ended.

Swiftly the doctor worked. "That's good. Here we go."

Spent, Jessie slumped into the mattress. The doctor smiled then held their son forward for inspection.

A tiny red-faced boy opened and batted bleary eyes a couple of times. The babe eyed them, rocked his tiny head curiously, as though saying, "So this's what you look like." Satisfied and exhausted, the infant closed his eyes and fell asleep. Then he peed on the doctor.

Doctor Adams laid the tiny one on his Mommy's belly laughing. "His hose works." Possessively, she reached for her son, gently touching the tiny cheek of the purple, wrinkled being. A surprised shock overtook Jessie. Her eyes went wide and she quivered all over.

"I need to push again." Jessie screamed with a question in her eyes.

The doctor quickly sat between her legs and grinned. "It is okay to push. There's another head peeking out."

Jessie gripped their son on her tummy and with Logan's help, secured the infant. She again scrunched and pushed with all her might. Letting out a loud bellow, the contraction ended. She fell against the pillow. Logan wiped curls from Jessie's damp forehead with stunned admiration in his eye. The infant slept contentedly on Jessie's tummy, as though nothing strange had happened.

Doc Adams wiped the new arrival off and held her up. "May I present your daughter?"

The astonished parents stared wide-eyed at a wee, wrinkled, pink baby girl. Her eyes opened and suspiciously with a snide smile, enriched her sweet, beet-red face. It looked as though she said, "Surprise!"

Once she and the babies were cleaned up, Jessie rested in bed wearing her favorite gown. A baby slept contentedly on either side. Comfortably propped on fluffy pillows, covered with their feathered comforter, Jessie entertained guests.

Logan sat humbly beside as Jessie did the honors, introducing Lu and Cable along with Rosie and her new husband, Ben, to their children. "Come meet our daughter, LuAnn Rose Pace. She is named after both of you, Lu and Rosie and Ann for Logan's mother. And our son, Ben Logan Pace, is named after you, Ben, and his father." Jessie smiled

Logan admired his wife as though a halo emanated from atop her head. Their guests soon left, so not to over-stay their welcome. Finally, the young family was alone.

"I totally underestimated you, my dear." Logan kissed his wife's hand, with a dreamy sigh.

"And I you, my love. Who would've thought our love so potent as to produce twins?" Jessie giggled like a school girl, wistfully observing their babies sleeping in her arms. "Put them in the cradle, so we can take a nap?" Jessie looked exhausted but elated.

Logan carefully picked each baby up as they wriggled at the intrusion and continued sleeping blissfully. Daddy placed their children gently together in the big cradle he had carved himself. The miniature beings immediately snuggled together, as they had in the womb. Logan covered the petite bodies with an elaborately embroidered blanket Jessie had crafted. They lay adorable, curled together like two cherubs.

Gracefully, she flipped the covers back and patted the mattress beside her. "Come, my love. Lay with me." Jessie smiled possessively.

Longingly, Logan pondered Jessie's request. He feared he might hurt her in her fragile condition.

"How can I refuse you anything, after what you've given me?" Logan lay fully clothed.

She wagged a naughty finger laughing wickedly. "No, no, my love. I want you naked, bare-assed, your body against mine. So strip 'em off, Buster." Demanding, Jessie's eyes sparkled.

"We can't make love. We must wait. You're in no condition. We must allow you to heal and use discretion."

"I realize that." She grinned, innocently. "That doesn't mean I can't enjoy my husband's naked body." Jessie's lust was evident but Logan began quickly stripping away clothing. Wanton desire showed unmistakable on Jessie's face. She licked her lips with pleasure at the sight of Logan nude. His masculinity, though relaxed, was proudly prominent. She shuddered, sending tingles through Logan's body. Logan's manhood jerked in response.

"My man . . . all male." Jessie's sultry voice whispered. Cautiously Logan approached. She reached for Logan unscathed and caressed his protruding shaft to a peak. As his body heated passionately flaming, she opened her lips and took Logan in enveloping him, with a moan of ecstasy.

"Ummm . . ."Logan's head lolled back. His eyes closed, reveling in the heated moisture of Jessie's mouth. She sucked him vigorously. Logan's powerful fingers tangled tenderly in Jessie's silky curls as he caressed her head.

Without qualms, Jessie brought Logan to climax, helpless in her hands and mouth. Logan gave in to the sensations, shuddered and gasped.

"Jessie." Logan's love filled her.

She urged Logan's exhausted body into bed aside her, contented and satisfied.

"I love you more than life itself." Jessie's voice was but a whisper.

"And I love you as much, my darling Jessie."

"Logan, you've protected and respected me, my friend and champion."

"I cherish you and our life together."

"You've given me a family and children. You have turned this house into a real home full of unconditional love. That is everything. Thank you, for making my dreams a reality," She whispered into Logan's ear.

Curled beside her, Logan's nose tucked intimately behind her ear, he fell instantly asleep, exhausted. Jessie had finally found self-forgiveness and with it belonging, family and love. The loving couple rested, looking forward to a wonderful life together. Tomorrow brought another adventure on their journey.

THE END

(1) Hymnal according to the use of the Protestant Episcopal Church in the United States of America written by George Washington Doann, born1799, died 1859, popular during the 1800's.

DISCLAIMER: This novel is a work of fiction as are the incidences, characters and their experiences, for the most part. A handful of actual historical characters, locations and events are portrayed fictionally associating with and interacting with fictional characters in the story. Both fictional and historical characters are portrayed during historical events in ways which could be feasible. However their experiences are completely from the author's imagination. Any similarities of fictional characters and events in this book to actual characters and events, is purely conjecture on the part of the author for the sake of entertainment only.

NOTE FROM AUTHOR: When I completed this story my friend and editor, Linda Rankin, was thrilled with the tale. Linda wanted more historical information, saying the story was like a great meal, and she craved dessert. She wanted maps and factual data about the historical portions of the book. So here you go, Linda. I've compiled these historical tidbits about characters enhancing Jessie's life. They may be found on my website at the below link and in my newsletter editions; so sign up today at my website. Enjoy!

www.lyndareesauthor.com

ABOUT LYNDA REES

Lynda is a storyteller, an award-winning novelist, and a free-spirited dreamer with workaholic tendencies and a passion for writing romance. Her dreams come true, blessing her with a supportive family. Whatever crazy adventure Lynda congers up, her loving Mike is by her side. A diverse background, visits to exotic locations, and curiosity about how history effects today's world fuels her writing. Born in the splendor of the Appalachian Mountains as a coal miner's daughter and part Cherokee, she grew up in northern Kentucky when Newport prospered as a mecca for gambling and prostitution.

Published in romantic suspense, historical romance, advertising copy, and freelance, Lynda is an active member of several professional writing organizations and judge of professional writing events.

Author's Note

I hope you enjoy my work and we become life-long friends. *Time for Romance!*

    Lynda Rees
    Love is a dangerous mystery

Get the latest book deals, exclusive content and FREE reads by subscribing to my newsletter.

Visit my website:
www.lyndareesauthor.com
Email:
www.lyndareesauthor@gmail.com

Also by Lynda Rees

Gold Lust Conspiracy

The Bloodline Series:

Parsley, Sage, Rose, Mary & Wine

Blood & Studs

Hot Blooded

Blood of Champions

Single Titles:

God Father's Day

Madam Mom

Find information about these books at website:
lyndareesauthor.com